MARGARET CAPE

MARGARET CAPE

A NOVEL

Wylene Dunbar

Harcourt Brace & Company

NEW YORK   SAN DIEGO   LONDON

Requests for permission to make copies of any part
of the work should be mailed to: Permissions Department,
Harcourt Brace & Company, 6277 Sea Harbor Drive,
Orlando, Florida 32887-6777.

Library of Congress Cataloging-in-Publication Data
Dunbar, Wylene.
Margaret Cape: a novel/by Wylene Dunbar.
p.   cm.
ISBN 0-15-100248-7
I. Title.
PS3554.U46339M37   1997
813'.54—dc21   96-48108

Text was set in Granjon.

Designed by Lori McThomas Buley
Printed in the United States of America
First edition
A C E F D B

To Jack

PROLOGUE

Rosamond, Mississippi, 1993 ✍ Chapin Finley Cape is dead—only forty-three years old when he fell down the stairs at Cape House, broke his neck, and died, causing a good deal of disorder among his peers and the lesser class as well, who are, strangely, even more disturbed. They are all swirling and noisy as mallards in a small pond protesting the arrival of a strange duck. Now they must think of Margaret, his elderly mother and a catatonic for nearly thirty years. No one suspected they would have to think of her ever again.

It is not that Chapin Finley's death is unexpected. He has lived his life assured to come to a bad end and it is testimony to Death's many commitments and Chapin Finley's portion of good luck that he lasted as long as he did. No, the troubling matter is that he never married and, as people do at an age when it hardly seems relevant, he neglected to make a will and, so, Margaret owns the land—five thousand acres of Delta land, "ice cream" land that produces two bales of cotton every acre. If she had simply died first, as is proper with a parent and child, all would have passed as it should. Now Cape Plantation will belong to no Cape.

Rosamond is unsettled because of this and not in the same way for each of its people. No town is like that. Yet, the town is placed so that it is appropriate to give it one feeling, although it is being too charitable to say that Rosamond is the most eastern point of the Mississippi Delta, which is what people in Rosamond *do* say. The town is, at best, a spectator to the Delta and its peculiar burden is that it sits at the intersection of three distinct regions of Mississippi—the Delta on its west, extending north and south in equal measure, and the Mississippi hill country to the north, and, east, the middle of the state, joining the others to surround Rosamond like the troops of General Forrest himself. Rosamond is given a choice of what it will be, then, and it chooses to be a Delta town. Yet, the streets and square are not sun-washed and hazy, but green, shady, lined by tall red oaks and sweet gums. Hill country dogwood and forsythia bloom profusely each spring and there is a new, four-lane highway to Jackson. Its choice made, however, the town will not be thwarted.

A Southerner fondly speaks of having "a sense of place" and means no more than the rules, only the rules, and especially here, in Rosamond, where the town's very identity rests on a pretension, requiring a certain concentration and not inconsiderable effort to maintain. But there is a reward: the answers precede the questions. Each resident is given a place and a purpose without even asking and, if the fit is not quite right, it is best to wear the shoe given. In consequence, Rosamond proceeds under a kind of First Principle which cannot be questioned without the risk of bringing down the entire edifice. At least, it was that way once, in that other time—before now when its people of every different sort sometimes seem to be barefoot together, trying to find their shoes again and every one of them is trying hard, knowing that the disorder must be contained or, else, trouble—seductive, but perilous freedom.

It is Margaret Cape who gives the particular truth to that, having brought destruction and near ruination that last time, although, admittedly, the situation was extreme. She was an outsider to begin with, a Yankee coming to Rosamond the young bride of an old man—Big John Cape—and all the awful other after. Rosamond made a place for her, but she looked to herself only, as if its strictures were unwelcome distractions, not the boundaries that made her anyone at all. It is twenty-seven years past that she paid for her anarchy, losing her life or the same as, out of sight and of mind at Cape Plantation since. The people of Rosamond smile sad smiles, satisfied to say this.

Even so, a few days after Chapin Finley's funeral, a rumor began that Margaret is returned, though such a view is unaccountable—what would be the point? Wasn't it settled for once and all then? But it was last Wednesday week, the eighth day of September, she was said to appear anew on the Square as if she were alive, not dead, although they know she has not been dead, of course, but the same as. "I was just coming past Bass's Jewelry Store and she was right there in the front," Chesley Cooper, the banker, said. "Her old manservant was helping her onto the sidewalk and having a time of it and I said, 'Do you need some help?' not knowing who it was until she looked up with those peculiar light eyes and I knew then. 'Thank you, no,' she said like it had been only yesterday and, I don't know, there was something odd about her." The others said, "There always was," and they shook their heads smiling to each other as if it were that other, more fathomable time.

PART ONE

Crab orchard red fieldstone forms the straight walk to Little Mildred Melton's home. It is dull pink-tan, not red, but the stone's name is "crab orchard red" and everyone knows what is meant is this very stone. At the end of the walk, near the curb, are two stone markers with iron rings as if to tie horses, and in oblong circles around them are masses of ruby mound chrysanthemums, which are, in fact, ruby red. The walk steps up to the arched entry of the only English Tudor house in Rosamond. Its design was set by Little Mildred's husband's grandmother, Sara. She had been only sixteen when her parents sent her for a year's free study in the Cotswolds, provoking criticism but that was the way the Dodges were, and the year became Sara's cornerstone, so that she drew on it constantly in conversation, in her thinking. It was no surprise that she would want a house to match her own foundation. Little Mildred and Frank moved in after Sara's death—when Frank III and Sara Cape were ten and eight—and Mildred has lived here the forty years since.

Little Mildred is at the back of the house, which faces the L-shaped yard that slopes under the shade of red oak trees and one native pine to a flat rectangle where she keeps her garden. Albert, who drives her and takes care of things, is at the lower corner watering a group of red leaf nandinas the sprinklers cannot reach and it has been dry, suiting the cotton but nothing else. She is pacing the smooth stone floor of the sunroom. She does not use the cane and never uses it indoors, except in public to avoid the inevitable and unsightly loss of balance. At home, there is always a chair near enough. And, if she should fall, what of it? She is not the bag of bones so many women, and men, too, might be at eighty-four. She can feel the firm bulge of her buttocks as she walks and her small breasts have not sagged so much and she can make her biceps show. She is not mannish, but resembles her brother, John Buie Cape, tall, dark, strong in a way that shows. "Your mama cut y'all out with a cookie cutter!" Big John had teased his children.

Little Mildred abruptly stops pacing and sits in the padded wicker chair painted pistachio green and takes the October issue of *Southern Accents* from the lamp table, riffling the pages. She stops at the flower-and-garden section, annoyed by an article on fall pruning by Sally Felcher, who knows nothing about it beyond what she has pestered Little Mildred to tell her at Mississippi garden club conventions and has forgotten half of that. She places the magazine back on the stack of others, patting their sides into a straight line, knowing what it is that makes her anxious. The waiting for results is the difficult part, even when one is assured of the right result. She has never been any good at it.

She pushes herself up out of the chair and walks to the glass, looking for Albert. Just like a Nigra to up and leave and not know any better. "God puts quality in or not before we're born," Big Mildred told her daughter. "It is our duty to watch over the lesser ones so they won't be a problem to us or themselves." Margaret. Poor, dear little Margaret. Even in her disgusting stupor, she has managed to be a problem! How much better for the Capes if John Buie had never laid eyes on her. How much better if Big John had never brought her to Cape

House in the first place. How much better for them all if Margaret had never been born.

"I guess I be goin' on, ma'am." The soft voice comes from behind her, and Little Mildred swallows the wrong way. She coughs hard to get her breath.

"Albert! Don't come up on me like that. Like a thief in the night. Did you feed the mums?" Albert grins at her fluster. He is short and young enough to enjoy creating a stir.

"Yes, ma'am. I did that 'fore noon. You not back takin' smokes?"

"Of course not. Well, go on then." She is reluctant to let him go and she does not know it. He does not leave. He comes past the doorway and into the room behind her chair, straightening a quartet of Walter Anderson prints that hang on the back wall of pecky cypress, dipping to scoop up a missed dust ball beneath the long iron and glass table below. It is the time of day that the outside and in begin to be the same light, after the afternoon and before dusk. Albert turns off the ceiling fan and switches on the print lights.

"Our frames goin' to need nailin' together again. I'll take 'em to Herbert's Monday morning. The Window Frame, they don't care you got pictures fallin' out the bottom. Jus' take your money. Herbert try 'n do a good job. If he don't, he don't want nothin' for it either." Albert looks around, satisfied. "Well, I guess I'm gone," he says, repeating himself.

"Oh. Today is Friday, isn't it? I just lost track of the days somehow. Hand me my purse over there by the sofa. Hand it here to me." She takes it and retrieves the money, holding out five crisp twenty-dollar bills, tapping the unopened pack of Salems to the bottom of her bag. "You aren't in any trouble, are you, Albert?"

"No, ma'am. I been too old for that for a while." He grins, placing the bills in his wallet, sneaking a look at his watch. He has less than an hour before he has to be at the hospital, where he has a second job helping doctors during emergency surgery. He has other work, too—cleaning doctors' offices on the weekends, selling cars or houses or appliances for anyone who needs them sold—all of it for different people, and there won't be any finding him in the white man's pocket, depending on just the one.

"Something I was going to ask you." She tries to remember but things sometimes slip away now. He waits patiently, as if he would stay for the night. She shakes her head. "It's gone. Good night, Albert."

"Yes, ma'am. I locked the front door and I'm lockin' the back door behind me. I'll be here Monday morning good 'n early."

When she hears his car—it is a late-model Oldsmobile and Mildred worries that he is dealing in drugs—she remembers what she had wanted to ask him. Margaret's man, Sam Adams. She is almost certain he has not done anything rash. He is one of the few old-days good Nigras left, not like Albert who sometimes seems to be laughing at her. Still, she would like to hear it from Albert, who will certainly know and, perhaps, tell her. What is Sam doing these days? Now it will have to wait until Monday.

2

Baldwin, Massachusetts, 1919, and after  You have a story, her father told her often. Each of us does, he said, and told her that hers would reveal itself to her, if she learned to seek it. When she asked what her story was, he waggled a finger and made her frightened with the worry on his face. He insisted her story, whatever it might be, would not simply show itself without her efforts and she was certain that if she did not find her story, that failure would mean catastrophe. She looked in every one of the dozens of books that her mother provided her. Peter Rabbit was there. Black Beauty, and the Princess and the Pea. But not one story about her. She listened to her aunts and uncles tell family tales like the ones about cousins Violet and Pansy and how they had eaten identical meals for forty years and how they each wore a fresh flower on opposite sides of their heads so that when they faced each other they were mirror images, refusing to marry because they loved the very same man and how their father, Uncle T (for Theophilus), had been unrelentingly terrifying within the walls of their rural home, while applauded for the generosity of spirit he displayed to neighbors, who would never think or speak of him beyond that description once settled. Margaret attended these stories well, but never heard hers mentioned. She listened as her mother read aloud newspaper accounts of the Teapot Dome scandal and, later, Tiriboschi's crossing of the Channel and the trial of John T. Scopes. As she grew older, she scanned the small tidbits beyond these front-page events, but there was nothing. She was twelve when she realized, with some relief, that she was in her story and a part of driving it forward. She began to look at things differently then. She looked for a story line, a sign, that might indicate where the future lay. Her search inevitably led her to adopt the demeanor peculiar to species of deer and other wild things, an intense watchfulness attended by delicate motion, ready to quickly spring in whatever direction she perceived her story to lead her. Her diminutive size and physical grace further accented this. Bronze hair and sallow skin combined with finely drawn lines to camouflage her so that when she moved, it was sometimes startling—something quite still, suddenly animated.

By age nineteen, Margaret Finley without exception wore clothes in one of three colors—an apricot cream shade, russet brown, and a slightly golden ivory color. After a while she began to wear the same color for similar activities. She wore the ivory for most social occasions. When she attended church services, she always wore russet brown and wore the apricot cream when she walked fourteen blocks to the library on Beeker Street with a stone lion at the front entrance and two globe streetlights to the rear. Yes, she read, although otherwise words were a bother. She did not keep a diary nor did she care to engage in idle chatter with her acquaintances. She had never been a letter writer and she did not have much to say, even to her mother or father. They did not find this odd, Dr. Finley and his exquisite wife, Anne Chapin, because Margaret had rich and revealing conversations with those around her all the same. These by an attitude, a posture, a deviation from her usual direction. So, then, when Dr. Finley came from telling young Margaret of his arrangements for her in the December nurse's class, he recounted to his wife the details of their conversation.

"I found her in my library and told her. She was surprised, at first," he allowed, "but, then, she said she had already been thinking of doing that very thing herself and wasn't it wonderful how we were so attuned to one another?"

"She wasn't annoyed with you for not asking her first?"

"Well, maybe a little. But, she knows I'm looking out after her interests here. She told me that, in fact. She said, 'Papa, I should be angry with you, but I just can't be because I know you love me and would never hurt me!'" Anne Chapin raised her eyes from her needlepoint to look at her husband; he saw this and understood but refused to back down. "Yes. She told me that." He repeated the lie daringly, defiantly. "And, I tell you, it did this old man good to hear those kind words from his little girl. My little Margaret loves her papa and she would do anything he asked just for that reason."

"She does love you, dear. That much is true." It was Dr. Finley's turn to communicate in silence and he turned sharply, leaving Anne alone with her sewing.

He had, indeed, found Margaret alone, reading in his small library, and he entered from the parlor whereas she sat facing the bedroom door. She knew at once who was there by the pipe smoke, which always lingered in his wool suits, this overlaid with Johnson's hair tonic and the faintest touch of formaldehyde from the clinic. She breathed in this contaminated ether and held it to her for a moment and, in her later years, his image would spring full-blown from an encounter with any one of those same peculiar scents. "What a pretty dress, Margaret." She looked up at him, then, with the beginning of a smile. It was an apricot cream dress, of course. She had decided to spend the afternoon reading, which was of sufficiently the same character as her trips to the Beeker Street library. He told her then of his plans for her, the nursing class and the rest. She was not struck by his audacity—she was accustomed to having him decide matters for her—but by the coincidence. She had been reading at that moment an account of Clara

Barton, who nursed the wounded troops in Civil War battles in Virginia and later founded the American Red Cross, and she said nothing, but rose, handing the book to her father. Agitated, she paced the length of the room, hands behind her back, imitating Dr. Finley's own manner when pondering an important decision. She had no need to either rebel or acquiesce. She would do as she had always done. She would examine a notion from the standpoint of where it would take her, look at it from an angle, heft it before deciding whether it was a part of her story. Then she would reject it or not, and her father would go along. This *was* a part, she decided. She would join the December class.

Robert Finley stood there waiting, holding her book. She looked at him now, standing quite still, absorbed by his only child. She came to him and took the book from his hand, placing her other hand on his shoulder and pulling him close to kiss him softly, at first on each cheek. But then quite suddenly, she placed her lips firmly, warmly against his and he thought he felt the tip of her tongue pass delicately over his teeth. She stepped back, without expression, and spoke. "Two solitudes" was all she said before turning to leave the room and Dr. Finley recalled at once the lines from Rilke: "Love consists in this, that two solitudes protect and touch and greet each other."

3

"Chancellor Cordeman's on line two." The intercom's announcement is startling in Niles Abbott's dark office and he stops midsentence at his computer, midthought even. Niles once described Dewitt Cordeman as a "legal deviant in a judicial raincoat," but he picks up the receiver immediately, following a lawyer's habitual deference to judges.

"Good morning, Your Honor! How can I help you today?" The jocular tone sounds the exaggerated enthusiasm, a rule of Titus County phone conversation, and only slightly betrays its disdain.

"What makes you think I need your help, Counselor? Seems I been making it fine a good many years without you." The words are teasing, lazy. Judge Cordeman is a man accustomed to having others make the effort to understand him.

"That's surely true, sir. Just forgot, I guess." Niles stops the click of his typing and pulls a yellow legal pad near, beginning a subject list of possible jury instructions in the Desoto Bank case he will be trying in a couple of months.

"I haven't seen you around much since you got back. Ol' Charley keeping you busy, is he?" Niles stifles a sigh. Charles Brandon, the silver-haired hero of Brandon and Associates. Even judges drop his name.

"He is, Your Honor. I—"

"We've been having us a time with that timber case," the old man interrupts, laughing only a few seconds until he begins to wheeze. Niles says nothing. The chancellor has smoked unfiltered Pall Malls since they were a dime a pack and he doesn't want to hear anything about it. "You know that case, Counselor?"

"Yes, Your Honor. Mrs. Blaylock." Niles writes "witness credibility" and "lender's duties" on his list, his bold scribble illegible to anyone else. Mrs. Blaylock is Charley's current damsel in distress, her fortune in hardwood timber stolen right from under her by Hardy Mall, Mr. Big News from the county next door. Charley prefers such cases. Baubles. Civil actions, a rare criminal one, something that he can take out and admire or show off to others. "You'll have some fun with that one, Judge."

"I guess we will. Well, I know it can't be as exciting as those big-city cases you had yourself down in N'Orleans." Cordeman coughs loudly into the telephone. They are both silent while the judge catches his breath. " 'Course, they don't have all the twenty-four-hour-a-day casinos up and down the river neither, like we got. You been yet?"

"No, not yet, Judge. No time."

"Yeah, well. You know Beetle Bailey, don't you?" There is a pause, almost imperceptible. "Buddy knows him real well."

Niles hears the pause but ignores the reference to his father. "The chancery clerk? Sure do."

"That's him. Won $14,000 at the craps table last weekend. I guess they'll probably watch him close now. You know, I hear they have cameras all over like in Vegas. Even in the john, someone said."

Niles sits back, pushing his steel-rimmed glasses atop curling, dark hair grown a little too long for Rosamond. The Mississippi Legislature won't even fund a secretary for its state judiciary. When Buddy dies and he is able to leave, he will go back to

New Orleans, where he won't have to entertain lonely judges.

"How's your daddy doin'?" Cordeman's voice conveys concern with a measure, Niles imagines, of pity. Diabetes had cost Buddy both his legs last year and, then, the stroke last November, most of what was left.

"Real well, Your Honor," Niles lies. "I'll see him in the morning."

"You tell him I asked about him."

"Yes, sir. Thank you."

"I always liked Buddy. He was the only member of the board of supervisors to come by my office to welcome me back to the bench after my bypass surgery and all that. Seventeen years ago last January. You know, I never went along with what they did to him."

Niles cuts the judge short. "It's all water under the bridge, Judge, and he's at peace with it."

"That's good. That's good to hear." Cordeman clears his throat and they are both silent. "Charley tells me you're the man on all these sophisticated real-estate deals."

"Charley said that? I'll have to ask him for a raise." They both laugh and sit quiet again, longer.

"You handle ward's business?" Cordeman's voice unexpectedly shifts, becomes deeper and authoritative, his courtroom tone. Niles's heart grabs, but he is also relieved. Local protocol demands that the point of a telephone call must be last and the judge is ready to get to the point.

"Pardon me, sir?"

"*Ward's* business. You know. Children, crazy people."

"Oh. Yes, sir. I mean, no, I don't really." Niles's secretary, Delores, expertly submits and withdraws five letters for his signature, his concentrated review unnecessary since he has typed the text of each himself. When she takes up the last and is leaving, she points to her watch and he nods, waving good-bye. It is after five o'clock. "I know what you're talking about generally, Your Honor. That's all."

"Good. That's all you need to know. Look it up in the Guardian section of the Code. You're a conservator."

"Your Honor wants me to be someone's conservator?"

"Wrong and wrong. The court doesn't *want* you or anyone else to be a conservator. The court would rather everyone and his brother was perfectly competent to manage their own affairs. But, that's not so, is it?" Cordeman breathes deeply then softens to a confidential tone. "And, I don't want you to be just *someone's* conservator. I want you to take conservatorship for Margaret Cape."

"Margaret Cape," Niles repeats, idly tapping the name onto the screen of his computer, where it glows back at him with the rest of the letters there.

"It's his mother," Cordeman says. "Chapin Finley Cape was Margaret's son."

"No, I remember." He is annoyed to be read so easily, although he does not really know Margaret Cape, but he knows *of* the Capes—Big John, the standard in a golden age of gentleman planters, his rogue son John Buie, whose life, with that of his older son, was short, both passing young in accidental death and on the same day. And, of course, he remembers Chapin Finley's death two weeks ago. The man was only forty-three and he fell down the stairs and broke his neck. It was something out of the ordinary, causing a little stir, and Niles specifically remembers the report in the *Rosamond Register.*

"What it is, we got a little problem with the land. Chapin Finley didn't take care of his business—he let the land get away from the line and we need to get it all straight, back with the Capes. The family—well, Little Mildred Melton anyway— they're all over me to take care of it. I figure you're the one can get it done legal. Probably an outright sale for a thousand dollars or some such."

"There are statutes, aren't there?"

"Oh, yes. Very definitely. Charley said you like to dot all the i's and cross all the t's. I want you to understand that is exactly why the court is asking you to undertake this very important task. Right and tight. That's the way it needs to be done or not at all. Well, that's it. Just let me know when you have something."

"Your Honor, just a minute. The ward. What about her?"

Cordeman seems surprised, as if he is thinking of this for the first time. "Nothing. Put her in Bayou Glen, I guess."

"What's wrong with her? Alzheimer's?"

"What? Oh. No, that's not it. According to Little Mildred, she's just not there. Looks up, but unconscious, like a zucchini with legs. We went with 'general lunacy.' That way, it's *all* covered, see."

"You've set it up already, then?"

There is a brief silence, then Cordeman laughs. "I have you in a shotgun wedding, don't I? But, Counselor, all you need to do, you need to go on and get the court a proper legal description of the plantation and get the lady into Bayou Glen or the like, where they can keep an eye on her. I don't mean ruin your weekend—she's got an ol' Nigra—but as soon as you can, hear."

Niles seizes the opportunity. "Your Honor, if time is really important here, there are probably several lawyers who are more experienced in these matters and could do it a lot faster. Stewart Ellis, say."

He hears the click of Cordeman's cigarette lighter, then the long breath inhaled. "No, I don't think so, Niles. This is a somewhat delicate situation. I understand the house is a damn museum and the court would feel more comfortable with somebody't knows his ass from a hot rock. Listen, I need to get on home. I promised Bunny Love we'd go over to Greenwood and Lusko's tonight, have a little pompano. Glad to be back, huh? I know your daddy is happy about it."

"Yes, sir. Give Mrs. Cordeman my regards." Niles puts "peremptory instruction" on the list and tears off the page for the Desoto Bank file.

"You got questions about Miss Margaret, just talk to Charley about it. He pretty much knows the situation. I don't want anything coming back on this, Counselor, understand? Right and tight. That's how this needs to be."

VOICES RAISE ON the street below and Niles leans to the side of his desk and peers through the closed blinds. The sidewalks are not crowded but, nevertheless, fully occupied at the customary places around the Square, no one walking in a straight line—a jarring, exceptionally rude thing to do—but rather moving in and out in graceful arcs from station to station around the perimeter.

At the Square's center, the side door at the corner of the courthouse swings open, and Dewitt Cordeman appears, his hair slicked, wearing the black suit he favors. The color is unfortunate, making his florid face and its lupine features look ripe. Niles watches the chancellor to his car, a dark Lincoln parked in a reserved space at the curb, where Cordeman bends to spit before opening the car's long door and disappearing inside. He drops the blinds and sits back heavily in his chair. "It's a different place now," Charley told him in New Orleans. "All the hard times has made people give up a lot of foolishness. You see women in the grocery store in jeans or shorts. I'm not lyin'. The club is real different, too. No ties during the day, now, and paper napkins. Hell, if you can believe it, they even got coloreds that ain't caddies in the Greenville Country Club! Couple of doctors." And the exception proves the rule, Niles thinks.

One car cranks its engine directly below his window and he hears the creak of its wheels turning to pull from the curb into the street. A shouted greeting follows and a car door slamming as someone gets in or out, the sound the same, but individual disturbances, nevertheless. There is not even an occasional angry blast of horns, no continuous playing of distant sirens, no soft roar of a busy city street. Except for that, Niles can almost imagine himself back in New Orleans, sitting in the Canal Street offices of Harkin & Wells, and even knowing he is not, he feels a certain safeness afforded by the distance between this second-story room and the street below.

"You talk like that place is some magical glade that transforms you once you set foot in it. That is totally, completely irrational. Do what you want to do. Follow your own rules." Julie said that on one of their first dates, when they were still exchanging stories and fascinating each to the other. "What if you don't have any of your own?" he asked her but, if she answered him, he doesn't remember.

The computer still glows orange and black. MARGARET CAPE MARGARET CAPE MARGARET CAPE it says and he tries to summon sympathy for an old lady with no mind, but there is only relief that she is an inactive, unthinking problem that can be filed and nothing to do until Monday. Niles stands to leave, punching keys to exit from word processing to the C prompt, then flips the switch on the power strip to "off." The blinds are closed tight and the office is almost black, but he knows where he is, taking his jacket from the sofa and walking to the door without needing the light.

4

Boston, Massachusetts, 1937  Margaret Finley fell in love
with Big John Cape while she was following the course of
nursing selected by her father at the Boston Veteran's Hospital
and Big John was admitted fully intending to die. He had
brought along his wife, Mildred, and received regular letters
from his son and daughter, John Buie and Little Mildred, both
of whom had remained behind in Mississippi.

His first few weeks were spent listing his extensive properties
and assets and completing a holographic will leaving instructions for the management of his farming interests and a cotton
gin he owned nearby, appropriate gifts to his longtime employees, a small bequest to the public schools of Titus County,
and the rest to his widow and children. His impending death
was liberating. He was free of the innumerable burdens and
duties he had assumed as head of a household, as a man even.
Energy that had been used for these purposes was now available
for others and he used these gifts as he had opportunity. He
permitted himself to speak openly to those who attended him,
to look at them and to study who they might be—a novelty
for him, a Delta man used to knowing others only in the context of their family and position. Margaret came to his room

often, to feel the warmth of his regard but partly in curiosity for she had never been outside Massachusetts let alone as far away as the Deep South and Mississippi. Big John spoke to her continually of his family and friends at home in Rosamond and on Cape Plantation. He told of them through stories and not stories necessarily of their own and it required all of her concentration to understand since each person he mentioned seemed to have a name already belonging to someone else.

"You see, little one," he explained to her one afternoon, "a name is a precious thing in a Southern family. I suppose that's one of the few things we had that the Yankees couldn't burn or despoil. And, just like your mama and daddy want to leave their most precious things to you, we want to leave our names to our children." He laughed at the intensity of her silent gaze. "I know it gets a little confusin' havin' the mamas and the little girls and the daddies and the sons all the same, but we have ways. We call the mama 'big' or the daughter 'little' like my own Little Mildred. Or we use the middle name, too, like my boy, John Buie. You see?"

As his stay lengthened, she came to his room more than her duties required. Margaret even allowed herself to place him in her story from time to time, but only in play, because she regarded his vows of marriage to be sacred ones. But when, while dining at Faneuil Hall, Mildred Cape choked on a chunk of pot roast and died, Margaret took it as a sign. Three months later, John Cape was released from the hospital, healthy as a horse, and they were married.

Big John emptied Cape House for Margaret so that she could fill it again with the fine furnishings they purchased on their honeymoon, traveling to Europe, then the Mediterranean countries, Egypt and North Africa, before crossing to South America, then home to Mississippi. Margaret arranged the rooms by countries, with the music room containing only what came from England, Ireland, and Scotland, and the great Front

Hall filled with French antiques and those of the Italian renaissance. The rest were furnished accordingly and the bedroom was Egyptian.

The Brazilians were the most beautiful of the peoples she
had seen, Margaret thought, although she had brought back
only photographs from that country. They were definitely unlike the Scottish, who with their heavy cloth and gray, sharp-
lined countenances depressed her as had the jutting room of
Edinburgh Castle when she stood looking out over the rocky
precipice and down into the city below, gray and cold and wet
like its inhabitants. The English, too, and the flowers did not
deceive her. They were an artifice that Margaret quickly saw
through. It was true that, on Portobello Road, she stood transfixed by the oil painting, a red fox, one paw up, looking out at
her and Big John found her standing there, looking to where
the painting hung on the dealer's wall. He bought it for her
because he loved her, of course, but even more because he loved
buying things for those he loved.

She had not realized when they married and departed for
an extended honeymoon that they would be spending any time
at all acquiring or buying such as they had done. Margaret was
raised in a family with a home already assembled. Her bedroom
bureau was Aunt Mary's, the dining-room table her grandmother's, the home itself had belonged to her father's childless
uncle and namesake, Robert Samuel. Even the muffler she wore
as a child had also covered the childish hands of her mother
and her mother before her. Big John's world was different.
"They didn't leave us anything," he told her and she soon understood that "they" always referred to the "Yankees." "They
raped our land and our women, then burned every possession
we owned. They swept across the Delta and left behind a barren void that my grandfather and my father and I to this day
have struggled to somehow fill and make life form there again."
Margaret wanted to believe, but how could the Yankees have
destroyed something that was not there? Most of the Mississippi

Delta, Margaret knew, had only been reclaimed from the river in the early part of their own century. Big John sighed. "Muffin, there is your little Yankee mind fooling you again. So literal."

"They sent their laundry to Portugal," Big John told her of the rubber barons who built the marvelous Teatro Amazonas, the opera house in Manaus, Brazil, a thousand miles inland on the Amazon and then, only fifteen years later, were brought down by the theft of their precious commodity's seed, which, it turned out, grew better in Malaysia. He said it with the respect and longing that he repeatedly accorded those things which were part of past glories unjustly brought to ruination. Even in decay, the theater was magnificent, she could not deny. They had already attended performances on two evenings, surrounded by the opulence of the deep rose and gold Baroque trappings in the enormity of its circular interior and multitude of balconies rising several stories above the stage. Gold-veined mirrors held chance portraits: a brightly gilded costume in an opéra bouffe, dancers moving in a blur to the swell of music, her own gloved hands resting in her lap. When, at the end of the second night's performance, John touched her arm, she rose with him, holding tightly to him as they moved into the flow of the others. She wore the printed silk gown and gold sandals he had bought for her in Paris, he in his black evening suit, and they glided with a faint rustle through wellborn Manauns and the soft clicking of Portuguese conversation to an arched entry and onto the tree-lined sidewalk beyond.

The day following, the *caboclo* guide took them expertly through the narrow *igarapés* and deeper into the shelter of the rain forest. Margaret sat motionless at one end of the small *catamarãs,* shaded by its blue awning, the box camera resting in her lap. Continuous light and shadow and the broad trunks of rubber trees on the bare floor of the forest passed slowly by her. From time to time, the guide pointed to wading white herons or flashes of gold high above—monkeys moving quickly between the trees—or his oarsman whispered *"papagayo,"* borrowed from the Spanish, and pointed to the silhouette of a parrot in flight across their path and Margaret sleepily raised the camera toward the attraction.

She had herself spotted a small herd of cattle half immersed in the black, acidic water of the Rio Negro when excited shouts of *"Papagayo! Papagayo!"* caused her to turn her camera back to the other bank. There, a small banyan tree with perhaps fifty green parrots adorning its branches like Christmas ornaments. They took wing almost immediately and she put down the camera as the buzz of their halting flight passed over her. A sign, she knew, and she was suddenly awake and alert now, watching when toward the end of their excursion the small shack had drawn everyone's attention, not for itself—it was much the same as a dozen other *palafitas,* river homes they had passed—but for its yard full of brightly colored flowers, set out with fully as much purpose and flair as a formal English garden. The oarsman pulled up and steadied the boat while they admired the unexpected beauty. Then, a slight movement to one side and Margaret turned toward a girl of ten or eleven, whose gold-and-brown hair softly waved back from hollow cheeks and large blue-gray eyes. Her skin, a deeper gold than her hair, was barely covered by a scrap of cotton halter above a short pink-and-green gauze skirt. She stood uncannily still as she balanced on a large log floating near the bank. In the boat, Margaret stood then, too, so that they faced each other, each making continuous, imperceptible adjustments to maintain her balance. Margaret raised the Kodak, focusing on the child's face, which looked squarely and unsmiling into the camera as the pictures were taken. She sat down, still watching the girl, who watched her, too, even as their boat moved away back into the tributary and toward the big river itself. Soon the trees and the grassy banks of the *igarapé* came between them. But, it was only when the boat reached the broad expanse of the Amazon that she turned back toward the river, feeling its soft pinch and roll beneath the red and black of the sunset.

5

"Someone really loves you. Guess who. Someone really cares. Guess who." Sam Adams sings with the radio and cooks Margaret's breakfast. The cast-iron pot is filled with simmering water and he swirls the metal spoon once in it, then softly drops the egg to follow the eddy's current. His concentration is fierce. This is breakfast and there is a task for every minute of it and no place for extra thoughts that trouble. He takes a long step to the counter across from the stove and back again, bringing the tray that is ready except for the egg. It is nearly the exact shade of rusty white as the kitchen counter and he is pleased to observe this. Having a sense of color is one of Sam's special talents or so his grandmother told him right away and she had always relied on him. "Does this hat go with my dress, Samuel?" she would say Sunday before church and no one else would suit her. His first job outside the fields had been at the florist, putting the shipments of cut flowers into water in the cooler and he arranged them by color so that the spectrum of the rainbow went from left to right. The owner liked him and when Miz Cape—the first Miz Cape—had needed a man for the house, someone with some sense and who came to work clean, he told her about Sam. The flat, dark gold of his skin pleased Miz Big Mildred, unlike the purple black of the bluegums—he shakes his head in disgust at the thought of them, Negroes who would never get out of the fields—and he took special care with his appearance, pomading his hair and growing a small mustache that sat like a chevron over his full lips. His hair has since become a natural frizz, receding back into a half crown, but he has kept the mustache.

Sam wets a cotton rag under the tap and rubs the tray's edges, but the color stays. It is the same with the counter, just not white anymore. Comet powder might scrub it clean, but there is no one to see it and that would be a dollar gone down the drain with the cleanser. Miz Margaret, she used to see it, used to like to sit in the kitchen and talk while he and, long time ago, Ella, cooked. It was right here at the table with the enamel top, too, right here that she went away. "Don't do it, ma'am. It ain't yours to pay for." He had begged her hard because he could see it happening in her eyes, blue-sky eyes behind a cloud that held his tearful gaze, eyes that could see the truth of a man's soul. "Don't go," he said but she placed her hand on his cheek so gentlelike and soft and shook her head just a little before her hand dropped to the table heavy as if it were dead and she was gone. He catches himself and pushes the thought away. "A thinking nigger is a man in trouble," Big Mama told him and it was good advice. Things are different alright, now that Mr. Chappy is dead and Miz Margaret is back, and maybe he should tell her everything but, then again, maybe he shouldn't. Everything is changed. Better, some say, but at least back then he knew his place, low as it was. No way to tell that these days, what he supposed to do. Whether like this he should let it out or keep his mouth shut. First, he will have to make up his mind whether to think about it at all and right now is breakfast and no time for anything else.

He retrieves his white jacket from the hanger, left otherwise on the wall hook. It is starched and smooth-pressed and he pulls it on carefully to avoid wrinkling. The cuffs are almost two inches above his wristbones. Each time they become frayed, he turns them under a quarter inch more, securing them with adhesive tape. He lifts the tray and holds it level although that is more difficult with his arthritis cutting up. Rain is coming. He is out the door and halfway down the long back hall before he remembers the radio. "Sam, you worthless dog!" he reproaches himself. He considers whether to return, but his arms are already trembling from the weight of the tray and he continues toward the bedroom, promising himself he will be extra quick in his duties so that he can turn the radio off when he gets back to the kitchen.

"Good mornin', Miz Margr'et." His voice is deep yet lilting. He sets the breakfast tray on the bedside and he uncovers the pot of marmalade and unwraps silver from the linen napkin, long fingers arranging every item on the tray in the same manner he has every morning for a long while. "It's a bluebird day, ma'am. Maybe you go out to the garden today, get a little sunshine. Maybe finally goin' to rain tomorrow. Be too late." He steps away, waiting for her, and sets his feet wide to steady himself on reedy legs beneath a back that bends over to carry the weight of seventy-eight years.

Margaret feels the gentle bump of the tray but lies still, slowly coming into consciousness. In a distant room, the radio is playing blues songs. Commotion. Noise. That was precisely the thing that confirmed her return. Not the sound of it so much as the hearing and the uncanny understanding. This morning, the noise is music and she knows at once what it is—the Greenwood blues playing on Sam's plastic radio in the kitchen—and she cannot just not know it. It intrudes without asking. It is inside, too. She hears herself thinking not only what she very carefully plans to think, but more. Before there was simply silence, suspension, not even dreams, and she unexpectedly remembers when they stopped—May 1966—there have been no dreams since then, she is certain.

"I got our car sittin' out front. Maybe you want me to carry you into town later on?" Sam lifts the tray and holds it toward her in offering.

Margaret pushes herself up against the square, down-filled pillows, looking at Sam and he accepts the invitation to place the tray for her. "No," she says and Sam snorts softly so that she raises her eyes to look at his face, but he is already at his usual course around the room, closing the windows to the side yard garden, running a sinkful of warm water, straightening the photographs on a wall of Cape ancestors, and, finally, going into the closet to lay out her clothes. "There," he says to himself or to her, punctuating each completed duty. Margaret picks at the coddled egg while she watches him.

"The mummy's tomb," she says, surprising herself, and Sam stops to look at her.

"What's that, ma'am?"

"He called it that."

"Mr. Chappy?"

She shakes her head. Not Chapin Finley, but someone else. She looks at the dark walls and tries to remember. They are very tall, emerald green, with a wide band of geometric figures along the top. A threefold screen hangs on the far wall, curious persons in costume painted on each panel, and, near the door, a wine-and-gold tapestry hangs from a cord attached at the ceiling. Her bed sits between the door and the long wall of windows, its mahogany headboard carved in angles and half as high as the walls themselves with a part-canopy extended over-head, ivory silk gathered inside its dome and gold cloth draped below to the floor. Egyptian! Everything in the room is Egyptian and he loathed that.

"His father," she says. "Nineteen forty-six."

Sam's step quickens a little as he brings a dress from the closet. "That's good you rememberin' like that, ma'am. It all be comin' back soon, now." He goes in twice more to bring out dresses before returning to her bedside for the tray. "I had an auntie once lost all her mem'ries. Messin' around with the wrong man. All of us tellin' her to throw him down, but she wouldn't. He come home one evenin' high. Didn't like the way she looked or somethin'. Hit her with a full pack of Falstaff and she couldn't 'member her own name for a year after."

"My name is Margaret Finley." She says it sternly, not intending that at all, but her voice is unruly from disuse. Sam shakes his head, chastened.

"I wasn't meanin' nothin' like that, ma'am. This here's different. Sure it is. You weren't never knocked cold. I jus' said about my auntie 'cause when her thoughts did come back to her, they came in a bundle. Maybe yours'll do that way, too." Margaret touches his arm.

"There is something I need to do, Sam," she says gently. "I can't remember what it is."

"I know, ma'am. You been sayin' that almost from the start. More'n two weeks now."

"You've been here."

"Yes'm. Right along. Where would I be goin'?" He laughs to jolly her, but her solemn countenance makes him quiet again. She holds his gaze in place and stares at his brown eyes, watery from age, and a memory is stirred. He starts to speak, then stops, looking away and she loses the thought.

"It ain't nothin' for me to say. What you should do or like that."

Her fingers leave his arm and rest on the coverlet. Sam stands still, forgetting to hurry while he needlessly arranges the silver and presses the linen napkin smooth with his fingers. "Maybe you jus' let me drive you into town and around again, you might see somethin'?"

Her eyes close and he waits for minutes before he takes the tray away, pulling the door closed behind, and she is alone again. She settles deeper into the pillows and opens her eyes. A small sun dog, brought by late September's light, dances on the ceiling, its shape changing as she watches, until it becomes a single, iridescent line, then vanishes. "What does it mean?"

she says aloud while something, almost a thought, comes to her before it falls away again. She rolls away from the window and reaches beneath the pillows on the far side of the bed, careful to pull the snifter upright from its shelter and drinks the remaining brandy in a single swallow. Mr. Mall may have smelled it on her breath as she smelled his cigars. She couldn't tell and it was her first thought that he was on a "widow's call," a mission of mercy performed by men for women who were suddenly without the comfort of their husbands. "You're jus' a li'l thing, ain't you?" he said, and it was very much the same thing as Ches Cooper said to her in 1945 when Big John died: "You frighten me, Margaret, you're such a fragile one. I always thought John might break you in two," and he took her shoulders to pull her close, breathing in her face until she turned from his grasp.

Her feet prickle with pain when she stands, more as she walks to the closet and the three dresses hanging from the door hook. The first is more dressing gown than day dress, made of creamy, ivory charmeuse, the long chains of rust unseen, hidden in the folds. Next is a shorter wool jersey dress colored russet brown, but Margaret chooses the third, the apricot dress, a frayed, cotton shift. She steps into it, pulling it up over her bare skin, her hopes rising as well that this, at least, will be the day she remembers how to decide what she is to do, so that she will be something more than confetti held to the wind. The dress hangs loose on her sharp bones, her arms bare and protruding like leafless branches of winter. She listens for Sam's footsteps to fade to a far place before she dares to cross the room and open the library passage door.

Cape Plantation, 1937 ✺ It was four months and ten days after her marriage, that Margaret Finley Cape walked through the door into Cape House on Cape Plantation. During their honeymoon, she had purposely avoided any thought of the house, even while she and Big John furnished it from countries around the world. He had talked about it at times, of course, but she had taken his words only as words, refusing to give them any life beyond that. Now, when she saw the house, she knew she had been right to do so. Her heart lifted when they rounded the last curve of the long drive, which wound from a pillared gateway through the grove of fan-shaped pecan trees, and she had, at last, come home. The house was enormous, but with her first sight of it, she knew that it was in reality a community of discrete parts, each of which she could easily fathom. For one thing, the exterior of the house suggested just that, didn't it, with its mix of white boarded walls and dusty clay brick ones in almost equal parts? She had trembled a little at the front entry as she climbed the granite steps between eight round white columns stretching up high above her to the second story roofline, the red clay wall towering with black shuttered eyes to watch her every move. But Big John had taken her arm before they reached the door and directed her instead to a side porch, down three steps to a walkway shaded by Moorish arches and a Japanese birch, through a wooden gate and onto a half-circle brick patio set in a walled side yard.

"This is the way you should enter your home," he had whispered into her hair as she gazed in wonder at the exotic mix of trees and flowering plants which filled the yard, surrounding at the very center an intricate wrought-iron gazebo, painted white. "Look here," he said and turned her to face four large French doors set beneath a long window stained with what appeared an English country scene. Through them, they entered a walnut-paneled library, empty except for a leather chair, a yew table, and the books, which filled most of the shelves on three of its walls. A fireplace was the centerpiece of the remaining wall and except for the ones they had just entered, Margaret saw there were no doors.

"Just a place to be alone when I needed it, somewhere where I could see who was coming before they saw me," Big John explained and Margaret understood. Then, looking to make certain they were alone, he lowered his voice to a whisper. "Now, I'm gonna let you in on a little secret, sweet thing. Look." He reached up to a brass sconce, one of a pair on either side of the doors and, suddenly, a portion of the shelves rotated, creating a doorway into the adjoining master bedroom.

"Herman Coker did this for me when he built the east addition and only he and I and Mil' knew about it. They're both gone, now, so just you and me are the only ones." Margaret's eyes widened and she insisted on closing the bookcase door and reopening it again and then repeating the procedure again and again until Big John grabbed her up laughing, "C'mon now. You're goin' to wear it out, muffin!" She laughed, too, and they returned through the garden to the front entry, where she walked, hopefully now, through the arched door into her new home.

Later they ate their supper—cold fried chicken and eggplant salad—on the screened porch along the back of the house, sitting beneath the fans and looking out over the nearest portion of five thousand acres of green cotton with the lights of the field hands' shacks far away, along the trees and turn row at the side farthest from them. Even the buzzing of the locust and mosquitoes was safely away, outside where they sat and with her eyes closed, hands wrapped in his, Margaret could believe that only the weight of the night's air, hot and moist, could reach them. Big John rose and kissed Margaret on the top of her head. He crossed the narrow porch to the screened door and outside to the steps, where he lit a cigar. Silently, he continued his review of the field while Margaret remained inside, watching him for a while and counting the fireflies that glowed then disappeared against the screen, mistaking once the burning tip of his cigar for one until he abruptly set off toward the equipment barn which housed his office.

She left then, smiling a little at Ella Adams, who came to clear the table, and when she had at last found the place where her dresses were hung, changed to one colored apricot cream and opened the bookcase door into the library. Two hours later she was still sitting, eyes closed, her arms wrapped around herself and legs stretching toward the empty fireplace, when Big John found her there and led her gently back to their room.

6

The dark center of the library proves she is still alive. More than that, if she sits very quietly, she alone exists there and it is only when she chooses—turning her face against the stiff leather back of her armchair, reaching her hand to the cool flat of the yew table nearby—that anything else is there at all. Death is quite different, she knows. Dead, what can be seen of her will alone remain. A stick on the ground, a mirror on the wall, a detail. It can be confusing in that way in the light, the dead and the live mingled together. Here, in this black room, her own life stands out.

She is eighty years old, or nearly so—eighty!—awakened from the sleep that has persisted over a length of time as yet unremembered. She has not been asleep, of course, but simply different, so different that the memories of the one person are not the memories of the other. If asked before, she would have thought such a void meant the butting together of the disparate parts, that her last memory at the age of fifty-three would be as fresh as the previous moment, pressing against her next memory that only happened to occur all these many years past. But it is not that way at all and, in fact, that previous moment's memory is as far away as if it had been in another's life altogether and in its place is a kind of discomfort, difficult to say, that prevents her from bringing that second any closer.

Outside, the multitude of things and movement bewilder her and disturb her concentration on simply being once more, although her first sight, ten days past now, was only Sam's dark face close to hers, its skin waxy, and remarkably the same as before except for the gray in the edges of his woolly hair. He had cried out, "Miz Marg'ret! You here!" in so full a voice that she jumped and the space around her and all in it rushed to the opening, shocking her newly found consciousness. But this was the most startling of all of it, that she awakened—well, it was not quite that, but like that—with a feeling of urgency and to a certainty that there was something she must do. That is it. Something to be done. She does not know what.

"What will you do?" her father had asked her, when? Oh, yes, that memory does come. She was only nine years old and they were standing outside Landrum's Market, three blocks and an alley from their house—it was in Baldwin, Massachusetts, such a small village, really—and a coarse-coated mongrel near the door and hungry beyond reason ate her penny for sea foam. She reached to pet its flat head was all and the coin dropped from her fingers into the snap of its jaws. "What will you do?" her father asked, teasing her, and she said nothing but took the dog home and fed it for two days, until her cent passed in its excrement and, by her thorough checking, was found. She washed the coin with borax soap and returned to the store for the candy, two days delayed was all, and it tasted the better for it. This is not the same, of course. She had known, then, what the object of her quest, quite humble, was. Now, she feels only the impulse to an abstraction. Act. Do. What?

It is late in the day and Sam is moving about in her bedroom, just beyond the corner door singing to himself. "They call it stormy Monday, but Tuesd'y jus's bad," he repeats continuously, the remaining verses of blues forgotten. Moments later, through the small grate in the west wall, his footsteps are in the entry hall and the bolt turns in the massive cypress door at the front of Cape House. There are no windows here to see, but she knows these late-day sounds. And there is something new, the weariness of age. That, too, tells her the day's time is going.

This is the tenth day since her waking that she has come to this dark place. It had seemed the thing to do, a place to re-trieve what memories she can, a blank space where intuition can keep pace with the senses. Too, she is hidden here. Sam once knew the library was here. In 1945 he walled the side yard windows and doors, not knowing about the other entrance and then, most surely, he has forgotten the room is here at all. It is dark except where the circulation vent cuts through to the foyer, and light there only when the doors to the Front Hall opposite are open and afternoon sun comes through its west windows. Not now.

"Where is he?" were her first words and Sam said, "He dead, ma'am. Mr. Chappy died." That was not who she meant, though she did not know who it was she did mean and so she said nothing. "We the only ones now, I guess," Sam told her and she saw their faces from before, all of them with an in-quiring expression but she did not answer until, at last, they faded and she and Sam were alone again. "How long?" she asked him and he said, "More than awhile," and she remem-bered it this morning—twenty-seven years. Twenty-seven years after something, and she drops the thought as abruptly as it came.

She sits with her eyes open and fixed on an invisible point across the room. She sees Sam bringing her breakfast two mornings before, her mother dressing to go out seventy years ago. She is walking in grass, her chest tight or, sometimes, her body loose and indifferent, then she is on a Boston street, warmly wrapped in soft woolens and her father clasps her mit-tened hand. When memories come to her, it is in no order and they stay their distance. On her fifth day here, she had suddenly recalled an entire conversation between her and a woman she later remembered to be Little Mildred, Big John's daughter, and during which she, Margaret, seemed to be someone else altogether.

There are hemp threads in front of the chair that she feels coarse against her bare feet and supposes the rug is worn away and that she must have sat here many times before. She pulls her legs beneath her and places the skirt of her dress so that it hangs loose over them. At first, her feelings were as distant as the memories but that has changed. Each day they grow stronger. She has known for a while that there is nothing more in this room except a droning, directionless energy pressing her to act—it is inside her now—and yet she has done nothing, coming here as the days before.

It is possible that there is no way to know what she is to do but she has the hope of some rule or guide. If there is one, it must be within her own memory and she has set herself to remember it. She has memories and more memories so far, but none suggests any way to order even a tiny part of the entirety. In the meantime, the past and present swirl together, an increasing burden. She is the centipede learning to walk, willing each of its hundred legs to move, and that will never do. And, there is fear. At least, she has decided that is what it is, this formless pushing back nearly equal to her impulsion to act, a stale dread that seems left over from some other time.

In the first confusion, she thought she must go to Rosamond. "Yes'm," Sam too quickly agreed. "That'd be good, you get out and see what's what," he said, but the thought was wrong. The hazy, strong light nearly blinded her as they drove along dirt roads, winding miles through an unchecked extension of flat fields, green with high cotton, and, in the town, the things and the people everywhere! Their faces turned toward her or purposely away—it was the same thing—out of brightly colored summer cottons, crowded together, indistinct, a Renoir painting. One even followed her home and into her bedroom. No, no. That was yesterday, not then. There are things disordered in her mind still. She thinks of the barker's voice he had and wonders if others would come, too. *They are coming.* She hears the feeling, increasing its force and, at last, understands she must leave here, must look in a new place for what she does not know and the thought fires her fear greater and makes her angry. Her face flushes and her eyes tear. If something needed doing, why couldn't it have been done before she reached this piteous state, before whatever had been that she cannot remember?

Margaret presses her fingertips to her eyelids. At first, she sees only the void but, after a few seconds, bursts of deep orange flicker across black space, then bright lines and streamers that transform to broad swirls of pastels and, at last, into a slowly turning geometric maze on a mustard field. She was a child of seven when she discovered the patterns and that they repeated endlessly.

She pushes up from the deep chair, straightening her spare body in the slow time it requires after being still so long. A soft touch startles her. It strokes the length of her legs, then is as soon gone. She stumbles away, unsure, but it follows her, brushing against her from one direction, then another. When she stops, the touching stops. Another person cannot be in this room, she is certain of that. The bedroom is different, of course. The big man had easily found her there yesterday morning, opening its door and walking right to her, she sitting braced by one arm on the bed. "If you will permit me, ma'am, your man said you was staying in. I'm so sorry you're feelin' poorly." He boldly came near her, the khaki shirt cloth across his large belly so close she smelled cigars and turned her head. "They told me last week you was gettin' out again, or I wouldn't have come at all," he said. She rose from the bed and walked past him, sweetly leading him away to the back hall and to the kitchen porch. "Would you care for some iced tea, Mr.... ?"

and he said, "Hardy Mall, ma'am. Yes, I believe I surely would."

She turns slowly in a circle, taking little half steps and extending her arms out into the black space, finding nothing, until the thought comes to her—and not by any reason but as if it is a memory or a gift from no one known—that the touching is only the movement of her cotton chemise, grown too large for her withered shape so that its folds fall loosely against her whenever she moves.

She has forgotten what she was set to do before and she turns again in a growing circle, reaching for the invisible chair. At last, she feels the sharp corner of the yew table and, left, the rounded arm of the leather chair and, touching it, she remembers—it is night and she was about to leave, going to her bedroom. She passes behind the chair, holding its high back until the tips of her fingers touch the shelves along the wall to the passage door. The commotion of her senses is rising, as if some small fissure within her has been suddenly widened allowing them a new, unobstructed path. She feels more distinctly the dress fall against her, then away, again, again, and she hears the dress fall as well, its soft slapping of her bare skin, and she thinks she smells the flat scent of cotton, too, until she is to the last of her newborn endurance to sense and she no longer moves, but is stopped in the darkness, somewhere away from the door. Standing still, she hears and feels only her own harsh breathing and the faint thudding of her heart, and she smells the must of the library. Her back is stiff and it aches. That is the very thing. She is to do something! She, an old woman, confused by her own faculties, who strains to walk from her chair to the door! She tries to laugh—it is the first time she can remember—but her voice catches, gurgles. Today she will be content to reach the passage door, nothing more, and she pulls one thin arm from the dress, and then the other. The chemise falls to the floor, stroking the length of her body a last time and she moves away, silently now, until she is at the corner of the library. She feels for the brass sconce and, finding it, pulls it down with both hands. The passage door scrapes open and Margaret Cape steps naked into the dim light of her bedroom.

Baldwin, Massachusetts, 1919 and after ❦ As a young girl, Margaret pursued her story as she would follow a path in an unfamiliar wood. She looked for markers to indicate she traveled in the story's direction, by intuition since there was only that to say that a sign had been found or, if it had, what it meant. Behind some tree or another, she would find what she sought. She would stand before it and be awed and, also, utterly satisfied at her part in it. That was it. The end. She rejected at an early date the notion that this unwalked trail was only the journey of her life's time here. The end of that course— death—was already known to her and there was no need to search for signs to lead there. Death would find her at the appointed time. Nor did she search for her soul although she feared, at times, she might lose it. Father Moran had started that.

"My little Margaret is a sensitive child. I must insist that she never be struck in any manner," Dr. Robert Samuel Finley instructed Sister Agnes Rose when Margaret was five years old and he presented her, for the first time, at the nuns' Parish School annexed to the cathedral.

The sister had a very large, soft face with a sharply bent nose and an extra roll of chin. Her voice was as high and clear as the steeple bells. "We will take proper care of the child, Dr. Finley," she responded firmly, but Margaret's father stood in place.

"Let me explain further. I have spoken personally with Father Moran concerning this matter, when he dined at our home at his regular time earlier this week. He gave me his absolute assurance that Margaret would not be touched and directed that I should tell him at once if it were not so." Dr. Finley moved toward the sister as he said this, so that he stood uncomfortably close to her. Margaret saw Sister Agnes Rose draw back and her sour look at the mention of Father Moran.

"Of course," she said and Dr. Finley knelt and kissed Margaret on each cheek before leaving. Sister Agnes Rose held Margaret's shoulder firmly in her grip until they could no longer see him, then said, "Come with me, Margaret Finley," and she led the child to a corner of a large classroom with hanging globe lights and high ceilings. She left her there and, each day thereafter, Margaret came to that place and sat quietly while the sister taught her students, from which group she excluded Margaret.

Under those circumstances, it was simple enough to slip away for solitary walks through the cool, stony halls of the church and not just the sanctuary but the myriad of storerooms and offices that could be found surrounding it. There was, to Margaret's delight, an atrium not far from her classroom where she sometimes found sparrows scratching in the dead leaves and, once, a garter snake slithering beneath the English ivy. That was how she happened to see Father Moran, because his study was along that hall between her classroom and the atrium. She was not spying as he accused and his anger startled her. The door was open. She heard his familiar voice and happily followed it until she was at the door to the innermost part of his offices. She pushed it open and he was there with Charles Santee, the round-faced boy who was three grades ahead of her and who sometimes brought messages to the sister in her classroom. The boy's eyes were filled with tears.

"Are you hurt?" Margaret asked him, but Father Moran, in furious tones, silenced him and ordered Margaret to go to the sanctuary and kneel in the first pew until he came. She forgot to kneel, but when he arrived in the sanctuary only minutes later, the priest had changed from an angry man to the jovial friend that she knew from his frequent visits with her parents.

"Margaret, my dear. Are you still my precious little brownie today?"

She nodded her head, but continued to regard him warily and seeing this his eyes flashed with what might be hurt as well as anger. The priest seated himself on the step of the altar. "Do you know what a secret is, Margaret?"

"Yes," she told him and she did know.

"That's good, child," he said and sighed softly.

"It's something I can only speak about to Mother and Papa. Or sometimes only to Papa," Margaret went on although she could not bring her voice above a whisper and she wanted very much to return to her isolated place in Sister Agnes Rose's classroom.

Father Moran looked at her. His face was so sad and she guessed she had done something very bad this time although she had no idea what her error could be. He rose from his place on the altar step and came toward her until he stood high above her and the folds of his black robe almost touched the tip of her nose.

"This is different, Margaret. This is not an ordinary secret. It is a secret of the Holy Mother. Do you know what that means?" She shook her head. "It is something you cannot tell anyone at all—not your mother, nor your papa. It is so secret, you cannot even tell yourself."

The priest backed away and walked a few steps toward the side door through which he had entered. He turned and, for a few moments, studied Margaret's childish face, confused and fearful. "If you tell what you saw in my private office just now, you will be telling the Holy Mother's secret. Do you know what will happen if you do that, Margaret?" Her neck was frozen in place and it prevented her from any indication she did not know and she was barely able to whisper, "No."

He smiled and came back to where she sat. "You will lose your soul, Margaret Chapin Finley. God will take it and hide it where you can never find it. You will be invisible and no one will know you ever lived in this world. No one will care. Do you understand, Margaret? If you tell—even yourself—you will vanish into nothing."

It was several months later when her father was reading to her at her bedtime. He chose *Alice's Adventures in Wonderland* and he read wonderfully, dramatizing each part as they went along in a way that reduced Margaret to giggles. But when he came to Carroll's account of the Cheshire cat, he suddenly pretended that it was Margaret who was gradually disappearing into a smile and she screamed and cried together, "I don't want to be that! Don't make me be nothing!" upsetting Dr. Finley so much that he grabbed her in his arms, almost too tightly, and he rocked her. "Margaret! Don't be frightened. You *are* something! You are not the Cheshire cat. You're not! You have a story of your own. Each of us does."

HER SATIN GOWN lies on bed linens that are properly turned back. A glass of water and an amber plastic pill bottle sit on the green marble shelf of the nightstand and, behind, a pint decanter full of brandy, next to a cut-glass snifter. She pulls on the gown—when was it made so difficult?—and sits at the dressing table, leaning close to the mirror beneath the small Tiffany lamp, studying the reflection of her face for minutes. The pale blue-gray eyes are familiar—barriers, not windows to her soul, clouds threatening a storm, although her smallness and quietude contradict the danger—but the planes of her nose and cheeks are changed, sharpened by the years, and her hair is not bronze, but dull and yellow gray, its long, thin strands pulled into a low ponytail and nearly invisible against her aged skin. She stares at her features impassively, committing them to memory anew. A thought and she holds one hand aloft. Sallow skin hangs between the knuckles, larger than she remembered, but the hand stays steady. Ah, she is relieved. No Parkinson's the way her mother suffered. She pours the snifter half full of brandy and gets into bed.

Sam's wife, Ella, once kept the Egyptian linen sheets starched so that they crackled pleasantly with every movement. Now Sam only carries them to Rosamond to the laundry and they are soft and silent as she pulls the top sheet and cotton blanket over her. It is she and her old bones who crackle now. She laughs out loud to think this and her voice is stronger, echoing against the high ceilings above her. He was her partner, the man had said before he left. "What with your boy passin' on, I thought you might be concerned. I'm here to tell you, far as with me, you stay here and it'll be business as usual for the time being." She nodded and offered him sugar for his tea and wondered what business was done with her son Chapin Finley, an oddly detached man as she had suddenly recalled and, Sam told her almost at once, quite recently dead. "How very nice of you to come, Mr. Mall," she said or meant to say, but Sam took him away, or he brought her here. She cannot remember how it was done just now, only that the man was gone. She turns to face the side yard windows, careful to keep the snifter upright. It is the dark of the moon and the yard will soon be black, even its whitewashed brick walls nearly invisible. The still air magnifies the sound of skittering lizards and insects beneath the open windows. Margaret Cape lies awake, sipping the liquor slowly, thinking, knowing she will not sleep for hours.

7

The worm is attached so firmly to the thick stalk of the tomato plant, it almost seems an elongated, green tumor rather than a different life, but Little Mildred sees it for what it is. She hates these fat moochers and pushes herself up from her mulching, two plants away, to come for it, grasping it delicately between thumb and forefinger, turning its razor mouth outward even though she is wearing thick cotton gloves. "Hah!" she taunts the worm and takes it back to where she was picking bugs from the lettuce—fall is always the buggy time—kneeling again to show it a last sumptuous tomato plant before it dies. She pinches the head hard and the green guts of the worm explode over her glove. She tosses the worm away from her before pushing her gloved hand into the dirt, letting the sandy grit of rich Delta soil scrub it clean.

She sits back to survey her work, brushing clean her long skirt before she stiffly raises up, using her cane to push her weak hip past the crouching point. A front is passing through and maybe fall will get here after all. It is cool enough that the dew has not steamed away and she shuffles, stiff-legged, across the wet grass to the hydrant near the old native pine, balancing herself on the wide soles of her deck shoes while grass trimmings from Albert's Friday mowing fly up to cling to her cotton anklets. She sets her tray of tools on the wood bench wrapped around the tree, and stoops to turn the valve, already attached to a soaker hose that Albert has placed upside down in her garden, but when she lifts up, she weaves sharply to the left, stumbling back to drop down on the bench. The dizziness does not last long and she thinks, maybe it will be a stroke that brings me down. She has wondered in these years past eighty just what it will be—diabetes, cancer, bad heart? Nothing has shown itself—she gave up smoking in the spring, but only because it had become socially unacceptable—her doctor proclaims her "perfectly fit." The difficulty is that no one in her family has died a natural death to give any indication what the Cape weakness is.

Her mother, Big Mildred, had died in an especially undignified manner, choking to death on a piece of meat although, thank the Lord, it was out of town. Then Big John and her brother, John Buie, died in sudden, unprepared ways, leaving her, as usual, to make it all straight. Why do people find it so difficult to live their lives correctly? Even as a small girl, she understood what was expected of her, what she should do, knowing not to touch anything but her own starched dress when she wore white gloves and the true story of the War and the mean-hearted degradation of the South in the guise of "reconstruction" that followed; that a lady was always kind to the Nigras, never using the vulgar term "nigger," or "redneck" either for the white trash, but nevertheless keeping a proper distance. What do people think, that they can act as they please, selfishly ignoring their duty and partaking only of pleasures? People who count are born to a place, a way of life and if those do not suit or one cannot fulfill what is required, then go away and let the rest of us be. She saves the most contempt for those who willfully stay and disrupt the aesthetics for others. If she attended a play she did not care for, she would leave, not talk over the performers or go to the stage and attempt to change the direction. It is all so very clear, isn't it?

She takes her time between the bench and the house. She knows her limits and that is enough for today. Below the single step to the fieldstone patio, the Carolina jasmine is trailing to the right, but not the left, directed by its circumstances. She clips the extra runners and the bush is symmetrical again. A lizard shoots up the porch column behind the jasmine and she removes her hat, fanning the wild creature away, cooling her face with the breeze. The dizzy spell is completely past but, just the same, she will have a little nap before lunch.

There were times she might have wavered. When Big John married Margaret, a child younger than herself, and then left Margaret to marry his son and Little Mildred's brother, John Buie, it took her breath away. Of course, in the '60s—always a bad decade for the South—Frank Jr.'s family had done its own part: his sister Edith, a continual embarrassment, with her fervent letters and guest editorials denouncing segregation or even the Citizen's Council of which Frank Jr. was a member. Happily, Edith received a supporting letter in reply to one of hers from an equally odd English professor at Ole Miss and she married him, living afterward in Oxford, where such subversion is expected and neatly contained within the walls of the university community, banking off one to another, never escaping into the real world to do anyone harm.

But Little Mildred has not wavered through all the difficulties and she is reaping the rewards, her children respectable members of the upper class of Rosamond, her grandchildren coming along behind them whereas Margaret's sons are dead. She has lost her nephew, Chapin Finley, it is true, and she was fond of him, rejected by his mother that way. And, yet, she thinks what Chapin Finley is putting her through! He had only the one small part to play, one line to say and that almost as if she were holding it written on a card before him and he had failed even that.

Six months back and before, she saw him often at the Rosamond Country Club after lunch where they both played

early cards—she, in the ladies' card room and he, in the back
bar reserved for men. She knew he was there even without
seeing him because of Willie Capps, the club's headwaiter, who
occasionally stopped with a tray of iced teas on his way to the
men's bar, carrying one double gin and tonic with a maraschino
cherry, Chapin Finley's favorite. At five o'clock, he switched to
bourbon, before 8:30 prime rib and home fries and more cards,
but he stopped coming and Frank III said, "Riverboats," and
then he was dead. Little Mildred is not so uncomplicated, however, as to blame his mother's blood in him for all the mess.
She has known his father and the other Cape men, too. Still,
once again it is left to her to set things right and do what is,
perhaps, her last duty before she dies, to make certain Cape
Plantation stays in the blood.

Well, she has tended to it, calling Dewitt Cordeman herself
to let him know what needs doing, and it is only a matter of
a few days and the property will be in Cape hands again.
Monday, she will call Bayou Glen to arrange a room for
Margaret. Perhaps they will pick her up so she will not have
to see her at all, except Mildred is mildly curious to see her in
her stupor, to personally accept the partial compensation for the
damage the woman has done.

The polished slate floor echoes the scuff of her shoes as she
crosses the sunroom and steps up to the carpeted hallway,
turning left toward the bedroom at the far end, where she
walks between walls covered with the duplicate lives of parents
and children. On the right, there is the photograph of Little
Mildred and her escort on the evening of her debut at the Delta
Debutante Ball in 1926 and, across, Sara Cape's own debut in
1963, also at the age of eighteen, but at the Southern Assembly
in Greenwood. Right, Frank Jr. is pictured proudly behind his
wife, who holds their newborn son, Frank III. Opposite is Sara
Cape holding her first baby and behind her, her husband,
Butler—without a tie. Little Mildred frowns each time she sees
it. The photographs get older, the photographed younger, as

she moves toward the bedroom until, at the very end of the hall on the right, are the pictures of her own infancy. She and John Buie are dressed for Easter, posed with their ponies or with the old yellow Labrador dog. Here is the one where she is only six months old, sitting in the small cart while four-year-old John Buie lifts the harness rails. At her back is a dark blur and she knows it is the large, strong hand of their Negro maid, who does not otherwise appear. She supposes Sam is getting a little creaky himself, one of the few "shufflers" left in the Delta, all old like him and their loyalty to their white people deep, but sometimes it seems as if these old Nigras live forever. She stares at her tiny self, the black hand pushing up her back and, then, reverses her path toward the sunroom. Her purse sits beside the sofa and she rests on the padded arm while she retrieves her checkbook. "Sam Adams," she writes. "One Hundred and no/100 dollars," and tears out the check, folds it, and puts it on the long table with her keys so she will not forget. There. That is it. She can think of nothing else to do and she will have to wait and see and hope for the best but, God, she hates the waiting.

Cape Plantation, 1938 ❧ "Well, you see, it was the last year or two of the War and the Yankees were coming down from Memphis regular," Big John Cape recited again the story he had told and been told a hundred times. "They knew all our men were up in Virginia or over in South Carolina and they'd pick some peaceful, undefended Mississippi village and bring in their brigands to burn and plunder and rape. 'Cause, what it was darlin', that was really their whole entire purpose." Big John arched his eyebrows and looked over his spectacles toward the fireplace hearth where Margaret sat listening, courting her disagreement, but she remained silent.

"See, what they say now is altogether a fabrication. The War wasn't about slaves or secession or any of that nonsense those Yankee books say. I'll tell you what it was about." He was breathing too hard and she leaned toward him, reaching out her hand until she could touch his. He sat back on the settee and took a deep breath before continuing.

"Covetousness, pure and simple old-fashioned Biblical envy, was what it was. They couldn't stand it—us down here in the warmth and beauty of Mississippi and them living up there in those dark and filthy cities. We were happy, living a good life with our mamas, our aunties, and our grandbabies. The Nigras were happy, too. Things couldn't have been any better and the Yanks just had to destroy it all because they were so full of hate and envy. Baby girl, I have to say, you may be the one thing of beauty those Yankee bastards have ever had, pardon my French."

Margaret smiled and squeezed Big John's hand, then turned and looked again at the soldier in the painting above the fireplace.

"Right. General Cape. Well, he was a brave man, darlin', he truly was."

Margaret looked again at the portrait. It was one of the few furnishings that had not been removed before she arrived but left hanging in this the most prominent position in the Front Hall. The General stood beside his horse, in full uniform, including an elbow-length cape that hung loosely over broad shoulders, with one hand resting on a walking stick and the other on the pommel of the saddle. A conventional pose, perhaps, but Margaret had been drawn not to the soldierly demeanor but to a quality of resolve, even stubbornness, that she discerned. And, yes, there was in his eyes something of Big John whom she adored, although the General was a spare man with the wiry gray hair and rawboned, stern countenance of an Irish wolfhound, unlike John, florid, stocky, and with a whooping laugh that delighted her.

"See, he was my mama's daddy and when all this was happening he was close to seventy years old. Just like me, muffin. But, Mama always said old John Buie was one who never knew his limits anyhow and he had taken on commanding the Home Guards in three counties including Titus, which, what that was, was any man or boy who wasn't already out fighting somewhere else. So you had the little boys and the old men, is what you had. And they knew that, see."

He rose and walked to the mahogany sideboard that she had brought from her parents' home and the bottle of bourbon he kept on a tray there. Margaret watched as he poured and wondered again how he could take in so much liquor without apparent effect. She recalled it had concerned her father, who, other than taking a small glass of sherry before dinner, did not drink spirits.

"That day, they were coming here to burn Wauchomee Bridge, for one thing, and anything else they found that they thought we might find useful. They weren't thinking about having to fight at all, 'cause, see, for a long time they had been just coming down here on occasional raids and pretty much doing as they pleased. But, the old General, somehow he got word they were on the way and he went out and over a couple of days found him some 'men,' about a thousand boys and granddaddies, and they waited for them Yanks out at a little Nigra church off Sperry Road—it burned down since, maybe thirty years now—and about a mile before you come to the bridge."

Margaret had been transfixed by the portrait of General John Buie Cape since she first saw it. The Capes were of Scottish descent and, quite naturally, he should have been placed in the music room, but she left it here instead. She knew he had something to do with her, although she had not yet decided just what. It was the way the painting arrested her attention, the way his gray eyes looked at her, and the way that everyone else seemed indifferent to him, regarding him as an amusing story, nothing more. He was hers in some way, she was very certain of that.

"Well, the General and his ragtag army hadn't been settled

there too long before here the Yankees came, fat and self-satisfied. Four thousand of 'em, their horses strutting down the road carrying those Yankee Doodle Dandies, and the furthest-most thing from their minds was doing any kind of fighting. Imagine their amazement when they rounded that turn—it was right there by where Harrison Sr.'s drive is—and a few hundred yards down, standing across the road, was this double line of courageous Confederates. See, the old man had a few of them out there in the open and the rest on either side, part in and around that church and the others in the cemetery across the road."

Margaret closed her eyes to imagine the confrontation, first as a Yankee soldier being caught unaware, his heart suddenly racing and his hand jerking up the reins, the horse's head tossing, and then as a fourteen-year-old Titus County boy, standing in the roadway, frightened but purposeful, his mouth dry, his fingers gripping the stock of his musket, nervously feeling for the curve of its trigger. She searched for the General and saw his face first, his eyes like John's, with the same look of amusement as he took in the startled Yankee troops.

"The General was up on his own Walking Horse stallion, sword in the air, and he just kept that horse dancing back and forth behind the line in the road. Then, all of a sudden with a bloodcurdling Rebel yell, he commanded his men to fire and that hired help from up North scattered like a covey of quail. Well, that was really all there was to it. Oh, the Yanks shot back from behind the trees and made a couple of halfhearted attempts to charge the line in the road, but after an hour or so they decided they would rather go back to Memphis and think about attacking some spot in Mississippi other than this particular one."

Big John sat back, chuckling, his eyes starting to close, but Margaret put her hand on his knee and he roused himself. "What is it, sweetheart?" Margaret looked again to the portrait.

"Oh. Well, the General came through it all in fine fashion

and everyone wanted to make a hero of him but he wouldn't have it. Told his family he didn't want to hear about it anymore. He said to my daddy that a man shouldn't be put over others just for doing what was his to do in this world, that all he had done was to keep his eyes and ears open so he'd know what that was when it came along."

That is how she finally came to know with certainty that she had come to where she belonged and where her story could continue forward. Here, in Cape House. It came to her at that moment, the moment the General's belief in his own story was made clear. She was to bear the General's descendants, no matter that he was dead, he lived in Big John. Her children would be the General's children, the children of the great soldier. She was comforted to have it all resolved at last and from that day until his death, Margaret fondly called Big John "General."

MARGARET CAPE STEPS cautiously from her bedroom into the back hall that reaches west toward the center of Cape House. She is eager to take this first venture beyond her room and the dark library, but her senses are heightened, like those of a wild creature stepping from the forest's cloak into an open meadow. Three oblong patches of light mark the course of the long hall, two of them extending from doors at either end of the kitchen porch on the north—a sunny room with square, nine-paned windows the length of its back wall—and the other from the open door to the kitchen immediately past. The table on the porch is laid for dinner, still hours away, but it is Saturday afternoon and she supposes Sam is in Rosamond, playing dominoes at Ike's Pool Room, and he likes to have everything in order before he leaves.

A gilt wood screen conceals the hall's corner, and around it, two extra side chairs sit against the wall, next to the closed double doors of the dining room. She reaches the second chair feeling feverish and a little nauseated. Rivulets of perspiration roll down her temples, and she sits down to rest, pressing the side of her face against the varnished casing of the doorway. It is only that she moved too quickly to this place. The distress will pass if she sits here quietly.

The chapel is close, between the dining room and the Front Hall and its single, carved door stands open halfway. Margaret pulls the door shut behind her after she enters, then inches down the center aisle and toward the raised altar, reaching from one pew to the next, distrustful of her slippers on the polished pine floor. Beyond the altar, a curved wall of emerald-and-gold stained glass transforms the afternoon's flat light so that it is colored and indistinct, like the pictures in her mind only days ago.

She last came here, when? Weeks past, years, she cannot know. The Cape Bible is on the altar table, atop three Asian silks, and she recalls that she sometimes read it or, as now, sat in the first pew with her head bowed and counted the nails in the boards that ran crosswise to the altar. When the daffodils bloomed in February, she brought bouquets and placed them in the chased silver chalice that sat beside the Bible and, once, in October, she placed full bolls of cotton under the table, taking a few strands from them each time she came until only the brown, dry pods were left. She cannot look without more pushing into her mind and she closes her eyes to stem the flow, but it does not stop and she remembers when it was she last came to the chapel. They brought Chapin Finley here the day of his death. Or Sam brought him, pulling him beside the last pew where she sat and she looked down on him. The bumping sound of his soft body being pulled across the boards was magnified by the near walls of the chapel. She can hear it still.

She moves her weight forward on her hips a little, relieving the pressure from the hard bench. "Mrs. Cape? Mrs. Margaret Cape?" Her name is called out loud and, still, the bumping continues. She turns in the pew and listens. She heard her name here on another day, but this is not quite the same. "Mrs. Cape? You in there?" It is not the body pulled along the floor, after all, but the booming voice of the big man Hardy Mall from a few days past and he is rapping at the front door of Cape House. Margaret tucks her feet beneath the bench and waits for him to leave.

The disruption unsettles her. People make everything more difficult. Big John said as much when he selected the silks on their honeymoon trip and brought them to Cape Plantation, the same silks she later placed on the altar. "See, sweet thing," he explained, "the fine Rosamond ladies put these in their houses. Not everywhere, mind, just two or three particularly noticeable places. Makes people think maybe they been somewhere 'sides Titus County." He laughed at his own disrespect and pulled her under his arm and she smiled to recall the warm strength of that embrace. " 'Course you don't need nothing like that. I'm the one needs these. Know what for?" He gave her time to guess but she shook her head. "Just a reminder. See this rooster in this one? He's an ol' cock like me. And this little waterfowl here all soft and gentle. That's you, muffin. This other one. The man holding up his sword? Now, I don't know what it was meant to be but it makes me think how he can end the others' lives in a flash and they wouldn't know what hit them. And that just reminds me, Margaret, is all," he sighed. "First thing, that how and when I die is out of my hands. Best thing for me to do is go about my own business until then. You see?" She did. "And, second thing, it says, of course, is 'People can mess up your own business.' "

The bench is too hard for her to sit any longer and she lies down on her side, curling into her knees. It seems unlikely that anyone will find her, but they are coming. She knows that and it troubles her a little that she knows.

The sun is midpoint on the stained-glass wall so that she lies in the shadow of the altar table and just below the light, looking up into its wide shaft hanging above her. It is comforting to be encased in the dark space beneath it, yet the light charms her as well. She extends her arm toward it but only the fingers

of her hand are illuminated, suspended apart from the rest of
her and moving in a graceful roll, each in turn curling to her
palm. "Margaret, is that you?" She hears the familiar voice
clearly and jerks her hand back from the light. Almost at once,
she knows that it is only a memory. Nevertheless, she raises
her head slowly from the bench until her eyes are above its
back and she can see all of the long room to the door. No one
is there.

8

Middle gray is a wise selection for the color of the cars of the Mississippi Highway Patrol, being the color of so many other things in the same country, especially in the Delta when the sky is working up to a rain. Sam spots the top of the patrol car before he is closer than a half-mile, but he knows already where to look for it. These last six months, he has driven this length of Highway 4 coming and going almost once a week and, each time, the car has been somewhere close to this corner. Sam is not frightened by police officers but respectful, in the way he knows not to turn his back on a mean goose. Big Mama said, "Stay out the man's sights," and his mother was shot to death and the man let the murderer out for money after five years and the whole lot of them, children and all, were locked up once on account of his father, a bootlegger in the '20s when it was illegal everywhere and not just big Baptist Mississippi.

Nowadays, like this officer in this car, the man might be a Negro, but it is no difference in the rules. Sam figures he is stopped for no good reason as much now as before. The black ones always keep their sunglasses on and Sam used to think, like the others, they in the white man's pocket, thinking like the white man wants because they scared, but lately he thinks some of 'em just plain like it.

He slows the Buick from fifty-five to fifty-two and passes the patrol car without looking. Looking got him stopped one time south of Clarksdale, but that, of course, was 1953 when he was a young man and a young man's look could be enough to kill him. He feels his pocket for the roll of bills, knowing that will certainly mean trouble for him with the officer, a short man, short and black making him doubly resentful. "Didn't you see my lights flash?" he asked Sam the first time he stopped him, both of them knowing he had never flashed any lights. This one stays here all the time now, catching speeders and DUI's from the Tunica casinos. It is a disadvantage to coming this far, along with the distance, but one of the casinos is on its way out, lifting anchor as soon as next week, and another has just opened, both meaning a shave of the house advantage, lowering the minimum bet amount and the winnings are better with less risk.

When the casinos first opened, he drove Chapin Finley everywhere, letting him have his drink in the backseat both ways, plus the free drinks all the gamblers were given in-house. They didn't have much to say to one another anyway and, yet, Mr. Chappy had done him one favor. He taught him the rules of blackjack and Sam is a good counter even with more than one deck. He always makes a little, sometimes as much as $300. Today, his take is a $153. Once, he lost $50 playing the $5-minimum table, because no casino was coming or in trouble enough to have a lower one. Fifty is his bottom limit and he stopped. That were Mr. Chappy's problem. No limits. Used to, he picked Chapin Finley up after cards at the club, coming to the men's bar to signal him it was time. At precisely 11:45, Chapin Finley would stand up no matter the winning or losing and say, "I don't want to turn into a pumpkin," and he was gone. But, that was before the riverboat casinos that now lined the Mississippi River from Robinsonville to Natchez, and, there, he had no limits of any sort, losing happily and in significant amounts.

He watches the nose of the patrol car for a long distance past. His heart catches when it suddenly moves out and turns into the road behind him but no lights flash, the blue light does not appear and he drives fifty-two miles per hour, his foot frozen at the proper pressure. The gray car follows only a few hundred yards before stopping on the highway, then backing into a field access drive and under its overhanging briars.

It is another hour before he turns from the state highway south onto the gravel road to Cape. He is later today than he intended. It is nearing three weeks since she waked, and he has already had to leave her twice to gamble. Used to, they left her often, him bringing Mr. Chappy two, three nights each week and staying until after midnight. When they returned, he always checked her good but she never moved from where she was placed. Once, by accident, he left her hand turned under her and it was the same for hours until he found it and rubbed the blood back. At least, that was the way it was the last six or seven years when he walked her around or she didn't walk. In the beginning, though, she was always wandering off and she being such a little thing was hard to uncover. The barn, they'd find her there sometimes, but more often she'd go up into the pasture somewhere and that were one of the first things Mr. Chappy sold off, the cattle. Things are different now, and with her thinking, too, even worse. She might be anywhere when he gets back. Last time he couldn't find her at all for an hour and, then, just like that there she was in her bed.

Still, he can't bring her along with him to these places. Himself, he wears his brown zippered jacket and the British cap Mr. Big John brought him when Miz Marg'ret first came to Cape and says nothing to the mix of people around him. They mostly come down from Memphis, he guesses, which makes him easier with being there, not as likely to be caught sitting next to a former guest at Cape whom he had served. It does not appear to bother the other Negroes who come, smoking Pall Malls and sitting one leg out, the other propped on the bar of stools at the slots, as if they are the same and as entitled to their folly as the whites who sit next to them in the same pose with Marlboros. But his daddy told him white peoples was like a herd of cattle. There's no reason you can't walk in the middle of them, but don't get too close to any one of them or look them in the eye and don't be making a lot of noise or they'll charge and run you down, and he concentrates on his cards and makes it his practice not to take a chair next to a white person. If one sits down there on his own, that is not his business.

He turns left into the drive. The dark is coming, but it is only just dinnertime and he has dinnertime duties yet to attend. He had left off thinking that she would ever be back and that meant there was no point in saying nothing about nothing and, yet, here she is and he is joyful but troubled, unable to remember any old peoples' saying ever told him that is useful in deciding what he should do. He supposes his people were just like the maid in the alligator story who quit when her boss brought home a pet alligator to raise in the bathtub. "I quit. I don't work for people who raise alligators," she wrote him in a note. "I would have mentioned it before, but I didn't think it would come up." Maybe there is nothing to do anyway. Everything is much the same, isn't it, except Mr. Chappy is dead and Miz Marg'ret is up walking around? Since Mr. Hardy Mall, no one else has come near and he sent him away good and tried not to consider the look Mall threw in his direction when he was out the front door.

Sam parks the Buick on the circle of the drive and comes through the front door into Cape House. He is already humming. He stops and listens but hears no sounds. He opens each door as he proceeds down the hall and sees nothing. She is not in the bedroom. He goes to the kitchen and pulls cold tuna salad from the refrigerator, preparing a half sandwich, and empties a can of fruit cocktail into a bowl. He straightens the dishes already on a small mat at the end of the kitchen porch table, then sets out to look for her again.

Her russet brown dress is wool jersey, which warms her. The chapel, too, as it lets in and holds the languor of the afternoon. Margaret sleeps, then wakens at intervals to see the hours passing by without her. The chapel door opens, closes, and it is only then that she notices she can no longer see the walls around her and the light through the window has faded to dull gray. She is sitting up when Sam enters for the second time.

"Miz Marg'ret, what you doin' in here? You c'mon now," he says, pulling her up with both hands. "I got supper all ready to go." She lets him lift her and take her elbow to steady her while they walk together down the long aisle to the door.

"He was here," she says.

"Who that?"

"The man who came in the morning. Mr. Mall. I didn't answer and he went away."

Sam is silent for a few steps. "Have you thought about what is he thinkin', you know, comin' out here when you locked up in here all by yourself?"

"I knew not to answer." She wonders at her knowing even as she tells of it. There is only a scratchy, uncomfortable feeling but it is out of reach. She tries to explain. "Someone held this out to me and I was waiting for something else instead and said, 'No, that is not the one.' It was very much like that."

"My cousin's boy, Poo Poo, he say Mr. Hardy a big man over in Tallahatchie County what maybe wants to be a big man here and everywhere, too. I don't know." He doesn't know. There is a Master lock in the kitchen drawer and he will put it on the gate in the morning.

Margaret feels her legs give way. She grabs the back of the

last pew to keep from falling. "Let me sit here," she says and sinks down onto cool wood, leaning her head against the curved back.

"You need your little pills, Miz Marg'ret?" Sam kneels beside her. "We was movin' too fast, I shoulda known better."

She shakes her head and wonders, at the same time, what the pills are. She keeps her eyes closed and waits for the sickness to pass. She remembers her last brandy was before breakfast and she wants another. Sam kneels beside her and she pulls close to his shoulder, so close a silky strand of her grayed hair clings to his wiry nap. At last, she pushes up, bracing her arm against his. "I want to sleep," she says.

"Yes, ma'am." He holds the door back as she steps into the hall and turns left. "I picked up some good whiskey today. A hot toddy'd be good to sleep on, wouldn't it?"

She smiles and pats his hand. "Yes. It would."

When Margaret is delivered to the bedroom and before he goes to heat the whiskey, Sam returns to the foyer. He pushes the thick cypress door to and turns the bolt twice, making certain he hears the solid thump and knows the lock will hold. "Taking sides between white peoples like sidin' 'tween a rat and a snake. Get bit and die either way, so stay back away," they said, but what if wherever he stays takes a side, and not just altogether between white peoples. What would Big Mama say to that?

Cape Plantation, 1945  "Man cannot understand, on his own, the great mysteries of life. Only God has ken of those and allows man understanding only to the degree he sees fit. We are nothing without Him and we can do nothing without Him." Margaret heard Father Moran say these words at Mass many times in her childhood and when Big John died unexpectedly she decided that perhaps he was right after all. She had noticed that events had a certain order, that she could sometimes see a plan emerging and, certainly, that is almost what the father had been saying all along. Still, Big John was dead and she had not borne a child.

Dying was not a mystery to Margaret, a doctor's child, who often heard her parents speak of death and who, at thirteen, had first witnessed the death of one of her father's patients. "Death is simply the term we use to designate the end of life, Margaret," Dr. Finley had lectured her on the return home. "It is a mere word for the absence of something; it has no faculty to affect you, my dear."

Cancer had slowly wasted Carlton Stowe, his bedridden final months producing the expected pneumonia, and she was willing to follow her father's direction to hold the old man's left arm firmly to the mattress while her father held the other, pinning the dissipated body beneath his own, and they held him there until the paroxysms finally ceased and the rising phlegm in his lungs had choked him and the arm Margaret struggled to contain lay heavy against her hands and she released her grip. But, following that, Margaret had to be coaxed to approach again the inanimate body to assist in combing his hair and cleaning the spittle from his face, which remained horribly contorted from his final struggles to breathe, and all the other preparations that had to be taken before the Stowe family could be permitted in the room.

"When the life left him, old Carl was nothing more than a piece of debris. We accord his body some respect out of deference to his survivors, but it is of no matter to him anymore." As he drove, Dr. Finley glanced back and forth from the roadway to Margaret, who silently attended his words. "Do you understand, Margaret? Carlton Stowe has become inert matter and the only way he, or it, can possibly harm you is if someone drops it on you."

Anne Finley was troubled when she learned the following morning what had transpired and even more so when, to reassure her that no ill had come to Margaret, her husband repeated what he had told their daughter. She detained Margaret from attending her morning classes and, instead, took her to the rectory at St. Andrew's, where they met with Father Moran, who spent almost three hours explaining to her the Catholic principles concerning eternal life, last rites, and the soul, but all too late. The metaphors used by the parish priest were charming but she had seen firsthand now the drool and disarray of dying, the smell of bodily wastes oozing from relaxed orifices, and the dispatch with which lifeless matter was removed from the sight of those still living. She had already accepted, for the most part, her father's view of things and her later work as a nurse only confirmed for her that the process from birth to death so closely approximated the lifespan of an ordinary weed that there was exactly the same likelihood that anything of interest could emerge from a decomposing human to take residence in a limbo or purgatory.

On November 1, 1944, Dr. Robert Samuel Finley died and it was not until that day that Margaret found any reason to mistrust their shared understanding of death, although it was merely a thought that came to her barely defined. While it was certainly true that Dr. Finley was lifeless, waxen, lying in the mahogany coffin before them, something kept her from totally equating him with a dead weed on a compost pile even though she was struggling to do so. Anne Finley had insisted on a High Mass, ignoring her husband's own request, or perhaps he had mentioned only to Margaret that he wanted to be cremated, ashes strewn under the hemlock tree in their side yard, with no "pagan rituals" of any sort. While Margaret believed that the nature of his funeral arrangements could not possibly be of any importance to her father now, she also knew that it was, in some way, terribly important and it was this contradiction which raised her doubts about their mutual position.

Big John died of influenza less than three months later and it was then that her doubts became certainties. It was purely selfish, she knew, but it simply could not be that he was obliterated without a trace. He was part of her story. She was to have the General's children. That could not change and, yet, he was gone.

Margaret considered these matters for weeks after Big John's funeral. She devoted all of her vigor to her speculations, leaving her bed only to sit in the library, where she would remain for hours until Sam or his wife, Ella, would come, rapping on the glass panes of the outside doors to fetch her to dinner or, more often, to bring her a tray until she had ordered them to stop and then for good measure had directed Sam to build a brick wall across the outside of the French doors and paint it white, so as to conceal that entrance for all time. She decided that the General's story must continue, though he had been dead some fifty years and, so, it must continue even with the death of Big

John, as would his own story. That was not touched by the organic processes of death and, more, there was the order that suggested the hand of something greater.

She once asked her father about the order of her story and its source. He had put his brushy face close to hers the way he sometimes did, so that she could feel his breath on her face as he spoke, and told her that she was not to trouble herself. "These matters will resolve themselves if you do your part. You must only seek and attend to that well. The rest will follow." To Margaret's surprise, her mother seemed not to know of the stories. "God is the only story," she said firmly. "He will do with your life as He pleases. Practice your faith, say your rosary and confess your sins, and leave the rest to Him."

Margaret built a chapel in which she could meditate on this dilemma and pray. She allocated a portion of the Front Hall and a portion of the dining room, creating a long narrow room with one entrance from the hall. At the far end to the outside was placed a curved wall of stained-glass panels, extending from floor to ceiling and encased in wide mahogany timbers, and whose effect was to transform the outside of the house with its two-story rectangular main section and the side yard and one-story wing on the opposite side so that it looked like a steamship sailing westward across the green fields.

A narrow shelf, waist-high, followed the curve of the glass wall. On this, Margaret placed a large polished brass crucifix, a sterling chalice for the communal wine refreshed each day, Big John's family Bible, King James Version, which she read daily and then left open to Hebrews 12:14, and a candelabrum with three tapers to be lit during the time she used the chapel. A small platform, two steps above the chapel floor, held a lectern, as she occasionally asked the parish priest from Greenwood to give Mass for her and the servants, and on the opposite side a large statue of the Virgin Mary holding the Christ child.

She entered the chapel each morning for an hour or more

to say her rosary and recite certain verses and then to remain silent and very still. She listened very closely so that she heard the beating of her own heart, even the blood pulsing from it, into her neck, into her brain, but she did not hear anything more. She supposed that she must be listening to the wrong sounds. It was the same with everyday sounds, wasn't it, where one fails to hear the ticking of the clock until stopping to attend to just that? Margaret continued to read Big John's Bible, the noisy ways in which the Almighty manifested itself to mortals—rain, fire, earthquake, the human voice, the coo of a dove. She listened for those sounds now, alternating her attention from one to another. Her concentration was so great each time that she often left the chapel fatigued and permitted Ella to bring her a small snifter of brandy, which she sipped while resting in her bed, a cool cloth on her forehead. She heard nothing but, inexplicably, her confidence was gaining strength and she was not altogether surprised when, during her chapel meditations, she finally heard a voice calling her.

"Margaret, is that you?"

She did not answer but rose from where she sat and stepped to the platform, crossing it to close the Bible before drinking the remaining wine from the chalice and, then, as she reached to snuff the candles, his hand grasped her wrist, holding it away.

"Margaret, what is this? Why are you here?" John Buie Cape III looked down at her, his sharp blue eyes flickering with the candlelight. She did not return his gaze but stared at his uniform, her lips parting slightly as she comprehended what was presented to her. A valiant soldier home from the war. Big John's son and the great-grandson of General John Buie Cape.

10

The rain comes hard Monday morning until almost sunrise and, on the Square, the dusty red brick of the Georgian courthouse is sodden. From his desk, Niles can see across the Square but his gaze remains within the limits of his banker's light. Since 6:30 A.M. he has been making his way, piece by piece, through the work pile stacked to the left of his desktop—reading new decisions of the Fifth Circuit and the Mississippi Supreme Court, revising witness examinations for the Barrett trial set for Wednesday, answering letters. He has a preference for Rosamond as it is from his window—deserted, its sharp lines blurred, streets glistening and viewed from above—but he does not need to see it to know what is there. Rosamond is home and it was much the same when he was a boy of eight as it is now.

He takes the next document from the stack and seeing what it is, frowns. His little surprise from the post office, where he stopped earlier, the rain still coming so that he worried he would get everything soaked between the building and his Bronco truck left idling at the curb. He went in anyway and there it was—a single, white business envelope, lying on the metal floor of the postal box, neatly squared to the sides. It bore the chancery clerk's return and was addressed "Niles Abbott,

Esq." When he tore open the envelope, he saw the order and Margaret Cape's name and dropped the document back in the box for Delores to pick up later with the rest of the mail. He was at the curb and the truck when he suddenly changed his mind and trotted back to the lobby, opened the drawer again, and took the order with him. It was just that the box had never been empty like that before, the envelope lying there, alone, as if it were waiting for him and he could not push that picture of it from his mind.

Saturday, he had looked at the statutes, then the file. The court's proceedings were rife with error and, so, he is not Margaret Cape's conservator, no matter the court's order, and that made the appearance of it in his mailbox all the more unsettling. At the office, he placed the order midway in his work stack as a reminder to call Cordeman, but here it is at the top already. He moves it a second time, again halfway down.

Metal scratches at the front door lock and the bolt thumps open. Niles looks at his watch. Ten minutes until eight. The sound of footsteps fades into the front downstairs office and he presses the telephone intercom button, then "2."

"Yeah?" Charley's voice is nasal—"Otherwise," he says, "I could have been Marlon Brando"—but his enthusiasm for the day ahead is clear. He's an "optimistic realist," he says. "I know things are bad, but I'm always hopeful they won't get any worse."

"Hey. Morning, Charley. You got a minute?"

"Sure, buddy. I'm heading over to Tony's is all. Come on down."

Seconds later Niles knocks on the open door of Brandon's office and Charley invites him in. His rangy body is a shadow against the street window behind his desk, a dictating microphone in an outstretched hand, balancing by one foot on the window's ledge and the other on the open bottom drawer of his desk. He faces his self-named "Wall of Fame," on which is arranged his diploma from Ole Miss law school, licenses, and photographs from bar conventions, United Way campaigns, and chamber of commerce dinners as well as those from fishing and hunting trips and two terms as state senator.

Niles drops into one of the blue leather club chairs in front of the desk, staring at the wall along with Charley. In his own office, he displays only his diploma from Yale Law School, '85, and a Donnie Finley watercolor, *One White Jacket,* depicting a scene in the interior of a favorite New Orleans restaurant. His Louisiana license from his six years with Harkin & Wells is in the drawer of his desk, along with a framed letter of gratitude from Justice Gray, whose clerk he was on the Fifth Circuit Court of Appeals. At one time in New Orleans, he also kept a large photograph of his wife, Julie, on his desk but now that she is no longer his wife, he does not.

"Did you get my research on the Mall case, your motion to compel?" Niles asks.

"Yeah. Thanks. Cordeman heard us Friday. Said he'd let us know in a few days." Charley continues to hold the microphone as he pages through the stack of papers in front of him. "I feel kind of sorry for him. He doesn't want to cross old Hardy, but he knows we're entitled to Hardy's financial records under *Merton.*"

"You really think the law will have anything to do with Dewitt's decision?"

The shadow head bobs up in surprise. "My man, you must have been practicin' in Louisiana entirely too long! Of course it will. This is Mississippi. There couldn't be a more different state from lawless Louisiana than Mississippi! The law is God in Mis'sippi."

"C'mon, Charley."

"No. I'm serious. Are we goin' to have to go over this again? I thought I convinced you down there in New Orleans, you all worried you were comin' back to some Byzantine place outside the reach of justice. Mississippi cherishes the law, Niles, reveres it. And every Mississippi judge, I don't care if he's a Harvard-educated intellect like Lincoln Eli or the bottom of the barrel like our Dewitt, every one of them is devoted to being a faithful guardian of the law. The difficulty, see, is in when they start deciding what the law is."

Niles knows that the difficulty is that it is impossible to stop Charley talking when he is in the rhythm of his own voice, like a stabled racehorse moving his neck in continuous imitation of the victorious reach toward the finish line. "Rosamond has changed," Charles Brandon assured Niles at their New Orleans interview. "I'm not interested in playing politics," Niles told him, and Charley said, "Yeah, I understand what with your dad and all." "I'll follow the law and practice with the same standards I would anywhere," he persisted, so that Charley finally laughed and said, "Buddy boy, if you're good enough, you can piss on the courthouse lawn at twelve noon. If you're good enough."

"The law is the law," Niles says.

Charley's laugh explodes from the dark. "Nah. You know better than that, boy. There's all sorts of law. Take for instance. There's the law of Moses, there's the natural law or, more often, its cousin, the *Mississippi* natural law. All that in the statute books and the cases—even that is up to interpretation. The trick is to get the judge to the right law to apply. See? Louisiana's different. All that Napoleonic Code rat's nest. I don't know. Maybe the judges there did want to follow the law, just couldn't figure out what it was and said the hell with it. Anyway, fortunately for our lady, *Merton* is the law in Mississippi no matter what kind of law you look at, natural or unnatural. Cordeman's got to apply it."

"Well, you'll never guess what else our fine guardian of the law has done."

"Appointed you conservator of the Cape lady?" Charley laughs at Niles's open look of surprise. "Dewitt asked me about it first, at the coffee club. Said he needed some intricate legal footwork—the family is on his back—and what'd I think. So, I told him you were his man and would do a superduper job for him."

"Thank you so much, Charley. Why couldn't you put him on to Stewart Ellis?"

"Stewart Ellis is a lightweight. Dewitt thinks this is important. Really, it's a compliment to you that he wants you to do it." Charley rises from his chair and, in a seamless motion, comes to the front of the desk and into the arc of fluorescent light. His hawk nose and prominent cheekbones suggest a Choctaw chief, and he is a sturdy, rough-looking man, too hairy, his hands too large for a man who works in a business suit. It makes his physical grace all the more surprising, mesmerizing. Niles presses deeper into the chair. "Think about this. You'll get to work with some regular people for a change. From the judge on down. That'll be good experience for you."

"Judge Cordeman is a regular person?" Niles is scornful.

Charley tips his head and flashes a dimpled grin, the one he uses to cajole. "OK, we all know Dewitt Cordeman is one sandwich short of a good picnic but he *is* the chancellor. He gets to decide practically everything—including my case against Mall, remember—without a jury. It won't hurt you to get on his good side."

"There's a problem. That's what I was going to say. They screwed it up already. It's going to take a lot of work to get it right."

Charley returns to the back of his desk and flips through more papers, his eyes averted from Niles. "Don't make this too difficult, Niles. Just do the legwork the court wants. You're not back at the law review debating the fine points of the law. Make a list of what she has and lock her up somewhere. Don't be making something difficult out of a simple one-two. She's unconscious, isn't she? Best kind of client to have." He pauses, inviting Niles's concurrence, but the younger man holds back, looking down to pick at a loose thread on the arm of the chair.

"Think of it this way. Cordeman says not only is the old lady a mental case, she has a medical condition—heart, aneurysm, or something, I forget—and she could croak anytime. Do a good job on this and he'll probably let you handle the estate, too. That could add up, you know."

Niles immediately thinks of several conflicts of interest in a conservator proceeding to handle his ward's estate. As executor, would he sue himself for breach of fiduciary duties as conservator? But, Charley paints the law with a broader brush and Niles can't call him on it every instance and he doesn't now. "He said you could answer any questions I had about her."

"That *I* could?" Charley grins, pleased in some way. "Nah, she's a little too old for even me. But, I will say this, there was a time I might hesitate to send a handsome, young stud like you out there without a pair of metal britches. I think you're safe now, though."

"That's it?"

Charley shrugs. "You can't tell about Dewitt. I don't know what he meant. She's not from around here. Did he tell you that?"

Niles shakes his head.

"Yeah. Back east somewhere. Connecticut, Massachusetts, I don't remember. Hooked up somehow with Big John Cape, old enough to be her grandfather's father and, then, when he passes, marries his son, who was still a good bit older than she was. Traded her virginity *twice* for the same plantation. It's probably a record." Charley stands and takes the hopsack jacket hung over the back of the chair. "You hungry? Come on over to Tony's with me."

Niles remains seated. "Well, here's the problem, though. Turns out I'm not really her conservator. In my opinion, Dewitt's order is based on insufficient process and the whole thing's invalid."

Charley returns to sit on the front of his desk. "I'll tell you my opinion. I think you need to remember law is like dancing.

Takes people to do it and some people do it better than others. I think, if you aren't careful, you're gonna end up with more law and less justice, if you know what I mean."

"If I take an invalid conservatorship, I could be sued for legal malpractice, at the very least."

"Now, see. That's what I'm saying. Who's goin' to sue you? Margaret Cape? She'll be dead before you know it. Her kin? They got to find their way down South and past Memphis first. Anyway, as long as you act in her 'best interests' what's the damage? I can tell you right now what her best interests are. Get her hair washed every Saturday, nails polished, Fleet enema, then beddy-bye. That's what they all want at her age." Charley slaps his knees and stands again. "I know this, Niles. There is nothing more useless in this world than an old lady and nothing that can cause more trouble. You get an inventory and put her somewhere she won't be a nuisance. Remember what I told you, every file gets opened, it's like a love affair. Easy to start, difficult to bring to a happy end. Now, how about the coffee club at Tony's? You need to meet these people, buddy boy. They're goin' to be thinkin' you went off to school and got Yankee disease."

Niles follows Charley out the door of his office but, at the last second, turns to the stairs. "Another time, OK? I have to run out to Bayou Glen and check on Dad. He won't eat or some crazy thing."

BACK AT HIS desk, Niles picks up the next paper from the work pile and, impossibly, it is the Cape order again. He tries to follow Charley's advice, just to see how it feels, purposefully turning the order face up, affixing a Post-it, scribbling "new file" for Delores's attention, and putting the paper in the "out" box, but he sits in his chair, unable to reach for any other work, feeling as if he has driven toward the ditch on a dare and must turn the wheels back up on the highway before it is too late. The electronic mail comes up on the computer's screen with the pressing of Alt-E and he quickly types a message to Delores: "Pls find Chan. Cordeman, give me #, place to reach." Niles presses F9 to forward the mail and retrieves the order from the box. Relieved, he pulls the next document from the stack to his left.

Cape Plantation, 1945 🖋 "Is that you, Margaret?" John Buie had asked her that very question so many times. She answered readily, at first, eager to appear before him. There was a pleasure in that, forgotten in the months preceding, of having another place his consciousness radiant upon you. Yes, Sam and Ella had been with her and Ella's nephew, who carried the coal and chopped wood, but it was not the same at all and not because they were servants or colored, which, as anyone in Titus County knew by that time, was of no consequence to Margaret. Nor was it the same with Little Mildred, who brought the younger children some Sunday afternoons, or her husband, Frank, whom Margaret had occasionally seen while he directed the farming and gin before John Buie's return. To them, she might be a lump of Yazoo clay as much as a thing with living sensibilities, no matter.

Her father had told her about being alone. "Each of us lives forever beyond fathom, Margaret. You are you and I am me and that is the end of it. Do not expect to be greeted at the portals of your soul by another. It is enough that the other acknowledges your existence." And, yet, he had not told her all of it because she knew she had touched the soul of Big John and he, hers. Then, John Buie, too. It was very close to that, at least, for a short while. Perhaps she had remembered it wrong and her father had only said not to attempt, rather than expect, to know another in that way and perhaps that much was true.

June was the time for chopping out cotton. John Buie left Cape House often then early in the morning to gather the hands and take them to their fields. Margaret had watched Big

John at the same task and heard his exuberant laughter while he joked with the Negroes, slapping them on their backs as they climbed onto the bed of the pickup truck so that one would almost think he envied them their day over his own. But John Buie gathered the men quietly and Margaret tried but she could not hear when he left his room each morning and descended the stairs before going outside to the office to wait on the crew.

He stayed out of sight most days and she wondered whether he had learned this at war. Yes, he had the responsibilities of the farm now to account for some of his absences, but he had too many things to do and places to go in the evenings, Margaret thought, for a man who had been away for almost three years. She waited in the Front Hall for his return those first few nights, rising expectantly when she heard him open the door and enter the foyer. But he only looked at her rather strangely, stumbling a little at times so that she knew he had been drinking whiskey somewhere and, once, he patted her cheek and his hand smelled of Shalimar and, then, he climbed the stairs to his room and she was left alone.

On that June morning, she sat reading in the side yard and, this time, when John Buie came out of the kitchen porch to his office she heard. She heard the field hands begin to gather and, finally, she heard John Buie's voice. Still, she could not hear the words he was saying and she peered through the wrought-iron grill in the back wall to see. He stood quite still among them, dressed in khaki work clothes, an obelisk in the group's center. His work shirt hung unbuttoned and loose outside his trousers, the short sleeves rolled up to expose heavily muscled arms and shoulders, his height and size accentuated by the slump-shoulders of the Negroes circled about him. A straw fedora shaded his face. Margaret rested her chin against the wall's plaster shelf beneath the grill to listen as he softly droned orders to the workers, her eyes half closing to the sound over the scent of jasmine from the garden behind her. Suddenly his voice rose as he wheeled toward one of the men, who jumped away like a dog fearing a kick, and Margaret started. But, of course, John Buie did not strike the man. Soon after, he climbed into the driver's seat of the truck, the men scrambling onto the bed to be carried to the fields to chop the cotton. Margaret waited until she heard the truck turn onto the county road and then she opened the back gate. She crossed the drive to the office and stepped inside.

She waited there for almost an hour. Ella came to throw vegetable peelings on the ground at the back of the barn and, once, Margaret thought Sam was coming to the office itself in search of her. But he turned at the last moment to go into the other side of the shed and came out carrying a saw, intent on some project in the house. After this, she retreated to the very back of the room, where the hand-tooled saddle Big John had used for Tucker was stored on a walnut stand. She pushed aside the blanket that lay atop the saddle and straddled it, pulling her sheer cotton skirt up off of her legs and putting her feet in the stirrups. She leaned back against the rough board wall. A large square window was high above her head and the room was warm already, filled with the sweet smells of oil and leather. She had come here often to Big John, bringing him a glass of iced tea or some ham and biscuits. The wooden desk had always sat toward the front and, across from where she sat, she could almost touch the oak filing cabinet where Big John had stored his important papers. He would search and file and fuss while Margaret sat on the saddle watching. "Don't you think I don't know there's a smile under there," he teased her. "You jus' keep on giggling at this old man. I'll fix you later." And then he would wink and make a sudden motion toward her and send her running breathless and laughing back to the house. The farm was quiet now. Margaret closed her eyes and listened to the flies buzzing at the glass panes, sleeping finally, until John Buie returned.

She woke to the crunch of the gravel drive beneath the tires of the truck, then its engine silenced, its metal door open and shut. She watched the office door as it swung back and its frame was filled by the shadow of John Buie.

"Is that you, Margaret?" he said, squinting to see her. "What are you doing, girl? Riding ol' Tucker in your dreams?"

Margaret swung her legs up on the saddle so that a bare foot rested on either side of the pommel. For a moment John Buie stared at her legs, exposed and extending from the soft pile of her skirt gathered around her hips. Then, abruptly, he turned away to the desk and began to rummage through the drawers.

"I'm kinda busy this morning, Margaret. Did you need to tell me something?"

She felt a sudden impulse to bolt to the privacy of her own bedroom but the saddle horn was available to hold herself in place and she collected the entirety of her will and strength to answer him deliberately and clearly. "No. I need you to do something."

He did not look at her. "Oh, yeah. What's that?" He continued to leaf through a logbook he had uncovered in the bottom drawer of the desk but the silence finally pulled his gaze to her again. She looked directly at him and could not, would not, say anything further now but she was certain he already understood.

"You know what Frank's been doing? Letting 'em borrow toward next week's pay." John Buie shook his head. "He gets that from his old man. Frank Melton Sr. always believed the best in everyone. The man was constitutionally incapable of suspecting that anyone might have less than an admirable motive. Crazy ol' fool." He looked away from her and methodically adjusted each of the six desk drawers until each was in perfect alignment with the frame of the desk. "You know his wife used that very thing to get him to marry her, told him she was pregnant. Hell, she wasn't pregnant. What do you mean, I don't even know if he had..." He looked back to Margaret, suddenly agitated, angry. "You women just never seem to learn. You know that, Margaret? You sashay any which way you please, then holler your head off if some red-blooded man takes you up on what you're selling." She did not flinch but looked at John Buie steadfastly now and without disguise. Big John had been an elderly man when they married. He was large and strong, but with the soft layers of flesh and rounded edges that came to all men in older years. John Buie, at forty, was as tall and large-boned as his father had been, but he had not yet lost the hardness and strength of youth. Margaret could see that in his face without even seeing his muscular arms and chest both plainly visible beneath the open shirt. Her eyes began to tear and she could not understand why because she was not, was not afraid and she shivered a little under his stare but she was resolute.

"You're not leaving, are you?" he concluded, almost sighing, but she could see the excitement in his eyes and she held his gaze steady as he approached her. He stood to the side of the saddle, touching her skin lightly with his left hand, his fingers stroking her ankle and pressing more firmly as he brought his roughened hand up her leg to the welt of her cotton panties. She placed her hand atop his and he raised his eyes to look at her face. Yes, she was certain now he did see her and a new swell of the exhilaration she had felt these last weeks rose up inside her. She continued to look into his eyes, cold somehow and deep blue, as she unbuttoned one by one the tiny mother-of-pearl buttons on the bodice of her dress, finally untying the satin ribbon woven through the top. She shrugged her shoulders to let the blouse fall gently around her waist then reached her arm behind John Buie's neck and gently pulled his head down to her small, rounded breasts until she could feel his breath heavy and warm against her bare skin. She leaned back then against the boards once more, suddenly absorbed by thoughts of as-yet-unborn babies suckling. His hand came under her then lifting her up, at the same time he swung his leg across the saddle, and with the other hand clutched the back of her long hair, holding her so that she could not move without pain. She closed her eyes tightly as he maneuvered himself to enter her. She had been afraid, after all, but the fear was mixed now with the surge of her blood and the pleasure of exquisite pain as John Buie's thrusts began to drive her rhythmically, repeatedly, against the saddle's rim and when he abruptly stopped, she grabbed wildly at his neck and shoulders to pull him toward her once more.

"Whoa, now." He laughed a little and looked at her through narrowed eyes, seeming to enjoy this moment more than what had preceded it. He waited interminably long minutes before he again began to thrust deep inside her and she cried out almost at once and wrapped her arms and legs tightly around him. She felt a slight shudder of his body then and he sat back. He did not kiss or stroke her but lifted himself off the saddle, zipped his trousers and wiped his face with his shirttail.

"You'd better get on up to the house now. Frank'll be bringing the men back over here in another hour or so." He left without further word or look and Margaret started to leave, but she could only turn sidesaddle before leaning back astride the saddle as John Buie had found her, and then asleep.

She dreamed of Big John and the first time they made love, almost a month after their wedding—"He's an old man. Don't expect much of him," her mother had told her before the wedding, but he was waiting for her sake, saying at last, "I didn't want you to bolt," as if she were some wild colt showing the whites of its eyes. They were in Greece, where they had stayed in Olimbía for several days while viewing the ruins. The room was sparsely furnished, but private, and the balmy Grecian nights had been perfect. Big John watched as she took her first sips of retsina and was so gentle that it made her smile to think of it even now. Big John lay on the bed and called to her to come to him. She tried but the room grew wider the more she walked toward him and then it was as if she were walking through loose piles of cotton and could not get her footing. Her father and mother were in the far corner watching with impassive faces and Sam and Ella looked through the window then ducked down, then looked through again. Suddenly, big arms came up behind her and she knew they were John Buie's. He lifted her toward the bed and laid her down beside Big John, who wore a soldier's uniform now.

She resisted. "I have to see the ruins."

"What, darlin'? You don't have to worry about that. I got them here. They're right outside the door, see?" And they were there and she began to feel vertigo and Big John laid her head on the pillow softly. "Don't you worry, muffin. Just rest here." She closed her eyes and when she opened them again she was no longer in their room but on the cold marble bench outside the Temple of Hera. John Buie stood looking down at her, an angry look across his face. It frightened her and she gasped and with that awoke disturbed and for the first time she noticed that she had cut the soft pad inside her knee on the silver epaulet of the saddle. She rubbed at it to soothe the pain as she began to rock slowly back and forth on the hard, polished leather of the saddle seat. She rocked in a steady rhythm, gradually increasing the pendulum swing of her hips and this time when she came, she did so in peaceful silence.

CHANCELLOR CORDEMAN IS holding court in Sumner and since there is no receptionist or secretary, Niles's call goes directly to the judge's chambers.

He would have preferred to bring the bad news by indirection, but Cordeman's mood will not let him do that and, so, he speaks quickly and with Yankee bluntness. "I've found a number of problems with the conservatorship for Mrs. Cape. It's not valid."

"What are you talking about?" Cordeman is challenging and incredulous at once and Niles lists in ready order the irregularities—a questionable petitioner, incorrect dates, the lack of compliance with the new notice laws.

"Is that it?" Cordeman's mood is uglier than before.

"He doesn't have an attorney signing the petition, and Chancery Rule 6.01 requires..."

" 'All fiduciaries must retain an attorney.' Nathan Bass is not the fiduciary. He's asking—as an interested businessman—that one be appointed," the judge explains, as if to a child. "*You,* you're the fiduciary and you're already a lawyer, and 6.01 makes an exception for that. That's the reason I always try to get one of you boys to do these things. Saves me a lot of trouble. *Usually.* Try to think these things through before calling the court with them, Counselor."

Niles ignores the implicit warning. "Yes, Your Honor. But the lack of sufficient process is the biggest problem."

"Of course." Cordeman pauses. "Problem was you weren't at the hearing to see that the Cape family was duly represented and, so, that cures any notice problems. Now, *she* wasn't there, but she is a damn turnip, so you draft an order for the court to sign, finding that she did, in fact, have notice. Good-bye."

"Wait. I mean, sir. Even if that would be enough for her, Judge, her next of kin would still have to have notice for it to be valid."

"I told you the family was there." Cordeman speaks sharply, but an edge of doubt has crept into his voice.

"The Cape family's her in-laws, Judge. Next of kin, as Your Honor knows, of course, means blood relation. Charley said she came from back east and I would assume it would be someone back there, unless she has some other children or grandchildren."

Niles waits, listening through the dead silence of a minute until Cordeman speaks. "What do you propose would correct these grievous errors of the court, Mr. Abbott?" he asks coldly.

Niles concentrates on keeping his voice neutral so he will not be thought to be talking down to the chancellor. "If, after reasonable diligence, her nearest blood relative can't be found..."

"Reasonable diligence so found by the court. Then what?"

"There is no alternative but to serve constructive notice by publishing for unknown next of kin in the *Rosamond Register*."

"Notice by publication?" Cordeman brays, his voice shrill. "That'll take over thirty days! You know that." The judge sighs and Niles hears the lighter click. "Son, let me tell you something. This is something, now, they don't teach you out of books or like that. Back when they came up with this thirty-day stuff, it took people half that time to get to the county seat. Made sense then. Now we got television and telephones and telefax and you can have a lot done in thirty minutes. Nobody needs thirty days' notice. Now, on the other hand, thirty days of a crazy old lady sittin' on top of one of the biggest plantations in the Mississippi Delta might as well be a lifetime. It won't work. Let's just pick one statute and follow it. I know you fellas always want to cover your ass, but you have to use good sense, too."

"I know it's a little inconvenient, Judge..."

"Inconvenient!" the chancellor bellows. "Hell, yes, it's inconvenient. I know. You don't care about that. No one does. This is the court's ass, think I don't know that? If everyone had died in order, the way they were supposed to, it would have been fine. But, no. And, now, just like always, I'm supposed to clean up the mess." Cordeman wheezes so loudly that Niles holds the phone away from his ear and still hears the labored coughs, the retching and spit into the wastebasket. "Things need to be wrapped up quickly, Niles." Cordeman's voice is barely audible, whispering a secret. "They get out of hand. You can never tell. Ches Cooper told Little Mildred Melton he thought he saw Margaret on the Square the other day and she told Cooper he was an old fart who needed glasses. Well, not in those words but you need extra words to say the same thing when Little Mildred tells you something." Cordeman's drag on his cigarette whistles into the telephone and he is suddenly upbeat, jovial. "Okay, Counselor. Have it your way. But the court does not have the resources to jump through all these hoops you're settin' up, Mr. Invalid Conservator. So, I don't care if you are her fiduciary, you be the one prepares the necessary summonses for the court and I'll have the clerk issue 'em. And, Counselor?"

"Yes, sir?"

"As soon as Margaret Cape is served with process, you get your butt on out there and get what you can underway, conservator or not. Don't wait for a hearing. She won't know the difference. You can start the inventory and have 'em carry her to Bayou Glen. Understood?"

PART TWO

An American holly grows against the house, pressing against the west end of the kitchen porch windows and a few of its branches extend as far as the window of the kitchen proper. Clusters of green berries already cover it and one day in November, when the berries are turned bright red, cedar waxwings will gradually gather on the roof of the barn across and, then, in the late afternoon, descend as one and pick the tree clean. Margaret sits at the porch's long harvest table, a collection of stories by Virginia Woolf resting on its edge, and she reads "The New Dress" for the fourth time since morning, when she remembered it was a favorite. It was only the second reading that brought to mind, as if she had never forgotten, how she knew things. Or how she once knew them and, presumably, still would now that she knew the way again. It is strange she can ever have forgotten that! Portents not of her making, but outside her and, yet, in a language that it seemed only she knew. They came only when they did, not at times expected and that made them noticeably different from the urges and intuitions that were always with her, guiding her not so much from her trust of them as from their persistence.

In that way, as an intuition and for several days, the pasture has been occupying her thoughts inordinately, persistently, but the gravel road to the gate is too far for her to walk. She would never reach the pond beyond, where she sees wood ducks circling above. She came here to this bright room when the inclination began, where she could see through undraped glass to the pasture, at least a part of it, but the feeling has not lessened. Instead, the very sight of it adds to the force of her intuition.

"I can't even look that way. I just see green dollars with little wings flying over the grass like butterfly moths." Chapin Finley had sat at this table, to her right, his large head lowered over Sam's duck gumbo and rice so that the thinning strands of his silky, blond hair grazed the stew while he held the bowl steady with delicate fingers.

"The pasture is part of the house," she said or, no, she had only thought it.

He finished the gumbo and pushed the bowl away, exasperated. "Margaret, do you know what sustains me? You don't have to answer, of course. I'll carry the conversation." He laughed then, a short, bitter laugh. "It's this, Mother. There will come the day when you must go away—surely that will be soon—and I will have to carry on alone." He had looked at her or, more, inspected her, tipping his head one way then the other. "On that inevitable day, I will at last be able to chart the course of Cape Plantation without you incessantly veering us willy-nilly. You, apparently, have never grasped what I have known for simply forever. That we have only one possibility and purpose in life, Margaret, and that is to live with some grace in this crude environment. To add, if we can, some aesthetic value to what came before us. That requires m-o-n-e-y. Q.E.D."

She looked at him, nothing more. She was certain of that. But, blotches of red appeared on his blue-white skin, the last facade of congeniality gone. "Don't judge me, Mother. You! We know you need little. You barely exist these days. I'm the one out in the world for the good of Cape. Not that you would ever know to acknowledge it. We dropped the club membership? Nobody has the least notion. I arrange to be invited by one or another just often enough to show our face there. Do you think I want to go to New Orleans every other month? Those dreadful wet, hot mornings giving a worse headache than you deserve from the night before? But I get seen there. It's a job just keeping up with where's the right place to be. If I lived like you all up there in your head, no one would know Cape or Capes even existed more than a figment of someone's imagination. Someone's underactive imagination."

"You don't think you might upset her, do you, talkin' to her like that 'n all, Mr. Chappy?" So, Sam was there, too, standing behind Chapin Finley and out of his view. His voice was deferential, but she saw the hard look.

"Now, don't you go mother-henning her, Sambo." Her son stood and patted the old man's back. "She doesn't have the least notion what I'm saying. Her elevator's stuck down there somewhere around the mezzanine." He laughed the laugh again, then lifted her from the chair and held her to his chest without effort. She saw them together. He was a large man, like his grandfather Big John, and she was, as he said, barely there. Her legs and arms hung loose and her hair touched her face in a way she would not have arranged. They carried her like that, and she realized that this memory was not very long past and that it was the first she had recalled of any of the dead years.

"It been a good while since you been up there." Sam looks with her toward the pasture. "I could take you up in the Buick. I don't know why it can't go anywhere a Hereford can." She spreads her fingers across the table's dull, uneven wood, bracing herself while the warm surge of new recollection moves through her again. They had carried her everywhere! She, knowing nothing, a limp cloth doll to be put one place or another. How open to harm she must have been all those years, sleeping without cover. Yet, here she is and Chapin Finley is ... dead. A smile tugs at the corner of her mouth and she purses her lips to suppress it. She will not take pleasure in another's demise, although it is true, perhaps, that she had not cared for him much. The thought of her own survival buoys her, nonetheless.

"Anybody in here? Hello?" Both of their heads turn to the open doorway and they listen. Now, the tap, tap on the front door sounds clearly and the scrape as it opens.

"Hello?" Neither Margaret nor Sam speaks, listening to the heavy steps and the voice come closer, until there is a metallic chinking and Sam recognizes the sound of handcuffs hanging from a belt.

"It the man," he says and it is only moments until the sheriff's deputy is there, folded papers in one hand. He extends them toward Margaret.

"Are you Margaret Finley Cape?" he asks. It is the usual sort of question when a summons is served, although this time the deputy asks more in wonder than from duty.

Cape Plantation, 1945 ✍ It was her mother who had suggested the similarity on the first and only trip she made to visit Margaret at Cape Plantation.

"He's like Homer. You must know that."

Margaret did not answer but sipped her iced tea, then pressed the wet, cold glass to her temple. It was insufferably hot, not unlike July, but feeling more so because she had so hoped for a respite from the summer's oven while Anne Finley visited.

Her mother's younger sister had married down in taking Homer, a boy from Lebanon, Missouri, and of no particular religion. Elizabeth Chapin met him somehow while he was serving as a navy seaman in Boston and the mystery of their meeting had subsequently been the focus of family concern after all was said and done and not the substance of their unfortunate life together. What is certain is that she fell under the spell of Homer Cash's considerable charm immediately. He did not even pretend to be a man of principle and, if he had, others would have laughed at him rather than the other way around, which was how it actually was. Rules were as inapplicable to Homer as to a flower, and that is what Homer was, a Missouri hawthorn sprung up in the small hills of Massachusetts, engaged in no more complicated purpose than to be what he was, which was oftentimes as much a surprise to Homer as anyone. While he wooed Margaret's aunt, taking her one day to the homey Irish café and pub in their neighborhood and on another sneaking her aboard his ship to see the steam boiler that was his chief responsibility and, on others, spending extravagant amounts of time lolling in the Chapins' front parlor, playing "Just a Kiss in the Dark" on the Victrola and listening to all Elizabeth had to say, he was becoming engaged to two other Baldwin girls to whom he had also taken a fancy. The matter continued rather uncomfortably for several months and was only settled when Elizabeth announced at one Sunday's dinner table, "I'm going to have Homer's child," her eyes shining with joy at having won the race and knowing that she and Homer would soon be married.

He was a wonderfully entertaining uncle who delighted and frightened Margaret at the same time. She could very well have avoided him altogether, as his laughter invariably marked his location, but it drew her to him as well. Spying her, he would swoop her off the floor and hold her hands in fists pushing them into her face while he taunted, "Stop hitting yourself, Margaret. Stop that, now." Margaret was afraid but so convulsed with giggles she could not escape.

She did not see at first how much like him was John Buie. John Buie was a somber man who rarely smiled and his games were not the ones Margaret had played as a little girl.

"You know I'm right, don't you, dear?" Anne sat rocking with Margaret on the screened kitchen porch watching the workers chop cotton and some were carrying water for the others along the rows. Margaret was not ignoring her mother so much as she was "considering the source" as Dr. Finley used to say and sometimes about Margaret's mother.

Anne Finley believed that nothing could happen that had not already happened with different characters and places before. Margaret supposed these came from her mother's own experience and that, mostly, within her own family. Indeed, Elizabeth was warned by Anne that Homer was nothing more than another Joseph Pruitt, who was Uncle T's wife's younger brother. Joseph was the delight of many a family gathering before he had suddenly taken it in his head to train for the merchant marine and then, after a few weeks, disappear altogether for twenty-five years, suddenly reappearing without a decent explanation. But Elizabeth married Homer anyway and he worked his entire life on the wharfs of Boston and never disappeared in the way Joseph did. Their marriage was alternately peaceful and violent and their family became large—four boys and a girl, who like Homer seemed to carry a little thrill with them wherever they could be found. It was only after their first decade of marriage that Elizabeth found Homer drinking coffee in the kitchen of one of his former fiancées and, put on the alert, subsequently discovered a private log of feminine names and necessary information in the drawer where his heavy socks were kept. When Homer awakened the next morning, he opened his eyes to Elizabeth standing at his side of the bed, both hands gripping a butcher knife raised above him and it was only because of his navy days, Margaret's father later speculated, that he was able to roll from the bed quickly enough to avoid any contact between his body and the blade as Elizabeth brought it swiftly down. Thus, he was spared death at the hands of his young wife, but not death itself. In rolling from the bed so quickly, he was unable to secure his footing and the small rag rug on the floor by the bed slipped, causing him to fall heavily against the bedside stand, which fractured his skull and, ten days later, ended his life. Margaret's mother had said then, "I told you he was like Joseph."

"No one's like anyone, Mother," Margaret said and rose to go find Sam and tell him that the patch on the screen had come loose, to fix it before the evening mosquitoes, and when she married John Buie Cape in late October, she did not tell Anne Finley that a baby was expected in April.

"NO, MA'AM. THAT check hasn't gone through."

Mildred replaces the telephone receiver in its cradle and watches Albert coming up the yard to the patio. He rolls the cord of the electric weed trimmer as he walks. She will try to remember to speak to him about that. He has twisted the cord until it resembles braided hair and, certainly, that cannot do it any good. "Did you give the check to Sam?" she'd asked him last Thursday. "No," he said. Then Friday, "Yes, ma'am." "Well, what did he say?" "Nothing, I guess," with an innocent look. As if that fooled her. Why couldn't they just spit it out? You always had to drag it out of them, every-thing. And, now, here it is Monday and the check has not been cashed.

She takes the telephone from her lap and replaces it on the end table, pushing herself up against the sofa cushions. This time of day, she and Frank Jr. used to sit with cocktails and watch the titmice and chickadees flit in and off the feeder, mourning doves collecting the sunflower seeds fallen to ground, and he would tell her about the day at the bank, who came in, who was borrowing or failing to pay. She could tell him a lot about the last few days—too much for someone Little Mildred's age—and a drink would be nice, but she does not ever drink alone. It is not something for a lady to do.

Very soon, on October 23, she will celebrate her eighty-fifth birthday and the children will host a party for her that she has already told them how to plan. Sara Cape has not developed into quite the hostess Little Mildred expected, and Frank III's wife, Paula, is only playing tennis these days. Her doubles part-ner, Mimi Dodge, is as fanatical as Paula and they have hired the club's tennis professional, hard muscles covered by practically nothing, to give them lessons in winning. They are nut brown and steely-eyed, a 5.0 Volvo team, that is what Paula tells Mildred, who thinks it unseemly to be publicly avid and even more so to assign a number to it. Frank III, well, he stands to the side with his wife, as if he is content to have her determine the rest of his life outside the bank. It is no doubt their father's blood showing and there is little to be done about that. I had to marry someone, didn't I? And Frank Jr. was clever enough to realize that his role was a limited one. He had been a good husband in that way and had really only lapsed the one time, with Frances Pratt, a bookkeeper at the bank. It was not even his doing, but hers, Frances having seen others of her station move up into the primary role and wanting to try it herself. The end of it came when Frank's father, Frank Sr., told his son in so many words that if Frank took up with Frances, married her, then he and Frank's mother would "stand by" Little Mildred and the children. Frank Jr. sensibly returned home and, twenty years ago, had the good grace to die before he became a nuisance.

"Here the *Register,* ma'am."

"Thank you, Albert." Little Mildred reaches to switch on the lamp, frowning as she unrolls the paper to the front-page photograph of Billy McLaurin, president of the other bank, Titus County. He is the one who spoke to her today, shooing her from the premises as if she were someone's colored maid. She had only been asking after Margaret's records, trying to find the social security and other numbers needed to admit her to Bayou Glen, but he insisted she go see the lawyer Dewitt had mentioned. Niles Abbott. She will do just that and get everything straight, you may be sure of that, Mr. McLaurin. She does not recognize the other men in the picture, but the caption says they are from Bali High Casino and are financing a shuttle service to their riverboat from Rosamond. She is disgusted. They are the camel's nose under the tent and will be inland before those fools in the Mississippi legislature have had the time to look up "camel" in the dictionary.

She has been reading for almost an hour when she reaches the last page, page ten, and the dozen or so public notices printed there. It is the second notice in the first column:

In the Chancery Court of Titus County, Mississippi
Nathan Bass v. Margaret Finley Cape
No. C93-605

TO: ANY HUSBAND, WIFE, DESCENDANT, ASCEN-DANT, NEXT OF KIN, PARENT AND ADULT KIN WITHIN THE THIRD DEGREE COMPUTED IN ACCORDANCE WITH THE CIVIL LAW OF THE STATE OF MISSISSIPPI OF MARGARET FIN-LEY CAPE

You have been made a Defendant in the suit filed in this Court by Nathan Bass, Plaintiff seeking the appointment of a Conservator of the Person and Estate of Margaret Finley Cape. Defendant other than you in this action is Margaret Finley Cape.

You are summoned to appear and defend against the complaint or petition filed against you in this action at 10 O'Clock A.M. on Friday, the 5th day of November, 1993, in the courtroom of the Titus County Courthouse at Rosamond, Mississippi, and in case of your failure to appear and defend a judgment will be entered against you for the money or other things demanded in the complaint or petition.

You are not required to file an answer or other pleading but you may do so if you desire.

Beetle Bailey had signed as chancery clerk, and the three dates of publication appear in the lower left-hand corner— October 4, today's date, October 11 and 18.

She reads it twice, then closes the paper without finishing the other notices. "Stupid! Stupid people!" she speaks out loud to hear it and to let out some part of her rising fury. She does not want to be so angry. It will make her dry skin itch from the heat and keep her awake, but her breath continues to deepen, pushing the sensation of ammonia into her nose and she is seething already deep in her gut. She stands and begins to walk the floor, thinking best that way what she can do. Dewitt Cordeman cannot possibly have placed such a notice, would not string together such a description of "Defendants" that the notice addresses. Nor Nathan Bass, that pathetic creature—his mother had once sent invitations marked "RSVP, please." Really! Someone else's crafty hand is shown and she will need to determine who it is, give him the information he needs to understand that this is not the time for blind justice, that Cape Plantation and Cape House belong with proper Capes, not such persons as described in the notice. It will not be necessary, surely, to violate the family's privacy but she will have to tell him enough.

12

Since getting Cordeman's process published, Niles has not thought of Margaret Cape or anyone or thing other than Peyton Barrett versus North Atlantic Casualty, his client. He has tried his tenth case in six months, having never tried a case by himself when he was with Harkin & Wells, and it is a consuming enterprise. It is five o'clock, Wednesday afternoon, when the jury returns with its verdict. "We, the jury, find for the defendant, North Atlantic Casualty."

Opposing counsel is on his feet. "Plaintiff requests the jury be polled, Your Honor." The company man looks at Niles, alarmed, but Niles shakes his head. The jurors are asked, one by one, if each agrees with the verdict. Nine must say, "Yes," and ten do, but the two dissenters are the first two asked and Niles grips the man's arm on the chair to reassure him until the polling is complete.

There are still minutes to wait, instructions for posttrial motions, dismissal of the jury before anyone else can leave the courtroom, the congratulations of opposing counsel, and the gratitude of the representative. At last Niles is in the Bronco and on the highway back to Rosamond. He removes his tie and pulls over at the first country grocery for two long-necks of Budweiser and a sack of redskin peanuts. In the fifty miles back to Rosamond, he reviews favorite moments in the trial—his opening statement, the cross-examination of the plaintiff's expert, the judge reading the verdict. For the moment he discards thoughts that Peyton Barrett is known to be a rich man who doesn't need more money, that there were eight women on the jury and that they are always good defense jurors when someone is complaining of anything short of death itself—once you've given birth, you don't like to hear whining—and, besides, the two younger ones clearly had the hots for him.

Halfway home, he empties the bag of peanuts onto his tongue and opens the second beer. He knows the road. Like his Delta friends, Niles spent half his school years driving long distances, often as far as one hundred miles for even a three-hour dance, and every road for miles is familiar to him, each with its own character. This one, passing north and south of Charleston is his "wild road," only, perhaps, because of its closeness to the hill country, the thick tangles of trees and several rivers that pass through. There is the Flowers' south place, where he and friends attended September dove shoots in college. Long before that, he was initiated into the rites of real hunting at the usual age of fourteen at the Burkhalter Gun Club near Prudence on this same road, but on the other side of Charleston. He sighted, then dropped a nice spike with one shot—the young buck crumpled to the ground as if his slender legs had suddenly dissolved beneath him—and the men carried the carcass to the lodge. Around the campfire that evening they brought a small bowl where the deer's blood had been collected and, dipping a thumb in the bowl, Raymond Flowers marked Niles's face with blood, the sign of manhood achieved. It was later that he learned the more refined touch necessary to shooting doves, delicate birds the size of plump robins and soft as if they were wrapped in gray panne velvet. On his last shoot, the fall he left for law school, he had found a live bird among those bagged at the Flowers' place. It was wounded but making muffled, choking sounds, dying too slowly and he stupidly tried to end the suffering by cutting its head off with his penknife. He grimaces, the peanuts sour in his mouth, remembering the lengthy sawing of tough gristle while the bird thrashed wildly. They still had the shoots, still baited the fields with grain and drank whiskey while they unloaded enough firepower to bring down a 747, and Harrison Tierney III had invited him to one last month, but he couldn't find the time.

The Cape Gin, a two-story steel building on the left, marks the ten-mile corner. He studies it with new interest as he passes, almost hitting a black cur dog that crosses in front of his truck before he looks back and swerves in time to miss it. It was close to here, he remembers, that he saw the most incredible sight when he was eighteen and at the same time of year in the same soft light at almost six, near enough to the Wauchomee Bridge to see the arch of its towers. A dark animal crouched to the left of the roadway, where the terraced ground sloped away from the concrete retaining wall and it was oddly shaped, too long and narrow for a dog. He had slowed and when he was almost even with the creature, it turned away to climb the slope, then, unexpectedly, turned its head back to look at him, full-face. He had stopped breathing and he can remember now the strange sensation of time slowing as he passed by, unbelieving. It was a panther, a red-fawn Florida panther, nearly eighty pounds of wild animal that the Delta supposedly had killed off thirty years before. It was too fantastic, and while he has thought of the sighting many times, he never told anyone what he had seen.

Niles opens his throat to chug the rest of his beer, pulling back pleasing thoughts of the trial, the way the skin heats in the moment of known triumph or, the same thing, in averting disaster. But the wild other is stronger, pushing its way back in and he sees the eyes as clearly now as he did then. He will never see another one, he is certain, but he looks closely around the bridge as he passes, just in case.

Cape Plantation, 1945 ✍ She knew with certainty by November, the first week in December at the very latest, but by then she was already carrying his child and they had married in October. Over those summer months, she showed herself to him willingly, foolishly, in their intimacies, reveling in the contact with another. Her mother's warning in July did not deter her. His urgency, his need for her was great and that would have unarmed her anyway.

"Tell me, Margaret," John Buie said softly one evening, "tell me about your family. You have some of their things here, don't you?"

And she eagerly showed him everything and told him from her heart. They went to each piece and she, stroking the polished mahogany of the sideboard, laughed when she told of how Father Moran came for dinner one Sunday and insisted on leaning back in his chair at the table while completely dominating the conversation until her father became so annoyed he jumped suddenly to his feet, startling the priest, who fell backward against this very sideboard and left a permanent scar. See? There? And her aunt Mary's own dressing table. "Was she as pretty as you, little girl?" And the beaten silver goblets that were her grandmother's and the leather-bound Greek classics that she read as a girl. She even showed him the garnet brooch that her father so solemnly delivered to her on her thirteenth birthday. John Buie took it from her hand and held it out to the light, studying the pewter setting, leaves winding round the cut stones. "Y'know. It's funny, isn't it? We don't think of little Yankee girls as havin' mothers and fathers, but just springing out of the ground like weeds. But, honeybun, you're just as familied and as deserving of respect as the best Titus County girls I know." He placed the brooch back into her palm then and closed her fingers around it. He wrapped an arm round her and with the other hand came up underneath her full skirt and roughly grabbed hold of her, pushing his finger deep inside her as he lifted and carried her to the bedroom.

Two days later or perhaps it was two weeks that she awoke one morning with a start and Sam was knocking at her door calling to her and telling her that she should come, but everything was already gone. So much so that even the spaces those pieces had occupied were filled by other similar things of an origin that Margaret could not identify.

"The things we have here at Cape should be Cape things, Margaret. You see, don't you? You're a Cape yourself, double over now, and we really shouldn't have anything confusin' that for us." John Buie had been so very calm and his voice so tender that she had doubted her sensibilities and fought to accept the reason of his words. Still, she asked, although very weakly, "Where?"

His calm abruptly disappeared, his irritation showing as he waved her off. He lit a cigarette and began to pull on his coat and make his preparations to leave for the day. "I don't know, Margaret. What does it matter?" It was Ella who told her later that she watched as John Buie directed his crew to load the collection of cherry and mahogany and walnut furnishings and the smaller things, too, onto the back of the big truck, tying a tarpaulin over the top, and Wilfred had called to her through the kitchen porch screen when they returned, "Tell boss it's in the river."

Margaret watched him leave without saying more, then ran to their room, which had been hers, and where the dressing table had been, taking up the small flow blue porcelain box that had been moved from the old to the new and looking inside to see that the brooch was still there. Grateful for it having been spared, she returned the box to its place, but it was merely an oversight and, the next morning, the brooch was gone, too.

He had not, however, remembered it all and Ella helped her move the largest of those—a spindle-back rocker, a small trunk filled with her books and childhood mementos—to a corner of the bedroom as Margaret instructed. She had been waiting until their marriage to tell him about the library as a special gift to him in the same way Big John had given it to her, but then had changed her thought and was going to tell him at Christmas. It would have to be foregone now. She told Ella to return to the kitchen, and only then opened the hidden door and pushed her cache through into safety.

She had given only passing thought to protection from others in the entirety of her life. Once, when she was small and her mother held her hand through the crowd at the railway station and it was by the enormous iron clock in its center that a man, a vagrant with grease in his hair and the smell of rot and vomit on his clothes, came suddenly toward her and Anne Finley screamed grabbing her up from his way. "Little missy, little missy?" he called to her as her mother carried her away to the train home. And in that way she had always been safe in someone's watch, someone to lift her out of the path of danger if any should present itself. But, this. Another who longed to devour her, who baited and stalked her, so that her own soul and her story, too, were in peril; she had come to understand that all was in the balance.

Later, Margaret sat at the kitchen table, stemming blackberries while Ella talked and gathered the pots and jars they would need to make jelly.

"Mens just like that, Miss Marg'ret. Always sniffin' and struttin' around like some dog. Same way, too. They either pissin' on somethin' or kickin' up dirt all over it. I know *that's* right."

"Ella!" Margaret scolded as firmly as she could, but then she laughed and felt the fear and pain subside. She had a friend once and remembered how their secret conversations sustained her. They spent afternoons in one or the other's bedroom or shopping at the emporium or playing in the park, long hours beside each other, comforted by the rare joinder of familiarity and acceptance. But Ella was not her friend. Nor Sam. Big John explained that right away and Little Mildred told her often enough that despite their seeming affection for her they loathed her and all white people and would as soon slit her slender, curved throat as look at her.

She thought of that when the minister's wife had come to her following Big John's death to ask if she would work with her in the Bay Clinic, a Negro hospital in nearby Hawkins, and she declined but with John Buie's return and her renewed confidence in her course she had thought better of it and went along to see what she could do to help. The thrill of it! Olive-green plastered halls lined with them, dust-covered from the fields, and the babies already lowering their voices the same as their parents. They needed her, too, and came to her room solemn, unsmiling and, yes, perhaps they loathed her with her white dress, white skin. But their hatred could not undo her nursing and when the treatment was done, the aid given, it persisted apart from her as well as them. Yet, it distracted her from the other and, if she had been mindful, perhaps she could have seen, could have drawn back in time except what of the children? The General's children. She could not see any way to bear them except through John Buie and there was never a sign to the contrary before they married. But, no matter. It was too late.

SAM SERVES MARGARET lunch, then leaves her sitting at the kitchen porch table. "Thursday fresh produce day at the Jitney. Just a little while in town, I be back," he tells her and it is clear enough that he expects her to remain in the chair where she sits, but when the sound of the Buick's motor recedes, she rises.

There are seventeen rooms in Cape House not counting the closets and the butler's pantry. It has been more than a week since Margaret left the dark spaces of the library, four weeks since she "awakened" to Sam's voice, and she has been in only four of the rooms—her bedroom and the adjoining library, the chapel, and the last several days, the kitchen porch. She forgives herself the narrow limits of her searching so far. After all, she was not for twenty-seven years and then, in the next moment, is, aging to nearly eighty in a single day. And, although she is here now, her father's temperamental heart is with her, too, and quickly beating toward its end. She considers that she may have returned from one death merely to be present at another, but it seems unlikely. Resurrection has always been a purposeful event.

Margaret leaves the folded papers on the kitchen table and shuffles her stockinged feet along warped, uneven pine boards, holding the table's edge until she is near the far door. The document is thick, on long white paper and its paragraphs speak of "mental weakness" and say she cannot manage her own business. She had read the rest eagerly, and several times since Monday, but it never revealed what her business is. She moves slowly, the floor creaking in like rhythm—truncated swipes on a fiddle—and Margaret is relieved to reach the more solid footing of the hall. How do people abide the commotion? Even by herself, the noises of everything else that is, all that surrounds her, is a constant intrusion to her own thoughts, which teem inside her. When other people add their voices to the noise of existence, it is deafening.

The bedroom windows face south to the side yard and Margaret steps gratefully into the sun-warmed room. Now, *she* is the commotion!—her own breathing is all she is able to hear and, in her ears, she can feel the fluttering pulse of her heart-beat. She drops down on the bed, sitting until she pours a snifter of brandy to the rim and drinks it a third of the way down. When she lies back, she turns her face to the windows and the side yard beyond. She remembers learning to talk all over again when she came here, mastering the soft lilt of a Mississippi voice, the faint suggestion of apology, an exagger-ated response to every comment. "How wonderful to be in my bed with you," she tries, lifting the brandy in a mock toast, but the voice is not familiar.

Margaret studies the changing colors of the leaves on the two trees that remain in the walled side yard. They are turning, but still mostly green. There has been no frost. She can see the very top of the gazebo roof and down to the surrounding iron rail, where chickadees and a Carolina wren alternate alighting. It is an hour past noon, perhaps. Time passes slowly when one does no more than be, walking through time, examining the minutes like interesting rocks picked up along the way.

The document's claims about her mind do not disturb her. Hadn't she overheard, without effect, her own son and his aunt Mildred saying much the same, although with words less kind? It was some time ago, just when is uncertain. "Madness is mostly convention, Margaret," her father instructed her when her cousin Joseph was committed to Bell House after his parents began to fear his brooding presence. "Its meaning defines those who assert it, not the supposed madman, don't you see?"

She presses back into the soft pillows and pulls her feet beneath the hem of her dress. She closes her eyes, listening to the rough edges of her own breath, waiting for sleep. There are no memories, only a feeling that passes over her and is gone, but she recognizes it in that instant. It is the feeling in the morning after catastrophe, in the first moments of waking when there is only the dead weight of unalterable consequence, the moment just before opening one's eyes and remembering what it is.

13

What touches the ground is beginning to rot, but most of the trees lie as they first fell, slender limbs extending from sturdy trunks, those dwarfed by giant root masses of dirt and tentacles not fitting for view but meant to stay beneath the earth. On this, the hill-country side of Rosamond, it is unusual to see sky and planet meet. Instead, the light comes from above or in small strips between hilltop loblolly pines or as here, once, in uneven patches among brittle sweet gums or sycamores and round-topped oaks and an occasional hickory or black walnut. This was one of the few hardwood bottoms left in Titus County before Hardy Mall brought it down, leaving the pines atop sloping ridges and their divides covered with scattered gray corpses so that, now, it resembles nothing so much as a mass execution—just afterward, before the crumpled bodies are pushed into a ditch and covered with dirt. Still, all the wood of value has been removed, taken out on Mall's trucks along the red clay logging road, its deep ruts dividing the open field then disappearing into the pines at the far end.

Niles Abbott waits in the Bronco while Charley stands foot up on a decaying tree trunk looking around. Margaret Cape is awake. "Yeah. Harry walked in—Monday morning it was— and she was sitting up reading a book," Sheriff Earnest told him at Tony's, where Niles and Charley were lunching on the meat loaf special. "Just got busy. I was going to give you a call this afternoon."

"You been here before?" he calls from the truck and Charley nods.

"Oh, yeah. Sure I have. Good lawyer always goes to the scene first thing. Remember that, Abbott. Never know what's gonna be important. I just wanted to take a second look."

Niles removes his blue poplin blazer and lays it behind the seat in the cargo area. Dewitt Cordeman had ruled in Charley's favor this morning, ordering Hardy Mall to turn over his financial records and Charley is ebullient, insisting on coming here from Tony's and Niles has the only four-wheel drive readily available. The windows are down but there is no breeze, only the tropical heat left over from September. But today is the seventh day of October and very soon, as if by magic, while the days swelter, the nights will gradually become cooler, crisper until by November, daytime follows their lead and summer is gone.

Mildred Melton is coming at two o'clock. He has put her off for days supposing she wants access to Margaret Cape's private matters after Billy McLaurin called him about her snooping in the bank. She had almost persuaded a gossipy teller to let her examine Margaret's accounts when Billy saw her and intervened.

Charley is back at the Bronco, kicking off red gooey clay from his shoes. "I don't know. Hardy and money are like twin brothers, they're so close, and he doesn't make many mistakes. 'Course wood is just one of the five dozen businesses he's got into. He's not particular what he does, just whatever makes the most money." It is Charley's way to think out loud, as if those around him have nothing but his activity to fill their own thoughts. "Knows everything. You won't see him dancing at the club. Nobody knows nothing there. He'll be over at the Countyline Market or the VFW fish fry. He's always one block

ahead of the parade. I think he wanted that hardwood on purpose but it's just a feeling. Think about it, will you?"

Cape Plantation, 1948 🐦 The duck's nest rested between the
root of the button bush and the pond, as closely to the edge as
permitted it to remain upon land and not slide floating away,
finally saturated and sinking to the bottom. The mallard hen
was watchful, sitting tightly on her eggs when they spied her,
occasionally reaching her bill down to pull the feathered twigs
and pine needles closer, protecting her unborn ducklings from
the nip of the spring breezes as well as unwelcome visitors.

"Buie. Come here next to me, but sh-h," Margaret whispered
to him and he scampered to her, squatting down and bringing
one finger to his lips in mimicry of his mother. She pointed to
the nesting hen, less than ten feet away, and they both crouched
motionless for minutes watching the hen, who watched them
as well.

"Bird?" he whispered, blue-gray eyes fixed earnestly on
Margaret's. She smiled at his childish beauty, and stroked his
golden skin and the cap of dark hair framing his face.

"That's right. But, it's a duck, Buie, a mama duck."

"Mama duck," he repeated and laughed suddenly, startling
the hen, who shifted positions.

"Sh-h. She's protecting her babies just like your mama looks
after you. You're mama's baby." She pulled him close and he
lay his head against her breast the same heavy way he had as
a nursing infant and she held him gently to her as they sat in
the tall grass, still brown and prickly from the winter. Ella's
little Caraly began to fuss in her basket and Margaret released
her son, patting his behind, and jiggled the basket until the
baby quieted, but the ducks on the pond began another round
of tumultuous breeding, drakes mounting the others of either
sex, pecking their heads relentlessly, continually down and under the water. The ruckus frightened Caraly, who began to cry
again. Buie interrupted his play and stood watching and she

did not stop him. Each spring she had seen the bodies of hens and drakes alike floating dead in the pond, victims of these exceedingly natural causes, and he was likely to see them as well. It was what happened.

Yet, she was vigilant. She knew now that his soul, his story could be stolen away without a trace to follow and until he could protect himself, she must carry that burden for the both of them. She would tell him as soon as he could understand and she was uncertain why her father had left this for her to discover perhaps too late. Still, she had known it by the time she bore Buie—John Buie Cape IV—two years preceding in April of 1946. He was a big-boned, strapping child, like his father, and after John Buie had brought her to the Grenada hospital, she labored fifteen hours to deliver, fainting three times from the pain. But each time she roused herself from her stupor because she knew that she must be watchful for him, for her unborn child, and later when he was placed still bloodied and whimpering in her arms, she rocked him and sang to him, stroking the downy black hair that covered his body, letting him suckle her little finger until he fell asleep.

She took his hand and bounced the basket in the other and continued around the curved bank of the pond. She had often come to the small pasture with Big John, bringing apples or carrots to the horses and then he died and Frank took the horses to stable with his own and there was never reason enough to come very often again until Buie. She listened for John Buie's pickup marking his return for the midday meal, but when they reached the small rise at the east end of the pond, she could see the truck had arrived without their knowing it and was already sitting in the driveway. Margaret clasped the baby's basket in two hands and hurried toward the house, Buie trotting at her side to keep pace, but John Buie had already finished his meal and looked sternly at her when she entered the kitchen porch with Buie, wet strands of hair clinging to their flushed cheeks.

"Don't take the boy out in the sun so much, Margaret. It's gettin' on to summer now and it's too damn hot. For both of you." John Buie emptied his cup of coffee and tapped his knife on the edge of the table, signaling Ella to bring more. " 'Course if you want to cook your own brains that's your business, but don't take my son with you."

"I care for him, darlin', just like you do. My goodness, you make it sound like I'm trying to kill my own baby." Margaret looked wide-eyed in his direction, tilting her head and with the suggestion of a smile.

"I wouldn't want to say *what* goes on in that little Yankee head of yours." He took the last stiff piece of salty ham, placed it between biscuit halves, and carefully wrapped it in his kerchief before stuffing it in his shirt pocket. "Just mind what I say and keep him inside." Ella came onto the kitchen porch with the coffee. She poured half a cup before he stopped her and rose, taking the cup with him. He watched Ella go and then lowered his face close to Margaret's. "And let Ella take care of her own little brat. She's s'posed to be workin' for us not the other way around. She'll take advantage if you let her."

Margaret smiled and kissed John Buie's cheek. "What would I do without you to keep me straight. You be careful now, hear?"

She sometimes wondered whether others did it this same way, but then it was impossible to tell, wasn't it? And what difference if they did not? If discomforting adaptations must be made, she would have to endure them but keep her purpose in sight all the while. It had not been so painful, really, once she had known what the transformations must be and when and she was allowed sufficient time for the change.

"Ella?"

"Yes'm."

"Change the baby and give Buie a little sponge bath. And tell Sam I need him to drive."

"Where you off to this afternoon, Miss Marg'ret?"

"And pack a bottle for Caraly and a box for us. We're going over to the Sperry Road churchyard. We can picnic in the cemetery."

Who was she now? When she spoke to Ella or to Sam? She did not want to think about it, really, she was not certain. She had noticed this very thing—that pretense bled into reality, leaving behind a stain that could not be erased. She considered the need for another separation of sorts, to provide a constant, a watcher to oversee the transitions from one to the other and to make certain things were put back in the proper places and as nearly like themselves as could be managed. She would go to the library, later, to think about that some more.

Margaret brought Buie to the cemetery, yes, because it was the scene of General Cape's battle, but also because it was a pleasant and peaceful sort of place. She did not believe in spirits although she did have a notion of something tangible left behind, not just when one died, but every moment thought, lived, breathed and she supposed that a little part of the battle was still here on these grounds.

Sam pulled into the gravel turnaround across from the burned-out remnants of the old church and parked the car near the blackjack oak that stood at the southeast corner of the cemetery. Margaret took Buie's hand and carried Caraly to the farthest headstone. They always followed the same path, as she walked the boundary of the cemetery, coming in row by row until she eventually reached the row immediately next to the road and, so, the car to take them home. Buie's journey was easily three times her own as he moved in a spiral around and through the graves, stopping to pick up small rocks or watch a trail of ants and before long Caraly would be old enough to do the same.

Margaret moved slowly, reading the stones as she walked, their plainness reflecting the meager station of the persons whose graves they marked. The Capes were buried as the need arose in a marble mausoleum situated on a small hilltop in the

Rosamond Cemetery to the east of town. Margaret visited there one time, when Big John was entombed next to Mildred Cape, and she had not returned. There was no marble here and many of the headstones were made from the large flat rocks turned up in cultivating the fields, their composition including Yazoo clay, which gave them a mulatto brown shade. The carvings were simple and limited to a name, years of birth and death, and occasionally a small decorative medallion, her favorite a crown.

She looked for L. J. Adams and Pearlie Adams, buried side by side near the center of the cemetery, and knelt to pull weeds from the sunken earth over the graves, remembering, reviewing what Sam had told her.

"L. J. Adams was my daddy. Pearlie, my mama."

"I thought Estelle is your mother."

"Big Mama? No, see, Daddy married her after my real mama died. Lamar, my brother, and me were just little fellas and Big Mama raised us up."

"What happened to your mother, Sam? Did she get sick?"

"No." Sam had brushed off his khaki pants and stood up then, shifting from side to side as he spoke. "What it was, well it's what learned me if there's trouble 'tween a husband and wife, just leave it alone."

"I'm sorry, Sam."

"No, ma'am. It weren't my mama and daddy having trouble, it were mama's cousin, Dorothy. She always about half wild and she'd gone off and married some field nigger from the next county. Clyde Curtis. He was either drinking or doing something gonna land him in jail."

"How awful for her."

"Don't go feelin' nothing for Dorothy, Miz Marg'ret. Daddy always said he thought she half liked bein' beat on. But, she finally had enough and moved in with us. One day, when Clyde was at work, my mama went with her to get the rest of her stuff. They were there in the back hall with the windows all alongside, and mama were walkin' through when Clyde stepped out from behind a tree and shot her dead."

Buie had tired and was resting, his head in her lap. She tried to imagine what it would be to lift a shotgun and kill another, and could not just now, but she would try again on the next visit to these grounds. In any event, Clyde had done it and he had been punished, a little.

"He went to Parchman but he was out in five years. White man, the fuzz, used to live up near Charleston paid his way out, they said. He went to work for him after that," Sam told her.

Margaret spread the blanket beneath the blackjack oak. She fed Buie the biscuit with butter and jelly, a banana, and a piece of pound cake Ella had packed, while she and Sam ate ham and biscuits spread with chowchow and mustard and the baby hungrily finished her bottle. She lay between Buie and the basket holding Caraly, singing softly to them both until they were asleep and she could close her eyes and sleep, too, and Sam waited at the car, sitting on its running board, while he carved a little bird from a piece of hickory to give to Buie.

"You must think I'm a fuckin' idiot," John Buie said to her. Margaret lay next to him in their bed and she faced the windows bordering the side yard. The moon was full and she thought she could see the outline of the *pyracantha* spread across the far wall like spectral fingers reaching toward the top to escape over. She had been almost asleep and she struggled to waken and to remember what it was she was to say.

"John Buie, don't talk that way!" she whispered, deciding finally. "You'll wake the baby."

John Buie snorted. "There you go with that Southern belle talk, like you were some tight-pussy debutante from Greenwood. You think I'm so stupid as not to know you're puttin' that on?" Margaret measured her breathing, concentrating to make it slow and silent.

"And even if I was, let me tell you, little girl, I can be places that might surprise you. You remember that, hear?" She turned toward him and his face was gray and angular in the moonlight, except for his eyes, which were still blue and glittered as he spoke. "That's right. I've heard you talkin' to my son and it's all different and, then, the next minute up and pull this shit with me. You're goin' to have him as fucked up as you are, you know."

There. There it suddenly was and it was really simpler than she had imagined. She did not need to be outside of herself altogether as she had sometimes feared, just slightly to one side and she could see it all. Yes, he was really quite dangerous and she would need to be even more careful to keep the separation precise but so long as she did he could never reach her at all. She turned back to face the windows, waiting until she heard his breathing deepen and become regular before she let herself return, watching now to see it was done in the proper fashion. She would take Buie back to the pond in the morning, and the baby, and perhaps the ducklings would have pipped their shells but, if not, she would come back each day, watching, watching until they did.

LITTLE MILDRED MELTON arrives promptly for her appointment at two, moving slowly with the help of a cane, but the confident euphony of her voice surprises Niles. She is smartly dressed in a cardinal red suit with a small gold locket affixed as a brooch on her jacket and wears a rectangular-faced Hamilton watch on her wrist, but no more jewelry than that. Niles guesses that she buys her clothes in Dallas or, maybe, New Orleans. They sit next to each other at the conference room table, looking at each other silently. Her metallic blue eyes are narrowed, exotic beneath the coarse black and mostly silver hair combed in neat half-curl bangs around her face. She is not thin in the way old women can be and, even seated, she towers.

He is the first to break the silence, to look away. "You wanted to talk to me, Mrs. Melton?"

She hesitates, not nervous, but measuring him. "Growing up here, you must know I was a Cape before I married my husband. Big John Cape was my father, John Buie Cape, my brother."

"You are concerned about Mrs. Cape, I assume."

"The Capes have been in Titus County for 157 years, Mr. Abbott, before it was a county even. One of the first governors of Mississippi, General James Seifert Foster, was a classmate of my great-grandfather Cape when they attended the university at Virginia before the war."

"Yes, ma'am."

"Before the hostilities began, he—my great-grandfather— was widely known to be an exceptionally learned and kind man. I don't mean to say he was a liberal, of course. He was an honorable man of principle. He had a rule. The slave families must be kept together. It was quite radical at the time, you can imagine, but he insisted on it."

"Yes, ma'am. Perhaps I could explain what a conservatorship is and what I anticipate doing."

"He was already an older man, but he was sent to South Carolina at the very beginning. He was a general. They knew his quality and were counting on it." Mildred Melton places the heel of her palm on the walnut table and pushes hard as if to move it. Her fingers quiver at the effort and the table stays where it is. "Another's error resulted in his men suffering a fatal ambush. The General was among the many left for dead, but the Yankees took their shoes anyway, I mean every dead man's shoes, just in case. That's how evil they were."

"Yes, ma'am. War can make us do things we otherwise wouldn't."

"The *Yankees,* Mr. Abbott! I have never once heard of a Southern boy stripping the clothes from a corpse, depriving a dead man of what dignity remains."

"No, ma'am. The General was alive, then?"

"Oh, yes. Quite. He walked home without shoes, without any treatment for his wounds. All the way from South Carolina they made him walk without shoes. And for what reason? For them. For the Nigras. That is the pitiful, only reason that man who was their most glorious and kind protector was made to suffer. And, I will say, it's been the same from that day to this. Have you seen the notice in the *Register?*"

"It's the court's notice, Mrs. Melton. Judge Cordeman is the one who had process issue." Niles assumes his most innocent look.

Her head jerks and she looks at him, her eyes steady, and she almost smiles. "You wrote it," she says matter-of-factly, although she has only inferred the truth of her statement this moment. "I knew it wasn't his doing. Oh, Dewitt Cordeman has done well for himself. The Cordemans have always been ones to try to rise above themselves but there is coarseness, middle-mindedness in their blood. I was in school with Gracie Cordeman and she was one of the best of them, homecoming maid two years in a row. Yes. After high school, she broke up Dexter Allen's marriage to the Tierney girl, then left him with two children to chase after that Leland author who lived in Montana and was back visiting his mother. He wouldn't have her, of course. No. Dewitt managed to get himself elected is all and just because he convinced all of the trailer trash and half the Nigras in five counties to vote for him does not suddenly give him mastery of the English language, let alone the law."

"Do you have some objection to the summons in the paper?"

"You are too young to know firsthand and, thank the Lord, no one has talked about it much for years, but all Margaret Finley has ever been was just a foolish old man's mistake. My daddy, Big John. He was the one who brought her here from Boston back in the thirties."

"The marriage didn't work out?"

"Oh, he was pleased enough, if that's what you measure. I suppose she was a pretty little thing, in a way. Had that throwed-away-child look that makes some men fall all over themselves. Cape men especially, it seems. I tried to help her fix up and dress right, but she just couldn't learn. It wasn't five years—no, it was 1944 or '45, I think—and he died."

Mildred clutches her handbag as if she is about to rise and leave, and Niles starts out of his chair to help her, before he understands she is not leaving to go anywhere. "I do wonder whether, in view of this unfortunate publicity, it might not be well to go ahead. Will there be anything you need from me to make the transfer, Mr. Abbott? It should be in my son's name, Frank Melton III."

Niles leans back in his chair, his right hand resting on the legal pad, and he does not look at Mildred while he speaks. "Mrs. Melton, let me explain my situation in all of this. I will be Margaret Cape's conservator. As such, I am charged with a responsibility under the law to act only in her best interests. It is true that the statutes permit me to sell her real estate, if that is in her best interest and the court approves the sale. However, those are facts that as far as I can see remain undetermined, at least until I have had a chance to talk to her."

"I am prepared to provide Margaret's care until she passes. That is her interest and her only interest. She has no loved ones to provide for. It is quite sad, really, but she is totally alone and the world will be the same after she goes as when she was here. On the other hand, if Cape Plantation is delivered, by this farcical state of affairs, to some stranger, a greater tragedy cannot be imagined."

Niles measures his words. "If there is a proper legal way to make the transfer and it is, in fact, in Mrs. Cape's best interest, I will not hesitate to recommend it."

Mildred Melton sits back, satisfied. She gathers her purse and cane. "I am very pleased, Mr. Abbott, that we were able to chat about the family and our home." She pushes herself up from the chair and Niles reaches out to steady her. "Thank you so much for your time."

Niles clears his throat. "I want to be forthright. I am not, as it turns out, Mrs. Cape's conservator yet and I won't be until the hearing on November fifth. So, I can't even propose transferring anything until then."

"You don't mean you are going to leave things as they are for another month?" She stands barely a foot away from him and, in her raised heels, is as tall as he is.

"I don't really have any say to do otherwise. As it turns out, it's probably for the best, now that she's awake. I'll need to ask her some questions, get some idea how she's functioning."

"Awake? Oh. She's always been awake. Some people got in their minds she was in some sort of coma and it has never been like that. It's catatonia, a sort of sleeping while awake."

"No, there is apparently something more than that now. The sheriff's deputy says she's reading a book, walking around. How did she seem to you when you last visited?"

Mildred Melton sits back down, opens her bag, and takes out a mint in plastic wrap. "Surely, Judge Cordeman told you of our estrangement and, even so, Margaret's situation these past years would not permit easy commerce."

"He was not specific. You have not seen her in...years?" Niles leans forward and she is starting to rise.

"Years. Well. Good day, Mr. Abbott." She is on her feet and moving away from him down the hall to the street door. Her step is quicker now, more sure and almost sprightly for an old woman with a cane. At the door, she stops and turns toward him. "Ah, yes. I couldn't place you. You're Buddy Abbott's son. He was one of the ones they put in jail, wasn't he?" Niles says nothing, holding her gaze until the corners of her mouth lift in an indeterminate expression and she leaves.

14

Margaret is troubled and she walks in the endless acres of Cape Plantation cotton, which continuously sprouts, grows green, fills with cotton, before being put to death and sprouting once more. The land is flat, the horizon so distant she will never reach it and marked by stone figures scattered throughout the field. Her shoes are the wrong ones to traverse the sandy furrows, which are dusty, then full troughs of water, then hard. She reaches the nearest figure, anxious to ask her way, but it is stone and says nothing, nor the next or the one after. Still, each one is known to her, persons once familiar who have ceased to be and have become fixed in this single form. She is very tired and she turns to go back, but a black wall has risen behind her so she is unable to retreat even one step and she resumes her journey toward the horizon, walking in and out of the endless statues. She drops to the earth, unable to walk farther, and the cotton continues its endless regeneration as she lies in its rows. Then, she is up again, but lower and walking on four feet, a formless, feral creature creeping steadily forward. Now the statues come alive and shout words at her, hold up signs with printing and point to the meaning. But, she is wild, feral, understanding nothing, yet knowing at last her path, moving confidently to her destination. The stone figures rock the ground to topple her, but she moves easily from side to side keeping her balance until the ground sways even more and she wakes.

"I didn't mean to wake you, Miz Marg'ret. I was just getting this up." Sam presses a cotton towel in rhythmic, firm motions against the coverlet next to Margaret. He had smelled the spilled liquor when he entered the room and went for the towels before going farther. He had already unpacked the week's groceries, purchased with his last casino winnings. When he came back and got within arm's reach, he saw the other, the watery vomitus pooled below her open mouth, some of it on her tongue and he feared she had choked until he listened for her breath.

She tastes the sour debris and Sam hands her a towel to clean it away. "I'm sorry," she says but he does not acknowledge the apology.

"I told him to come, the lawyer you said was on the papers. You just go on back to sleep now." Sam drapes a dry cotton blanket over her and takes the glass and decanter with him when he leaves. Margaret watches him out the door, listening until his steps turn from the hall into the kitchen before she turns back the cover and gets up to go to the library.

NOVEMBER 5 WAS the date the papers specify she should "appear and answer" the petition and she had found his name on the summons page at the very end in the corner. She had not seen it on the first reading because it was not typed or written in ink there, but impressed into the page, the reverse of the raised clerk's seal and written in the same hand as the clerk's signature. "Call Niles Abbott when served," it said.

Inside the library door, she reaches out with her left hand to the wall of shelves, moving carefully along them until she reaches the opening and the cabinet and turns toward the chair. Her hands ache a little. It is not the arthritis. She can definitely tell the difference and, if she could not, would have known when stroking the knots across her fingers gave no comfort. Sam has told him to come. The feeling she remembered with Little Mildred so easily returns, her self slipping across a divider worn down through constant crossing and she hears two voices at once, one sweet and smooth, the other not. Praline sauce on ice cream, hard leather soles scuffing down a brick street. "Mr. Abbott?" She practices the greeting out loud as she walks toward the leather chair and, then, again, "Mr. Abbott?" She softens the *"A"* a little and says it another time with more lift on the last part of his name until she has it right and she is the Southern lady, a Rosamond matron. "Mr. Abbott? I'm so very *pleased* to meet you."

The knowledge comes to her before she reaches the chair and Margaret stumbles at the suddenness of it, waving her arms to keep her balance in the dark. Her story. It has not been found. Of course, that is the urgent task that confronted her on waking and there is not much time. "I have a story. I must find it." She says the words aloud with as much certainty as if she had never forgotten and turns back to the cabinet. She feels for the small scrolled frame, taking it and turning to the west wall and the vent. There is a small light coming through this day and it is afternoon, the brightest light for the west of the house. She kneels, not without difficulty, but by leaning heavily against the wall and sliding slowly down until she is resting on the floor. She holds the photograph out in front of her and she can see the gold-dark face of the Brazilian girl staring back. A river Indian from Brazil, balancing on a log. The brown face and light eyes, her preternatural calm, capture Margaret now as then. She is a sign for her story, yes. Of what, Margaret has never determined.

Cape Plantation, 1949 𝕤 It had been in August or early September and she could not remember past that day the month or time that he found her in her room just as she was preparing to enter the library to sit awhile before bed. Blessedly, she had not yet opened the hidden door. She was wearing an apricot cream dress, of course, and she had seen him leave early in the evening, but now he crept up behind her so softly that she had no sense of him until he grabbed her arms with a holler and lifted her high above his head.

"Come here, you little fiest pup! Have you missed your daddy, umh?" He dropped her on the end of the bed and sprawled across her, the weight of his body pinning her. "What? Cat got your tongue? Let's see." He pressed his face close to hers and the smell of whiskey was so strong she was afraid she would retch. She pushed him back and struggled for air, but he grabbed her arm roughly and sprung to his feet jerking her up with him.

"Don't you ever push me away, you sorry bitch!" She staggered from the force of his words, the anger in his voice, and when the back of his hand struck her face, she had not been able to close her eyes. He was at her wildly, grabbing the front of her dress and tearing it apart then pushing her down again onto the bed, where his massive forearm braced beneath her chin to hold her. He knelt, forcing himself inside her, using his free arm to pull Margaret's body to his as he savagely slammed against her until he was satisfied, she near unconsciousness. She did not know that he had left her until she heard his laughter and that of his closest friend, Junior Tierney, in the hall outside. She heard their voices fade slowly away and did not move until the hallway had been silent an hour. Holding the torn dress together, she made her way to the library door. Safely inside, she stayed until morning.

Chapin Finley was born the following May and on the anniversary day of John Buie's return to Cape Plantation five years preceding. Margaret knew it was a sign and, all things considered, not propitious and, so, she kept an eye on the little one and kept him a distance from Buie, whose good and proven heart she guarded. They were different children, she saw immediately and that little Chappy was better left to himself more.

Or, at least, with Ella who had half nursed Caraly until she was almost two years old and could continue with Chapin Finley, allowing Margaret her time with Buie and for other things. It was not the time for a baby and she was glad to be finally delivered of it so that she could return to what most concerned her, that being Buie, her nursing at the Bay Clinic, and her constant guard against her husband. And there was another thing as well that had been growing in her despite her effort to place it to one side, but she could not. It was an extra care about the meaning of her story and not the story itself. The question had always been there, of course. "If I weren't here, what would happen to you and Papa?" she asked her mother soon after her twelfth birthday. They were ice-skating in Chadwick Park. At thirty-two, Anne Finley was stunning, with rosy cheeks and dark hair and wrapped in a stylish green coat with fur cuffs and collar. The older boys flirted openly with her and she gracefully ignored their admiration in a manner that promised that she might, nevertheless, acknowledge them if they persisted.

"Margaret, has your father been filling your head with ideas again?" she had asked with some irritation but Margaret shook her head. "We would be sad if you would ever leave us, darling, of course. Let's not speak of it further." The square-jawed, blond boy skated by a little too closely and Anne Finley pointedly turned away from his sanguine smile, lifting her chin, which, as an incident only, showed her becoming profile.

"But what if you had never met? If I had never been Margaret at all?" she persisted.

"I haven't the least notion of what you are saying, Margaret. We have met. You are our precious child," Anne Finley said sternly, removing one hand from the fur muffler to tuck a straying curl into her cloche. "If you weren't Margaret, you wouldn't be our child. We would have another child. But you are and we don't and that is the last we shall talk of this."

Her father had been no more helpful. "What would be

different if you didn't exist? Everything would be different. Don't you see that? Everything. The question is wrong, Margaret." And, after a time, she let it go and thought only of the story and what belonged there. But now, the inquiry had pressed upon her again. What did her living mean beyond the sum of events comprising her life?

She felt sad at times that there was no one to help. She came to understand that very few even knew about the stories and that, probably, it was just as well not to tell the others. John Buie knew only enough to be a threat to her, understanding in an unarticulated way that her story kept her forever separate from him and gave her a power to exist apart from his will. That, she thought, was what drove him after her. Little Mildred once found her reading in the garden, a collection of stories by Henry James, and rebuked her, saying, "There is only one story. That is the story of the Lord Jesus." Margaret had startled Little Mildred by asking, "What is the story?" and Mildred left without saying, left her wondering. "I really don't fault you in any way, Margaret," she said a later day. "Really. I hope you understand that." Little Mildred held Sara Cape out from her, by the shoulders, to get a good look, yanked at the stiff polished cotton skirt of the child's jumper, then set her to one side, done with her for the moment. "There was even a time that I thought the world began and ended with me, the way you do. I was, I don't know, sixteen or seventeen at the time."

THE COMPTON BUILDING has housed extra Cape possessions since at least 1918 because Little Mildred remembers going there with her mother, Big Mildred, to exchange her child's bed for "something more suitable to a young lady." In that year, there was a single wood door—Big John installed the metal one later in the '40s—through which they entered a cavernous, two-story space, with exposed crossbeams and two or three double-hung windows high on each of the long walls providing light enough to see, although not the colors so that everything appeared black and white. The floor was solid heart-pine boards on cypress joists, and swept clean. Big Mildred sent one of the servants to dust and clean once a month regardless and, two times each year, Big John sent a field hand to spray for spiders.

Little Mildred and her mother moved in a circle around the room's perimeter, the valuable, if unneeded, family furnishings arranged there as if for display. Occasionally they stopped at a piece that provoked special memories and her mother told her its story while the two field hands Big John dispatched to help them leaned against the wall near the door. No one was in a hurry.

"This one seems very nice," Big Mildred said at a single bed with a Victorian arched canopy and Queen Anne legs, but Little Mildred shook her head and moved ahead to a larger double bed with a thick cherry frame and solid tester. "This is the bed you like?" Her mother was skeptical. "It's so bulky, honey. Maybe a little...well, masculine."

"Not when it's dressed," Little Mildred insisted and her mother allowed that, with the proper bedclothes, it might transform from outright masculine to "handsome."

"I'm not certain this particular bed is right for someone who's still a little girl," she said affectionately, "but if it's what you want." It was and the hands loaded it on their truck and Weeze, Little Mildred's nursemaid, washed it with soap and water then rubbed it down with lemon oil. That evening her mother came to see Little Mildred in her room, to say good night and to tell her the special story of her bed. "Do you know whose bed this was, darling?" and Little Mildred shook her head, not knowing but sensing she would soon be immersed in the history of it, bathed in the warm comfort of ready meaning. "It was the General's and Kathryn's, his wife. So, you know what that means," and even though she was only ten years old, Little Mildred did know: there is a price for having one's worth and place guaranteed, a heavy responsibility. Still, all of her life she has borne it well. She kept the bed when she married and to this day it is the one in which she lies down to sleep every night.

"Did you remember to bring the key, Albert?"

"Yes, ma'am. I got it right here."

Little Mildred and Albert stand beside the car and the Compton Building. It is nearly noon and the salmon stucco of the exterior reflects the sun, making them squint at the light, always brighter anyway in this part of town with no trees, only rows of squared, unembellished buildings in proximity to the railway depot and tracks. "Check to make certain you have the right key. I don't want to climb those steps and be locked out." Albert trots up the rusted grid steps to the door and puts the key in the padlock.

"It the one, Miz Mildred," he says and she comes up after him.

It is not as light as she remembered or perhaps the windows have sooted over through the years from passing trains and other pollutants. And, too, it is fall. Still, she can see the many bulky pieces covered with canvas tarps or furniture pads, not as disordered as she has feared, but not the immaculate storage her mother kept either. She would like to go around to visit the pieces, recall the pleasantries of the earlier days, but there is not the time. "Start pulling out anything with papers, Albert."

He circles the room and pulls three cardboard boxes full of files and manila envelopes to the front, center space. "That's it, I think," he says but Little Mildred laughs.

"You didn't know my father and my brother, Albert. They were very different men except in two things and one of them was that they never threw away anything." Little Mildred walks to a large bundle, covered with a quilted pad and pulls it up to see. It is a mahogany linen press with three bottom drawers, two half-drawers, and a double door at the top. She taps her cane against the bottom drawer. "Open this."

Albert pulls open the drawer. It is filled with scraps of material and the next up, as well, but the third drawer and the two smaller drawers contain loose paper of every sort. "I shoulda known. You right, Miz Mildred," he says.

"Yes and I want every scrap out of here." She precedes him around the room pulling out drawers, opening doors or pointing to them for him to do so. When they have reached the front door again, more than forty containers of papers stand open. "Go by the Piggly Wiggly in the morning and get some cardboard boxes. Make sure they are clean. I don't want any with fruit juice or roaches. Bring them here in your pickup truck and pack every bit of paper in this room into the boxes. Put them in the truck and bring them to my garage." Margaret is awake, walking around, and she must take precautions even if the act is unlikely. She does not know of any instance Margaret has ever come to the Compton Building since that one time but, no matter, if she should come now there will be nothing to find.

15

"**G**ood. You're back." Delores meets Niles on the steps as he returns from the bank. "Several people have called."

"Anybody important?"

"Not really. They're all in your E-mail."

Niles locks the door behind her. At 5:30 the law office is empty. He locates a Budweiser in the coffee room's refrigerator and sits down to a new accumulation of paper on his desktop, a dozen file copies of letters sent over his name, a letter, and one set of Request for Admission to be signed and go out in the morning.

After the meeting with Little Mildred, he has turned up some useful information. Margaret Cape has two bank accounts at the local Titus County Bank, neither of which has a balance of over $100. She receives two checks each month, less than $500 total, both pensions for veterans. Each of her husbands had served his country in the military—the Spanish-American War and World War II—and Niles congratulates himself on having the foresight to send notice to the Veteran's Administration of the conservatorship proceedings. Billy McLaurin, the bank's president, didn't have a lockbox for the Capes, said they had never kept one. In fact, it was one of the persistent rumors that Big John's grandfather had buried his valuables underneath Cape House and that all the Capes had followed suit. Even had there been one, Billy suggested, Chapin Finley would probably have used anything valuable; he lived high.

Niles also paid a visit to Bass Jewelry Store and Nathan Bass, the man who brought the petition in the first place. He wondered why and Bass told him it was because of a debt he had carried for quite a time, for resilvering back in the spring of 1966. The surprise came—it still unnerves Niles to remember it—when Bass had produced the IOU signed by Margaret Cape, his means of avoiding the statute of limitations on open accounts. It was the signature. Niles thought it was his own when he first saw it. It was the same bold, illegible scribble he used, but when he looked closer the letters could be made out and they spelled "Margaret F. Cape."

He pushes "E" on the keyboard and a list of messages appears on the computer screen. He begins to scroll through them, deleting or forwarding them on to Delores with instructions. "Someone to see you" is the fifth message and he recognizes the name of Margaret Cape's servant immediately. "Sam Adams stopped here, about 4:30. Mrs. Cape needs to see you AT CAPE HOUSE. I told him tomorrow (Fri.), 2 P.M. (You said you wanted to start inventory.) OK?" Niles tips up the Budweiser bottle and sucks out the last foamy remnants of the beer. He is uneasy. "There are two cases," Charley has told him. "The one you take and the one you get."

Hawkins, Mississippi, 1955 ✍ When Margaret came back to Bay Clinic, Buie was almost nine and she said she came only because Ella would not go otherwise, insisting it was only her "high sugar" causing problems, that there was nothing the clinic's weekly doctor could do. Ella had confidence instead in her nightly nip of Dr. Tichenors mouthwash—3 percent grain alcohol—and was satisfied with that. But Margaret knew Ella had already twice fainted dead away while about her kitchen chores and Sam continually complained that Ella would "tear up at nothin' at all." Of particular concern to him was her attitude toward their four children—Caraly and the three older brothers. "She don't beat their butts no more like they need. They do what they want and she jus' sit there," he told Margaret.

Sam drove them all, Ella beside him in the front seat, Margaret behind her, with Buie sitting next to her and Caraly on his other side. Margaret kept her expression grim and murmured occasional reassurances to Ella, but she was secretly thrilled with the return to Bay Clinic and knew as well that John Buie shared her secret and fumed, thrilling her more.

At the start he had encouraged Margaret to come, solemnly repeating the words of responsibility Delta planters felt for their lessers. "We have to take care of them because they can't do that for themselves. We use their bodies—that's the gift they were given—and, in return, they use our minds and character—our gift—to stay healthy." But he soured on the notion and when Buie was two and Ella had stopped nursing him, John Buie forbade Margaret any further trips to the clinic.

He woke her to tell her or thought he did, as she was not sleeping but faced away from him toward the windows, thinking things through. "I've decided you shouldn't go to Hawkins anymore," he declared, and she did not reply but her thoughts shifted to this peculiar statement and what it might mean. "Don't go." Of course, she understood that much and that it was meant as a command rather than a request or interested advice. Still, the essence of command is threat, an implied warning of consequences should the order be disobeyed and that was a part of what eluded her. The other part was common to every instance in which John Buie set such private rules and that was why he thought to do so, why he thought he could reach across the impassable chasm between them to will her acts as well as his own?

In her time at the clinic, the women came first to see and perhaps trust, before the children and only after those, the men.

They filled the narrow wooden benches—bent between unsteady supports—that lined the walls of the central hallway. "Eulalie," she called the name without seeing any particular face in the dim corridor. At the far end, the painted door to the street gave some light and air, too, propped open with loose bricks from the building foundation. Otherwise, there was the one hanging bulb, with a twist key switch. It was not enough to distinguish among the dark bodies, some golden or mauve but most were black coffee, dusted gray in patches from the field unless they oiled their skin carefully and many had given up that vanity. "Yes'm." The woman waited to follow Margaret into the first examination room, a toilet once, now used for a pine table and metal chairs. A stethoscope and blood pressure cuff rested on a tea towel draped over the dry commode. She pointed to one of the chairs, and the woman sat down, knees nearly to the floor as she balanced on the edge, wanting to leave, it seemed, even though she was the one who gave up a day's dollar wages to come.

"Where is it?" Margaret kept her voice steady, flat. In her first interviews, three years before, she began by asking, "You're not feeling well?" in sympathetic tones, but that was inevitably followed by sniffling or outright crying. "The Nigra is like a little child," Little Mildred had advised her. "If you baby them, they just whine all the more." Margaret thought not, that it was more something to do with loneliness, so lonely, alone by oneself, that there is no point to feeling anything at all, so that when sympathy comes it is like an unexpected visit to a shut-in who is too grateful to see another and cannot rein in the rush of feelings so long unshared. Eulalie, bare-armed in a dull plaid shift, appeared muscular and healthy, but bruises, even deep cuts from an errant hoe, were barely detectable on such dark skin. "Where is it?" Margaret repeated the question, and the woman looked up at her from the bottom of her eyes, then raised her hand to her throat, brushing it lightly with her fingers before dropping her arm again.

"Does it hurt?"

"No'm."

"Is it difficult for you to swallow?"

Eulalie raised her eyebrows and giggled. "No'm. Everythin' go down good."

It was a long questioning before Margaret came to the correct guess—each time it was such—that the woman had a cough that kept her awake, her baby in the crib disturbed, too, by the noise, and it was starting into her lungs. "Do you work in the field?" Margaret asked her, suspicious she was breathing the sprays for insects or weeds or the spray that killed the cotton plants before harvest, but Eulalie worked inside, cooking for the field hands and, on special occasions, for the planter himself. The dove shoot each September was the largest of those events and she always cooked for days in preparation.

"Does the baby cough?"

"No'm. He fine."

"Do you have other children?"

"Yes'm."

"Do any of them cough?"

Eulalie thought long on the question then said, "Yes'm. They do," as if surprised and in wonderment that Margaret knew these intimate details of her home. Margaret supposed, then, why the woman coughed, her children, too, or in all likelihood why. The shotgun shacks, four-sided and unfinished salvage wood, were rife with spiders and the field workers often brought home the used chemical cans and doused their own homes with the poison. Eulalie and her children were inside the most and they were being poisoned with the spiders.

"Take some borax and water and wash down all the walls," Margaret told her before sending her somewhere else to wait for the doctor and, too, "Bring your children by so the doctor can look at them," and Eulalie said, "Yes'm. I will," so sincerely, but Margaret knew that she might or she might not. This was the woman's first visit to the clinic and she would have to decide whether she trusted the advice to follow it and whether she would next bring one of her children when sick. The child would be as quiet as she, any obstinacy beat out by his mother before it posed a greater threat to him from some white-someone-else more powerful.

Nevertheless, it was then—Buie so small, she going to the clinic two, even three or four days each week, the longest hours during the summer—then that she was struck full force with the feeling of certainty about these choices, even though she was still a young woman of thirty-five whose life was presumably far from over. She nursed and she mothered, her days used up completely by reaching, needy hands. She had borne the General's child. She nursed as Clara Barton had, needing to come to this place to do either. There was John Buie, it was true, but this was Earth, not Heaven, and he was a necessity to the other, as Evil to Good.

Then he decided for her that she should leave the work, never go there again. Her mother had often warned her against tempting Fate, but Margaret thought herself guarded by the brevity of time she allowed the feeling to come and always in different places and times, never the same. And, it was not quite right to say it was really a feeling at all, surely nothing that was self-indulgent or excessive. Instead, it was a thing seen, a part of her life entire, and she could be romantic over the notion, as if she were traveling in the forest of her signs, upon the back of a well-bred mount whose head bobbed correctly, gracefully in front of her, and along the way the forest opened into meadows from time to time, and on either side of the same road. She turned the horse across and around the meadow, although never stopping, and rode in a warm breeze through clumps of reedy grasses, mashing fragrant wildflowers, stepping to the side of moss-covered rocks. The ground was firm, the horse recently shod, and her touch on the reins turned the animal this way or that as she pleased. That was what she saw sometimes. But other times, she saw herself seeking a promised

haven on a different sort of road, one that crumbled away behind her as she strained to push forward against something
unseen. Not wind. There was little of that in the Delta except
for the change of seasons. But there was something that
whipped her around if her shoulders were not squared as they
should be and it was only as she used the last of her will and
strength to push into it that she found the warm sanctuary, a
dry, soft hollow on the leeward side of a rock or tree where
she could sit with drops of water streaming from the cap of
her hair, chill bumps on her gold skin, and she could sit there
until she was rested or as long as she liked. It had been promised and found. She smiled at either of these sights, although
she tried not to do so. "Will I know when I find my story?"
she once asked her father and he said, "What would you
think?"

On this day, it was seven years past the last patient she had
calmed or cajoled and Margaret preceded Ella down the familiar hallway between the benches of others waiting, passing
them by without looking, refusing any thought of their needs.
A square-bodied woman in nurse's white came into the hall,
placed pale, freckled arms on broad hips while she looked up
and down the rows, then singled out Ella and Margaret, motioning them into a large, bright room where records were kept.

"What've we got today?" she asked Margaret only, who answered for Ella. "She is very tired and, at times, she seems to
limp on her left foot." The nurse took a sample of blood and
removed Ella's shoe and cotton sock, exposing hard calluses,
split and oozing, that covered the ball of her foot. "She could
lose this," the woman said, and Margaret said, "It must be
diabetes," not looking at Ella who had begun to cry.

Margaret left Ella to the nurse and stepped again into the
hallway. "Don't go to Hawkins again," he had said, and she
called the doctor's office to tell him she would not return and,
then, what of her certainty, her story? But, today she was back
for some time and the next Tuesday and then Thursday after,

and then twice every week, she returned to the clinic to work until, without warning, the clinic was itself ended some nine years later during the summer of 1964.

NILES ABBOTT PRESSES the Bronco's horn again, longer this time. Through the locked gate, he can see fifty yards of the S-curved driveway before it turns left and disappears into a pecan grove that lines either side. No one inside Cape House, he supposes, can hear him from this distance. The old man will remember the two o'clock appointment soon enough and Niles rolls down the window to wait.

It is another bluebird day, with a clear, prairie sky, warm as summer but without the usual sticky haze of humidity and chemicals. He slouches in the seat to let the sun on his face, then seconds later sits up again, needing to make his list of points to review with Mrs. Cape. He reaches for the red rope folder containing her file and pulls out a legal pad, writing several lines quickly, then tearing off the sheet, folding it, and tucking it in an inside pocket. He slides back into his previous position and stares straight ahead at the gate for ten minutes until, at last, Sam Adams pulls it back to let him through.

Niles waits for him at the front door of the house, while Sam short-steps slowly up the driveway toward him. Sam is panting when he reaches the porch steps. "You could've ridden with me. Didn't you see me wave?" Niles asks Sam, who smiles and shrugs, but says nothing. He opens the door to let Niles pass through into the darkened foyer, then steps around him and through the door at the far end. Niles waits in the dark, shifting his laptop computer from hand to hand until, after a few minutes, the old man returns.

"Miz Cape jus' up from her nap. She gone to freshen up now," he says cheerfully and pushes back double pocket doors along the left wall, causing Niles to narrow his eyes at the sudden infusion of sunlight. "You sit over in here, Mr. Abbott,"

Sam gestures toward the light. "I'll get you refreshments." He leaves again but Niles remains in the foyer, able to see what is there now. The room is dramatic, its walls Chinese red, with framed prints and silks hanging in groups on every side and as far as he can see up the walls of the stairway ascending to the second floor. There are only two pieces of furniture, each oriental and old. He sits down on the smooth black bench next to the front door, balancing the computer on his knees as he boots it and begins to type their descriptions. Delores can come next week to inventory what he doesn't get down today and take Polaroids of everything. Then, an appraiser. He makes a note to ask Charley for a name.

Sam reappears with glasses and a decanter on a silver tray, and Niles follows him through the opened doors. The warm colors of the foyer give way abruptly to glittering gilt and ivory in a room as big as two and requiring three double-tiered chandeliers for light. The room is crowded with antique furnishings—very fine, very old French or Italian, perhaps—but there is something else, too, and Niles stops inside the doorway, momentarily stunned by the deterioration that flows over the room like a vestige of the constant tide washing over a beach. The smell of damp mold is so strong, he gags.

"What is this room, Sam?"

"This is the Front Hall, Mr. Abbott. She only use it for the special times. You the only special now for a while."

Niles glances at the old man but there is no hint of irony in his expression. He remains intent on the tray, his long, spindly fingers deftly arranging the brandy and snifters and a plate of cookies on a low parquetry table placed between two settees, sea green silk and dark mahogany, set up on fragile, intricately carved legs and identical except for their unique patterns of fungus and water stains. They sit at right angles to the wall's center, a magnificent fireplace framed in veined marble and, on either side, six double-arched windows extending from the floor to within a foot of the high ceiling. He can see now that it is these that form the source of the room's decay, their gold drapes spotted with mildew and in shreds near the hem below. The afternoon sun shines unobstructed through them and their panes lie in shattered pieces on the floor below. Underfoot, the fine Heriz is a collection of blue and persimmon threads no longer bound to one another but merely resting in juxtaposition on the water-spotted floor. There is no need to inventory because there are no longer any individual items to list. The room is a single entity now, unprotected and weathered by the elements as one.

He feels a little queasy, always the one with the weak stomach, and today he skipped lunch. He sits down on the settee facing north and pours himself a little of the brandy. Its warm smell masks the pungent mildew and, feeling better already, he sits back and raises the snifter to examine the liquor's chestnut color in the sunlight. He sees her then, his rankled stomach grabbing a little from the surprise. She has been here all the while, of course, in her soft ivory satin dress, gazing down at him, protected from the elements by her position above the fireplace, dominating the room, and the only excuse he can make for not seeing her before was that he has been so intent on inventory and furniture styles that he failed to enter the Front Hall in the manner one ordinarily would and which fashion would have immediately brought the painting into view.

Niles sips and studies Margaret Cape at twenty-five, thirty-five? Certainly, forty at most. She is beautiful, but all women are in portraits they or their husbands have commissioned. Kathryn Cooper, his high school girlfriend, once told him, quite seriously, that having one's portrait painted was a necessary confirmation of position that had to be done at a particular time—late enough for a woman to have produced at least one heir, but not so late that her youth and freshness had faded and she was forced to wear all of her major jewelry in compensation. Margaret Cape, Niles thinks, had timed the portrait perfectly. He cannot look away and the sense grows that he has seen this thing before, the very same but different. She looks at him serenely, her lips slightly parted, blue-gray eyes wide, inquisitive. The bronze hair piled loosely atop her head is only a shade darker than the golden skin of her face. The artist had posed her by an elaborately carved side chair, perhaps one in this room, Niles thinks. Her back is to him, her hands rest easily on the chair's back, and she stands head turned over her shoulder, feet apart, one leg extended out...as if she is fleeing something or someone and only stopped for a moment to get her bearings. No, that is not quite right. Where has he seen this? Niles looks at the face again and, yes, he can conjecture fear there, the strong chin set in defiance but the eyes pleading for rescue. He laughs at himself, embarrassed; he shouldn't be drinking booze at teatime.

"Mr. Abbott?"

At the sound of the soft voice, Niles starts and automatically stands. When he turns, she has already crossed the room, her eyes large and fixed upon him, and the memory is shocked into his conscious. The panther had struck the identical pose, its head turned toward him while the body poised to spring away. He remembers the eyes offered the very same expression, not fear after all, but eyes sometimes mistaken that way, receiving and present eyes, their intense thought the polar opposite of indifference. *I am a live thing here. You are one, here.* She extends her hand toward him. He watches it reach to him, careful to enclose it softly in his own, much larger. "I'm so very *pleased* to meet you," she says and he looks down into the suddenly familiar eyes of Margaret Cape.

16

He stands until she seats herself on the settee opposite him with the brandy easily in reach and she quickly pours two fingers in a snifter. She sits back, cradling it in both hands to warm the liquor, then lifts her chin to Niles, who accepts the cue to sit. The look of him appeals to Margaret, not in a seductive way, although she smiled, surprising herself, when he finally turned and she saw that he was an especially handsome man. It was before then, when she had let Sam bring her to the doorway of the Front Hall, where the young lawyer waited, head tilted up toward her portrait, his dark hair thick and curling, very like her own Buie's. "That him," Sam whispered to her and she left his arm at once, wanting to touch the one who earnestly studied the painted image from someone else's thought of her, the portrait that had taken the General's rightful place. She wanted to turn his face, living toward living. "No, here," she would say to this person like her, alive in a dead room, and he would touch her, too. She did not, of course. It was a benefit of age's infirmities that she had time to reconsider her desires before she reached him and remember the dangers and, so, had only offered a greeting.

"Yes, ma'am. I was admiring your portrait. It's very nice, Mrs. Cape."

"Oh, do you like it?" Her voice is soft, but well rehearsed now, duplicating the melodic quality of Rosamond matrons. "I never cared for it really, but John Buie insisted on hanging it anyway."

"Well, I'm afraid I have to agree with him, ma'am. It's really very nice." Niles looks again to the painting then back at Margaret, who sits watching him execute the rituals of conversation. There is enough similarity to know she is—had been—the young woman in the portrait. Her size and the delicate structure of her face are the same. Yes, she is much older, the soft bronze hair mostly gray now and she is not wearing ivory satin today, but a dark wool crepe suit, too big for her atrophied body. He smiles at her and it is a warm gesture, friendly even, but the dispassionate appraisal from his eyes contradicts it and Margaret, understanding that the mouth is the face's liar, ducks her head and continues her lines.

"Ernest Langer painted it when he was still living with his sister in Yazoo City, before he moved to New Orleans," she says. "Let me see, I believe in 1956. Well, it doesn't matter, now, I suppose. He just painted buildings down there, someone said, the Quarter, you know."

"Yes, ma'am. I've seen his work before. He was really talented." He smiles again at her and, at the same time, searches her face for signs of lunacy but she is not "noticeably crazy," Charley's interpretation of non compos mentis. "NCM. Noticeably crazy Mississippian," he would joke. "Don't count, see, unless you can see it. Otherwise, Whitfield would be a city, not an institution, and one of the larger ones at that." It is good, at least, that she is small and quiet-natured, easy to handle in the way the nursing home prefers.

Margaret holds a porcelain plate toward him and a linen napkin in the other hand. "Have one of these madeleines, Mr. Abbott, won't you? Sam made them fresh today. He's likely to get his feelings hurt if we don't eat them." Niles hesitates, then takes the napkin and one of the small cakes, downing the rich, buttery morsel in one bite and reaching for another. Margaret stares at him, captivated by the unexpected fervor of his appetite and she remembers reading somewhere: "Don't feed the bears." Still, she extends the plate toward him once more and he takes another cake.

"I didn't get any lunch today," he explains, brushing the crumbs from his trousers and onto the napkin, suddenly feeling self-conscious. She unsettles him, she is too still, barely moving as she listens to him speak or even when she is speaking and, yet, he feels as certain she would move quickly away from him if he alarmed her in some way. She leans forward to set the plate on the small table, then reaches for the crystal decanter and he notices that a narrow ridge of dust extends across the top of each shoulder of her suit. "Here, let me do that for you," he says, taking the decanter from her hand and standing to pour the brandy.

She lets him fill the snifter halfway before raising her hand to stop him, then sits back on the settee. It is more difficult than she imagined it would be. More effort is required to sustain this sort of pretense than simply separating herself and giving over to another way to be for a time. She is not willing to do the latter anymore, however. This is the last of her and she wants to be present for all of it, but the strain just now is considerable for the little given her in return. He resembles Buie in a few, small ways. That is all and it explains, perhaps, her attraction to him but no more. The likeness alone is not enough to direct her or explain why Niles Abbott intersects her story just now. A sign will certainly come, but is there the time for waiting?

Niles moves forward on the seat cushion and leans toward her, bracing his forearms against his legs. "Mrs. Cape, there are a couple of things I'd like to go over with you, you know, about the conservatorship and all," he says, measuring his words. "But, since it was you who called me, I thought, first, we better see whether there's something special you wanted to ask?"

Margaret considers the question. If she speaks her thoughts directly to him, they might move quickly together toward the meaning of this junction for him as well as her, but that is not a reasonable hope. It is doubtful he knows he has a story and he will filter whatever words she speaks through his own rules of meaning, Rosamond rules and words having no capacity to express what she intends. What can be said, anyway? He resembles Buie a little. That is all she is given and, for the rest, she must wait.

"No, there's nothing," she says.

Cape Plantation, 1956 ☙ Her father told her about the place different ways, different times. He was a man who did not care to use axioms or even the same expression over and over. What was the point? If there were anything that bore repeating, he said it afresh, from a separate vantage, like the infinite visions of an eye circling its object.

He had startled her and her mother at five o'clock on an October's Sunday stroll near the duck pond in Baldwin park. "Look!" he shouted and stopped short so that Anne Finley, who rested her arm on his, was pulled backward and nearly toppled. "Robert Samuel!" She said it in a low voice and it was a reprimand and yet she looked the way he pointed, as did Margaret. A man and woman sat on the far bank, he half below her with his elbows back into the Bermuda grass, eyes either closed or drooping far. The light was odd just then and their clothes blended too well as if they were varying shades of brown in a sepia print, except that the woman toyed with a periwinkle blue scarf that seemed electric in comparison. Before them and in parallel configuration, a pair of white ducks swam by on the dull brown water exactly between the green pads of two water lilies, giant Brazilian *nymphaea*. "Ah," her mother sighed. "It is a painting." Margaret thought that her father would cry, his pleasure was so magnified. He grasped Anne Finley by her dainty shoulders as if he were about to kiss her lips in public but he caught himself. "Her mother! That is the reason my little Margaret has sight into what is special. Exactly! A painting is what it is."

Other times, other things, the same. The abounding place. That is what he called it. He showed her moments but it was not a moment, nor a place either. "It is an idea inside you, inside me, and everyone living. The animals and plants, too. Yes! What is the look? Plants have more time for ideas than the rest of us." The abounding place, he told her, was the supposed object of life's longing, a place where the cavities and hollows inside us filled to above the edge, the surface tension holding the last of it and we were sated, steady. "Don't you understand what it means, Margaret? Beware it! Beware."

She forgot what he said even as he said it. Who could remember that? When Buie was ten, she was on the very brink of the place he had warned her against and she had no notion. Perhaps she confused her father's description with self-satisfaction or dull contentment and neither applied in any measure to the life she was passing at Cape Plantation. It was already summer in May, a usual occurrence at cotton planting time, a time requiring John Buie to be away each day until dark. Ernest Langer came at midmorning to work on her portrait and that had been going on for several weeks. He had appeared at the last of April, ready to work, and John Buie summoned Margaret to the Front Hall to tell her. "Mr. Langer here is going to paint you, darlin'," and, from the doorway, her eyes cast about the room because she had seen no one else, but he was there, the artist standing in front of the long windows looking decidedly arty, his hands clasped behind him, feet apart, while he gazed at some unknown, unpainted beauty outside. He wore the khaki pants common to Delta farmers, but two sizes too large, a white collarless shirt, and a soft, loose jacket that hung halfway down his thighs. "Just now, Mr. Langer is occupied bein' sensitive," John Buie explained to Margaret in a stage whisper and the man turned laughing, but looked only to her.

"Mrs. Cape? I'm delighted to meet you at last." He tipped his head, his long forelock hanging to one side, and gave her a courtly half-bow, then stood back and appraised his subject. "If I can capture one portion of your singular beauty, I shall count myself successful." His face was not the delicate one his initial stance promised. He had rounded, country features and his skin was noticeably pocked. Still, it was kindly enough.

"My wife doesn't talk to us, Mr. Langer."

"Oh, I see." The painter nodded, sympathetic to some unstated suffering.

"I mean, she can talk but she expects us to read her mind, anyone who might care what she's thinking. I'd tell you what she's thinkin' right now, but I've gotten a little out of practice."

Langer reddened and coughed into his hand, then pretended to be gathering together his paints. "Well. If it is agreeable with the lady, we can begin today." He held his hand to Margaret and she walked across the room to him, passing John Buie without acknowledgment. "Why don't you sit here on the settee and we can discuss some ideas for the portrait. Here." He patted the cushion next to him and Margaret sat on the very edge. "While we have this light, let me try some colors next to your skin. You know, it's quite interesting. You're almost a pure burnt umber, with the white added, of course. Maybe a little ocher. Most pleasing." Langer held up a series of small tubes, their metal cases distorted by a hundred bends and creases. "I think I can get it fairly quickly. Now, let me see your eyes." Margaret lifted her chin and looked at him squarely and his own eyes widened. "Oh, my. How singular."

She did talk, of course, but what she said was not what John Buie cared to hear and, so, it went unnoted. She had a strange feeling about the painting but she was unable to say why and so merely suggested that it was an unnecessary extravagance. "If it is, it is my extravagance, not yours. What do you have to throw away?" He stood by the closet—there was a tufted stool outside the door—and folded his dirty clothes as he removed them. Unless he had his own plans in the evening, he did not bathe before retiring, but waited until morning and Margaret read his mind better than he read hers. "I'll tell you this, Margaret, and not because I have to but because you are the mother of my sons and there may be some small part of you that will do the decent thing for them. My wife—the wife of John Buie Cape—should have her portrait painted by a fine artist and it should hang in the Front Hall. My boys should have a mother painted by such an artist. Now, I am going to have that no matter what life you are choosing to live for yourself. I am going to have my life as it should be."

Langer had told them he would be finished within three weeks and the last of those would be spent in his own studio in Yazoo City, where Margaret would be brought one time for final corrections. But, after four weeks, he still painted at Cape House and his easel and drop cloth stayed put in the middle of the Front Hall so that no other use could be made of it. Even John Buie—who waved away every inconvenience from the man far beyond his usual tolerance—wondered aloud whether Ernest Langer was the artist everyone supposed and began to repeat his epithets about his manhood, although not so strongly as before. Langer did seem in some disarray, especially to Margaret, who saw him more than the others. He was on his third canvas, having angrily abandoned the two previous ones and it was clear he blamed her for his failure so far. "You must let me see you!" he exhorted. He tried any number of foolish fantasies—"You are the beloved of a great knight who has risked all for your honor and it is the first moment you see him returning to you after years away"—trying to make her look some way or other that she could not give to him. She thought she followed his directions precisely and sat very still until her back and legs cramped, smiling to just the degree he encouraged, but it was not what he wanted and he was losing hope in finding it. "You hide from me, Margaret Cape," he scolded her and she was glad he, at least, did not see how the entire enterprise disturbed her. John Buie had said "my life" as if it were a thing of a particular sort to be selected or not, and she remembered something her father told her about taking a certain time out of her path from birth to death and making that her "life," everything else referring forward or back. "It negates itself, takes all the life out, don't you see, Margaret? When something is set, so full there is no impulse to move, it is like the funereal body filled with formaldehyde and just as dead. Why else does every religion postulate the time of perfect fulfillment after death, not before? Think about it, Margaret. It is life in a painting, nothing more."

"Are you uncomfortable?"

"A little," she answered and accepted the unspoken invitation to stand and stretch.

"Be careful. Don't wrinkle." He had insisted on going through her dresses and she worried he would select something for her that was wrong, but he had picked the ivory satin, the color that she herself felt was right for being painted, which was certainly closer to a social occasion than it was to going to church or reading a book. She stood and walked away toward the large windows on the west wall, pulling back the sheers to see the fields spanning the space between her and the curve of the earth, not so very far after all, she noticed. She looked for a long time, turning a side chair set between the windows and leaning on its carved back, Langer saying nothing to disturb her.

"Don't go in there, Buie. Your mother's bein' painted." John Buie's edged voice came through the open door and she turned looking back over her shoulder, searching for Buie's face, but she only saw part of the figures in the darkened foyer, their trousers and the larger man's arm stretched across the other's chest, holding her son from her. "That's it!" Langer's shout startled her and she looked to him stepped away from his easel and standing with arms stretched wide. "Thank you! Thank you!" He blew kisses to her and he did not come back after that day nor require a further sitting, painting Margaret exactly as he saw her then, at her moment of consummate caution and care.

"I guess that sonofabitch is as good as they say," John Buie allowed, examining the finished painting. It was a painting of her, alright, he said and he hung it in the Front Hall "so everyone can share the burden with me." He took away the General's painting, never telling her where, and she was so relieved to have the painter gone and the painting behind her that she never thought about what her father said about the abounding place. She had come to that place where she filled herself even while she required constant repair to wounds from her life otherwise. She filled herself with the love of her child, Buie, being his mother and raising him safe and it was who she was and she did not consider that it was something to beware.

NILES PULLS THE list and a ballpoint pen from inside his jacket. "There are several points I want to mention," he says, spreading the long yellow sheet on the table between them. He wonders whether she notices the likeness of their writing, but she only looks at him, waiting. "First, let me say that I don't want you to be apprehensive about any of the proceedings ahead. The purpose of law is not to hurt, but to take care of people and their legitimate needs," he says by rote and draws a check mark on the paper to the side of what seems to her a dark blur. "Now, as you know, a petition has been brought asking the court to appoint a conservator for you," Niles continues, looking up at her now for a response and she nods. "In about a month, on November fifth, there will be a formal hearing and the chancellor has told me that, on that date, he plans to appoint me your conservator." She sits silent, acquiescent it seems, and he takes a deep breath, satisfied the worst part is past.

"You are going to protect me," Margaret says directly and he laughs a little, surprised, so that she asks, "It's not so?"

"No, I didn't mean...yes, I am your protector in a manner of speaking. Yes, of course. I just don't want you to think there is any notion you are in some sort of physical danger, that someone is out there wanting to do you harm." He is sincere in his effort to reassure her, suddenly more concerned than before as if merely saying the word brought the thing into being. There is an injury in the way the others are treating her, as if she were a nuisance because she is old and unreliable, and his indignation rises until he remembers Buddy and he tempers his judgment of the Capes. He smiles and is glad when she smiles slightly as well, shaking her head. "Well, what I was going to say concerned the inventory. You see, ma'am, I am— will be—charged with looking after your assets and not only your personal welfare. You know, your possessions, property and all."

"Cape House?" she asks. The pace of the conversation has increased somehow, confusing her a little.

"Yes. Exactly. And what's in it and any other real property you may have. Which brings me to another question I have. Could you give me some idea, Mrs. Cape, what land you have besides this house?"

She looks at him blankly and seconds pass. No response comes to mind. She needs more time to speak, to phrase things in the other way. At last she lifts the plate of madeleines toward him. "Please take this one last, lonely little cake, won't you, Mr. Abbott? I don't want Sam to fuss at me about it."

"No, thank you, ma'am," he says, marking the list. "Don't worry about it. I can check the land out for you. I'll do a search at the courthouse. Don't worry about it," he repeats, still looking at the paper. "That's mostly all. Oh, I almost forgot this.

Do you have any other children besides Chapin Finley?"
Margaret's head jerks slightly and, seeing it, Niles recognizes
his error. "I know he recently passed away. I'm very sorry, Mrs.
Cape. I just have to ask these things. What about grandchildren?" She says nothing and he stares into middle space thinking of other important matters he did not have on the list.
"You have accounts at Titus County Bank. What about other
accounts, CDs, lockboxes?"

Margaret shakes her head, closing her eyes and trying to
regain concentration. She is feeling tired and she has questions
of her own already, more than she can answer and now he asks
more. She has wearied of the questions, of him being here, of
being here herself. She misread the sign and it was a mistake
for Sam to summon him here, that is all, and she needs to be
alone again, to reconsider what is to be done. She moves forward to the edge of the settee.

"We can go over these things later. There's no hurry," he
says, noticing the movement. "What I will do right away is
make an inventory, a kind of list of everything, and if there is
anything you need to have done, I'll go ahead and take care of
it. For instance, I noticed you need a little repair on these windows before we get another rain. I'll send someone around to
fix them, with your permission, of course."

Margaret opens her eyes and looks at him. "Repair?"

"Yes, the broken windows. Would you like me to send someone to replace them?"

She rises and seems disoriented at first, and Niles comes
halfway up to catch her, but she does not fall. She walks toward
the enormous west windows, turning toward the one to the
right of the fireplace until she stands at the center of its glass.
The windows did break one time, but that had been years ago
in late afternoon in May and the sky turned yellow brown just
before. She watched from her bedroom looking out at the side
yard when the first small pellets struck the ground and then
stones increasing in size until the entire yard was covered with

hail, cream-colored ice stones as large as hens' eggs. It began and ended within minutes and, later, Chapin Finley shouted through the bedroom door, "Mother, it got some windows on the other side. I'll get Dew's to take care of them."

She pulls the drape to one side, exposing the stained and tattered lining. Beneath its hem, the floorboard is soft and rotted. "The windows are broken," she says and realizes she does not remember anyone had ever come. She turns back and touches the edge of the rug with her toe, the threads separating and lying where they are pushed, and there is a strong smell of mildew. The furniture, too—she can see it now—has been damaged from the storm or from the exposure that followed.

"You didn't know?"

The baritone voice startles her and she sees that he is watching her with the same look of appraisal he let show in the beginning. She flutters her eyelids closed and gathers herself to respond. "Oh, yes, of course," she says lightly, coming back to him. "But, when you're alone in a large house, Mr. Abbott, things can get away from you. You know how that can be. The General and I bought these in Paris," she says, touching the carved frame of the settee and seating herself on its edge once more.

"The General, ma'am?"

"Yes. My husband. That was what I called him, although it was his grandfather who was actually a general, General John Buie Cape." She looks up at the painting over the mantel. "His portrait used to hang in here instead of this one. General Cape's, I mean. But it was lost. I mean moved."

"Oh, really? I'd like to see it someday," Niles says, genuinely interested. "He's sort of a legend around here, you know." He leans forward, again resting his forearms on his knees and Margaret moves back the same distance. "My mother's grandmother on her father's side was a Buie," he persists. "She's kin to General Cape some way. I can't recall."

"To the General?" She suddenly leans toward him again,

their faces so close he can see the dusting of powder on her cheeks and that the shading of her eyelids is no more than discolored skin fortuitously accenting light eyes. "How odd that you would have the General's blood in you."

"I wouldn't call it 'odd,'" Niles laughs. "I'm probably related in one way or another to half the county." He raises his eyebrows, smiling an invitation to speak, but she does not accept. He tries again, broadening his accent to convey affability. "It's just like they say, Miz Cape. Everyone knows everyone else in Miss'sippi. If you don't know somebody, don't worry 'cause you're bound to be kin to 'em at least."

He is trying to charm her, she knows, and it has the same pleasant feel as charm always does despite the nature or intent of its perpetrator. She studies his face a moment, then rewards him with a flirting smile and sits back. "I'm afraid I need to rest now, Mr. Abbott. I'm so sorry."

He folds the paper and nervously pushes it at the base of the plate. "As I said before, the chancellor wants to make certain you have any assistance you may need. So he thought—and I agree, of course—that you might want to go ahead and let us make arrangements for you at Bayou Glen. Now, that is."

"I'm afraid I don't understand what you mean, Mr. Abbott," she says pleasantly.

Niles clears his throat. "Arrangements, you know, so you could move in there. It's a kind of retirement place. Very nice. My father stays there. They've got a TV room and a courtyard. There's even a gas grill on the patio for cookouts. So far, they only have a semiprivate room available, but we could put you on the list for a private as soon as one came up." He is speaking too rapidly and he realizes he has pushed the cookie plate to the edge of the table until it is in danger of toppling off the other side. He reaches for it and sets it back. "I'm sorry," he says, but she has abruptly risen and her eyes are wide, with the same ambiguous, compelling expression as her portrait, and she looks so much like the young woman painted that Niles's breath catches in his throat. Then Sam Adams is there, reaching his hand to her and steadying her as she walks away. "It's been such a pleasure meeting you, Mr. Abbott. I think it's simply *marvelous* that a young man such as yourself has come so far. Do come see us again," she says and rests her arm on Sam's until they reach the doors and she looks at Sam, who nods and leaves her side, walking back toward Niles.

"I'll see you out the gate, Mr. Abbott," he says.

17

She waits beneath the stairs until they are through the door, then returns to the Front Hall and looks again, but it is the same. She had not imagined it only because he was there and she is tired, more tired than she can remember. The mahogany sideboard here, near the door, only needs oil but across the room, closer to the broken windows, the game table is no more than kindling and it is the same for the rest. If she did not notice before, she could have deduced it. Dead things like these need sealing for preservation, whereas what lives cannot be preserved at all. Instead, the living are...what form does protection take for them? Perhaps, the General and others like him? Niles Abbott has the General's blood but that is not enough or else she is too spent to see.

She comes to the facing settees, choosing his side to seat herself and she sees it at once. The paper lies on the table where he left it folded and tucked beneath the plate of madeleines as some secret love letter might be. She draws it out, unfolds it, and spreads it as he had, taking the magnifying glass from her pocket. The script is uncannily familiar to her and she nods as she reads the words.

> Taking care of people/needs
> Inventory
> Land?—how much
> HOME—11/5

"Miz Marg'ret? What you doin' back in here?" Sam helps her to her feet. "You gonna pay the price for today already. You need your rest." She does not oppose him, but lets him take her slowly out of the room and down the back hall to her bedroom, seating her on the edge of the bed. She pours a glass of the brandy and lies back into the soft pillows. He was right. The hurting does not wait long. It comes within minutes and spreads itself quickly across her, bearing down on her, crushing her chest and her body, a needy lover with no time for playful advances.

Margaret drinks the brandy in a single shot and buries the glass beneath the pillows. Sam was right. She needs rest now, now that she knows what is required of her and the time that is left. The note on the paper is simple but complete, and it tells her the path to follow. That is the meaning of "HOME," she is almost certain. And, since there is little time for mistakes anymore, it is a welcome touch of assurance that the note is written in her own hand.

THERE IS A message from Vernon Pettis, the new attorney in Charleston. He is a University of Virginia law graduate, not from Mississippi but Maryland, and he is Negro.

"Why would he want to come down here to Mississippi? That's what I'd like to know," Stewart Ellis commented at the recent Titus County Bar meeting and repeated for the twentieth time the story about how Pettis's first appearance in court, the circuit judge confused him with a criminal defendant and told him to "get back with the fella representing you." Niles has dissented from this talk, but he dials Pettis's number, hoping for the answering machine so that he will have discharged his duty to call without having to work through a conversation.

"Vernon Pettis," the clipped, accentless voice says after the first ring and Niles sits upright in his chair.

"Vernon. Niles Abbott returning your call."

"Yes. Thank you, Mr. Abbott." Pettis does not return the informality and Niles immediately regrets his presumption. "Mr. Bailey, the chancery clerk, said I should call you. I saw the notice about Mrs. Cape."

"The court plans to appoint me her conservator."

"So I understand. That is why I believe you are the appropriate person to alert."

"Oh, no. Alert? I hope it's not that bad." Niles laughs but Pettis does not join him.

"I wasn't certain what you might be planning at the hearing on November fifth and, after conferring with my client, we agreed it best I contact you."

"What is it?"

"My client has an ownership interest in certain properties that may have, in the past, had connection to your ward. He does not wish that they be mistakenly considered at this hearing."

"Oh? What properties are those?" Niles pauses, on the defensive now. "Mr. Pettis."

"It's actually a composite of several farms, together which have been known generally under the designation 'Cape Plantation.' "

Niles leans forward in his chair, all thoughts of beneficent whiteness put aside. Pettis is just another adversary worthy of his best offense. "Your client claims to own Cape Plantation? Who is this client?" he demands.

"Taking your questions in sequence: first, my client *does* own Cape Plantation and, second, I am not at liberty to divulge his or her name at this moment but I am in possession of the original deeds and looking at them now."

"Well, you do what you think is necessary, Mr. Pettis. The chancellor is going to dispose of those properties at the hearing one way or the other."

"Very well. We had hoped to avoid the expense of court proceedings, but my client will not have his title clouded. I have an answer prepared to file Monday morning. Thank you, Mr. Abbott."

Niles cannot wait until Monday and he takes the firm's courthouse key out of Charley's middle drawer. In the land records room, he finds nothing showing any transfer of Cape property during the previous ten years. Given the chancery clerk's casual record keeping, however, Niles knows to look further. In Beetle's office, he sorts through the unfiled stacks of papers on the desks and in counter trays. In the third drawer from the left, behind the chancery clerk's counter, he finds what he is looking for. A photocopy of a quitclaim deed from Chapin Finley Cape dated April 3, 1993, transferring all of his right, title, and interest that he may possess in a five-hundred-acre parcel to Hardy Mall. He does not need to look further to surmise there are others and that probably, just as Pettis said, they total all of the property called Cape Plantation.

PART THREE

At the three-way junction, Sam turns in his seat to look at her, his eyebrows raised, but Margaret shows her palms to him and refuses the decision. "I guess Ruleville be as good as any, wouldn't it," he says, turning the Buick south onto the highway to take the longer of two routes to Bay Clinic, the one that turns back north at Ruleville then passes Parchman, the state penitentiary. She remembers that it was the same then, when he brought her to the clinic twice, sometimes three times, in a week. She would decide the course at the moment required, no sooner, going north through Sumner one time and the other way the next or the same, again but when he chose, it was the southern route by Parchman and no other. "It he'p keep me straight knowing the mens inside and me sittin' out here," he says. " 'Member what the old peoples say—'God don't like ugly.' "

They are late starting from Cape House. She tries each color of dress in succession, but none is right. She is not going to read or to chapel or to be social. It was the same on the day Mr. Abbott came, two weeks ago, not a visit for an ivory dress but a different occasion altogether, an uncertain meeting with a stranger and nothing fit. After a time, she turns from the colors to what she wore when she came to this same clinic to work although John Buie made the selection then. "You can't dress up for them like they were regular people. It'd give 'em the wrong idea," he told her. "Then come home and put clothes in our closet you wore around colored people all day? What're you thinking, Margaret?" He sent Ella to Levin's to buy khaki trousers and work shirts for her and instructed that they be washed in town with Ella's laundry then folded in a drawer in the kitchen and brought to Margaret when she needed them. His acts were in accord with what she knew of him and she let them alone, trying to shield herself from the corruption that might come when the regularity of shameful deeds makes them a necessary reference point. She wore the clothes, but for her own reasons. Sam found them as soon as she remembered and grinned when she appeared with the pants belted to the last notch and the sticks of her arms protruding from rolled-up shirtsleeves.

"Look at you! Make me think of the old days, 'cept you 'n me both need some fattenin'," he says.

The Delta bows out from a narrow start in Vicksburg and extends north a hundred and fifty miles to Memphis, but it seems to her narrow, constricted in some undefined way. Before they reach Ruleville, the regular succession of flat cotton fields, two or three shotgun shacks for the blacks, concrete block houses for poor whites, and a whitewashed mansion with Grecian columns of various orders repeats itself a dozen times. The gray sky increases the feeling, a ceiling across it all getting lower by the mile. They come to Shelton, a plantation town of a single street with rusting, one-story buildings on either side and a score of solemn, dark faces congregated around cars and lampposts and corner signs, watching them pass. She looks back at them, too, and the stores behind continually swallowing them up, then spitting them out again.

Sam is agitated by her decision to come. She can see that in the way he holds his body rigid and chews at his lower lip. "It ain't no more, Miz Marg'ret," he protested and tried to dissuade her journey. "Ain't no use goin' jus' wear yo'sef out." It was unlike him to push against her that way, but she had spent long days thinking it through and she told him to drive her there. "Taking care of people/needs" the note said and she had taken care of people like these at Bay Clinic. She watches through the car window without knowing what she might see or when.

"Let's stop for a cold drink, Sam."

"Not Shelton, ma'am. It ain't the same's it was. Bee's Grocery on down the road another mile or more."

She does not argue. Everything changes and she is glad of it because only what lives changes or effects change, complicating her task, certainly. She wonders about the usefulness of a journey to Bay Clinic as it might be this moment; what she would know is Bay Clinic as it was, at least before it became a burned-out shell. She cannot remember much of the moments of her time there, except that needfulness was the floor and ceiling and walls around her and the people's faces.

Sam brings her a can of iced tea from Bee's and an RC Cola for himself and salted peanuts in the skin. At Ruleville, he turns the car back north and, in a short distance more, the arched entry to Parchman appears on the left. MISSISSIPPI STATE PENITENTIARY it says in white wrought iron and signs on either side of the road say EMERGENCY STOPS ONLY. Sam slows the Buick to half-speed as they pass through the zone. "Still there," he says and she looks through the arch or beyond in clusters of white barracks, the cell blocks in camps dividing the flat fields, but there is nothing to see.

She remembers Sam's warning and tries to prepare herself. Not to do so is a privilege of the young and strong-hearted and she is neither of those, but she cannot imagine what she will see when they come to Bay Clinic.

"Peoples finished their eggs, comin' out now." Sam waves his arm to the road and fields, but she sees only green, mechanical pickers moving in rows of cotton and soybeans in oblique angle to the highway and an occasional car or truck or cotton wagon met or intersected. There are a few walkers, except next to town or county stores and, then, only children, black children leading smaller ones and sometimes turning to look, their hands fiddling in front of them. The sameness from mile to mile, year to year, is hypnotic and the single difference she can see is that the red-tailed hawks used to circle the rabbit-rich fields but now they perch on electric wires or a tree near the highway, waiting for the work to be done for them. "It's not pretty, honeybun," Big John told her. "But it just has to be that way. All this 'ice cream' land and pretty, too, we'd be run over by every Yank and his aunt Sally. See?"

"You're lying. You think it's beautiful," she laughed.

"Lying, you say!" He regarded her with mock offense, then sighed and pulled her close to him. "That's so. I do. And the others here feel the same. It's what puts us here and not elsewhere. See? You have to be peculiar to live in the Delta and like it. That's why I brought you here, sweet muffin. Figured you'd fit right in."

"Hawkins, Miz Marg'ret. You sure 'bout this?" Sam shifts in his seat and slows the Buick to match the thirty mph speed sign. "Jus' turn around and go on back wouldn't be no problem."

Cape Plantation, 1957 ♨ "Let him go, Margaret." She did have her hand resting on his shoulder as he stood on the back steps looking up at his father, who was waiting. His small hand rested on the wrought-iron railing in the same way hers rested on him and she saw again how they were hands alike with long, graceful fingers, the little one crooked in toward the rest. She looked squarely at John Buie and gave Buie a gentle push away.

"You are so melodramatic, darlin'," she said slowly, drawing the words out in exactly the manner she had heard Sara Love

Tierney do Sunday afternoon over cocktails at the Coopers. It did not fool John Buie, but that was not what she intended. "His mama couldn't keep our little man from his first duck hunt if I tried, could I, sweetheart." Buie reached his father's side and turned back to look at her. He was utterly calm, smiling the ironic smile that was older than his eleven years, and he said, "Don't worry, Mother. I've got the best shot in the Miss'sippi Delta to teach me." John Buie swelled at this flattery and grabbed Buie from behind his neck, playfully pushing his head forward, down. "You come on, boy. We're gonna bring yo' mama home more dead ducks than she's ever seen alive on that mud hole yonder." They turned, separating at the back of the pickup and getting into the cab. Buie waved through the dust as they left.

She could hardly bear to have her son leave her protection, especially with John Buie from whom she took care to keep her concern secret. Yet, in the strange logic that makes trustworthiness increase with disinterest, she had told her inner care to a total stranger. It was the Sunday before at one of the intimate dinners Pressgrove and Baby Cooper staged every few months for three or four couples at one of their three Rosamond homes. The old Brooks home, copied from a raised plantation house in New Orleans and left to Press by his grandmother, was the favorite for entertaining. "Don't dress," Baby informed those selected and they all understood without more that the lack of neckties would be more than compensated by the ladies in delicately painted scarves and faces, wearing triple solitaires and linen "afternoon" dresses.

"Junior and Sara Love are comin', too," John Buie had told her when they drove into town Sunday. He shook his head in disgust. "I saw this coming a mile off. All these years, see, the Tierneys weren't highbrow enough for Baby. SL's just a good girl, likes a good time. Doesn't get her ass in a sling if things get a little rowdy. You don't see her talking all that intellectual bullshit like the Coopers do. *Pretend* to, anyway. But, hey, the girl gets herself painted by that fag artsy-fartsy from Greenwood and, all of a sudden, she's Baby's best friend."

Margaret lay her head against the car window. The wave of her bronze hair against the glass blended with the beginning autumn. September strained her resources. The cotton neared picking and, in synchrony, the blood of the planters neared boiling. Like the others these days, John Buie was, as Ella said, "full of hisself," and the weight of him was that much harder to bear. The Coopers' invitation surprised her and, while she was never given a choice not to go to social outings as her husband chose, she came readily this time. "Why did they invite us?" she wondered aloud.

"Me, Margaret. They invited *me*. You're gonna get that straight one of these days, I know." John Buie dropped his right arm from the seat back and tapped her sharply on the shoulder. "Press Cooper knows Junior and me are tight, probably. Or maybe they think I'm gonna take one of those pasty-faced writers on, pay his keep like them," John Buie snorted, his eyes narrowing disagreeably, an expression familiar to her. "If that's it, they are fuckin' out of luck, missy."

They were last to arrive—a minor social coup—and Baby led them to the interior courtyard, where Press was serving drinks to the Tierneys and a man and woman Margaret did not remember ever seeing before then and would never see again.

"Margaret, John Buie," Baby held her by the arm as they approached the group. "You know Sara Love and Junior. Have you met the Camptons, our friends from Memphis?" Margaret shook her head, but John Buie pressed in front of her and extended his hand to the man.

"John Buie Cape. Nice to see you," he said looking down to Mr. Campton, wearing wire-rimmed glasses, a smallish man with a strong jaw and large, yellowing teeth.

"E. C. Campton. My wife, Dudley," he said, more to Margaret than John Buie, who replied in kind for them both. "Dudley. Nice to see you. My wife, Margaret." Margaret looked briefly at their faces in greeting, taking a small step away as she did and almost into a towering areca palm, one of a dozen lush, green potted plants positioned around the perimeter of the courtyard. The greenery flourished in the heavy humidity of the season and Margaret imagined she could see it inching toward its ultimate goal—obliteration of the dusty brick floor and every other visible part of the small patio. John Buie stood easily with Baby near the Camptons, who had seated themselves again. Junior and Sara Love sat on the brick wall of the small lily pond at the courtyard's center and next to the butler's cart Press Cooper was using as his bar.

"Why don't you tell Press what you and Margaret would like to drink." Baby pushed John Buie toward the bar table and again firmly gripped Margaret's arm pulling her toward the Camptons. "Margaret, Dudley's father was John Ellington, the editor of the *Memphis Scimitar* when Boss Crump ran things. Mr. Ellington was one of the chief supporters of your Bay Clinic when they first tried to get it started back in the thirties."

"Baby said you are doing some interesting work there," Dudley Campton spoke evenly, precisely. She patted the seat of the glider next to her. Margaret sat down, letting her dark gauze skirt fall over her knees and against the polished cotton of Dudley's red capri pants. The other woman sat comfortably, one leg tucked under, her elbow propped on the back of the glider, and she fidgeted alternately with her hair and an ornate gold medallion hanging on a neck chain over her black turtleneck. A red-and-white-and-black silk scarf hung loosely over the other shoulder. "Daddy felt it was enormously important for the Delta. He thought it was a first step in bringing us all together. Do you think so, Margaret?" She looked expectantly at Margaret, who stared back at the starkly white face and thoughtful black eyes beneath black bobbed hair. She could not place the accent. It was almost British, with a faint suggestion of her own Boston speech. She was struck with the sudden notion that Dudley, like she, was somewhere behind the large eyes, watching another Dudley converse in an alien tongue. She looked at the woman even more intently until her subject finally smiled, amused. "Well, do you?"

"If you do find out anything she thinks, be sure and tell me, will you?" John Buie held out a stemmed glass of sherry toward Margaret, who started when she heard his voice. He took a seat in the cast-iron garden chair next to them, crossing his legs wide and the toe of his shoe was inches from the arm of the glider, where Dudley rested her hand. "E. C., I feel like we've met somewhere. Are you with the cotton exchange?"

Campton laughed. "Hardly. I wouldn't know a cotton boll from a bowling ball." Dudley joined in the laughter and Margaret smiled uncertainly. John Buie sipped at his bourbon and kept his steady gaze on Campton.

"What *do* you know?" he asked, and E. C. returned the look.

"Oh, not much. Then again, I guess knowing *that* is knowing something."

"E. C. teaches philosophy at Rhodes," Dudley explained in a whisper to John Buie, who rolled his eyes and rose "to get more ice" for his drink. Dudley turned again to Margaret and, Margaret supposed, to Bay Clinic but, instead, she asked, "Do you and John Buie have children, Margaret?"

Her faced flushed with pleasure. "Yes. We have a little boy, John Buie. Buie. He's just eleven."

"How nice. E. C. and I have just one, too. Alice Anne. She's twelve, now. It's difficult not to spoil them, isn't it?"

"Oh. Yes," Margaret said nervously, realizing her mistake. "But Buie's not our only child. We have one younger. Chapin Finley. But..."

"Buie is your heart?" Dudley laid her hand on Margaret's shoulder, stroking it lightly. "Don't be afraid to say it. That happens many times. It's well that you know it." The soft, low voice, its odd articulation, charmed Margaret. She was finding it difficult to keep the separation in place.

"He's *good,*" she said haltingly. "He has a certain quality. I mean..." This was not the proper way to mention her child. Margaret struggled to remember the correct words, the phrases. The rumble of John Buie's voice distracted her. He was near the Tierneys now, standing over Sara Love, her body elongated on the lily pond wall. "John Buie! You are a *mess!* Do you know that?" She laughed up at him, swinging her crossed leg toward him in mock threat.

"He never gives you any trouble?" Dudley offered.

"No, it's not that. Oh, he doesn't, of course. It's something different." Baby left her seat by E. C. She was going into the house, and Margaret hoped that meant dinner was about to be served. She had not yet given herself words to define Buie's quality. When he turned eight, she told him of his story, correcting what had been omitted for her, and warned him there would be predators who would try to steal it. But he had merely smiled at her and reached up to touch her shoulder in a gesture of sympathetic concern. He could not possibly have understood what his expression suggested, yet he sensed immediately when she feared for him and took it invariably as a burden she bore and which he would like to ease because he loved her. It was not *his* burden. "What goes around comes around, Mother," he parroted Sam's favored assessment and his faith in this natural justice contented him, if not her. If he recognized the threat from John Buie, it was only as a kind of thrilling challenge, a dangerous obstacle to be rushed past or outsmarted. The cat jumps over the sleeping dog. The boy nimbly grabs the rattlesnake from behind its head.

Margaret was not waiting at the door when the hunters finally returned at dusk. She sat in the Front Hall sipping brandy and thinking of the portrait of General Cape, Buie's namesake. "I have your little soldier back, safe and sound," John Buie taunted her from the doorway and, taken by surprise, she instinctively looked for the child. "He's not here, he's out back, showing Ella the ducks to clean. Boy's a fair shot. Might be a credit to this family someday, you don't mess him up, first."

"I GOT THE key." A plump, brown arm reaches past her for the lock and Margaret steps aside to let the girl open the door—glass and metal, pneumatic, with painted letters although what they say is not clear to her without her big glass. She looks across the street to Sam, but he is in the Buick pulling away. "I'll go get gas while you're lookin'," he told her, still nervous somehow, anxious to be another place. The difference in the clinic building was obvious when they turned the corner down the block and, except for the familiar L shape and high pitch of the roof, Margaret might have believed the structure was a new one altogether raised up on the ground where the clinic once stood. It was painted white—shiny white—and around it was the deep green of well-watered grass and, next to the building, curving beds of colorful vinca in front of yews and tall, slender erocoides. New storm windows had replaced the wooden ones, and an aluminum and glass pneumatic door, the green, wood panel door that had entered the clinic. A white sign, with a rainbow logo in primary colors, proclaimed DACOM.

She follows the girl into a bright, square lobby with blue-green tweed carpet and glossy cream walls, lined on three sides by molded plastic chairs. The light is artificial because the windows are another leftover from the clinic, small rectangles high on the wall placed there to protect privacy and, now, for no reason at all. Below them are two desks sitting at right angles to the wall, behind a rail and a gate that the girl opens and, her enormous hips swaying, passes through.

"God a'mighty, I can't believe Friday already," the girl exclaims, dropping a ring of twenty keys and a white paper bag onto the left desk, then pulling open its bottom drawer and pushing her duffel purse inside. From the topmost drawer, she takes a desk plate engraved GLORIA BURTON and places it exactly at the center front of her desk, then falls heavily into the chair with a sigh and rolls herself up under the desk. Gloria looks at Margaret. "You lost? They told me not to be givin' out directions."

"I wanted to see what was here," Margaret says and that is true, although she has seen what is. There is nothing, except that it is changed, fantastically changed, and not that, really, but just that it is changed in a way not expected. It is very cool here, unlike the wearying heat outside and in the car, no longer air-conditioned, and she feels the tightness in her legs and feet and the fatigue of the morning's journey. She sits down in the chair nearest the rail.

"Look away. I didn't think you was wantin' no job," Gloria says cheerfully and she smiles at Margaret at the same time she takes the telephone receiver up and dials. She cushions the headset between chin and shoulder while she opens the white bag and takes out a tall paper cup, sweating from the cold drink it holds and, also, two sandwiches wrapped in tissue. She places the bag on its side, patting it down, then opens the sandwiches—sausage and biscuits—on top. "They some more Cokes in back, you want one." She motions with her chin toward a wide hall that leads back into the building. "Hey, girlfriend," she speaks into the phone. "You come get me at noontime? Uh-huh. Yeah, my car broke. Freddy got it over his shop. Uh-huh. OK, then." She hangs up the phone, satisfied, and picks up one of the sandwiches, taking half of it in one large bite.

"Is this an employment agency?" Margaret asks.

"Nuh-uh. That's not it, 'sactly." Gloria chews while she talks. "What this is, is DACOM. You know 'bout DACOM?" Margaret shakes her head. "D-A-C-O-M. Delta Area Casino Operations and Management. It were called DACOP for a while—Delta Area Casino Operations and Personnel—but the 'COP' part was scarin' off some of our applications." She takes a brochure from the desk tray and hands it over the rail to

Margaret, who shakes her head and returns it. "Oh, I can tell you what it says," Gloria laughs. She reads from the brochure. " 'DACOM is a collective project of Mississippi riverboat casinos to hire and train dealers and other key employees.' This is goin' to be a slow day. Friday always is. People ain't lookin' to get no job this close to the weekend, know what I mean? Now, Monday. Oh, my goodness. Mondays, everybody is a hard worker."

Margaret looks around the room again, but she does not see anything or any reason that she should come here, as the list most clearly—to her, at least—specified. Still, it is a list, not a single line and she will surely need to complete all of it before she can hope to find her story. Gloria eats and, at the same time, chats easily about the DACOM office, its recent opening. The casinos will change life for Delta people, she says, especially the black people. It is odd to hear such an opinion from a Negro girl, expressed openly to a white person like Margaret. That is one thing that does come to her at first glance along with the change in the clinic building and, this, this interchange with Gloria is a fantastic change as well. She was accustomed before the dead years to such conversations with a wall between the speakers, the Negro face impassive, closed, anxious only to have the talk over without incident. Even Sam, who has grown from young to old with her, measured his words and perhaps he thought she couldn't tell or didn't notice, but he was mistaken. Gloria Burton is so different from the dusty, hollow-cheeked field workers who had come to the clinic as to belong to another time and, Margaret realizes that, of course, she does.

"Do others work here with you?" she asks Gloria.

"Oh, yes, ma'am. They wouldn't want me runnin' things. I'd be closing the door at noon before long." She laughs, a girlish, high laugh that makes Margaret smile in return. Gloria neatly folds the sandwich papers and places them into the paper bag before dropping them in the basket at the corner of her desk. "You from Clarksdale?"

"I worked here. Years ago."

"Here?" Gloria giggles. "We just had open house last month. Congressman, supervisors, all the preachers. I mean! It was everybody. Wait. We took some Polaroids." She pushes up from the desk and reaches to the corkboard hanging on the wall behind, unpinning several photographs. She extends her arm toward Margaret then suddenly pulls it back, dropping the pictures on the desk. "Oh, shit." Gloria looks past Margaret toward the door and sits down quickly into the desk chair. "Here Emmaline." In one motion, she pulls the computer keyboard to the center of the desk and begins to type.

"Good morning, Gloria." The voice is low, clipped without accent, and before Margaret turns, the woman is in front of her, leaning across her and over the rail. "Put these with the Greenville file, please," she says to Gloria, who says, "Yes, ma'am," and then the woman backs away a few steps and straightens her jacket before addressing Margaret. She speaks in the same low voice—an even voice, distinctly unfriendly. "I'm director of DACOM. Is there something we can do for you?"

Margaret looks into a braided leather belt on a khaki dress. The rounded corners of a navy blazer hang to either side and Emmaline's athletic body, almost six feet tall, towers above Margaret. Like Gloria, she is Negro, but her skin is a shade lighter and more gold than brown. Her posture is perfect and controlled and, despite her unfriendly air, Margaret is struck by her beauty. "Is there?" she repeats, in a tone of voice not necessarily unpleasant, but with the same superior attitude a parent uses to question a child. Margaret had heard John Buie and other men like him use that voice many times. "I don't know," she answers and, it is true, she doesn't. Emmaline tips her chin in silent comment and leans over Margaret. "I see."

Gloria interrupts. "She ain't hurtin' nothin' just sitting there if that's what she wants. It won't bother me none."

Emmaline pushes gently up on Margaret's elbow. "I wish we

could visit but we have a lot to do. I'm sure this lady understands, don't you? Here let me help. Did you come in a car?"

Margaret stands, then steps away from Emmaline, twisting
her arm loose and facing her. The young woman still has on
sunglasses from when she entered and a flat briefcase with a
long strap hangs from her shoulder. Margaret looks at the
glasses seeing only the blurred outlines of her own pale reflection. Emmaline stiffens and steps back. "I don't mean to offend
you, ma'am, but if you don't want to associate with African
Americans, you are in the wrong place."

"Associate?" Margaret blinks her eyes, befuddled. This is a
change, as well, with such a conversation never occurring in
her presence before and she struggles to think what it could
mean. She has no difficulty with Emmaline touching her, or at
least not because they are different races, and that she is mis-
understood is of no concern to her. She does not expect to be
understood, has never been understood. It is the other thing,
the change. There are parts of Emmaline's talk that are somehow familiar. There is a certain derisiveness to what is said.
When Sam's wife, Ella, talked to her children it was always in
that tone of voice, almost hostile and as if she were disgusted
that she should say anything to someone so unimportant as
they. "Don't you think you might hurt their feelings?" she had
asked Ella once and Ella had stared at her as if she had spoken
in tongues. "I'm sorry," she says to Emmaline and walks toward the door without assistance, reaching to push it open for
several feet before she is actually there.

Emmaline hears Gloria's disapproving "hmmph" behind her
but when she turns, Gloria is knitting her brows in deep concentration on the blue screen of her computer. Emmaline
watches the old lady move away from her and angrily pushes
down the rising dismay that sometimes plagues her. "You're
too quick to be the judge," her mother told her. "That didn't
come from my side. I know peoples jus' goin' to be people."
And, yet, hadn't old Miss Olivia Hooker passed by her mother

at the funeral—it was Miss Olivia's brother who died and her mother had cleaned his house for fifteen years—and pushed her hand against her mother's chest, as if she were a door, or as if she were somewhere she should not be. Her mother's eyes—the surprise, then dull pain—it was impossible to forget that. And, in the ARCO station when she was nine years old and buying a cold drink, the weasel-faced attendant stared her aside for the white man behind her. It was true the man, a red-cheeked trucker in the sleeveless western shirt buttoned by pearl snaps tight across his belly and with his sweaty strands of thin hair hanging below his ears, squirmed some, but he had said nothing, nothing! She boldly sat the Coke on the counter and left, holding her chin in the air but shaking for fear long white arms would reach for her and she would be harshly scolded or, at worst—and Negro children knew those possibilities well—suffer the fate of Emmett Till. "There are bad white peoples, but jus' as many bad black ones," Gloria says now in these more forgiving times and it echoes Emmaline's own mother, who had always seemed oddly indifferent to the humiliations, the injustice that burned at Emmaline: "Think about the nigger that shot your great-grandma like a dog. You rather be in the world with him or some white man that puts his skinny nose in the air when you walk in? Somebody's nose, that don't have nothin' to do with me the way I see it. But I can be shot alright."

Emmaline reaches the door before Margaret and holds it open, ignoring Gloria when she returns, directed to the privacy of her own office, where she finally removes the sunglasses. She likes to wear them whenever circumstances allow. They cover her eyes—light, "cloudy day" eyes her mother called them— and she doesn't get the peculiar glances, demands for an explanation she doesn't have.

19

Not despite what has happened with Hardy Mall, but because of it, Little Mildred attends the Friday, October 22
luncheon meeting of the Rosamond Garden Club. It is called
that when, in fact, the true name is the Jane Fortescue Delta
Botanical Society, agreed upon only after a three and one-half
hour debate at the regular monthly meeting in March 1973
following Mrs. Fortescue's death from a stroke suffered while
she was naturalizing daffodils and, previously that same year,
was named president-elect. She was already seventy-three at the
time, but the club's presidents are, by tradition, advanced in
years and it was her time just as Little Mildred was seventy-
five when she began serving an unprecedented three years as
the club's president. Before Hardy Mall made his claim to Cape
land, she had planned to be absent from this one meeting, a
joint meeting with the Charleston and Greenwood clubs held
in a second-floor banquet room at the Holiday Inn, seventeen
steps to the top, covered in puce tweed carpet, but she cannot
do it without her absence saying, in effect, things that she does
not wish to be said. There is only one way to address unseemly
problems, as are all attacks on the family that diminish each
member, and that is to proceed with life as if there were

nothing at all and the public being simple-minded soon finds it impossible to hold the abstract thought that there is in the face of a visible representation that there isn't.

She stops at the third step and lets the younger woman pass her. "Excuse me, ma'am," the red linen suit with the short skirt says, seeming to be the age of fourteen, her brown bob swinging as she goes. Little Mildred smiles warmly. "Certainly, dear," raising her eyebrows and feigning breathlessness at the girl's rush for anyone who might be looking to see. And, they are looking, she knows that with certainty. She puts equal weight on the rail beneath her right hand and the cane in her left, easing the burning knot at her hip joint without anyone knowing it bothers her. It is fortunate, she considers, that the Creator put our thoughts up in the head along with the sense perceptions and emotions. All there, mostly inside, for no one to see unless she wants it so. It is almost too unpleasant to be this old and able to see the whole of the drama unfolded. And the oppressive waiting for the rest of it. Will Sam remain silent? Might she count on Margaret to die, but not too soon? If only, if only swims in her mind as she sees a hundred junctures where the slightest deviation of direction could have prevented this unfortunate consequence and the worst of it is that she herself is a principal part of at least one such juncture, maybe more.

"Mildred! I was so afraid you wouldn't be able to be here." Evelyn Cooper descends to the seventh step and grasps Mildred's hand and the silver knob of the cane as one. She is uncertain whether Evelyn knows about the problem with the plantation or if she is referring to her age, but Little Mildred knows that both diminish her in the eyes of the other in the same way, a kind of embarrassment, a failure.

"Evelyn, dear! Aren't you sweet?" She allows her hand to be lifted in a court gesture as they climb the stairs together, although it increases the strain on her hip to do so. "Thank you," she smiles when they are at the top and out of the doorway. Evelyn moves her hand to Mildred's upper arm and gently pushes her toward the wall.

"The children's invitation to your party tomorrow evening is darling! Sara Cape was in the flower shop yesterday and she is just precious, so excited with all her plans!"

Little Mildred nods, narrowing her eyes to see beyond Evelyn and the others coming in. There is a mix from the other clubs, creating a confusion that is a relief, under the circumstances, and she will not have a cigarette. When she was a young member, everyone smoked, something graceful to do with the hands. She gave it up almost a year ago when she noticed she was the only one still lighting up.

"Ches was *so* concerned," Evelyn says, her voice low, and Little Mildred knows then that it is Cape Plantation modulating Evelyn's expression and that Ches has been telling about Hardy. If she confirms the weight of the difficulty, she diminishes herself and the Cape family further both by the revelation and the public intimacy. If she denies it, however, it may be said that she is daft with old age and doesn't appreciate the gravity of the situation.

"Isn't that just like Chesley? He is such a lovely man, Evelyn. He really is." Little Mildred gazes innocently at Evelyn and the eyes around the room cut to them and away. Ah. Evelyn is the Rosamond's group representative in this discovery. "Olivia," Mildred calls to a small woman passing them who turns with a smile that becomes apologetic when she sees she has interrupted Evelyn. "Please tell Clarence the tomatoes are wonderful. I'm having such a grand time with them. My children think I have a green thumb and what I have is Clarence's tomato plants!" Olivia beams, pleased, reaches to squeeze Mildred's hand, then moves away quickly.

"Hardy Mall should have been jailed years ago," Evelyn says. Little Mildred nods but does not speak. "You know he swindled Ches once." The words are barely out and Evelyn downplays the error. "Oh, Ches was just beginning and it would never happen now, but he did."

"Really?" Little Mildred's open eyes acknowledge Evelyn's indiscreet revelation, but before Evelyn can recover her composure, Mildred presses further. "Well, tell him he needn't worry about this. Someone is always after what you have when you have what we do. We learned a long time ago how to protect against it."

"But doesn't he own the entire plantation? That's what he says. I mean, Ches mentioned some little thing. Of course, I don't know the details."

Little Mildred sighs. Evelyn is not going to let her off the hook but she cannot make the decision right here and now. What had Big John been thinking? She has wondered that for over fifty years. It was not that her father took someone younger than she as a bride, another daughter really, but that the one he chose resembled Little Mildred not at all. "Darlin', this is Margaret." He pushed his prize toward his daughter, holding her out by the shoulders like a new puppy at Christmas, and she remembers that Margaret let him move her, but looked straight up at Little Mildred with her odd, devil's eyes and raised her chin in a way Little Mildred understood to be a statement of superior position. At the thought of it, the anger rises in her the same as it had that day. It was their father's foolishness, Margaret, who had forced them to a deception— she and John Buie. Still, her brother did not need to marry her, although he insisted that was "the safest course" and Little Mildred had not believed him even then. She saw his hungry eyes on Margaret, his hands cupping her shoulders, too long, too intimately, when he spoke to her and his perverse desire to bed his father's widow. Thank the Lord that I am not a man susceptible to these sicknesses, bitter pleasures that turn in on themselves like a dog eating its own vomit!

"That's what he's saying, that Cape is his," Evelyn repeats and Little Mildred looks her and, so, the Rosamond Garden Club, in the eye as she responds.

"Perhaps Mr. Mall thinks that, but he is mistaken. Cape Plantation is safe and secure in our family where it belongs. I do hope, however, that he has at least enjoyed his little fantasy." Evelyn's head moves up and back, her mouth open as if to speak but saying nothing. When, after a moment, she chooses her reaction—"Oh, Mildred, I am so happy to hear that. I truly, truly am."—Little Mildred sees she has succeeded in forcing their allegiance. Evelyn follows her to the second row of chairs and sits beside her, and the others begin to take their seats nearby. She will have to pay the price if she wants to make her lie the truth and she has not decided whether that is the best course. Either way, she is eighty-four, one day from eighty-five, and what can they do? Send her to Parchman? She shifts her weight in the hard seat of the chair, lifting her bad hip barely from the metal. So many fools! Chapin Finley needed only to do nothing but outlive Margaret by a day or, failing that, provide a will. Yes, he carried a special burden, with his ailing mother who doted openly on Buie, yet he had failed in every respect, living beyond his means and not only in the usual way. Then, when Frank III had refused him loans, he had gone to the odious Hardy Mall. And that stupid lawyer! Stirring the pot at exactly the wrong moment. This is why women live longer than men, she is certain, to clean up after they are gone, take care of the messes. Well, she can do it. She can retrieve the will John Buie hid away—there is no question he kept it, a pack rat like his father! But what about Sam? And what if Margaret should hang on like the last leaf of winter?

She holds her right hand palm up and pats the left on top as the afternoon's speaker is introduced. He is a columnist for the *Clarion-Ledger,* the Jackson paper, who will speak on curbing the threat of chinch bugs in centipede turf. It will be a pleasure to listen. She doesn't have centipede, only Saint Augustine.

Cape Plantation, 1962 🪰 "Who is she?" Duke Tierney's young wife, Mary Ivan, asked seeing Margaret at the Clarksdale Country Club in the winter 1962. It was the yearly Planter's Ball and Margaret was forty-nine but still the sort of woman that made it a fitting question, although neither Mary Ivan nor any of the others who had recently joined Delta society knew the edge Margaret walked. Rather, when she entered the marbled foyer, bare shoulders above an uncut length of ivory satin wrapped round to a few inches from the floor and her delicate arm hung loosely on John Buie's own burly, tuxedoed one, she seemed as fragile and beguiling as a butterfly in its chrysalis hanging from the woody branch. Women gave her sidelong glances, unwilling to grant her effect, but the men stared openly as is their way and, well, she had some of her mother in her, after all. They watched her pass and stroked themselves with lewd imaginings of hot encounters with this unfathomable woman at the same time they stood respectfully aside for the man who could own her and still take his pleasure with others he happened to find, then discard, some of whom were in that very foyer.

This was the twenty-fourth Planter's Ball she had attended, seven as the wife of Big John and this, the seventeenth with John Buie. She thought it odd that she remembered the number and nothing else at all and, still, there must be something because every incident was utterly familiar. John Buie asked about a drink for her and left her for the bar. She entered the ballroom alone, twist-shouldered her way through the throng, and positioned herself next to a small group at an angle that made it seem as if she were possibly a part of the conversation to anyone approaching, but not so close that the group itself would give her any notice. John Buie found her, bringing the glass of sherry she requested, although vodka collins was the smarter drink for a lady, handing it to her straight-armed while he continued his conversation with a fellow planter and, his duty done, left until dinner.

In the domed foyer, long tables were arranged in a circle, each topped with several displays of goods to be bid on in a silent auction, beside each a lined pad and a pen, and guests signed their names and the amount bid. When the bidding ended at eleven, the last and highest bidder was the successful buyer. Margaret sipped her sherry as she moved from item to item, paintings, watercolors, line drawings, a gift certificate for a weekend at the Peabody, a string of black pearls. She stopped at a photograph of a simple building with asbestos siding, sitting in high growth, an electric wire extended to its chimney end. "It's a Nigra church," the voice behind her said and she turned into the wide chest of a young man almost six and a half feet tall. "I was over by Leland looking at a used picker and I saw it and the light just happened to be right." They looked at the photograph together. There were several bids already, the highest $35. "It's very nice." Margaret smiled at him and he lifted his glass and smiled back. He had white blond hair and red cheeks and, but for his exceptional size, the presence of a puppy. She reached for the pen to make a bid, which seemed the polite thing to do, and wrote $40 next to her name. "If you don't have the high bid, I'll make you a copy," he offered genially, and she nodded and said again, "Very nice."

Ella died on the last day of July and the funeral was a week later. John Buie and Little Mildred and Margaret and the children attended the service, which began at nine in the morning and was not concluded until one P.M. "Jesus, God Almighty, you get 'em together and the music gets goin' they just can't quit," John Buie complained, but stayed the length with the rest of them. He was Ella's white person and it was right that he should see her to her grave. After the cemetery ritual, Little

Mildred greeted Sam and each of his and Ella's four children—the youngest, Caraly, was thirteen—and pressed a dollar bill in each of their hands as she passed them. Sam tapped the first one on the back, who said, "Thank you, Miz Mildred," and the others followed the example. Margaret did not know the three boys, Ella's sons who worked other jobs, but she stopped at Caraly, whose almond eyes were brimming with tears, and she pulled her into her arms and held her tight. "Your mother was a good person, Caraly," she told her and the girl said, "Yes'm. Thank you, Miz Marg'ret," and Margaret kissed her forehead and squeezed her hand again before John Buie pulled her sharply away and into the car and they left.

In September that year, a black man climbed the gray steps of the Lyceum at Ole Miss, the antebellum administration building that had been the hospital for both Yankee and Confederate soldiers during the War, and he asked to enroll. His plan was revealed some time earlier, that he would ask to be the first Negro student to enroll at the university and, over the months, objection was made, not in a unified voice but like a tide gathering power as it rolled toward the shore, until the weekend before his coming, the governor of Mississippi had rallied the Ole Miss crowd at the first football game of the year, played against Kentucky in Jackson. The few critics said they were reminded of a Munich beer hall and Hitler but John Buie returned full of the cause and, thus, even Margaret in her purposeful solitude did not escape the force of events. "That nigger wants an education. We'll give him an education." John Buie was drinking more, raising his voice to an almost frantic note that Margaret had never heard in him before. It was the same for the others. "What is it about the sixties that every hundred years the Nigras make trouble?" Little Mildred commiserated with him and Junior Tierney and Sara Love, his wife, shook their heads and had another bourbon.

When the registration of James Meredith went sour and emotional whites, some from Mississippi but an astonishing number from Tennessee and Alabama, too, rioted and two persons died, Margaret could see the felt release in John Buie and the others, but it was only for a short while. The change was made and, if nothing more, their conversation no longer contained the Civil War accounts she was accustomed to hearing nearly every day—the tragedy and courage of Pickett's Charge, the possible treachery of General Longstreet, the many lost opportunities of the South to win the War that made the speakers improbably conclude that the South rightfully should have won and, so, its cause was just. Instead, there was a new talk, intense, threatened, but hopeful, too, as if a new war was begun and there might be yet a chance to correct the errors of a hundred years before.

"Do you know Pledger Fulton and Charles Cooper?" Buie asked his mother on one weekend's walk to the pasture and Margaret nodded that she did. "They were the ones burnt the cross outside Ebenezer Baptist Friday night. They wanted me to come with them. Said it was just for fun, but I said I wouldn't."

Margaret trembled to think of him outside her sight, living in the world as it was. "It's very dangerous right now, Buie."

"Yes. You know, it was funny. I didn't know for sure what I would do and then Pledger said, 'Come on tonight. We're gonna decorate the nigger church,' and I said, 'No, I don't care to do that.'" He stopped in the path and touched her shoulder. "Don't be afraid, Mother. That's what I figured out right there when I said that to Pledger and Charles. They're the ones all filled up with fear, crazy and dangerous like a fearful animal."

"It might be better if you didn't tell them what you are thinking," she said and, at the same time, wondered how she could still say this to her son when it was her own path and the one that had made the confines of her true soul so small, allowing only her care for him, that almost anytime it might disappear without anyone's notice.

"MY MAN, IT all depends on you tomorrow night." Charley enters Niles's office without knocking and drops himself onto the sofa.

Niles looks up from his work and smiles to conceal his irritation. Time, he considers, would be better partitioned in the same manner as parcels of real estate, with particular owners and a chain of title but, as it is, it seems a kind of public park where anyone can decide to take a stroll.

"Yes, Niles, you are charged with this month's 'suck up' detail. Sibyl has been planning this Memphis weekend at the Peabody for four months—even got the Romeo and Juliet suite—and there is no way she will cancel for the Meltons' party." Charley has found a wayward paper clip and uses it to retrieve excess earwax.

"Charley, no. I can't. Really. I am loaded up to here. I'm not kidding. I need the entire weekend to work." Charley continues to delve with the paper clip. "Don't do that," Niles warns. "You'll get an infection."

Charley lays down the clip. "You *will* be working, old man. Working on securing the First Southern Bank business, which, as we speak, is being hustled out from under us by the Cotter Purdy firm in Jackson. Frank III is on the board, you know. And—listen to me, Abbott—Paula Melton wants in your shorts bad. I can tell."

Niles sighs, laying down his pen and pushing back from the desk. "As a matter of curiosity, Charley, have you ever gone to one of these things just for the hell of it?"

"Go ahead. Stick up your nose. Somebody has to think about where your next file is coming from. You don't ever worry about that, do you? Think your fairy godmother brings 'em, I guess." Charley tosses the used paper clip across the room and neatly into the wastebin. "When I was first practicing, I sat around reading paperback novels half the time. No business! This fancy office didn't happen by accident. Don't ever think you're so good, hotshot, that you don't need to make the rounds."

"I thought you said, 'If you're good enough, you can piss on the courthouse lawn at noon and no one will care.'"

"That's *after* you make your rounds. Besides, I thought this would make you happy. Get you a chance to be close to your beloved old lady."

"What are you talking about?"

"Oh, yeah. That gets your interest, doesn't it? I don't believe it." Charley shakes his head. "Frank Melton III and his sister are giving their mother, Mildred, a birthday party. Little Mildred Melton. She's the one you were talking to about Cape until everything hit the fan. And, your wonderful Margaret Cape is one of the family."

"I don't think so, Charley. Mrs. Cape would be the last person Mildred wants at her party."

"Well, whatever. You've had almost a month to get over that business. I'm really going to be disappointed in you, Abbott, if you don't care enough about this firm to be at the Meltons'."

It has not been a month, but two weeks since Vernon Pettis gave him the surprising news that Hardy Mall owns Cape Plantation, and Charley is right to sneer. He is unable, somehow, to let it go. He had called Cordeman early the Monday morning after but the chancellor was unexpectedly detached. "Hardy owns it? Well, what do you know. OK, Niles. I appreciate your help, but looks like the court won't need you after all."

"Doesn't Your Honor want me to go out to Cape and talk to her and Sam? I don't think they know anything about this."

"No. The family can take care of that kind of thing. There's no need for you and me to get in the middle of handling some old lady. We can be thankful for that. We take it on ourselves to tell the old lady, she drops dead of shock, and, then, where are we?"

Niles could not let go. "Perhaps, she needs to have a guardian *ad litem* appointed under the circumstances, someone to particularly represent her in this matter, and shouldn't someone check the title, read all the wills, just to make certain Chapin Finley was actually the owner and entitled to transfer the property to Hardy?"

"Sure. Maybe someone should. But that's not your business nor the court's. Mildred Melton is no fool. I'm certain she'll have someone check it out if there's any reason to do so. And the court doesn't believe in guardian *ad litems*. Too much Latin. No. Just be glad you got one less thing to worry about. Thank you, hear?"

Niles worries about it. He does not trust Little Mildred to act in Margaret Cape's best interest. He doesn't trust Hardy Mall either. Yet, he cannot fault Mall, cannot say he stole Cape Plantation. Chapin Finley traded it away for value received, just as the law provides.

"I don't know what Hardy would want with Cape. He likes to turn the fast buck. He did buy the Griffin plantation in Bolivar, but part of it is on the river and, you watch, he'll sell big to one of the casinos before long. I do know the chancellor is satisfied Hardy owns the property, the family believes it, so who cares why or what the old lady thinks? She's on the way out. You've finished your part. Now move on." Charley urged him to get back to his other work, work on the Blaylock case. On Monday, Pettis had finally delivered Hardy's financial records.

"I told Delores to put them in the extra office upstairs," Charley said. "Hardy didn't do us any favors. He just threw those papers in there like he was putting trash in a Dempster Dumpster. He's being pretty cavalier, not like him. Makes me wonder maybe he's got woman troubles. Anyway, twenty-two boxes of it. But, you know what? I know there's a Shetland pony in there somewhere, Niles."

"Are you pretty much ready?"

"If you can find me a pony, we're gonna knock his dick in the dirt. Did I ever tell you about the time I defended a guy for capital murder and the aunt of the woman he killed brought a gun in her purse to the courtroom?"

"Yeah, I think you did."

"Well, what happened was that, see, she was going to use it on him and, I don't know, maybe me, too, if the jury's verdict wasn't to her liking. So, I got wind she had done this and let the sheriff know at one of the breaks and he stations himself at the end of her row. The jury acquits my guy and she doesn't do anything after all, but nobody knew what might happen for a while. It was something!"

"I don't think Hardy will have a gun on him, Charley. Of course, as big as he is, he might just get up and beat the tar out of you."

Charley's eyes were flashing, his fingers moving. Trial is set for Wednesday week and he is at the gate and restless to begin. "Carter Sims from Indianola tried to punch me one time. Didn't like my objecting to something. Or, what it was, he said I had used up all my objections. I think he knew he was losing and wanted to turn it around. Anyhow, I remember he had to crawl up on a chair to swing 'cause he only comes to my shoulder."

"I'll do my best to find you something, Charley," he told him but, so far, he has found nothing that can help Mrs. Blaylock and every minute he spends in the company of Hardy Mall's records is a minute thinking about Margaret Cape.

Why did Chapin Finley use quitclaim deeds instead of warranty deeds, why did Hardy accept them? The deeds do not guarantee that Chapin Finley actually had title to anything, saying only that "Whatever I own of this land or later own, I give to you." Of course, Mall had not risked much in the bargain. Niles had found the records of some of the payments to Chapin Finley and $75,000 was the most he had received for five hundred acres of land worth four times that much.

"I just feel I ought to do something," he says to Charley, who has found another paper clip.

"So, what are you going to do?" Charley is irritated, restless to move on to something he deems worthwhile. "Remember, Niles, this is a law office, not the law review, where we can sit around all day discussing the finer points of nonexistent situations."

"I'm not sure. I guess I'll do what the law tells me to do."

"What? You think the law is Madam Marie the palm reader over on Highway 8? The law tells you what you *can* do, Niles, not what you should. Use your head. You're too smart to make a dumbass remark like that. The law isn't an airplane you set on autopilot. You. You got to drive it where you want it to go." Niles stares at his books on the far wall, his jaw set, chin up. Charley reads the barrier and changes direction. "Listen, Niles, none of this is your fault. You aren't even her conservator. Maybe what's happened is too bad, but it's legal. Chapin Finley needed money—everyone knew he was gambling high stakes—and he sold the plantation to Hardy because he could, the law let him. It doesn't matter that he shouldn't've done it. Now, I can tell you what *you* should do, though, and that is move on. You don't have time for somethin' that ain't your business, buddy boy. OK?"

20

He guns the Bronco to sixty-five as soon as he hits the west limit of Rosamond. Now that he has decided to make the trip, he wants to be there immediately. Charley was not approving. "I'll be at Cape House," he told Delores on the way out and Charley said, "Uh-oh," from the office behind, where by some unexplained acoustical principle, he hears everything at Delores's desk. "Niles, come here a second."

Niles stood in the doorway, refusing to come farther. "What is this hard-on you have for Margaret Cape?" Charley demanded.

"Nothing. I just realized I may have given her the impression I was her legal representative." What had she said? Her protector.

"Thank God she's in her eighties," Charley said. "Did I ever tell you about that woman I got involved with handling her divorce? Lot of trouble, Niles. Occupational hazard."

"It's not that. I want to straighten the representation thing out if no one has said anything to her. You know, 'reasonable notice,' Rule of Professional Conduct 1.16."

Charley laughed at him but he left anyway, knowing that it may be a rationalization—that it *is* one—but it is, nevertheless, a reason to see her sufficient to withstand assault from the Capes or others. Why he needs any reason remains unanswered and he does not permit himself the dreamy thought that he goes to look for it.

He turns at the Cape Gin and drives the mile and a half to the gate to Cape House, swearing when he spies the lock neatly in place. There is room to drive around the post, but that is pressing the scope of his authority and he pulls the Bronco to one side and gets out to walk. The house looks even larger than it had before. The preceding night's rain has pounded the remaining leaves off of the pecan trees, leaving them starkly bare and the front of the house visible, towering over its surroundings and the austere Delta landscape, with nothing to detract from its immenseness.

Sam's Buick sits in front of the steps and Niles hears the popping of the cooling motor as he comes near. Before he is up the steps, the front door to Cape House opens and Sam greets him. "Where your car, Mr. Niles? We just come in, didn't see you."

"The gate was locked. It's OK. I can use the exercise. Is Mrs. Cape where she can talk?" Niles starts to move forward into the doorway, but Sam steps outside first and shuts the door behind him. Niles gives a short laugh, but Sam does not respond, walking head-lowered past Niles and down the front steps.

"She sleepin', need to rest," he says. "You come on with me, Mr. Niles. I'll walk with you to the gate." Niles hesitates, then trots to catch up with the old man.

They walk beside each other between the black bark of the bare pecan trees and over the crunch of gravel and Niles gives a brief account of things to Sam. Sam asks him, "Who did Mr. Chappy sell out to?"

"Hardy Mall. At least, that's what Mall's lawyer claims."

"Uh-huh." Sam watches the ground while he walks. "Do Miz Little Mildred know?"

"Yes. She knows. I called her and I think the chancellor probably told her, too. Why?"

"Oh, it nothin'. Nothin'. I thought she ought to know, bein' in the family and all. How long she know?"

Niles looks away, embarrassed. "For a while now. Maybe a week or two."

"Uh-huh." Sam does not look up.

"Sam, if there is anything you can tell me to help Mrs. Cape, I wish you would. I mean, I don't represent her, but I don't want to see her put out by Mr. Mall either."

Sam looks at him and his brown eyes are kind, tired but Niles sees the wall between the two of them that won't come down as easily as that. "No, sir. They ain't nothin' I can think of just now."

Cape Plantation, 1963 ☙ On November 22, 1963, Margaret entered the chapel in the late morning and it was already afternoon. The sacred things sat on the shelf behind the altar and she moved idly from one to the next, picking up the chalice, feeling the band of raised figures, then setting the cup back in its place, looking to something else, somewhere else to turn her attention. She came more often than before, now that protecting herself and Buie was most of what she did. Her younger son, Chapin Finley, was not at risk. He had nothing to steal, nothing to destroy. The effort took from her, used her, and like a wounded animal retreating to its den to heal, she came here for the solitude that helped her survive. She preferred the library, of course, but she could not enter it easily anymore without detection and John Buie sometimes seemed to be everywhere at once. This weekend, at least, would be a respite. Junior and Sara Love had taken him with them on a gambling trip to Las Vegas.

"I told 'em you wouldn't be going. It'd be too much fun for you to want anything to do with it," he told her and she said nothing. She packed a Samsonite hanging bag for him with extra khaki pants, starched white shirts, underwear, and socks, and when Sara Love called to tell her that Tory, Sara Love's younger sister, would also be with them, Margaret added gray dress pants and the blue cotton sweater that matched his eyes and made certain he took the bottle of English Leather cologne someone had given him at Christmas. She did not want him, did not want anyone that way anymore and, so, she could as easily pack his bags for a weekend of intensive infidelity as she did the boys' for a Little League tournament.

Still, the feeling came. She sat down on the carpeted step and leaned against the chapel's lectern, closing her eyes and letting what remained of it stand out more clearly but the sensation was almost gone. She could leave the chapel in another hour at most.

"It was out of town, Margaret," he told her the first time, quite openly and confident he met the standard of rectitude expected of Rosamond men, while she stood, pregnant with Chapin Finley, holding the dainty handkerchief casually left in his duffel and feeling the invisible body blow that left her breathless. For days after, she endured a weighted numbness, as if her senses were taken somewhere else for a while and burlap bags of the Delta's sandy soil put in their place. It was a puzzle to her then although she knew she felt sometimes drawn to him in spite of his dangers, but intimacies he might have with some other one were disconnected from her and she could not understand why the feeling came nevertheless.

It was not shame, although even Ella averted her eyes each time as if in kindness and it was very like that when she was with others in outside places. "Come sit here by me," they would say and sweetly take her hand, pulling her down to them. "Are you doing OK, darlin'?" And their creamy lips opened across white teeth that somehow drew strength away from her until they were more dazzling than before.

When the sun was halfway down the stained-glass wall, she left to find Sam to bring a little brandy to her bedroom before the school day ended and Buie and Chapin Finley were home again. She pushed open the heavy oak door and Sam's full, baritone voice filled the hallway in a half-wail, half-shout. She ran at once to the kitchen but he had come to the end of it and sat silent at the worktable, his mouth gaping and arms outstretched with the palms up reaching to her. His daughter, Caraly, was there, too, and she stood stony-faced behind him, without touching.

"Caraly! Sam!" Margaret cried and he grabbed her arm with his large, bony hand, the sandpaper palm circling her wrist.

"Miz Marg'ret," he sobbed softly. "What goin' to happen to us now?"

"Please tell me what it is," Margaret said kindly and reached her other hand to his shoulder.

"Not me, ma'am. Not so much. But the chil'rens. What they goin' t'do?" He looked hopefully at her, as if she might really answer him and she looked for explanation to Caraly.

"They shot the pres'dent, ma'am. School let out. It so bad." She faced Margaret squarely then. "They didn't want him helpin' niggers no more, I guess," she said and Margaret said, too, "I guess."

She left them together and, taking the brandy, went to her bedroom. When she closed the door behind her, she gladly shed what she was wearing and wrapped herself naked in the soft cotton quilt her aunt Elizabeth gave her when she married Big John. "You know, I jus' realized something," John Buie had said to her in the summer. "That nigger lovin' sonofabitch Kennedy came out of the same soil as you. Why doesn't that surprise me, Margaret?" He stood bare-chested by the side of the bed, his skin nut brown from four days of wading and fishing off the Gulf shore wearing only swim trunks and carrying a shark stick. "Now, I found me a real Mississippi lady this time," he said, eyeing her for any response, but she had made none. "Hotter than a new bride. Wore me out. 'Bout out, I'd say, anyway."

Margaret sat on top of the coverlet, the quilt warm around her, and swallowed the snifterful of brandy in one gulp, then poured a second and sat it on the night table. How very odd to have one's life end in just that way, the deliberate act of another. Must it mean that the one, without entitlement, prematurely ended the other's story or could the story have been complete and the killing a final stroke? She supposed that could be and, yet, the contingency in such an intersection of lives was breathtaking. The victim need not know, should not know perhaps, but surely the killer required a sign and something singular and as stinging as a slap in the face for an act of that magnitude.

"Out of town" no longer restricted John Buie in the same way and someone from a neighboring plantation town was acceptable. He had used the office in the barn more than once and, Margaret supposed, the house would be next.

"Y'all are becoming a spectacle. If you can't keep your husband happy, why don't you let him go?" Little Mildred had demanded. "It wouldn't be so bad, Margaret. You could make a new life for yourself in Jackson or Memphis or back home with your people."

"Buie," Margaret said and Little Mildred looked surprised.

"Buie? My dear, he doesn't enter into things at all. He would stay right here in his home and little Chapin Finley, too. They are Capes and they belong here. But, you can go wherever you please," she said, then added, "They could come see you, of course. I'm certain they would."

Perhaps it was true and she could safely leave him now. He was nearing eighteen and would be starting Ole Miss in a year. No, there would have to be more. He was so certainly a part of her story and its meaning that she must use the greatest caution. She would need some clear sign before she relinquished protection and there had been none of any kind.

"Mama! Did you hear?" Buie rushed into the bedroom without knocking. "The president's been shot! He's dead, Mama."

"Caraly told me, honey," she said, pulling herself up from the pillows and onto her side to face him.

"She knows?" His concern was the same in voice and expression. He had never hid himself the way she did and that made stronger her drive to guard him. "Sweet Caraly. She must be low. I wanted to be the one't told her," he said, looking sadly at Margaret, shaking his head. Yes, he was almost a man now, already taller than his father with the same dark hair and olive skin but his eyes were like hers, blue behind a veil of gray. "They laughed, Mama."

"Who laughed, Buie?"

"The others at school. I told him they had no business doin' that. That he was our president, too."

"I'm glad you said that, darling." Margaret caressed his hair and cheek, still flushed with indignation.

Buie took a deep breath, looking down, then suddenly laughed and looked at her, his eyes displaying mischief in the way of Big John so that she thought of him and smiled. "Know what else I said?" She shook her head. "I told 'em, if nothing else, my mama was from Massachusetts, same's the president, and that I would have to consider it a personal insult requiring action if I heard one more snicker from any of their ugly pusses. That shut 'em up then."

He stood up from the bed and walked in a mock swagger to the doorway, making Margaret smile to herself as she leaned back once more into the pillows. "Buie, darling, I love you so much. You must be careful."

He stopped where he was and said, "I know, Mama," then closed the door and walked back to the bed to sit by her side, wrapping his arms about her. "It's jus' that's all they understand sometimes," and he pressed his cheek against hers, breathing softly into her hair and they lay together that way, without speaking, until she slept.

SAM STANDS OUTSIDE the bedroom door and calls in, his face sideways to the cracked opening. It seems that he is giving his mistress privacy and he means it to seem that way but it is he who wants to stay out of sight. She can read his face like a newspaper, always has, and today he has many thoughts to keep to himself. "I'm goin' now. You settled, Miz Marg'ret?" There is no answer and he opens the door a few inches more, leans his head inside. The room is still light enough—it is only six o'clock—and he sees her small figure beneath the bedcover, facing the windows. "Miz Marg'ret?" he whispers and the figure does not move and he comes farther into the room until he is at the foot of the bed and her reclining profile is in his view. Her hair is tied away from her face and she is wearing the same khaki shirt she wore to Hawkins this morning. He suspects she drank herself to sleep even before he sees the empty snifter half under the covers. She needs her drink. He knows that, knows that and is glad she has the hooch to smooth things over. Life rubs rough on a lady like her and she needs something to get her through. Himself, he can get by with a little Easy Times last thing at night or, sometimes, if there is a wedding or a funeral, he might take a nip in the day. He approaches her quietly and pulls the cover over her shoulders and takes the empty glass, then thinking better of it, puts it back again.

He takes the car out slowly when he leaves, scratching away from the gate and onto the county road. At the corner, he remembers the gate left unlocked and he turns the Buick back in a wide U to tend his error. "Don't let your mind wander," Big Mama told him. "You need all you got where you are." But the thoughts take him away sometimes, anyway. He swings the gate to and loops the padlock through the iron links of the chain. It is a nuisance to have to do that every time, but her all alone that way, he needs to keep the gate locked.

He drives hard to the Lucky Seven casino, faster than he ought, but he is eager to get inside and tend to familiar work that will fill his head and push other thoughts away. He remembers the officer too late at the junction of Highway 4 and Highway 61, but fortune is smiling and the patrol car has not yet arrived. It is too early for drunk gamblers on their trips back to Hernando, Memphis, Crenshaw, and the other hundred places they may go. From the intersection, the highway takes him down, down into the bed of the Mississippi River until he turns into the small service road for a final descent to the casino parking lot, two-thirds full already. By Mississippi law, the Lucky Seven must be, and it is, a riverboat, afloat and connected to the Mississippi by navigable waters, but there is no danger of seasickness when aboard, the casino set in a hollow dugout filled with water for the purpose and as solid as any Wal-Mart. He bypasses the valet and parks the car himself, walking back to enter beneath the four-lane marquee with LUCKY SEVEN across it in twenty-foot letters made of giant red-and-silver sequins. Inside, the thick carpet repeats the colors in curving leaves and pretty women, white and black and in-between, wear stiff red skirts up to the stride, with fishnet stockings and high heels and silver bustiers so tight even the spindly ones look like they could nurse a baby.

He circles the floor, but no seats are open at the blackjack tables and he stands back to wait, watching the others play. They are still playing $3 limits and the tables won't clear until the limits raise to $5. He fingers the paper in his pocket. Little Mildred has sent him five checks now, each for the same $100. "What this for," he asked Albert when he brought the first one and the young man grinned and said, "I thought you'd be tellin' me that. You been givin' Miz Melton some of your goodies or somethin'?" "She *your* boss," Sam shot back to him and Albert said, "Nobody boss Albert." In the weeks after, he had brought four more, like the first, each time with a face more sullen than the previous occasion and pushing the folded paper roughly into Sam's hand. "I wish I could make money doing nothing at all. What you got on her anyway?" "Nothin'," Sam told him, but he was thinking along the same lines, knowing Miz Little Mildred hadn't suddenly developed a gold heart giving out cold cash for the good of it.

A cheer goes up at the craps table nearby and he moves closer. Someone is a good roller and the numbers are coming. "Cocktail, sir?" She is a white girl no more than twenty-two with white teeth and red lipstick, her blue eyes almost lost beneath the black gummy mascara on her long lashes, calling him "sir" and he does not know what to say. He has come up learning how to be a good worker, how to stay out of trouble and that is all, no more. It had been enough once and how could the old folks have guessed back then that he might need something more someday? Some way to think through things when work was over and trouble wasn't holding on to his collar every second. No matter to them, they died in time, but he is here with Negroes standing ahead of whites in the line at the grocery store buying cottage cheese and yogurt and other white peoples' food, some wearing suits and driving foreign cars and a lot, like here, mingling with whites at leisure. Miz Marg'ret, Lord, what a shock it must have been to her. "Sam, there were two young Negro girls in the clinic, all dressed up and so official." When she asked him, he thought his heart would stop until he remembered how long she had been away and she added, "Is it so other places?"

"You don't want to know it all, I'm tellin' you. They's some good peoples 'round but then you got the others just takin' advantage," he told her. "My cousin, Poo Poo? You remember him? He was just fifteen, sixteen. He'd help Mr. John sometimes for the dove shoot, carryin' the mens to the different fields?" but she did not remember him. "He assistant to the manager at John Deere over in Greenwood. So he's up pretty far. They's been a lot like him, I guess." The old-timey folks never thought it but he lives past their time and he is here with it, here with pretty white girls calling him "sir." She smiles at him and tips her head as if to say, "Well?" but she is deferential and does not say it aloud. "Bourbon," he says on a sudden impulse and she writes his order on a cocktail napkin and bounces away. Spaces are open at the craps table after the roller finally sevened out and a new, untested roller is throwing the dice. Each roll, Sam watches where the bets go down and where they don't, the dealer's stick moving the dice back to the roller. "Five dollar e-o," someone says and the dealer repeats the bet and moves the chips to the center of the table. "Odds on the six." "Odds off this throw." "Press the eight." Everyone talks at once in the brief moment between rolls, but he can learn the rules if he watches long enough and maybe he will. He doesn't know. "Here's your drink, sir." The girl is back and he takes the bourbon putting a fifty-cent tip on the tray. "Thank you," she says brightly and moves past him to deliver the rest of the drinks she carries. He comes closer to the table and sips, watching the action from behind the roller—a boy wearing a Memphis State T-shirt and khaki shorts. "Winner five!" the dealer shouts and a cheer erupts among the players and they raise fists in the air, take a swallow of their drinks, pat backs. The young man turns to grin at Sam, his face rosy with drink and luck, and he reaches his open palm up and toward the old man. "Alright, man!" he says and Sam hesitates, then raises his hand to slap the other and says, "Alright."

He has worked for the Capes at Cape House since he was nineteen and there are too many things he knows to pick out just one. He had just about figured she wanted Mr. Chappy's weakness kept from the light, but then Hardy Mall had made his claim and everyone is going to know anyway. Still the checks keep coming and she knowing for maybe two weeks, Mr. Niles said. Yes, there is the one thing but he pushes the thought away. If she knew about the girl, Miz Little Mildred'd already be dead on the spot and, if she weren't, she'd be sending a lot more than a C-note. Whatever. He is getting in the middle of too many white peoples' business. Between Miz Marg'ret and Miz Little Mildred, then Mr. Hardy and him being the kind to act on you gettin' in his way. Maybe it's a good thing, Sam thinks, not being able to decide, not saying nothing. He best stay out of it, just take care of Miz Marg'ret and keep groceries on the table. That is plenty for a man his age and he can die in peace.

"Cocktail?" It is another girl, not so pretty as the first. "No, thank you," he says. "Where the cashier's box?" She points to the far wall that looks a city block away. He walks toward it, fingering the folded checks in his pocket and refusing two more offers of drink before he reaches the counter. "Can I cash these?" He asks and a broad-shouldered man with a mustache that curls up on each end takes the papers and smiles at him. "As many as you want, sir," he says and, not knowing what else to say, Sam purses his lips and nods as if it were ordinary to him.

21

Little Mildred Melton stands to the right of her son, Frank III, and to Sara Cape's husband's left. They receive guests for her eighty-fifth birthday party, standing on clipped Saint Augustine just inside the gate to Frank's patio garden, but so far there are only a few guests to greet. It is too early, yet. The invitation is for six until eight and it is only twenty minutes past six. They are brave to have an outdoor party this evening, she thinks, her suggestion that the club might be a wiser choice rebuffed by Frank's wife, Paula, who can't seem to be outside enough; who stands, two men away, luminous in the dark evening, her creamy silk short-cropped blouse worn loose over fluid pants of the same material, fitted tight around her hard midriff. It is the fashion this year in the Delta and every woman within ten years of Paula's age will wear a version of the same costume to this party, each in her own best color. "I'm so pleased you could be here. Thank you." Little Mildred offers the tips of her fingers to Ches Cooper and accepts Evelyn's half embrace. Two young women pass, royal blue and rust Paulas, white teeth gleaming, not touching Little Mildred as if her age were contagious. Paula is gold and ivory, gold-brown skin beneath a triple-wide gold choker that vees into her clavicle, and the gold repoussé bangle bracelets that Kathryn Cape wore one hundred years before. Triple diamond stud earrings flash below her mahogany hair in its model's cut and a matching but larger triple solitaire ring flashes below. Little Mildred frowns at the presentation. She is too thin, too muscular, too dark, and seems almost euphoric, but Mildred remembers the vexatious power of a woman's nature and supposes the physical must surface somehow. She, after all, was married to Frank III's father and knows the generations vary little in Rosamond.

The weather has been unseasonably warm, balmy even, but fall temperatures might turn cool overnight and even if they don't, that only means big, black Delta mosquitoes will be here, worse than the cold. Still, she thinks the grounds pleasing with citronella candles lining the top of the stucco garden walls like an old Santa Fe hotel, a small bouquet of gardenias resting between each pair. More citronella torches burn at intervals throughout the yard and, at the far end, the fire pit is lit for warmth next to a large striped tent, in the event of rain.

At half past six, seven cars arrive at once and the receiving line is full. Niles Abbott waits his turn, dressed appropriately in a navy blazer and gray pants. "Niles!" Paula Melton reaches out polished, brown arms to his shoulders. She touches her lips almost to his earlobe as she pulls him in, placing his right hand in that of the rosy-cheeked young man next to her. "Niles, this is our son, Frank Cape Melton. Cape, I want you to meet Niles Abbott, one of our most prominent young attorneys. Cape is just beginning law school, aren't you, dear?"

Niles shakes Cape's hand with a firm grip, smiling. He recognizes him immediately as the friend of the boy Charley represented in the spring for indecent exposure—Holmes Noblin. Cape and Noblin had been seeing how many open car windows they could find and then urinate on the interiors and Noblin got caught. "Get away. It's a trap," Niles laughs, but Paula is already directing the next hand to Cape's and Frank Melton III, six feet six inches not counting his wiry brown and gray curls, looms before him.

"Abbott! Good to see you out of your office for a change! I haven't seen Charley?"

"Hey, Frank. I'm sure Sibyl called Paula. He and Mrs. Brandon hated it, but they're going to have to miss tonight." Niles remembers his mission. "What it was, a client called him at the last minute to go to Memphis for the weekend to meet with some company directors. We go all over now, you know."

"Yeah, well. Tell him we missed him."

"I will. Good to see you, Frank." He starts to move on but Frank reaches out a long arm to grab his left shoulder. He winks as Niles turns toward him again.

"I guess you got your hands full these days, baby-sittin' Margaret," he says and Niles presses his lips together, smiles and nods, but keeps moving down the receiving line. A few minutes later, he reaches the end, having skirted the cluster of guests around the honoree, and looks around for a bar. He requests a Budweiser and takes it to a spot between two clutches of conversing guests to nurse it and consider Melton's statement.

Little Mildred sees Niles Abbott enter, sees him greet Paula and the others and, then, neatly avoid her in his move through the receiving line. She did not invite him but they had added her list to the party list they used for themselves, one prepared with Frank's bank in mind, as well as including enough young people to make it pretty. She had named mostly other old women who, like her, were never asked otherwise only for being nice, but were required to have money, too.

There are three tables set along one side of the narrow yard, each lavishly covered in autumn leaf fabric, the bottom crumpled on the ground as if someone measured incorrectly, but it is only to show an excess of means, the same as fat on Henry VIII. At the center of the tables, towering arrangements of fresh flowers defy the dead leaves in the cloth and simultaneously pay tribute to Little Mildred's gardening prowess. Niles moves along the tables to graze on boiled shrimp and *rémoulade* sauce, hot spinach dip, slices of beef tenders in buttery fold-over, yeast rolls. He pauses every few seconds to greet acquain-tances and, inevitably, every guest at the party and thinks of the fearful, churning force of a Mississippi River eddy, but Buddy would love this. Everyone here had been his friend back then and even through the trial, deserting him only after jail left its taint. "I thought I was doing the right thing by everyone. The parts I bought were the best ones anyway, so the county got its money's worth, Jones got his business, and I got some-thing, too. Way it turned out tells me something was wrong with my thinking." Niles cannot tell if he still thinks about the conviction, the time he served. Before the stroke, he had said he had let it go and Niles should do the same.

The crash and sound of breaking glass pulls every head to-ward the house. One of the waiters, a young black kid in a white coat, has collided with a guest, a big girl. Niles recognizes Christine Butler, the new assistant district attorney, standing next to her boss, the district attorney, Evan Martin, and his wife, Kay. They had only met for a brief introduction at last month's county bar meeting and, then, she had worn a khaki, loose-fitting suit that he thought godawful. Tonight she is wear-ing a solid black dress and a brightly colored blazer that even Niles knows is unstylish, surprising himself by the observation. With her apple-cheeked child's face and a thick mop of hair, she looks pretty good, nevertheless, but he tightens when she spots him and heads in his direction.

"Hey, Niles."

"Hey." They stand next to each other but look at others, surveying the crowd. "You know the Meltons?" he asks.

She looks at him, amused. "You don't think I circulate in their little circle?"

"No, I just mean you're not from around here, are you?" He feels his face redden, but it is already dark and she won't see.

"No. Well, from Mississippi, yeah, but over by Egypt." She

pauses to sip her drink—Coca-Cola it looks like—and stares at him with a curious look. "From the county, you know. Spent my childhood watching animals screw in the barnyard, that kind of thing."

"Uh-huh." Niles nods his head in response, but scans the crowd for a reason to excuse himself. No one. "Can I get you another drink?"

"Yeah, thanks. Diet Dr. Pepper." He turns to leave but square, buffed fingernails tighten around his arm. "Let me come over here and talk to these two, bright people! Look at you. Aren't you both just the cutest things! And all those brains, too!" Their hostess turns to Christine. "Darlin', I'm Paula Melton. We are so delighted to have you here this evening! Delighted to have you in Rosamond, too! We need some young women who can keep up with these men!" Paula releases her grip on his arm to pat his cheek, her gold bracelets jangling in his ear. "I see you've met Mr. Gorgeous, here."

"I'll sit over here, Frank." Little Mildred takes her son's arm and follows him up three, short steps to the raised patio and a padded lawn chair. She took three Motrin before six, but her diseased hip has won the contest.

"Can I bring you a drink, Mother?"

"Yes. A vodka tonic please, dear." She is at a good vantage point, high enough to scan the faces clustered over the yard, and she finds him within seconds. He is talking to Paula and that Butler girl. Lord, that outfit! Who had invited her?

"Here you go, Mother." Frank hands her a double vodka tonic and a paper napkin, printed in the same pattern as the tablecloths but in different, blending tones. She takes a big swallow and raises her eyes over the rim of the glass to where Niles stands. He seems to be here only to be seen, he does not seem purposive, does not seem to know anything but that sort of thing is difficult to see. She takes another swallow.

Paula turns her gaze to the younger woman. "Christine— it's Christine, isn't it?—well, Christine, let me tell you something. Not only is Niles one of our most distinguished young lawyers—you knew he attended Yale?—but he is also one of our most eligible bachelors. He has to beat them off with a stick, don't you, Niles?"

"I don't know about that, Paula, but I do think I need to beat my way over to the bar and get Miss Butler and me another drink. May I bring you something?"

"Yes, well, I want you to do that—not for me, no, no—I need to check with cook about some more catfish pâté. But, first—wait, Niles, I want you to hear this, too. Christine, my father, Carlton Sanderson—his brother was the Supreme Court justice Winn Sanderson; you may have studied about him— my father roomed with Evan's father, Evan Sr., when they were both students at State."

"Oh, no. Really? Big Mr. Martin was at the office just this week." Christine and Paula share open-jawed amazement at this coincidence. Niles sips his drink, looking between them and he sees Little Mildred studying him. She averts her eyes almost immediately but it is too late. He begins to move toward the bar and, too, in her direction.

"No, Niles, wait a minute. That's not all. Christine's father is George Butler. Am I right, Christine?" She does not wait for the answer. "Well, you will not believe this, but my aunt Olivia Hollings was a Pettis? And the Pettises came from over by Egypt? Well. Aunt Olivia was herself born in a house right there on the edge of town. They use it for the country club now, just suppers and so forth. Anyway, that house where my aunt Olivia was herself born is directly across the street from the Methodist church and the rectory where Christine's father lived as a little boy." Paula smiles and gives each a tilt of her dark bob but her eyes are past them. "Kendall Povall? You have not paid the slightest attention to me! Come here!"

WHAT CAN SHE say to him? Everything is impossible. "Mr. Abbott, none of this really concerns you, does it? I realize you are a very bright young man who is naturally curious, however, so I will tell you that my father left Cape Plantation to my brother, John Buie, and when he died, he passed the property to Chapin Finley." He will not believe her and, if he truly knows nothing, he will become suspicious.

Niles asks for Christine's Dr. Pepper, but declines another drink for himself. The look on her face convinces him his instincts are correct. Something is there, but Charley has said it's not his business and what can he say? "What little secret are you keeping, Mrs. Melton?" And he could not say anything straight out, not here, not now. The event has an internal structure, inside rules, and it surprises him, but he feels bound even without having agreed to them.

Mildred watches him move through the crowd. She might preempt his doubt. "Well, I know you won't believe me. I'm just a silly old lady. Why don't you take a look at the wills yourself. Big John died in 1945 and John Buie in 1966," but what if he responds, "That's a good idea. I will"?

Christine has moved to another conversation and Niles hands her drink around her shoulder and waves good-bye. The crowd is thinning—it is after eight—and he is able to walk nearly a straight line to Mildred's chair. She does not look at him until he is leaning toward her and she raises her chin with a fixed smile. "Mr. Abbott. I'm so glad you could be here," and she does appear to be that glad.

"I'm afraid I hear thunder, ma'am," he says and, together, they look west and to the faint pulse of lightning.

Cape Plantation, 1964 🪶 Margaret was very nearly eighteen years old before a man, or even a boy, looked at her with the sideways glance whose meaning she knew or had nearly guessed, having accompanied her mother out many times. Her small size, she supposed, raised a presumption of childishness that, in those times, was almost never overcome by a closer examination. "Pretty little girl." She heard that often enough and she only felt bemused indifference, knowing as youth knows that there was time for everything. She knew enough to imagine already. Her father said to her, "Go to your room and remove your dress," and she did, leaving her cotton camisole and slip and she waited. When he came in, he looked at her a long time before he spoke and he sat on the edge of her bed while she stood in front of him. She was thirteen. "Your mother and I love you very much, Margaret. You are our only child and we want your happiness. Do you know that?" She said that she did. "If I could go with you each step of your life I would. But, of course, I cannot." He was solemn and he looked like a portrait to her just then, his black hair and gray temples in the shadows of her room, his body stiffly upright in a gray wool suit. "Come close to me," he said. "I want to show you something," and she stepped between his knees and he rested his hands and their long, steady fingers on her shoulders. "There are truths that cannot be told, Margaret. You must learn to feel them. Do you feel my hands on you?" He began to stroke her bare arms softly, then moved to her neck and, with one finger, delicately traced her lips and nose and eyes. "Close your eyes and think only of this feeling. Do you feel it?" She closed her eyes. His hands were warm and dry. They moved surely across her with reassuring weight and not the discomfort of a light touch. "This is how it feels to be cherished. Do you feel it?" She nodded and he smiled, satisfied. "Don't ever forget. It is a rare thing, that."

Curren Burnbridge was the first permitted to escort her from the house—she was sixteen—and it was to the Christmas Eve party at the parish hall. Their evening together was, more than anything else, a series of tasks to be executed. He took her hand when they came down the snowy steps from her parents' brownstone house and walked along the street. She raised her hair above her mother's graded beads and let him remove her coat inside the entry. She grasped cotton gloves in her right hand and her beaded bag, and took the eggnog he brought to her in the other, sipping it, smiling her thank-you. "You look lovely, sweetheart," Anne Finley whispered and she exchanged a smile with her father, who shook his head, and she understood this was not any of her story, but another altogether outside her and into which she stepped temporarily to read a part, a pleasant diversion, but no more.

It was altogether different the summer of her eighteenth year when David Sterling slid his book toward hers and nudged it, making her look up to see him across the library table. "Sorry," he whispered, with a half-smile, mocking her and petting her with the same look. She turned her face away from him in the same gesture she had seen her mother use when a man other than her husband was intimate with a glance, and, when, after a time, she discreetly looked across the table once more, he was gone. "I love him," she told herself but no one else and she was quite certain. Each day but Sunday, they met at the library. Or, rather, she came there and, sometimes, he came as well. It was the only place, in fact, she ever saw him at all and she believed in a part of her that he was always somewhere in its ordered Renaissance spaces, moving in and out among the polished fruitwood tables, stepping from one golden, dusty window light to another along the length of the checkered floor. On one day she was in the second half-floor stacks, selecting readings on nihilism when he appeared in front of her. " 'In revenge and in love woman is more barbarous than man,' " he said, quoting Nietzsche with his cryptic half-smile, and for days after, discounting any insult, she marveled at his erudition, his knowledge but, most especially, that he had called her a "woman."

Buie was eighteen when he knew he loved Caraly and Margaret knew as well, not by conjecture but because she had seen them holding one another and kissing with the lush ease that comes when passion and respectful affection are improbably conjoined. They were standing in the small landing to the kitchen's outside door, around the corner but she saw them when she entered the room from the hall and stopped, leaving again before they knew. Buie's dark hair and soft curls pressed against Caraly's own black hair, pomaded stiffly back from her face and the dark brown of her skin was markedly different but pleasing next to the gold of Buie's own. Nostalgia rose in Margaret, the first she could remember, and she envied them exchanging their warm breath and touching that way, but that was her only thought and she let them be.

"Would you come to the Front Hall with me, please?" John Buie asked her, weeks after in an open excess of courtesy, surprising her by his presence in the afternoon at a time he ordinarily would be at the cotton gin. She followed him from the chapel where he found her to the Front Hall and Little Mildred was waiting for them and already seated. "Mildred has been kind enough to come here and try to help us avert a catastrophe."

"Margaret may not know to what you are referring, John Buie," Little Mildred said in the same manner she often conversed past Margaret to others, and John Buie stopped his steady pacing the length of the room to erupt in derisive laughter.

"Oh, she knows. Yes. You may be certain that little Miss Margaret knows."

Mildred ignored him and explained to Margaret as if she were a child being told something delicate. "Buie has been, well, paying some attention to that Nigra girl, your help's girl."

"Caraly," Margaret said flatly and John Buie wheeled to glare at her.

"I told you, Mildred. The cause knows its effect."

"Be that as it may, something needs to be done before it goes any further than it already has. Pray to God, that hasn't been very far."

"But, if Buie loves Caraly..."

"Don't ever speak that way of my flesh and blood!" John Buie interrupted before she could finish and strode to stand over her where she sat and she thought he looked fearful. "A Cape cannot be in love with a nigger. Do you understand me, Margaret? No decent white man would so much as touch one. In all my years working around 'em, I can say I never took even a second look. And, don't think they wasn't tryin' to get me to all the while. That's all they think about, all of 'em."

"Margaret, dear," Mildred spoke gently, instructing her. "If God had intended we mix with the Nigras, he would have made them white, don't you see? He made them look different so that we would know they were the cursed race and to stay away. I'm very fond of Nigras, the good ones anyway. They can't help what they are and we have a duty to look after them where they can't help themselves. But, we can't treat them like a white person or they'll just take all of us down to where they are."

"Don't bother, Mildred. She can't hear you. I can see that little bitch sashaying around, pushing that big, round butt in Buie's face. He was just weak, is all. You know what made him weak? You, Margaret. Your Yankee blood in him is a hurdle he'll be jumping over the rest of his life."

Little Mildred moved forward on her chair, reaching her arms toward Margaret. "Buie would be completely cut off from everyone, Margaret. No one will want anything to do with him. And, it would be the same for her. That's the way they feel about it. They don't want their people mixing with the whites either. They know it's not right. You let it get started, there would be no stopping it. And then where would we be? Do you want Buie to be an outcast?"

Margaret sat before them, both standing now, John Buie with his hand braced on the mantel and Little Mildred, behind the settee across from her. They stood silent and watchful, as if petitioners waiting for her decision and she the queen whose word would be the law. Her agreement was clearly wanted, although she did not understand why that should be so. She did not think this love sinful as Mildred said, remembering her father had told her, "The word of God is most abused as the only reason of a fool." It was the last thought that won her. She did not want him to endure the loneliness of a life separate from others. She had freely chosen her solitary path, but somehow she could not wish the same for her son. Her thought was only this, whether Buie's and Caraly's love were a thing that could be taken even if it should. Sometimes she had sat by her David for hours, sharing chapters of *Beyond Good and Evil* and, later, *Thus Spake Zarathustra,* at once letting the same words and thoughts inside themselves. They read from the same book, his fingers resting on the edge of the pages, turning them only when she gave silent assent. It seemed in that way as if they had already touched before it was nearing September and at the end of the day, she went to the long cloakroom for her umbrella and turned to find he had followed her inside. He took her by the shoulder, his grip firm, and sat her on the boot bench in the dark corner of the room. His face was shadow, no more, but she felt his warm breath and when he reached his arm around her and pressed her child's body against him, she heard the soft moan and never knew whose it was. "What do you want me to do?" she asked them and John Buie looked at Little Mildred.

"John Buie's already talked to Sam and he's going to send her to stay with his sister down at Tchula." Little Mildred walked around the settee and resumed her seat across from Margaret. "Buie'll be at Ole Miss for summer school in another month, so it's really just a matter of turning his attention in that direction."

"Mildred thought we could give a party, invite some of the young ladies and young men he'll be seeing at school."

"Not just from Rosamond, of course, but all the good Delta families. We'll have to think of some appropriate reason. I don't want anyone thinking we are trying to bolster Buie's prospects for rush in the fall. He doesn't need bolstering. The fraternities will be falling all over themselves to pledge him."

David, her love, so young, died unexpectedly in the winter of 1932, a great, sad mystery to Margaret, although her father said it was surely food poisoning and it was subsequently that he made her arrangements for nursing school. Then Big John, and he lay in the grave as well. Her loves seemed always to die before their time and, now, she would kill another's.

Margaret nodded and rose from her seat to leave. "Something else, Margaret," John Buie said and she stopped without turning, knowing her necessity was to be admitted at last. "Buie'll likely come to you about this sooner or later, figurin' you'd be on his side."

"I know," she said.

MARGARET LIES ON her side facing the open windows to the side yard. She watches the storm close in and breathes in the thick, moist air. Thunderstorms in the Delta are never as spectacularly thrilling as the ones she remembers from Massachusetts and her childhood. Father Moran called them "God's lesson in humility, lest we forget," but her father scoffed at this idea. "I never feel so exalted or closer to the Maker as when these primordial forces revisit us," Dr. Finley said. "They remind me of the beginning of time and the evolutionary processes that have brought us into existence." She stills her breath to hear, but she feels nothing.

"Inventory" is the next line on Mr. Abbott's list and she knew at once that the thing meant was Buie's room, but she refuses the fact. Instead, she has looked through the first-floor rooms of Cape House in turn. The dining room was strangely bare—a table, chairs, and the Turkish brass side table, nearly nothing else—and, yet, she has no memory of what is missing. A tantalus set sits on the brass table with an empty holder for one of eighteen, tiny liqueur glasses. She remembers it breaking, nothing more. The chapel pieces are mostly present, she only supposes, but she knows with certainty that the music room is quite defrocked. The room is only a small square, perhaps fifteen feet, its walls covered with a dull rose paper and a triple crown molding at the top. A five-armed chandelier with yellow porcelain roses wound around its bronze frame hangs from the ceiling. The grand piano is there and the stuffed settee covered in satin with wide stripes and fine carved Chippendale chairs with needlepoint cushions—a London music room and not so unusual for that, except that the rug had been rolled to one side to expose the heart-pine floor and that had been chopped through, neatly and in precise rows, in potholes.

Sam had shrugged. "Mr. Chappy come in here a good bit before he died. Maybe he lookin' for the treasure." The piano sat solidly, one pothole per leg, but there were only two paintings and, for once, she remembered something missing altogether. Her favorite, the fox, was gone. Now, his room is the only one that remains and, still, she has not gone up the stairs, entertaining a new hope that there is something else required by the call for inventory.

She listens to the roll of thunder. The patter of rain sounds first on the far wall of the side yard, then moves slowly across the yard toward the open windows of Margaret's bedroom. The lightning is close now and she stares into it, narrowing her eyes at the glare of the pulsing strobe, trying very hard not to think at all.

22

The cold front follows behind the rainstorm and the heating plant that had last done work in April is cranking noisily when Niles unlocks the office door. The rattle of the furnace is accompanied by an ashy smell as if the building were still heated by a coal burner, but it must only be mechanical memory. They are all-electric, now. He is dressed for the weather in cotton socks and jeans, a Tabasco T-shirt from New Orleans that says *"Laissez les bons temps rouler"* and a dark flannel shirt. He often wore the same collection in law school and today, too, is a New England day in the Delta, a day to be spent inside a warm, stuffy building looking out to the clear cold.

He is feeling upbeat and elects to make a fresh pot of coffee rather than microwave Friday's leftovers. While it brews, he picks up the next stack of Hardy Mall's papers to review, putting on his glasses and staring intently but knowing all the while it is not working and in less than five minutes he has forgotten the coffee and Hardy and is padding through the chancery clerk's office and into the room of land records.

The history of Cape Plantation is laid out in less than a page of the Sectional Index. U.S. patent to the land was sold at the 1830 auction to Mitchell Scott Brumfield and, fourteen years later, John S. Cape bought 1,120 acres "more or less" from him, including the property on which Cape House now sat. In 1850 Cape transferred all of it in two equal portions to his sons, John Buie Cape—the General, Niles is certain—and Robert Connell Cape, who sold his part to his brother in 1859 and twenty years later "Kathryn C. Murrah" sold or gave away a few small parcels of the same property. The land has apparently passed by inheritance since then—a transfer that will be recorded elsewhere. Niles goes to the smaller chancery file room adjoining to look for the General's estate file. He does not know the date of his death, but he had been alive enough for his Civil War heroics and Niles begins with the clerk's docket for 1865, searching the *C*'s in each year thereafter until 1873 when a Petition for Appointment of Executor for the estate of John Buie Cape was filed on August 23. The file number is C-654 and Niles retrieves the bulky folder from the file cabinet.

The General left Kathryn Cape, his only child, all he had, the estate papers referring to her as "Kathryn Cape Murrah aka Mrs. William Spencer Murrah" and she took the land in her married name. The decree closing the estate was filed on December 12, 1873, and included a confirmation of title to 2,020 acres of land. She is Big John's mother, he suddenly realizes, wondering at once why Big John's name was Cape, not Murrah. The Capes would never have a bastard child or, if one impossibly appeared, would have the good manners to conceal its origin, bastardy being one of two claims no good Rosamond family will permit, the other, miscegenation. Ten years earlier Bo Flowers's uncle Guilford, drinking at the Country Club bar, imprudently suggested that Harrison Tierney III, who was bedding Guilford's wife, had Negro blood in him. It is true that Tierney's hair is black and unusually thick and curly; with his olive skin, it was enough to give Guilford's claim legs and when the rumor inevitably presented itself to Tierney, he uncased his father's twist barrel dueling pistols, drove to the Square, and left his car running in the middle of the street while he calmly walked up to Flowers and shot him dead. No charges were brought since anyone who had the authority to do so regarded the act as reasonable under the circumstances.

The answer is in the 1874 record of William Spencer Murrah's estate instead. His will leaves 1,200 acres of Delta farmland to his wife, Kathryn, and their five-year-old son, John Buie Murrah. The record of Kathryn's estate appears in 1902, where everything was left to her son, whose name had changed to John Buie Cape II and Niles suspects the General's daughter seized the opportunity of Murrah's death to carry on the Cape family name. Under Mississippi law, no formalities would have been necessary. He totals the acreage. Five thousand acres. Niles is stunned by the size of Cape Plantation and, at the same time, his blood rushes with the anticipation of hidden treasure. "Big money, big lies," Buddy used to say.

He finds Big John's own estate in the 1945 docket, remembering Mildred Melton's mention of the date of his death. The file is thick and he leafs through the pleadings to find the will. He sinks a little when he sees that Robert Sanders had been the estate's counsel. He was a rare combination of legal scholar and pragmatist, well known for trying, and succeeding with, innovations no one else imagined. Whatever he drafted would be virtually unassailable and although he has been dead thirty years, lawyers still keep copies of his pleadings for reference. The will is in the middle, "Last Will and Testament" is its caption, no more. He scans the paragraphs quickly. He mentions his two children, leaving Cape Plantation in its entirety to John Buie Cape and a quarter interest in a life insurance policy totaling one million dollars. Little Mildred was given the balance and a long list of furniture, jewelry, and other personalty "when her mother deems fit," odd language since her mother predeceased Big John, but it does not invalidate the will. He looks at the file again. Robert Sanders had prepared the will, but he was not the lawyer handling the estate. Frank Morgan Sr., a Greenville attorney, had done that. Niles scans the remaining paragraphs for anything else that might affect the land, but there is nothing until the signature page, where Margaret Cape's signature appears with John Cape's, each witnessed by two different witnesses, whereas only Cape's own signature and two witnesses is required. Niles looks at the page numbers, but they are sequential and the type is the same. Still, it is odd that the will would mention a dead woman and fail to mention one very much alive, who then signed the will herself when that is not legally necessary. Extra steps, unnecessary steps. Things that Robert Sanders was not known to do.

Niles remembers that he was just a kid when John Buie Cape had died and he easily locates the estate file on the docket. June 1966. C66-0321, but the file is not in the appropriate drawer and there is no "out" card indicating it has been checked out by an attorney. He returns to the docket book and looks for the last document filed. It is the Order Closing Estate, dated October 4, 1966, and beneath it in parentheses the notation he suspected: "File sealed by Chancellor's Order of October 4, 1966."

Cape Plantation, 1964 🙿 When Margaret thought of herself at all now, it was only because of the dangerous circumstances in which she had come to live. "No one feels sorry for you," John Buie told her. "I'm the one that gets the pity, livin' with the likes of you." It was undoubtedly true. She did not feel sorry for herself, although neither did she pity John Buie, nor feel anything at all about him. She felt her life in quietude and, sometimes, with a vague sense of having done with a magnificent creation. She had borne the General's child and, for this time after, her own fate was of no moment, that mantle having passed to Buie. It was only his life, his story, that had meaning as she brought him to manhood.

He was eighteen and almost a man. She wondered if her own life would end soon. Surely it must if her story were, as she believed, complete with the mothering of this child and it disturbed her to think this, not because she feared dying or even being dead, but the thought seemed to cast light on the structure of her suppositions and threatened to reveal an imperfection. They went to the pasture before the summer began and Buie moved to Oxford and the university. "We're going to have a party before you leave for summer school. Is there anyone special you would like to be invited?" she asked him without meeting his eyes and pretending, instead, to watch the cow path they followed toward the pond.

"You will stand aside while he whips me?" he said.

"Your father has never struck you." It was a question and a declaration at once and Buie laughed gently and looked sidelong at her bowed head.

"I don't mean that. It's something else I've thought about sometimes. What if we had lived earlier, in the presence of some great evil like slavery? What would I do to undo it? Haven't you thought that sometimes?" She shook her head and he sighed. "Well, I have, Mother. I've imagined I am there when some fellow planter brings his slave to be whipped and what I might do, what I could do. It's not so easy. I know what I would do if it happened today, but the question is not the same. Then, not now. Would I stand aside or not? Do you see?"

"You would be of a different time, too."

"Yes! That's it. I would be someone in that time, not a visitor from our time and our thoughts now. I would have the thoughts of then and I can almost forgive them because of that, except there were always true voices to hear, Mother. There always were."

"This is not the same," she said, wanting him to believe her and leave thoughts that endangered him.

"I don't mean disrespect, Mother, but I know you do not think that yourself. If I pretend I feel as the others do, I'll be shutting out the true voices now."

"You would be completely cast out from your friends, your father, from everyone. I don't want that for you."

"You want me to be as they are?" Margaret looked back to the path as Buie pushed his face closer to her. "I know it must be hard for you. I see things, always have. I won't be with Caraly if you say no. They would blame you and I won't put that burden on you unless you tell me you are willing to take it."

Buie waited a moment before he decided to speak again and his voice was harder. "You don't know why this is so important to Daddy, but I do." Margaret looked at him.

"He doesn't respect Negro people," she said.

"No, that's not it. He doesn't, but that's not it. I wouldn't know, either, 'cept Frank III overheard Aunt Mildred and Daddy discussing it when we were just starting high school and he told me."

Margaret turned to him then. "What is it?"

"Well, part of it I knew forever. That the General—you know, our famous ancestor—had a lot of incentive to fight for slavery like he did. He had a weakness for the colored women he kept. I used to hear the men joke about it sometimes in the Front Hall standing in front of the portrait."

"What then?"

"But there was more to it. When he and my great-great-grandmother had their one and only child, Kathryn, people kind of raised their eyebrows. They said she was too old to have children, that Kathryn was a half-colored baby the General fathered by one of the slaves."

"Your father's grandmother."

Buie laughed. "Exactly. Daddy might have some Negro blood in him, if it's true. They spent a long time living down those rumors and he doesn't want it raisin' it's head again. It would, of course, if his son took up with a Negro girl."

They were at the white oak and she sat on the new grass while Buie stepped down the path to throw bread crumbs to the mallard ducks. She could see to the horizon in any direction, the pasture the highest point for many miles. What was it about altitude that insulated a person from the difficulties felt closer to the level of the sea? She watched the ducks bob for the crumbs, Buie brushing clean his hands and checking along the bank for hens on their nests.

"There are only a couple of hens left," he said, climbing the bank.

"They are more at risk from predators than the drakes, I suppose."

"How do you mean, Mother?"

She shrugged her shoulders, regretting her comment.

"No. That doesn't work with me. I know you meant something."

She gave him a teasing stern look. "I mean they have all of the predators that the drakes do and they also have the drakes, themselves."

"The drakes might kill them mating," he said and she nodded. It was only the middle of May, but the summer heat was unsuitable for sitting in the outdoors and he helped her stand and they walked back toward Cape House. "What will you do when I'm gone?"

She looked at him, startled, before realizing he only meant away to school. "I will miss you, darling."

"No. Maybe I shouldn't say anything."

"That doesn't work with me," she mocked him, laughing, and he laughed, too. "What is it, Buie?"

"The way you hide yourself from Daddy and the others. I understand why, but I'm not sure it's what you ought to do. What's the point? If you can't show yourself now, when will you ever? It would almost be as if you never existed at all, except that I have been here with you, but now I'll be gone." They were almost to the gate and she stepped ahead of him to open it. "Mother, I don't want to upset you, but we have to take the consequences of who we are, what we believe. Don't we? Whatever they might be? If you don't show that, don't share it, it's like a plant out of light that just dies away."

Margaret looked at him, her face stony, her heart frozen by fear. "You'll tell me if you think of anyone to invite?" she asked and, when he did not reply, she walked alone back to the house.

MARGARET COUNTS THE stairs. There are twenty-one. She has not tried them since, when? It is nearly impossible, she supposes, but the list said "Inventory" after the other that led to the clinic and she knew, at once, that it was Buie's room upstairs. There had been no need to go to Bay Clinic. This morning she recalled that she knew already it was gone. She was there on the last day of its life and Dr. Saris, an Indian man from Ruleville, stood on the top of the two concrete steps outside the side door. She watched him turn the lock and he said, "That's that, Margaret," and she was pulled away. No, that is wrong. There were no locks, but he had said, "That's that, Margaret," and it was the last of everything and she is surprised she can remember this much of it.

She looks to the top of the stairs. Twenty-one. The children had played a game with the stairway each birthday, taking the step that corresponded to the age achieved and getting closer each year to the top of the stairs and adulthood. She closes her eyes and sees the boys small, struggling up with one hand on the spindles for safety, and larger, trotting lightly, confidently up the staircase, but neither ascends to the top.

Her breath is almost even again. She has been sitting here for nearly an hour, following the walk from her bedroom, down the back hall, and into the foyer to this spot. She had prepared for it carefully, taking one shot of brandy to warm her and placing the little bottle of pills in her pocket, then moving slowly, slowly along the hall. But her heart seemed less willing each day to carry her, as if the more her life poured back in, the heavier burden she became for it and when she reached the foyer, the pressing at the center of her chest became a clenched fist squeezing at her heart so that she stumbled back and sat down roughly on the hall bench. She had retrieved a tablet from her dress pocket at once and placed it under her tongue and it had its effect, but it takes more time today than before.

Margaret opens her eyes and the dim light of the foyer is sufficient to see most of the furnishings and wall hangings that crowd the room. They, of everything in Cape House, have best survived the wear and tear of the years. What is kept at the center is kept protected, she supposes, then immediately qualifies her conclusion. A fire started here would destroy these things first, no matter their central status. No, the place most protected depends on the source of danger and that these things have been placed here is mere fortuity. If placed in the Front Hall, they would have slowly deteriorated along with the rest of that room.

She shifts positions on the hardwood seat of the bench and wraps her arms around herself, tucking her hands underneath. An oak riser snaps—the air is cooler today and this room always reflects the change of seasons first—and she looks back to the stairs. It is not the physical difficulty that has made her delay the climb, but rather the object. Buie's room. Her child, dead—she remembered that from the beginning—and how he appeared and that she loved him. But, there is something about the rest that she willingly lets be and if she climbs these stairs and goes to his room, it will not lie still but rise up and then what? And, yet, the sign has brought her here and she must follow it or there is no hope to find her story.

Sam left her after lunch and he said he would be gone until late. She cannot wait for his help and, anyway, he is nearly as old as she and would be no more than a hindrance. Margaret grips the arm of the bench and braces herself to rise. She walks to the foot of the stairs and the first step is easier than she expected and she is to the fourth stair step before she stops for breath. "Four years old!" she laughs. She moves up three more steps and stops again. "Seven!" she barely utters the word beneath her breath. Then, three more, but too quickly this time, and the pressing, squeezing in her chest begins to rise again. No matter, she has the little pills. It is only then, reaching into her empty pocket, that she remembers she left the bottle sitting on the bench below.

23

"C'mon everybody. Let's have some fun. You only live once 'n when you're dead you're done." Sam whisper-sings the words in the dark, sitting on the bottom step, where Margaret lies on the floor beneath him, his legs on either side of the pillow he placed under her head. He does not have the strength to carry her that he used to, little as she is, at least not so far as from here to the bedroom. He guesses it is four or five o'clock in the morning by now, being after midnight when he came in and would have missed seeing her, except he cut on the light to make extra certain the front door lock caught and saw the ivory color of her dress on the stairs.

He licks the palm of his hand and holds it beneath her nose, then over her lips. Yes, there is breath cooling the wet. She has moaned once or twice, but mostly she lies still, breathing like a bird that has stunned itself against the glass, so faint he fears it will stop at any time. Sometimes, they sit a spell and fly away. He has seen that. More often, the stunning brings them down. He will not leave her before the sun comes. The old peoples say old man death can sneak up in the dark and don't like the light so much.

The phone cut off in August and Mr. Chappy said it was "a little cash-flow problem" and that he would get the money to turn it back on, but he didn't and, then, the fall. Sam chastises himself. He should have taken the very first check from Miz Little Mildred right to the telephone office in Rosamond. Let her think whatever she wanted. The telephone isn't even all of it. Dr. Taylor had left him a list of prescriptions for her in the summer, his last visit, but he didn't take all the pills they offered him for himself at the County Health Department and he did alright so he wasn't sure she should take all those medicines even if he could've bought them, which he couldn't, just buying the heart attack pills and hoping for the best.

When he found her, she was on the fourth step, folded over to one side and facedown, as if she sat first before passing out. She was climbing the stairs and he knows where she was going. How do she know to go there? It was the same with Hawkins the other day, the old clinic. And the pasture, too. She has a sense for it somehow and it has given him a scare before. When Mr. Big John first bring her home with him, even then, she could catch you up on things, thinking inside your head as well as her own and knowing someone's head is knowing how to bring them down, but she didn't do it. "She just ain't got around to it yet," Ella said just like the old peoples who thought it foolishness to put your trust in a white person's heart. But, if she never hurt him, talked to him good and true, what was the use in putting a different thing in her heart? Someone call you "nigger" and treat you like something they found on the bottom of their shoe, that weren't what they wanted either. Let peoples, even white peoples, do the right thing. Don't catch 'em coming and going. That was what he told Ella.

Through the long sidelights on either side of the front door, Sam sees the thin, red line on the far horizon, divided in a dozen parts by the black silhouettes of the pecan trees in front of Cape House. Margaret still sleeps, but he thinks her breathing is firmer. He brings another flannel sheet to wrap over her and bolsters her with pillows along her body. He will go to the hospital and get Dr. Taylor before his rounds and he can use the telephone to call. He stops himself. There is no one to call. He will call Niles Abbott, the young lawyer and just let him know. He had asked Sam several times already, "Are you sure there isn't something else you can tell me?" Like her, almost, he seem to know without being told.

He opens the front door slowly, lifting up on it so it will not scrape the floor. She is still lying just as he arranged her, but he stops and comes back, unfolding the extra flannel sheet and floating it out and down over her, then tucking the edges under her feet and the pillows. He takes his comb from his pocket and bends to smooth the hair out of her face and push it back into the rubber band holding her ponytail. "There you go, ma'am. All ready for company."

Cape Plantation, 1964 🎵 Freedom Summer was what the summer in 1964 Mississippi was called, even then, but not by Margaret who was in her own summer and, of course, not free. It was in June that she had any glimpse of what transpired outside the bounds of Cape Plantation and Buie had begun summer school two weeks before, an early start for his first year of college. There were the conversations, true, and more of them than before. "They want a war, we'll give them a war." John Buie gathered fellow planters near the door of the Front Hall while Margaret and their wives sipped frozen daiquiris on the settees. "Ours say that none of the local ones care anything about any of it, it's just all those Jews and outsiders coming in from up north," Sarah Carter whispered and the other wives nodded. Margaret was uncertain whether she joined them, she could sometimes pass through an entire evening watching only now and again, while the words and movements flowed without thinking. She hoped that she had not and it would not have been noticed absent her express contradiction since the unanimity of thought on these matters was as assumed as in a war. There was our side and their side and nothing

could be more clear. But, if it were a war, it was one of words
and cars, mostly. Early evenings, after dinner, John Buie went
to the front step one, two, even three times and a pickup's
engine idled while he talked with the men inside. They smoked
cigarettes, the blue smoke mingling with the truck's gray vapor,
and he rested his arm on the open door, leaning toward them,
laughing. Later a different car came, and a man opened his
trunk and gave something to John Buie. She could never see
but only heard these things from the side yard or the bedroom
or, once, when she was in the music room, quite by accident.
And, there were the other cars, the ones that John Buie or the
others claimed to see passing through with "agitators" and
"Jewboys" but she never saw those.

There was somberness, too, more than the usual and when
she found Buie, home for the weekend, huddling with Sam
and Caraly in the kitchen, they stood apart when they saw her.
"Is there a secret?" she asked, playfully, and Buie put his arm
around her and said they were only discussing how nosy Miss
Margaret could be and Sam said, "Oh, now, Mr. Buie!" and
laughed and, yet, it was metal laughter and they were all still
quite grim despite it.

That was June 18, when they had finished supper, and she
left the kitchen after last instructions to Sam and she saw them
at the front door. John Buie had his hand on the open door
and the others—there were four of them—filled the opening.
They were not his usual friends but county people, lean and
eyes narrowed, looking at her. "The mosquitoes," she said and
John Buie invited them into the foyer, closing the door behind
them, but they kept their hats on and she saw the last one
carried a shotgun. "Margaret, this is just business. You go on
to bed." She nodded and passed from their view but stopped
out of sight to listen. They wanted Caraly. "Sara Love Tierney's
girl and the Carter's girl—both of 'em—were heard talkin'
about her, how she's been carryin' on with white men. Them

Jewboys got here last Friday and she done all of 'em by Monday, that's what they're sayin'." John Buie's voice was low and she could not hear the words clearly, but he seemed to be trying to dissuade them because they were arguing. "That's the thing, Mr. John, it's what they're sayin' so it don't matter that she done it or not. They *think* she done it and we got to make an example of her so that the rest of 'em don't think they can get away with mixin', too." "What do you have planned?" she heard John Buie say and they said, "Nothin' hurtful, just a whitewashin'—she wants to associate with white folk—then, parade her down Main Street to let 'em all see her and know what's what. That's all." There were more murmurs and she heard him coming through the foyer and into the back hall. He walked toward the light of the kitchen, but she spoke to him from the dark hall. "What are you going to do?"

"You go on to bed, Margaret. I told you that before."

"Don't give Caraly to them."

He stepped toward her, his look menacing. "Are you telling me what I can do in my own house. You don't tell me what to do, is that clear?"

She moved closer toward him, until her face was lit from the kitchen door and a look of surprise fluttered briefly across his face. "Tell them she's at her aunt's in Tchula."

"That's where she should be alright. But she has her ass up here again, just coincidentally on Buie's weekend home. Might be a good thing to bring her down a peg or two. I don't think she's got our message."

"If you bring out Caraly, I will tell them or anyone who will listen about your grandmother."

"What the hell are you talking about?" He laughed, but she had hit the mark and lifted her chin in determination. "Everybody knows that's just gossip from people jealous of the Capes. Go ahead. Tell whoever you like." She started past him to the foyer and, for a moment, he seemed to step aside, but then his arm yanked her roughly back and his face was close to hers. "They're ready to roll. I can't tell 'em to just go home. They want some kind of action." She stared back at him, not wavering. "I'm going to tell them now," she said and his eyes flickered with some thought and he seemed to soften saying, "Wait here. I know what to do," and she watched him turn toward the foyer and, only then, saw the shadow in the kitchen doorway. Buie walked to her, his face concerned and loving but when he put his arms around her, she felt such overwhelming doom that she feared for him more than she ever had before. It was the following morning that she knew the feeling came from elsewhere. The telephone rang before eight o'clock and John Buie answered. He came back to the kitchen porch, his step lighter than before, and took his place at the end of the table. She waited until he chose to speak, a strange voice intoning the last, vibrant measures of a fugue. "That was your Dr. Saris on the telephone, Margaret. Wants you to help him over at Hawkins. Seems some good ol' boys firebombed your nigger clinic last night. Imagine that."

NILES IS AT his apartment, reading the *Clarion-Ledger* when Sam calls.

"Sam? She's alright, isn't she?"

"Yes, sir. But she took sick on the stairs while I were out and she mighty weak."

"Do you need me to call the doctor?"

"No, Mr. Niles. That where I'm callin' from, Dr. Taylor's place. He weren't at the hospital, not his day or somethin', they say. I came to get him, make sure he come fast. He puttin' on his pants now."

Niles suppresses a chuckle at the thought of Grady Taylor's indignity, awakened at six A.M. on his day off by an old black man coming right up to his Country Club Road home. "Sam, I'm goin' to check something about Cape at the courthouse today. That's probably the best way I can help. Find a phone and call me at the office as soon as the doctor leaves, tell me what he says."

"Yes, sir. I'll do it."

Sam calls the office a few minutes after nine. Margaret will recover with a week or two in bed, but she has probably added damage to her heart that might kill her the next time she over-exerts. Niles thanks the old man and tells him to call him if he feels he needs to. But, he adds, of course, I don't represent Mrs. Cape.

At 9:45 Niles leaves for his appointment with Chesley Cooper at First Southern, detouring through the courthouse. Entering the north door, he has only the length of the straight, wide hall to the south door and then across the street to the bank. The chancery clerk's office is the last door on the left before the exit and Niles steps inside. Beetle Bailey stands be-hind the counter, squint-eyed and stringy, a Styrofoam cup of coffee in one hand and a half-smoked Marlboro in the other, his posture reminiscent of a banana.

"Hey, Beetle, how you doin'?" Niles leans against the counter as if he has nothing better to do and plans to stay awhile.

Bailey eyes him suspiciously and takes a last drag on his cigarette. "You visitin' the little people today, Abbott?"

"Well, I guess not, Beetle. Otherwise, I wouldn't be standing here talking to the most important person in Titus County, now, would I?" Niles flashes as big and genuine a smile as he can muster.

"Yeah, well..." He knows Beetle doesn't believe it, knows good and well he is being manipulated but that he likes it just the same.

"Beetle, what it is, I have a question and I know if anybody can tell me, you can."

"That's what my wife says, too. Nah, wait. What she says

is, 'Beetle, you *think* you got all the answers.'" Bailey opens a new pack of Marlboros, taps out and lights another cigarette. Niles steps back from the counter as the fresh cloud of smoke billows around Beetle's head.

"It's really two questions. First, has an estate been opened for Chapin Finley Cape? You know, the one..."

"The answer is no," Bailey says with satisfaction. "What's your other question?"

"OK. This is harder now 'cause I'm taking you way back. John Buie Cape. Chapin Finley's daddy. I know an estate was opened, but was there a will?"

"I can answer that, Counselor." Dewitt Cordeman comes up from behind Niles and places a hand on his shoulder.

Niles turns to greet the chancellor. "Hey, Judge. I didn't know you were in Rosamond today." They shake hands.

"We got us a custody battle goin' upstairs. I told 'em I needed to take a potty break. Beetle, you got any coffee back there?"

Suddenly, Bailey is a cocker spaniel puppy. "Yes, sir! I made it up myself, used the premium today, 'cause I know'd you was comin'. You stay here, Your Honor, I'll get it." He stubs out his cigarette, moving the ashtray off of the counter and hurries to the coffee cart in the file room.

"Niles, when I get my coffee here, you got a couple minutes to come upstairs?"

"Sure. I'm s'pose to be at the bank in a little while, but I've got time yet," Niles lies. Chesley will be put out but no lawyer refuses a judge's request to sit and visit.

He follows Cordeman to the judge's chambers, one of several small, square offices off the dark hall behind the courtroom. Judicial economy, imposed by Mississippi's meager resources, is the guiding principle in the court's furnishings as well as in its rulings. The chancellor sits down behind a standard-issue metal desk, flat steel gray out of harmony with the warm gold of the wallpaper, a print with old-fashioned coffee grinders. In the corner, the judicial robe hangs on a wire hanger on a plain wooden coatrack and three metal folding chairs sit in front of the desk. Niles chooses the middle one.

"Now, before I tell you what you want to know, you tell me something."

"You know that I will if I can, Your Honor."

"What does John Buie Cape, dead all these years, have to do with Miss Margaret and getting her affairs all tied up in a bow? In fact, the court is not even certain it will appoint a conservator for Miss Margaret under these new circumstances, in which case, what does he have to do with anything?"

"Well, I have reason to believe that Chapin Finley Cape may never have owned Cape Plantation. If he didn't, his quitclaim deeds to Hardy Mall transfer nothing, because he had nothing. There really isn't anyone in the family I can rely on, so I'm having to go through the land records."

The chancellor sits back. "Ah, I see. Are you representing Mrs. Cape?"

"No, sir."

"Someone else in the family or Mr. Mall?"

"No, sir."

"You'll have to excuse me. I fail to see where you come into this at all."

"Well," Niles talks more slowly, trying to think of an answer he can give. "The petition specifically addresses Cape Plantation by name, Your Honor, and asks for its disposition. As is the case with every lawyer, I am first and foremost an officer of the court charged with a responsibility to present vital evidence I may have to the court that it might not otherwise hear. Therefore, since I have become aware of these facts bearing on the ownership of the very property upon which the court seeks to rule, it is incumbent on me, as an officer of the court, to present it." Niles takes a deep breath and lets Judge Cordeman consider what he has said, counting on his not fully understanding. It is several minutes before the chancellor speaks.

"I know how thorough you are, Counselor. Everyone does. Everything by the rules. That's the reason I 'specially wanted you to take care of this little matter to begin with. I didn't want any questions left hanging but, now, let me say this. There's thorough and then there's thorough. I don't mind telling you I don't plan to approve the petition appointing a conservator for her. You can go squirrel hunting that day if you want. No need for you to waste your time even."

Niles waits. Proper deference requires him to refrain from pacing their conversation. That is the judge's prerogative.

"John Buie's estate. I handled it myself. As the judge, I mean. It was one of the first things came up after I took the bench back in '66." Cordeman leans over the desk toward Niles, settling into his story. "There was a will. Left everything to the boys and since the older one was already dead, Chapin Finley took the whole pie."

"What about his wife?"

"Didn't leave her anything. Don't ask me about people's personal business. 'Course she's entitled to a child's share under state law, but she was already out of it and no one brought a challenge in her behalf."

"Did the will leave Cape Plantation by name, or did it say 'any real property I may own'?"

"I don't remember. You'd have to look at the will."

"I would like to do that, Your Honor, but it's sealed."

Cordeman chuckles. "You're wondering, now why is that, aren't you? Sayin' to yourself, seal a will? What the hell for? Well, you're right! Wasn't any reason at all except for one thing." The judge gets up, closes the door, then comes back and sits on the front edge of the desk. "Now, this has to be between you and me, 'cause I sealed all those records due to the sensitivity of the situation." Niles nods and Cordeman continues. "Paternity suit. Little girl over at Drew was the mother, her daddy and mama were friends of John Buie's and the Capes. Good people. I don't think they would've ever brought it up this way normally—public and all. But he was already dead when the baby—a little boy—arrived and all that Cape money and such." Cordeman rises from the desk and retrieves his black robe from its hanger. "I ruled against 'em. You start anointing every bastard child after the fact, you're asking for a full docket. It may have been his, maybe not. Today they'd probably be wantin' to exhume the poor SOB's remains for DNA testing. We didn't have all that then."

"He'd be twenty-seven, twenty-eight now?"

"No. Fortunately, the kid got caught up in a cotton picker when he was ten or eleven, chewed him right up. So, that was that. No loose ends." Cordeman pulls on the robe and zips it. He takes a hand mirror from the desk drawer and smoothes his slick hair, studying his reflection for a few seconds. Niles stands and began to back toward the door. "I know Your Honor needs to get back on the bench now, so, if I may be excused, I'll just..."

The chancellor puts the mirror away and closes the drawer. He looks squarely at Niles. "Tell Beetle I said you can have a copy of John Buie's will. Satisfy yourself, Counselor, by all means. Then let's leave it be and we can all go home. There's no need to make a federal case of it, hear?"

"Yes, sir." Niles opens the door, stepping aside, and Cordeman strides confidently through, his black silk robe rustling softly as he passes.

24

Niles finds the documents at seven P.M. on Monday before the trial begins Wednesday and Charley was right in suspecting Mall's intent. He had cut Mrs. Blaylock's hardwoods on purpose. Hardy's records were not obvious but almost so, once they are grouped in the proper way, a story, really, from beginning of his contract to Alabama Wood to the ending of the fall of the Blaylock oaks. AlWood's contract is standard for the industry, promising a certain sum to be paid to Mall for wood and his reciprocal promise guaranteeing delivery by the dates listed in the contract, pine pulpwood the most of it, and subsequent receipts and deposit slips verify his delivery on the dates specified and payments received in turn. By the date he began cutting near the Blaylock place, he had supplied everything he was obliged to except for one parcel—three hundred hardwood logs needed by Alabama Wood for hardwood pulp, the kind necessary to make fine paper, and Hardy had promised the logs at the lower pulpwood price, but he hadn't found a cheap source. The day he cut Mrs. Blaylock's hardwoods, he had one more week before the contractual penalty of $4,500 would be imposed. Two days later, Alabama Wood verified receipt of the hardwood and Hardy recorded the payment deposited. "Q.E.D.," Niles says, tapping the papers together.

He puts copies of the key documents on Charley's desk with a note: "You were right. Have fun."

Forty-three cases, in alphabetical order, are included on the active file list and Niles scans the entire number, then begins again at the top with the Barrett case. The plaintiff has another week to appeal and, in the meantime, he only needs to wait. He pencils a check to the left of the entry. *Blaylock versus Mall* is next and he lines through it. His part is complete. "Margaret Cape" follows Blaylock and Niles hesitates. The chancellor has told him he will deny the Petition to Appoint Conservator and that gives Niles no further role to play. Officer of the court? That is what he told Cordeman and it is true each lawyer bears that duty to aid the court in its dispensation of justice, but doing what, how much, is never settled. Busybody, Charley would say. He places a question mark to the left of the file and places the list to one side. It is probably better to begin with the day's mail anyway.

Niles frowns at the first letter on the stack, the form from Bayou Glen the director called him about on Friday. Buddy has not eaten more than a glass of milk and mashed potatoes for ten days and they want permission to force-feed him, a tube directly to his stomach. Niles had stopped in to see him, this morning before breakfast, to make another try, coming in the back door and walking, unnoticed, unseen to Buddy's room, where Buddy lay sleeping faceup in his bed, a neat rectangle beneath the thin spread, his colostomy hanging on a steel hook at the end of the bed and Niles knew a catheter hung, unseen, on the opposite corner. One more tube in him and he will resemble nothing so much as a bagpipe.

Niles stares at the form, complete except for his signature, then turns the papers upside down and places them to his left, deciding that he will stop by Bayou Glen again in the morning, then decide. The next letter is a survey from the American Bar Association and, relieved, Niles takes twenty minutes to pencil in bullets beside his firm's size, his primary areas of practice, and areas that he would like to see addressed by the ABA, and, thirty-five questions later, thirty-five decisions made, he is in a rhythm and sorts through the rest of the mail quickly, reading and responding to fourteen letters, leaving the drafts in Delores's directory for her to address and print, outlining a pretrial order for the Desoto Bank case. When he finishes, it is ten o'clock and he has checked every entry on the list, except the one—Margaret Cape.

He has seen John Buie's will and he had the same as promised Cordeman that would be the end of it. It was an unusually succinct document, barely more than one page, sufficient to renounce any previous wills, establish the testamentary capacity of the maker, and to leave "all of which I may die possessed" to his sons, per stirpes. Cape Plantation was not mentioned by name, allowing it to pass under the general language of the will, which would apply as much to a brass candlestick as five thousand acres of land, not the usual custom, the will of a planter being a rarely missed opportunity to speak and control from the grave. The court, therefore, had not been required to make any judgment regarding the ownership of Cape Plantation, and his pleasure at finding that had revealed his true motives to himself.

Niles lays down the pencil and takes his fountain pen from the drawer. Someone tampered with Big John Cape's will. He feels sure of it and sure that Rosamond supplied a righteous reason for it. Whatever that reason was, however, it will not do. Buddy taught him that without meaning to and he pushes down the anger, the wondering ever after how much of what he wore, ate, was, had come from Buddy's illegal acts; the knowing that, no matter, he was bound to be purer than Caesar's wife or have it said, "Like father, like son." But, it is the same whatever way he decides, isn't it—Rosamond's way, the law's way? He wants no adjudication, no res judicata to stand in the way when he finds the true will of Big John and the true owner of Cape, except that he will not do any such thing because Charley is right. He has no standing under the law, no role. It is none of his business. Margaret is not his client and, too, she is so sickly and near death that it would be a kindness to let her be and let Cape pass into the maw of Hardy Mall unchallenged. He uncaps the pen and brings its tip squarely to the paper and draws a thick, black stroke through the name of Margaret Cape and, to the side, a note to Delores: "Strip file, close." He is all the way to the Bronco in the city lot, placing the key in the door to open it, before he turns back. He does not bother with the lights but takes the stairs swiftly and retrieves the list from his tray, folding it in thirds and stuffing it into the pocket of his jacket. If there is a reason for doing so, he cannot think what it is.

25

"Miz Cape real sick," Albert had said Monday. He met Dr. Taylor on the way out, Albert on his way in to give Sam his weekly check.

"What do you mean?" Little Mildred asked him and he said, "I don't know, but everyone had their sad face on and I says to old Sam, 'What's happenin'?' and he wouldn't say much, so I know it has to be."

She has been doing some thinking in the three days since, a lot of thinking about the situation with Margaret. It is a relief, in a way, to be thinking of her again. Until that day twenty-seven years ago, she had needed to think about her every day. And, then, suddenly, she had not thought of her for all these years. Until now. She has been thinking, of course, what would be best for everyone, including Margaret. Margaret is at the end of her life as she herself is, although Margaret is evidently quite ill, whereas she is still well and serving as the chair of the Garden Club Historical Committee and hosting the Baptist Fellowship Meeting today week. In any event, Margaret's interests are, for that reason, only a small part of the equation.

It has been difficult staying away from Cape House all these years, the home where she grew to young womanhood, where her parents—Big John and Big Mildred—had hosted parties and dinners and people who knew how to be gracious and comforting. But her thinking has brought her to the conclusion that she needs to go there and to have a little talk with Margaret.

Albert drives her, taking the car around the side of the post when they come to the locked gate. "I have to do that every time I come," he says. "Who they scared's goin' to get them?" She walks through the front door into the wide hall, not seeing the devastation in the Front Hall or other rooms, but she smells the must and she sees the peeling paint on the large columns on the front steps. Thankfully, Sam must be gone—how often did he leave Margaret alone? You can't always rely on even the good ones. She makes her way to the back hall and the bedroom, because it seems Margaret was always in the bedroom, appropriately enough, and yes, that is where she is today.

Margaret hears the tap of Mildred's cane and her footsteps without knowing who is coming and there is enough time to hide the brandy decanter under the pillow. She places the snifter under the covers alongside her leg for support. When Little Mildred enters the room, she does not knock and takes a chair beside the bed, Margaret recognizes her immediately and a new memory comes at the same time—Chapin Finley's voice and Mildred's, too, in the hall outside this very room and they are discussing her, saying she was mad and a drunk but, thank the Lord, it seemed no one knew.

"Margaret, dear, how are you doing?" Mildred asks pleasantly as she lowers into the chair. "God, you look awful!"

"I'm very tired."

"Well, I don't wonder that you are. All that's happened these last few weeks. Chappy's dreadful, dreadful accident." Mildred pauses and looks at Margaret for a few beats of time. "And, all this other unfortunate business."

Margaret turns toward Mildred, spilling the brandy so that her knee presses into a warm moist area of the sheet. "Business?" she says.

"You know. Your conservator. I've met him, of course, and tried to set him on the right path, but it is never well to let these matters get outside the family. And, well, Mr. Mall."

"Yes," Margaret says, no more than that, and rolls back into the pillow once more, turning her head to the side-yard window. Mildred is pleased that Margaret seems so tractable. It is not that she ever had contradicted Mildred openly or argued or said much at all. It was the opposite, really, the passivity, the silent passivity, that can be as stinging as a slap in the face the way Margaret is, or was. Perhaps age or illness or her weakening mind have brought her to this better state and, if so, there is something to say for being mad.

"Margaret, do you remember Mimsy Sneed?"

"I don't think so."

"Well, you wouldn't, I guess. She was such a lovely person. A Webster from Greenville. She married Harvey Sneed, Mr. Sneed's son, lived in that house around the corner from Frank and me?"

Margaret shakes her head.

"It started after Harvey died. Just dropped dead of a heart attack when he was only fifty-four. His daddy did the same thing. Well, next thing we knew Mimsy was wearing dinner napkins on her head. Only her mother's linen, of course. Still, it was odd." Mildred pauses while Margaret pushes herself up in the bed, resting back against the large, square pillows.

"At first, she would just go around the house and yard, you know, but it got worse. Her poor children. Julia was in the garden club with me. What was there to say? They did everything they could but nothing stopped her. Do you need some help, Margaret?"

Margaret shakes her head no, closing her eyes. She needs to say something. "How awful for them." Yes, that is it. Margaret smiles, pleased she remembers.

"One day she married her second cousin from Mobile and

moved away, just leaving her family to face everyone by themselves. I guess she's still there." Little Mildred stands and traces the perimeter of the room, stopping to inspect the photographs on the far wall, shaking her head at the Egyptian panel. She comes to the foot of the bed and looks at Margaret. "We've become old girls, haven't we?" she says and Margaret opens her eyes and returns her look, amused. "It seems it was only yesterday that we were turning heads. Yes! You do know that Junior Tierney went into a near swoon every time you came into a room?" Alarm cuts through Margaret's body although she remembers nothing to explain it. "What's the matter, dear? Is it your heart?" Mildred says, and Margaret sighs and nods. "And I attracted my own share. Yes. Not the sort like Junior, all full of those male feelings, but the more refined, thoughtful man. I always suspected our Pastor Davis of having some wayward thoughts in my direction." Mildred sighs as well and they are silent together for some time. Margaret feels a certain familiarity in this conversation, with Mildred speaking of such an unlikely subject as men's sexual attraction toward them both. She often had done this when they were alone. She told Margaret about other men's advances or her own husband's performance in bed. Once she had claimed that she had conceived a son because Frank had been overcome with jealousy over attention she received at a football party in Oxford and when they had returned home had made love to her with unusual vigor. "It's well substantiated that the closer a man spills his seed to a woman's ovaries, the more likely it is she will conceive a son." Margaret supposes that her telling such things to Margaret is a kind of disrespect, something she would not repeat to the genteel and proper sensibilities of other Rosamond matrons, but what can it matter being repeated to a Yankee whore?

"I am so grateful to have my son, Frank Jr.," Mildred says as if she had been thinking Margaret's thoughts with her. "When I think about your sons being gone—such fine boys—

and leaving you with no children, no grandchildren, I am so sorry."

The words freeze in Margaret's consciousness. "Children? Grandchildren?" The young Mr. Abbott had asked her that although it was not one of the lines on the list. "Inventory" was the next she had tried to act upon and still must and, then, "Land?—how much." Still, she wonders what it can mean for Mildred to mention words so close to what had been said by him. She sits up and leans toward the foot of the bed, so that she can see Mildred's face better when she asks. "Children? Grandchildren?"

"Oh, Margaret. I am so sorry to have brought it up at all. Please try to put the past out of your mind." Mildred falters at this last unfortunate phrase. "Let's talk about the present." Margaret lies back on the pillow, wishing Mildred would leave so she can have something more to drink but Mildred sits in the chair again and talks over her for more than an hour, telling her gossip no more than a few weeks old and concerning persons whose names she recognizes and many more that she does not until Margaret thinks the rapid feeding of names will trigger more memories than she can hold but, strangely, Mildred's voice, what she says, is like a memory but in three dimensions, whose realness shuts out the possibility of others.

At last, Mildred hoists herself from the chair and takes a step away from the bed as if she were preparing to leave. Instead, she moves toward the end of the bed and around its corner toward the side yard windows. "I always loved this room. When I was quite small, I would come here in the early morning to Mother and Daddy's room and it was so beautiful then, all chintz covers on the bed and beautiful rose wallcovering and swag drapes and I remember she kept the most wonderful assortment of colored perfume bottles on her dressing table. When I came into this room, it was as if I were walking into my own future because I always wanted to be as good and beautiful and fine as my mother was."

Mildred stares out the window for some time. She is bent over and seems shorter to Margaret, who remembers her as a tall, imposing woman with a military bearing. She turns and walks toward the door, stopping halfway through, as if she has only just thought of what she is about to say. "You know, Mother gave us the most valuable lessons in living our lives decently and to the glory of God. She always said it was false pride to put oneself before God. That God put us here with His plan for us and our only duty was to follow His rules for our lives. If you didn't do that, you might as well be nothing at all or, worse, you were a hindrance and a burden to those around you who were doing their best to do what they should. If you follow God's law, she said, His order and plan unfold right before you. She was such a lady. She knew how to handle her help and that is becoming a lost art, I assure you. They all loved her, but she wasn't too familiar with them. She kept herself a proper distance. And, she had all the social graces. 'A lady knows when to leave,' she said, and it's true, Margaret." Her silence makes Margaret open her eyes meeting Mildred's steely gaze. "You and I can agree on that, if nothing else, can't we?" she says sweetly, and Margaret smiles and nods.

"Doctor said Miz Marg'ret can't have visitation." Sam's deep voice makes Little Mildred jerk back and she turns stiffly to see him behind her.

"Sam," she says in two syllables. "How very nice to see you. Is that a new shirt you're wearing?" Frank III had called her Monday with the news Sam had cashed all of her checks. At least that part seems settled.

"No, ma'am. It ain't," he says coldly and his eyes daringly meet Little Mildred's. She is unaccustomed to looking at the gold-brown of African eyes and it is she who looks down, unclasping her purse, then closing it again.

"Well, Margaret, I need to go on anyway. No rest for the wicked." She pushes past Sam without saying more, and he follows her to the front door and holds it open until she is through.

Margaret listens to the footsteps away from the bedroom, waiting until the front door scrapes shut before she dares extricate the brandy decanter and the empty snifter by her leg. She tries to fill the snifter but is too weak to lift the decanter over the glass with one hand. She puts the glass down and takes the decanter in both hands and lifts it to her lips, letting a generous swig of brandy pass through. It burns her throat and she coughs, but at the same time a gentle warmth spreads through her body and she lies back into the soft pillows and closes her eyes to sleep. There is much to consider in what Mildred has said and, still, Margaret knows that she is at a disadvantage just now since she is "under the brandy," as Sam says. Mildred advised her to die—that was it, wasn't it?—but how can she do that short of suicide and her Catholic upbringing makes that thought unpleasant although not determinative. She is going to die before long without her own doing. The way she knows that interests her and she remembers her mother's last illness and how she had fussed over her, trying to avoid any acknowledgment of her precarious state. Anne Finley had laughed at her, which surprised Margaret, because her mother was something of a vain woman and Margaret would never have guessed she had accepted that literally every person comes to an end of her life. Yet her mother laughed and, immediately contrite, said, "I don't want you to hurt, Margaret, or to be alone. I'm sorry for that. But this is what God wills for me." Margaret smiles to remember her own mother had spoken of God's will to her, as well. She said that death was not the fearsome thing to her that it might be to those younger, whose time was not ripe. "It is the advantage of living to one's old age. One is ready...and willing."

Is she herself willing? Is that what Mildred intended to advise, to be willing, to let go of living so death could enter? Her father, the doctor, saw many deaths and he and her mother argued sometimes because he said that his patients could control their living or dying for months even years and her mother thought that heresy. She will need to think it through and, yet, it is already a good thing, Mildred's coming. It reminds her that her time is growing short. She has followed the list only one step and the second, "Inventory," is still waiting.

Cape Plantation, 1965 🔊 "Wear this," he said and she took the dress, mossy green velvet, fit narrowly to the waist, with tapering sleeves and a dirndl skirt. Three crystal dome buttons were spaced down the front of the blouse and she wore an ivory silk slip beneath so that, the color was still right at the closest to her, next to her skin. It was not Christmas, only December 22, but it was Sunday. "The Cape family always has Christmas on the Sabbath," Little Mildred explained every year the twenty-fifth failed to fall on Sunday. John Buie had bought the dress the day before, when the tepid gray Delta winter had unexpectedly turned frigid, and he had given himself wholly to the occasion. This morning they wakened and snowflakes were falling, the courtyard already more white than brown. "Do you remember the last time it snowed on Christmas, Margaret? Buie was knee-high to a pup and we still had Ella. She cooked up everything she knew—oyster casserole, creamed potatoes, those flat, folded rolls she made. The Tierneys and their kids came over. Chocolate chess pie. Remember?" Margaret nodded, wondering that his spirit had lifted so far, and, for his childish enthusiasm, smiled a little.

"Let's go get the tree!" He roared through the house and up the stairs like the winter wind itself and banged on his sons' bedroom doors. It was early, eight o'clock perhaps, and Buie and Chapin Finley sluggishly complied with their father's re-peated urgings to "hurry up, the day's wasting." At last, the three of them descended the stairs, all dressed wrong for the venture, wearing deck shoes with cotton socks and khaki pants, their gloves and tweed or corduroy blazers the only accommodation to the snow. John Buie motioned for them to follow him into the winter but Buie paused at the door, and looked back to her where she was standing at the turn in the hall.

"He means to go to the pasture and chop a cedar."

"I know he does," she said and saw something in Buie's expression that troubled her, a sadness she thought, but she shrugged and let him go. She wasn't up to fighting for the life of a tree. They were gone nearly an hour before the three of them came, snowy and cold, bearing a ten-foot cedar and their snow tracks wet the foyer to the chapel, where John Buie flung back the door with one hand while holding the tip of the tree in the other. He was red-faced and too cheery, as if he had been drinking, although Margaret knew he had not.

"Jesus H. Christ, it is fuckin' cold out there!" John Buie exclaimed, as he set the tree on the altar, pressing it into the tub of wet sand, turning it this way and that until the view from straight on was symmetrical. "There. Alright, tree trimmers, it's all yours. I've got to clean up," he said in the same peremptory voice he used with the field hands and left Margaret and their sons in the chapel, bustling past them to more important business.

"Let's do it differently this year," Buie said, and Chapin Finley looked at him, suspicious.

"How do you mean?"

"I don't know, just different." He regarded the tree, still green and full from living. "It's dead, isn't it? We could display it as a kind of sacrifice in reference to the sacrificial role of the Christ child. Quit pretending we didn't chop it down and kill it, just lay it down on its side and drape some memorial decorations over it."

Chapin Finley glared at his brother. "You think 'cause you're a big college man now, over there at Ole Miss, you can talk blasphemy? You better not let Daddy hear you talkin' that way."

Buie laughed and patted his little brother's arm. "I'm just funnin' you, old man. Why don't you do the whole thing? You've got a talent for it," and Buie walked the aisle to the door, where Margaret had stood watching them. He winked at her and smiled, but she saw the dark look again and it was not his own sadness as she had thought before, but more a knowing of a sadness that can never be consoled.

Chapin Finley did have a talent for decorating the tree and when he had finished, the tree was barely visible beneath the weight of tinsel, antique wood icons, and enormous, blown-glass balls in red and blue and green and clear, reflecting the glittering lights he had carefully woven inside the tree itself, so that it seemed the center was afire. "Good Lord!" Little Mildred said when she saw it, and directed Frank Jr. and Frank III and Sara Cape to place the presents around the base.

John Buie presided over dinner with the assurance of a Caesar. "Thanks for bringin' Lily B. to help Sam, Mildred. He does alright for the few of us, but he's pretty basic."

"Lily B.'d be hurt if we didn't eat her cookin' on Christmas. Frank Jr. brags on her, you'd think someone gave her a million dollars."

"Boys, I ever tell you about the General's cook, nursemaided Daddy's mother and Daddy, too?"

"No, sir, I don't recall it," Chapin Finley replied.

"Name was Cho Cho. That was what she called herself. Daddy said she picked that to sound theatrical, exotic, show she wasn't just a field nigger. She raised up Kathryn, that was your great-grandmother, and she was gettin' on to seventy when Daddy came along and she took care of him, too."

"Did she take care of the General, too?"

John Buie paused, roll wrapped around a piece of ham, and stared at Buie. "She took care of our entire family. Just like a member of the family. That was what they didn't understand. They come down here and say 'free the slaves,' 'free the slaves.' And, 'course, we know that was just a ruse to come bust up the economy so they wouldn't have competition, but let's say that was the real reason, what do they do about it? I'll tell you what they did. They shoot and kill a lot of decent folk, black and white, and then they go back up North and declare everything is fine. Well, hell . . . excuse me, Mildred . . . what about Cho Cho and the rest of 'em? They didn't have anyplace to go, nothin' to do, and they already had these close, family relationships with their white people. What about that?"

Sam entered the dining room from the kitchen door carrying a silver basket filled with new rolls. He set it on the sideboard and removed the used basket from the table, then moved slowly around the table, clockwise from John Buie, so that each person was offered a hot roll.

"Are you still enjoying Ole Miss, Buie?" Frank Jr. introduced the new topic of conversation.

"Yes, sir. Thank you."

"What year are you now?"

"I just finished first semester as a sophomore, sir. I'll be a three-semester junior next term."

There were approving murmurs around the table. "Will there be anything else, Mr. John?" Sam bent close to John Buie's shoulder, looking out toward the table and not in his eyes.

"No, Sam. Tell Lily B. the food is delicious. You, too. I know you had a hand."

"Yes, sir. Thank you, sir," he said and was gone back to the kitchen.

"Buie, let me ask you something I've been wondering."

Buie read something in his aunt's voice and put down his knife and fork and waited. "Yes, ma'am?"

"Have you noticed any sort of decline since the change?"

"What change is that, Mildred?"

"Letting the coloreds in. It's been, what, three years now and I was wondering whether they've been able to keep up standards."

"Well, I'm not sure I'm the best one to ask about that."

"You don't have any of them in your classes or your dormitory?"

Sam pushed open the door carrying a silver pitcher, sweating from its icy contents and quietly moved from place to place refilling the glasses.

"Frank, I hear the Tierneys are buying a beach house down on the coast. Did they finance through you?"

"No. I think he went in some partnership or group that's getting financed out of Gulfport or Pascagoula."

"Sam, bring in the Grand Marnier and the liqueur glasses before we have our dessert." Sam nodded and hurried back to the kitchen. When he returned, he took the necessary number of glasses from the tantalus set on the butler's tray and distributed them around the table, then went around a second time to pour the Grand Marnier into each glass.

John Buie stood and raised the glass toward the others. "Moments like this put me in mind of how fortunate we are to be a part of this family and the honor and responsibility we each bear as Capes. I toast my sister, Mildred, and her fine family, my two boys, and my lovely bride, Margaret."

When he was seated, Buie stood halfway up, pausing as if to decide, then stood all the way and raised his glass. "Thank you, Father. I have a toast as well." The faces around the table looked at him expectantly, their gold skin polished bright. "I toast the newest Cape. My wife. The beautiful Caraly."

"I'M GONE," SAM says and gives last instructions to her to stay in bed and rest. He leaves her early lunch on a tray, water and a glass on the nightstand. "I be back by darkfall." She lies awake and looks out the windows to the side yard. There is a little breeze blowing the Japanese birch, its leaves still clinging. The front door slams shut and she counts his steps to the car, two, three and the metal hinge squeaks when he opens the Buick's door and again as it closes. She sits on the edge of the bed and takes the pill bottle from the nightstand before she even stands, holding it in one hand. This time she knows how careful to be.

She has hours. Sam will not return soon, so she sits for rest at the bottom of the stairs before climbing even one and, then, again each two steps. The risers are close when she sits among them and the damages from Chapin Finley's fall, fresh. Sam had finally told her, she persisting until he explained the cause of Chapin Finley's death. His resistance was puzzling but when he said, "He fell down the stairs, ma'am, broke his neck," she *had* felt strange, very close to wishing she did not know and, here, sitting on the stairs, slowly climbing them, she cannot put him from her mind. It is as if he is still on these stairs with her and the thought paralyzes her for minutes that he was the cause of her earlier mishap although she knows it was only her heart, only that.

Chapin Finley's room is to the right of the stairs that enter in the center of the upstairs hall. She can see his door above the floor from the twelfth step and is relieved that it is shut tight, a shadow line beneath, no light. Still, she moves to the other edge of the steps and holds to the left banister until she reaches the upstairs hall. It has taken her more than two hours.

There are six bedrooms, three along each side of the hall, and a large bathroom at the end. Buie's room is on the east side of the hall, the same as his brother's but at the far end, and the paneled cypress door is swollen, but it is not locked. It is a long narrow room with a closet on the right wall just before the bay window at the far end to overlook the side yard and, inside, the light is startling after the dimness of the stairs and hallway. Along the north wall, she walks toward more windows, but these viewing Cape fields and the pasture to the east. When she built the chapel after Big John's death, before she married John Buie, she had considered putting the chapel in this room but anticipated correctly that the stairs would be an unacceptable obstacle in her later years and decided against it and, when Buie was six, he chose the room—his father's room as a child—for his own.

Now, no one lives here. It is a deserted city of boxes, those occupying the center of the room, set side by side and askew, some low and long, others much taller. Several Jitney Jungle sacks sit gathered in a corner, papers layered to their tops, next to them more boxes, stuffed full, then closed and bound with twine. The bedroom furniture is still here, but along the perimeter, barely seen. Margaret follows a narrow trail to the flat-topped steamer trunk pushed against the north windows. She sits on it, staring at the collection of cardboard containers and lets the sun's warmth sink deep. She picks up a shoe box sitting on the floor at her feet and dusts the lid with her hand, reluctant to look further, then sets the box down, replacing it carefully in its dust print, and looks for a better place to begin. He didn't live here when he died and his room is different because of that. Perhaps that is why she remembers that detail while being unable to recall anything else about his death. He is dead and he didn't live here when he died. That is all she knows. What will these things help with that? They are what he left behind, things not most dear or he would have taken them along when he went away, where? A mahogany and satinwood bowfront chest stands on the wall to the left of the windows, closest to the corner and she decides, for no reason, that she will begin there. She pulls out the bottom drawer and it is filled with soft folds of unmatched material, next to a rattan box and a pair of scissors. She opens the box, its top spread in two hinged doors, and inside are papers stuck with needles and a small satin pincushion laden with straight pins. Other accoutrements of sewing are jumbled together—a tiny brass thimble, strands of many colors of thread, bias tape, the like. Margaret studies the drawer and its contents, puzzled. These are not Buie's things at all. They belong to whom? Unlike Anne Finley, her mother, Margaret had not been skilled with needle and thread. She had never sewn decoratively and any mending was left to servants. Ella! These were hers and, in a rush of memory, Margaret sees Ella sitting in a room, not this one, and small children pulling at her sleeve or the hem of her dress that she kept pulling down again over her knees. There were Negro children, Ella's own, and a white boy and another. Ella is dead, too, and before Buie so how had her sewing things come to be here? Perhaps she herself had placed them here when Buie left or Sam might have done it. She can't remember or doesn't know.

The next two drawers tell her that the chest was emptied when Buie left, then filled with what was taken from other closets, other places to make more room. Still, they contain things that were his, neatly folded shirts and pants in progressive sizes, following his own growth from a child of two or three until he was more than ten. Chapin Finley was a larger child from the start, big and barrel-chested. Buie was fifteen before he outsized his younger brother, growing almost four inches in one year and his shoulders were broad but rangy, unlike Chapin Finley. He had not become a man. Margaret pushes the drawer shut. He is dead. She acknowledges the fact almost as a single, declarative sentence, without context or meaning and it is, perhaps, not wise to think too long on the reason for that.

The top drawer is heavier than the others and she stares down at yellow boxes and green canvas strips without comprehending until she remembers—Buie's hunting clothes. The ammunition is in the boxes and dull green metal cases, beside a round tin of waterproof matches, camouflage waders, and a shirt and khaki vest. Duck hunting. He had hunted only when John Buie had encouraged him to go along on the early morning forays or to the Rosamond Duck Camp, where Junior Tierney had a lodge. He had left the clothes behind and, so, perhaps he had been telling the truth when he said he didn't care for it when they were sitting on the step together, just outside the kitchen porch, and the night was clear and Buie leaned against the railing. She could see his eyes, kind eyes but oblivious to the dangers she saw and that had worried her for him and, then...It was too much, out of control. Margaret presses her fingers to her eyes to force the memories away, to slow them. She has only felt a painful edge on entering the room, an edge that has widened and deepened until she is in profound agony, undirected and unspecified. "Inventory" the list had said and she had seized upon it as a means to come here, to revisit this pain that she does not even remember beyond its name.

The boxes seem larger than a few moments before and she twists through them as if moving among party guests, trying not to jostle any one of them unnecessarily. She floats her hands over them as she walks, hoping for some feeling from something there to draw her to one rather than another but they are only boxes. She opens the narrow, closet door and pulls the string, but the light is burned out. She ruffles the winter jackets hanging from the rod, catching her breath when she sees that one is John Buie's uniform from the war. The closet extends into the dark each side and she leans into it looking one way, then the other. A reflection of something light is at one end and she steps toward it. It is almost suspended in the black, difficult to see. She leans closer and is only inches away before she recognizes the form. A face! Her heart pumps in rapid beats and she backs out of the closet and into the room, through the boxes, roughly bumping against them until she is at the opposite wall. She puts the little pill beneath her tongue and edges along the north wall. Her heart jumps again when she passes the cheval mirror and she shakes her head. Such fear at nothing things. The bed is at the corner, undressed and covered with shallow boxes of papers. She pushes them away until there is enough room to lie down. When she does, she is careful to turn away from this room, from everything, and faces the wall to sleep.

When she wakens, it is late afternoon and the brightness is

faded. Sam will be coming home soon, but she is certain what to do and walks back along the north wall to the dresser. She retrieves the matches from Buie's hunting clothes and moves easily through the boxes toward the closet, stepping inside and to the left, still in darkness. She braces her arm against the wall and comes to her knees. She strikes a match and it fires at once, making a soft glow around it and to the end wall, not so far as she thought and, there, yes, it is a face. She holds the light for as long as the burning flame permits, looking at the familiar eyes, the hand draped gently across the horse's neck, and he looks back at her, too, the painted face of the gallant General John Buie Cape.

26

Margaret sits down to breakfast at the end of the table on the kitchen porch. Sam has placed a single straw mat there, with an ironstone plate, its gold trim rubbed nearly through, and what appears to be restaurant silver. What has become of the sterling? She remembers the pattern because she and Big John selected it in Paris. Tiffany. Audubon. He serves her meal already on the plate—sliced tomatoes from his summer garden, probably the last, a coddled egg with a spoonful of pickle relish and a half-slice of white bread toast. She eats slowly, alone. Sam eats the same meal in the kitchen, coming in every ten minutes or so to see if she needs anything. She can hear his radio playing, still the Greenwood blues, and she looks through the windows to the lightening fields as she eats. Last night she was able to see across half the section of rows, the pallets of harvested cotton scattered across them. This morning the fog has not yet burned off and she sees only the near rows and, beyond, the shapeless, black bush of the shelterbelt. "Land?—how much." That is what the list says.

She has never known anything much of the cropland and it is all cropland except for the pasture. Big John had told her once that Cape Plantation contained thousands of acres—she recalls that much. When John Buie was alive, he farmed the

same land and managed the gin—inexplicably, a shiver runs
through her—and after his death, she supposes, Chapin Finley
did the same, but there is no longer an opportunity to discover
that. She was in her "dead years" all that time and when she
awakened, he was already dead forever. She stares harder
through the windows to the black fields beyond. Small squares
of light shine in random patterns at the far reaches of the cotton
field, where shotgun shacks are still used by the field workers.
She has seen them in the fields for days, starting to harvest the
cotton, the beetlelike pickers moving slowly through the field,
plucking the bolls and spinning them into the teeth of the
cylinders.

Sam steps down the bowed wooden steps from the kitchen
onto the porch and she turns with the creaking.

"Sam?"

"Yes'm. You need somethin'?"

"Who is working the fields?"

"These ones 'round the house?"

"Yes, those."

"Yes'm. It Walter Threadrum's crew from cross the river to
Helena. Custom crew."

"Why are they working here?"

"I never knew nothing. Mr. Chappy the only one knew 'bout
it and I reckon they the same mens here last year."

Margaret places her chin in her hand the way she did as a
girl and it is strangely comforting. "Do you know how much
there is?"

"Cape land, Miz Marg'ret? They's a good bit onct, but it
ain't got nothin' to do with us now. I told you what Mr. Niles
say. Mr. Hardy got it."

"Yes. I remember." She can remember more, and more
quickly, than when she first wakened. If she brings a picture
to her mind's eye and waits, it begins to move and change into
new memories. Each time she tries, it becomes easier than the
time before and she is less concerned that it will whirl away

out of control. She tries to think of all she can remember about Cape land. The pasture. She always comes back to that and, strangely so, since it is only eighty acres out of thousands and altogether different than the rest. It is a high place, the only one in sight on the plantation and she took the children there. She can almost see the three of them—she, Buie, and a little girl—who? Oh, yes, Ella's Caraly—and they move together along the narrow path, the sharp points of field grass pricking their legs, but at the rise just before the pond, the memory suddenly stops and she does not try for anything more.

Sometimes Big John took her for a ride around the fields, down the side roads and turn rows while he spoke of a particular farm and when it had been acquired. Cape Plantation was unusual in that it was almost all connected, he said, an almost fan-shaped conglomeration of farms that Big John still referred to by their given names—Shaw Farm, Bayou Farm, Black Bear Farm—because they were acquired that way. She rarely left the truck although they often stopped, pulling into an access drive and Big John walked up and down the rows of cotton or, sometimes, soybeans, stopping to inspect a particular plant while she rested her chin on her hands out the window and watched him. He talked the entire time, never stopping to give her space to say anything if she wanted, which she did not. It was if he had things to say, to tell her and there was little time to do so. What had he said? She pushes herself to recall but different thoughts, contradicting thoughts, compete for her attention and she is confused until she begins to hear their different voices and knows that one voice is Big John and the other, John Buie Cape. Big John speaks of the land in spiritual, romantic terms. "The land creates us and sustains us, not the other way. People're always gettin' that backward. And after several generations in the same family, growin' one family the way it does, there is an exchange between the people and the land that creates a sacred bond between land and family that shouldn't be broken. That's why we're so careful to carry the land through Cape blood, you see." John Buie's perception is different. "Land is the measure of a man's worth. You can crow all you want, but you ain't got a barnyard, who gives a shit?"

"I carried the picture down like you said. Last night." Sam spoke from behind her and she nodded. "You want me to get some hangers, put it up in the bedroom there?"

"No. You put it by the door to the side yard?"

"Yes'm."

"That's fine. Leave it there, please." She knows that is where it is, has already placed her hands on it twice since he brought it, but she cannot reveal its importance, fears for it and hides it. She is dumbstruck in the General's presence in the same way as when she had first seen the painting. And reassured, therefore, that she is moving toward her story. John Buie had tried to hide the painting away, keep it from her, if she remembers correctly, although no reason for his act has come to her. Her confidence is rebounded and she will have Sam take her to the pasture after all, but in a day or two, perhaps. After she has spent the time she needs with the General.

Cape Plantation, 1966 John Buie was calm, acquiescent even, in the months after Christmas, when he had crushed the liqueur glass into the palm of his hand at Buie's announcement. Margaret watched him warily, but his acts bespoke only a strange indifference to his older son marrying a Negro girl. Indeed, he drew Buie closer to him, speaking to him of the responsibilities of a married man, persuading him to give him the documentation of marriage, the license and a certificate, for "preservation with the family's important papers" and to keep his marriage secret for a time "for Caraly's own safety." It was 1966 and the danger was not exaggerated. She watched, waited, unable to read what he was thinking and her apprehension grew. "I think Buie needs to go on and leave school, get started learning what he has to know to farm," John Buie said over breakfast and she said, "It's only a year more," but John Buie shrugged and lit a cigarette.

Buie started work at the Cape Gin in January and John Buie moved his things to Buie's room and slept there every night. It disturbed her to be shut out of her son's room but it was also a relief to Margaret, who nevertheless found it unsettling to be alone at night, listening to the noises of every sort both inside and out of the house, and she began to drink more than before to quiet them, to dull her senses to sleep.

John Buie gave Buie and Caraly the use of the house on Black Bear Farm, the farthest from Cape House, it was true, but it was also the largest of the farmhouses and removed from nearby shacks so that the secret could be kept. "Anybody asks, they won't, but if they do, she's your maid, helpin' with your laundry and cookin'," John Buie advised his son and, for once, encouraged Margaret to spend the time she pleased with Buie and, sometimes, he was there when she visited but, mostly, she kept Caraly company.

"If she lived, Mama wouldn't like it any more than Mr. John or the others, I know. And, I tried to push Buie from my heart at first, but he told me it was foolishness. 'Caraly, life is lonely enough without pushing away people you love and who love you,' he said and, I don't know." It *was* lonely where they sat on the back porch of Black Bear House, looking to the furrows of the barren fields surrounding them. There was one clump of willows just in sight, in a low place. They sat on the railing, each leaning against a supporting post. "Buie say—*says*—he'll bring us some rockers soon," and Margaret looked away toward the willows. John Buie would not allow Buie to select furniture from the warehouse. "Capes only do that when they marry or are fixin' to marry. We don't want anyone talkin' now, do we?"

In February Caraly stayed at the house and Buie attended the Planter's Ball with Margaret and John Buie. "I can't keep this up any longer, sir," Buie told his father in May. "Sooner or later, people need to know and I'll just have to take the consequences." "What about the consequences for Caraly?" John Buie asked. "I'll make certain she's protected," Buie said firmly and he could not be convinced this time. The time had come. It was May 1966.

NILES SITS ON the first bench behind the bar of the court, his corduroy coat buttoned against the air-conditioning that makes Clarksdale's cavernous courtroom too cold for the transitional weather of October. He is alone in the long walnut pews, but a dozen or more spectators gather in the unlit corner at the front wall, sitting in folding chairs or standing near the clerk's table. They are courthouse employees and a couple of younger lawyers from the district—Christine Butler waves at him—and he knows they come because they want to hear Charles Brandon argue Mrs. Blaylock's case. The lawyers hope to see something of Charley's they can use in their own cases, but the others are there for the pleasure of it, just to see excellence, some reassurance in the midst of days and weeks of lesser lawyers and their awkward struggling for mere competence.

Charley salutes and winks when he sees Niles, then leans forward again over the counsel's table, his lips moving in silent rehearsal, stopping only for occasional notes. Old Mrs. Blaylock sits beside him and stares at the door on the front wall that leads to the judge's chambers, waiting with the others for the chancellor to return from lunch. Her left arm is in a sling. She fell over the weekend and sprained her wrist. "God. Sometimes I can be one damn lucky dog, you know it?" Charley exulted after she called to tell him of her injury and it is true that the contrast between her and Hardy Mall is startling. Niles has never seen Mall this close, close enough to see the half-moon of damp khaki along the collar of the poplin jacket next to his stout neck, his bulky frame overflowing the government supply captain's chair and forcing his knees apart. Next to him, Vernon

Pettis, a small, dark brown man with wire-rimmed glasses—
referred to as "Ghandi" behind his back—is no more than a
pipe-cleaner man.

Charley is the first up, standing when he hears the doorknob
to the judge's chambers turn and a moment before the bailiff
says, "All rise." Chancellor Dewitt Cordeman appears in black
robe, climbing four steps to take the high bench and the others
in the courtroom stand then, too. "Is the plaintiff ready to argue?" he asks, looking at Charley who says, "Plaintiff is ready,
Your Honor." The chancellor nods and Charley steps smoothly
from behind the table and to the lectern. He lays the legal pad
of notes on top, then rests his hands on either side. "May it
please the court," Charley begins and the chancellor, pleased,
says, "You may proceed, Mr. Brandon."

"There's only one question in this case, Judge, and that's did
he do it on purpose? Hardy Mall admits he's the one that took
Mrs. Blaylock's trees, cut 'em down and hauled 'em away and
sold 'em for profit. 'It was a mistake,' he says." Charley steps
away from the lectern and crosses to stand before the defendant's table. He looks at Mall, who sits, head cocked to the
side, a smile curling the corners of his mouth. "Now, Your
Honor, I was prepared to believe Mr. Mall, here, and let him
pay my lady fair value for what he took. Oh, and a little penalty, too, for being so careless as to go on someone else's property and kill their trees. A man can make mistakes. I'd be the
first one to say that was true." Charley's arms are outstretched
in forgiveness, Jesus embracing the sinner. "But, Judge, when
I went to the scene of the crime, so to speak..."

Pettis is on his feet. "Your Honor, I'm going to have to object
to that now. This is not a criminal proceeding and Mr. Brandon
has no evidence of any criminal wrongdoing by my client."

Charley drops his long arms and rolls his head in an amused,
sidelong look at Pettis, but he does not respond. He returns to
the lectern and leans comfortably against it while the chancellor
addresses the objection.

"Mr. Pettis, I don't think Mr. Brandon meant to impugn your client in any way. It wasn't meant serious."

"Judge, whether or not he meant it seriously, it is prejudicial to Mr. Mall to have his acts described in the record with words appropriate only to a police action."

Cordeman frowns. "Now, now. Just hold on a minute. There's no jury in this court to be prejudiced. You're not saying, are you, that the court itself will be influenced into some ir-rational thinking by Mr. Brandon's oratory?"

"Well, no, not that, Your Honor." Pettis steps back, uncer-tain. "I just wanted to make a point for the record."

"No one asked for the court reporter for final argument. Is that right, Mr. Brandon?"

"Plaintiff made no request, Your Honor."

"Did Defendant make a request the court has overlooked, Mr. Pettis?"

"No, sir. I understand that a record could be made if we needed one, and we all signed it or something, I'd have to research it."

Cordeman waves his hand in dismissal. "Let the court say this and I think this is all that needs be said. The court is well aware of the rules of evidence and the rules of procedure and, in listening to argument by both counsel for plaintiff and coun-sel for defendant, the court will apply those rules automatically to eliminate any irrelevant, prejudicial, or inflammatory re-marks. Without the need for interruptions to object. That's one of the benefits of the chancery court, where the chancellor sits as both judge and fact finder. Streamlines the process, you see?" Pettis nods and sits down. Charley waits for Cordeman's nod before continuing.

"As I was saying, Your Honor, in the very beginning, I was prepared to forgive an innocent mistake and accept restitution for my client. Then, I went to see the scene of the . . . civil tort. Something wasn't right, Judge. Let me show you what I mean." Charley walks to the easel and turns over the large poster board. On it is sketched an engineer's survey of Mall's property and Mrs. Blaylock's property, outlining the area of trees cut. "You see how Mr. Mall cut his trees on his property all in a group, looks like a big rectangle almost. But instead of keeping going with the rectangle when he got to my lady's land, he skipped up here and took a patch connected just by the corner. Now, if he had kept going with his rectangle, he would have cut Mrs. Blaylock's pine trees. By doing what he did, he got all hardwoods. I know he said that was because they stopped the one place on Wednesday and made a mistake where to start on Thursday, but I just wondered whether there might be a more logical explanation."

Niles looks at Mall for some reaction, but he sits stone-faced, the increasing dark stain on his collar the only indication of concern. In the two days of trial preceding, Charley had asked him to identify documents including the ones Niles discovered, had introduced the documents into evidence, but had not confronted Mall with the conclusion drawn from them. "Why should I do that? Give him a chance to explain? The papers speak for themselves. They're in evidence and I'll spring what they mean in final argument." Mall shifts in his seat, looks at Pettis, who purses his lips and writes notes on a piece of paper.

"You're saying Mr. Mall was in a tight 'cause he needed hardwood pulp to meet his contract with Alabama Wood and he used your lady's trees to help himself out?"

"Your Honor states it better than I could. That's it to the letter."

Pettis gives a decent argument but he is hampered by his own intelligence. It is clear to everyone in the courtroom, including Pettis, what the documents mean. "The practice of law would be near perfect without the damn clients," Charley says and, watching Pettis struggle to defend an unworthy Mall, Niles sees his point. Still, it is a delicious moment when the arguments have ended and lawyers and spectators alike sit unnaturally silent awaiting the chancellor's decision. Quite properly, Cordeman leans back in his chair and looks down, reviewing notes of the trial, and he is the very picture of judicial discretion. No matter. The predicate is laid for a mighty verdict against Hardy Mall and Niles imagines escalating damages and punitive damages as the minutes pass. It is nearly ten minutes before the chancellor moves forward over the bench, resting robed elbows in front, and he is going to speak.

"Why don't you take some time and see if y'all can resolve this," he says. "If you can't, then I'll take it under advisement." With no further comment, Cordeman rises and steps down four steps from the bench and around the corner into the hall that leads to his chambers. Niles watches Charley, who rises slowly and buttons his jacket then gives a half wave, half salute to the bailiff before turning toward the pews, his face fixed in a smile. He pushes through the low swinging doors at the bar and stands over Niles.

"Can you believe that lowlife motherfucker doesn't have the balls to stick Hardy?" He is still smiling, nodding at passersby—"Good job, Charley," they all say—but whispering his fury to Niles.

"What are you going to do? Try to settle?"

Charley shrugs. "That's what Dewitt wants—takes him off the hook—and if I don't go along, I'll pay down the line." His face brightens. "Maybe I can get Pettis and Hardy to be the bad guys."

"I really wish we could talk sense on this like the judge says," Charley says, returning through the swinging gates and approaching Pettis and Mall with his body loose, nonconfrontational. "It's about to worry my little lady to death."

Mall's eyes narrow at Charley, but Charley looks only to Pettis, as if Hardy is invisible. "What kind of numbers were you thinking of, Mr. Brandon?" Pettis, as always, is formal, correct.

"My lady is too good, I know you can see that." Niles remains seated, watching the exchange. He and Charley have discussed the value of the case often enough, the hardwoods worth $35,000 in sawlogs, with treble damages under the statute, $105,000. The likelihood Cordeman would impose punitive damages, Charley had thought, was more than half, but he would only impose them as a fine, not by taking a measure of Mall's substantial worth as the law required. Charley figured $10,000–$25,000 as an optimistic view of punitives, raising the value to $130,000.

"She is willing to settle for $335,000, plus court costs, of course."

Niles raises his hand to camouflage his smile at this ploy, an unreasonably high demand that will make Pettis and Mall the obstructionists when they refuse it, but Pettis does not answer at once, turning back to Mall to confer.

Niles looks at Charley, who has seated himself on the corner of counsel's table and is chewing his thumbnail, a sign of his concern at having misread the situation. Certainly, he expected a laugh, an attempt to cast his offer in a bad light, not the seriousness with which the two had taken his suggestion. Pettis turns and—another surprise—smiles. "Mr. Mall is not prepared, of course, to pay your client $335,000," he says and even Niles hears Charley's sigh of relief. To have his first offer accepted, especially an inflated one, would have been certain proof he does not understand something important. But Pettis continues. "Unless, that is, you can do something else in addition to dismissing this suit."

"What little favor might that be, Mr. Pettis?"

"We understand that a client of your firm, Mrs. Margaret Cape, has raised some question concerning the ownership of Cape Plantation, which belongs under law to Mr. Mall. He would like to have those questions withdrawn."

"Just that?"

Mall gives Pettis a nudge. "Well, yes. He would require, of course, some written acknowledgment of the withdrawal. Execution of an appropriate quitclaim deed, duly authorized by the court. He has tried to convey this to Mrs. Cape before, but has been unable to reach her. Perhaps a courtesy stipend to Mrs. Cape for the inconvenience. I'm certain the chancellor would agree if we all were in agreement."

"I can't imagine there would be any problem, if the property does in fact belong to Mr. Mall," he says, talking slowly while he thinks. "I'll have to talk to Niles Abbott. Mrs. Cape is his responsibility. The chancellor would have to give his approval, of course." All three men look at Niles, who manages a poker face although he is as stunned as Charley by this offer and by its implication—that Cordeman had told them Niles was questioning ownership.

"Of course," Pettis says, politely, and Charley nods a curt nod, pushing the last stack of papers into his wide briefcase. He presses his thigh against the low swinging gates and walks toward the tall double doors at the far side of the courtroom. Niles rises and falls in behind him, almost colliding into Charley's back when he stops short of the door. Charley presses the top of his head against it, slapping the wood with the flat of his palm and Pettis and Mall turn to look.

"The casinos want it. That's it, isn't it, Hardy?" Charley is gleeful when the expression on their faces confirm his conclusion. "Hoo, hoo! God Almighty, you've still got it, Charley," he says, winking at Niles and laughing with satisfaction as he opens the courtroom door with a flourish and passes through.

CHARLEY DIRECTS NILES to his office and closes the door. His face is flushed and he is giddy. He grabs Niles by both shoulders, pulling him close as if he were about to embrace him. "Do you remember the Simpsons selling that bottomland above Clarksdale?"

"To the Lucky Seven?"

"Right. They had fifty acres or so, but right on the river,

and they went to meet with the casino lawyer to negotiate a deal. We'll ask him for big money, they thought, three million, maybe take two. You know what they ended up gettin'?"

Niles shakes his head. His shoulders hurt from Charley's vise grip. "Three million?" he guesses and Charley erupts in laughter, finally releasing him.

"Hell, no! Three million? *Three* million? Try twenty-five million dollars. See, the casino's lawyer sits down and before they can say anything, he says real official, 'We've looked at this closely and my client is unwilling to give any more than twenty million dollars,' and ol' Duross Capp—that was the Simpsons' lawyer—very wisely takes the Simpsons into the hall before they faint and they come back in and say, 'We really need to have twenty-five,' and the casino guy says, 'OK.'"

Niles stares at the older lawyer, not comprehending. Charley stares, too, but into the middle distance. "Know what, old man?" he says. "If the casinos want Cape—which we know they do—and if there's funny business with the will—which we know there is—then, you and I, buddy boy, are in high cotton."

PART FOUR

27

Little Mildred taps a Salem cigarette from the full pack and lights it, drawing the first puff deep to fill her lungs, careful to keep the lit cigarette held high and above her ear, the way they were instructed in Chi Omega. So. No one objects to Hardy Mall, all agree he owns Cape Plantation. So. He will sell Cape Plantation to the casinos or lease it for forty years, or whatever they do. For millions of dollars, maybe ten million, Niles Abbott said. Hardy Mall. She knows him, of him, anyway. He is a young man, maybe fifty-five, and from Tallahatchie County, out from town. He is not anyone, but he has become a reason to finally decide what she should do.

She watches Albert gather the hoses in the backyard. It has taken her three years to train him to keep watering the shrubs into October, even November to protect them from damage from the cold when it comes. He is coming straight up the slope, pulling the long loops of rubber hose behind him and she keeps her eye on those until she is certain he will not snag and break the low branches of her azaleas. Purely accidental that he doesn't, of course, they can't keep their mind on their business for a minute. Still, she is fortunate to have him. He is better than most. Little Mildred pushes up out of the chair. Her hip feels better with a little walking and she moves around the perimeter of the sunroom, pausing to fluff a pillow on the sofa, to straighten a print, but it is no use. The thought presses into her consciousness anyway. Oh, well, what is the good of lying to oneself at this age? It is this matter of Sam that worries her mind and suppose Niles Abbott told Sam about the casinos, too? The prospect of such money might be what it takes to shake loose the damning secret, if he has one—it makes her heart flutter just to almost think it. Perhaps it will be her heart that takes her, she thinks.

"Can I do somethin' else, Miz Melton?" Albert speaks through the screen door. "You need me to get the lights on? Mighty dark in here. You don't want to fall now."

"Did you take Sam his check today?"

"Yes, ma'am, I sure did."

"Has he asked anything about it, said anything?"

"No, ma'am."

"He never said, 'What is this for?'—something of that nature?"

Albert frowns. She has recited Sam's exact words the first check he got and he wonders whether he is being tested. "Well, now you say that, I do remember him saying that, something like that, but maybe just the one time."

"What did you tell him?"

He is certain now that she is testing him, but she cannot know what he said to Sam, otherwise she would have thrown him down already. "Nothin', really. Maybe 'For your expenses,' you know, something like that," he lies.

"Alright. Good night, Albert," she says and Albert, much relieved, quickly departs.

Sam has cashed the checks, has said nothing, but she is uncertain whether that assures there is nothing to say. There is nothing specific she can call to mind but that is exactly what alerts her, the nothing where there should be something. The girl just disappeared so very suddenly after everything and it was only a month more before Sara Cape's wedding. She had so much to do to think of everything. After the wedding, she and Frank Jr. had departed for several weeks in Europe with the Harrises and it just left her mind. There seemed no need to go borrowing trouble, anyway, and she had let it be.

It is different now. If Cape Plantation is to be recovered, if she decides to take the risk, the pot will have to be stirred and that is always likely to bring up what is on the bottom. The will has to be found or it is no matter anyway. She cannot believe that John Buie destroyed it although she advised him then to do exactly that, but it is not in any of the boxes Albert packed home from the Compton Building. She has searched through them paper by paper. There is one other place but she would have thought it too risky. Still, she saw him once put a letter from one of his women there and, so, he might have done the same with the will, tucked it between the brown paper and the canvas bearing the image of their illustrious ancestor, General John Buie Cape.

Cape Plantation, 1966 🐦 She was just finished dressing and stepped into the back hall on her way to the kitchen porch, where Sam would bring her iced tea and she could read while the porch was still cool. May had already brought the sticky heat of summer and she pinned her hair off her neck, securing it while she walked, so she did not notice him until he spoke, but he was already there, waiting it seemed, at the dark end of the hall. "Buie fell. Off one of the rafters at the gin," John Buie said and it caught her unaware, a sharp and sudden blow taking her breath away. "He's dead, so get a suit jacket and shirt and tie together and I'll have Sam take it all to the funeral home."

He stayed where he was, in the shadows at the turn of the hall, and she stopped, too, a room away. They silently regarded one another, their arms hanging straight to their sides, but she saw his fingers working and came closer to him, slowly, slowly until she saw the details of his face, too, his eyes, intense blue

eyes, and they were so strange to her that she knew she had
not looked at them for a long time before. "He fell," she repeated, and he sighed and looked away.

"Broke his neck. He just stepped wrong. It was an accident,
Margaret." His words were gentle and smooth and there was
nothing in them, but he looked back too soon and his eyes were
flickering, burning with feral excitement, and she saw them
and she knew.

"What happens to yesterday?" Buie asked her when he was
seven, startling her with the same question she had once asked
and she gave him her father's answer, "It's here with us, just
beneath today, holding it in place," but it satisfied him as little
as it had her. "No, it's not," he said firmly and left her for
hours before coming back. "It *is* here," he said then, in resignation. "But different, so we can't ever find it again."

"Get up! Don't be a stupid fool!" John Buie said angrily,
grasping her elbows hard and she saw she was next to him,
her hands clenching the khaki cloth of his shirt and one of the
pockets was torn. "You're the last one needs to be carrying on.
Wasn't for you, Buie'd be with us doing the things he should.
You're the one got him off track."

She nodded, uncurling her fingers, holding her palms up in
a gesture of submission and he released her but she quickly
stepped back, turning sharply to run through the kitchen porch
and out the door to the pasture road. John Buie shouted after
her but she would not hear his words. She thought of nothing
but the road and its gravel surface, the odd-shaped quartz
pebbles and, once through the fence, only the fresh mounds of
green grass left over from spring rains. Patches of red sedum
were blooming on either side of the cow path that led to the
pond and she stooped to examine their clustered flowers as she
would have on any day and to listen, but the ducks were quiet.
The commotion of mating season and its occasional violence
was done. It was time for nesting.

She topped the small hill and the pond was in full view.

Between, John Buie's Hereford cattle grazed on both sides of the path. There were week-old, white-faced calves and the bull watched her warily as she walked, uncaring, through the herd. She had protected Buie's life, cared only for his life, and it had been so for such a time that she no longer remembered what might threaten her own. It seemed unfitting, in fact, to still be here, walking anywhere at all, as if she were an actor in a play whose curtain had come down while she remained on the apron of the stage in error. She stopped in the path, thinking she heard someone behind her but it was only the ground under-foot echoing her labored gasps for breath. The bull snuffled and moved one foreleg, widening his stance, and she forced herself to move along the path, down to the pond and away from the spring calves. Faint ripples curved to the left across the brown water and she traced them back to their center, three mallard drakes dunking and resurfacing beneath a native pine fallen into the far corner of the pond. The pine's shallow roots still fed it and green needles clung to the smaller branches and twigs, shading a bream bed beneath, where the ducks disturbed the hatch. Margaret walked slowly along the bank, idly looking for the mottled-brown hens on their nests, as she had once looked with Buie and Caraly, but she saw none.

She moved toward the corner where the ducks fed and, one by one, the drakes preened for her, raising their chests from the water's surface, flashing their iridescent violets and greens, then swam slowly toward the center of the pond. The pine extended fifteen feet or more into the water and she stepped onto its root end and balanced herself as she walked along the tree, shaking above the water, braced by unseen branches speared into the mud below. She had almost reached the cluster at the tree's top when a peculiar motion drew her to a stout branch curving upward a few inches above the water and she cried out, losing her balance and startling the male ducks who lifted from the water in a flurry of wings and flew to the far bank. She steadied herself and bent to see better the soft brown creature that surprised her, a mallard hen in a swaying crouch, its speckled feathers blended with the red-brown bark of the tree and only an arm's length away. It did not move and she saw that it could not, its head barely supported by tiny vertebrae and dry, torn muscle exposed to view, the neck pecked clean of skin and feathers by the males in their ceaseless competition to recreate themselves. The hen's eyes looked like black holes and Margaret thought they had been pecked out as well until she stepped closer and saw that the holes were masses of black Delta mosquitos pressing around the sticky, glazed eyes, feeding through their thin membranes to blood-filled capillaries. The hen lived, yes, but only that, nothing more, stripped of all future possibilities save her own death and even that was outside her in its way, something that would come when it pleased and not by the creature's will.

Margaret reached toward the duck, her movement on the log suddenly fluid, surefooted as a cat's, every part of her unified in the single act of capture. The soft, brown feathers were motionless, the hen waiting, waiting and when Margaret grasped her, she felt a faint shudder, no more, and the duck's head hung limply against her forearm, its plump breast pressed against her ribs. She turned slowly and retraced her steps along the tree until she was on the bank again and listening for minutes to a distant baying as it became a loud, keening wail and she realized it was her own cry.

She walked along the bank, holding the warm hen against her, her tears ruffling its downy back. She searched the ground as she walked, stopping where the bank widened into a circle below the half bluff and the white oak, but the dirt was too fine, silty from the tread of the cattle herd and its rolling. She took the cow path up the incline to the tree, but the cattle came there for shade and the dirt was the same. She turned and started for the house, looking until she found what she sought and knelt in the path, placing the hen gently in the dust and holding her back with one hand, taking up in the other a sharp-edged fieldstone, pinkish brown and as large as two fists. She turned the stone until the sharpest edge faced out and brought it down hard on the last thread of the duck's neck, but the neck pressed into the dirt without severing and the firm, warm body wriggled, and Margaret raised the stone again and seven times more, crying louder with the increasing force of her strokes, the cattle wild-eyed and restless, bawling back at her bawl. At last, the duck's head lay separate and pressed into the sedum's dense roots at the edge of the path and she released stiff fingers from the body, sitting back on her calves until the sobbing stopped and her breathing slowed.

MARGARET SITS ON the smooth, red leather in the center of the backseat while Sam drives the Buick over the gravel road to the barbed-wire gate. He removes the twisted loop from the top of the gatepost at the same time he lifts the post out of the bottom wire.

The sage grass is high and brown and the late October rain and leftover summer heat have bent the shorter fescue into a soft, dense cover so that it hides the ground beneath and the car shakes as it hits unseen bumps and gullies. The pasture's terrain resembles the hill country northeast of Rosamond and stands out from the flat expanses with stunted trees that mark the surrounding Delta. It is, in fact, the highest point for forty miles in any direction, an enormous eighty-acre hump, shaped like a turtle's back and once suspected of being an Indian mound filled with sacred corpses. That thought was left behind some time ago, for a reason Margaret does not know, perhaps inconvenience more than inevidence, yet the land has been left alone and never tilled. At the pasture's center is the pond, sitting below a half bluff that is taller than a man with the large white oak above and it is to that particular place that she asks Sam to drive.

The wood ducks she saw before are on the water and feeding at the banks but, always shy, they fly off with the approach of the car while the more trustful mallards—two drakes and their three hens—stay. Sam opens the back door to the car and offers his hand to her and she lets him pull her up, feet extended first in court flats, unsuitable to the circumstances but whose graceful lines, nevertheless, complement her slender ankles. "Watch where you step, ma'am. It's kinda tricky."

She moves slowly toward the edge of the bluff, and on the water, the mallards move a like distance away, less friendly than when she brought the children each day to feed them. She reaches the oak and places her hand on its ridged bark. Sam leans against the Buick's front fender, half sitting there, as if that old habit were last followed only the week before and not many years ago when, even then, she was not certain why she came, a New Englander to whom this barren piece of Delta wilderness provoked neither aesthetic feeling nor some pleasant nostalgia for the discoveries of childhood. The children, yes, that could be a reason, their breathless astonishment at the most ordinary things, but it was not. Big John had known, had told her why he came. He came to this remarkable rise above the surrounding flat fields because here he could survey the enormous expanse of Cape and "breathe in history."

"The river had it first, then the Choctaws, but ever since, nobody 'cept Capes," Big John said, looking out over his land, his eyes moist for only a moment before he turned to her in mischief. "And, the tree hangers. Have I told you about those, little darlin'?" She shook her head, laughing as he put stout arms around her and lifted her in one brisk motion away from the oak. "I think I saw one just now. A long ol' rat snake hangin' down from that branch over there. He'd love a little warm bird like you for dinner. You're goin' to have to be more careful, muffin. Keep a look out."

Margaret steps closer to the edge of the bluff and onto the cattle trail worn there. She follows its silty path until it begins a sharp descent toward the pond, then stops to see, if she can, what it is that again draws her to this place. She stares across the pond's metal-brown water and over the sage, taking a wider stance to steady her legs, already weakening from the walk. Below the untenanted pasture she can see the rosy brick of Cape House, empty, too, although around it the flat fields are filled with cotton in bloom, killed brown and awaiting harvest. And the dust. Dust is the signpost of people. Dust in the field, a field hand on the green tractor. Dust on the road. She sees the dark car slowing near the pasture's edge. She looks down to her feet and gently kicks at the trail, making her own small cloud of dust, which springs up for a moment, then slowly settles back on the smooth leather toes of her shoes.

"Miz Margaret? You doin' alright?" Sam steps toward her and stops.

"I won't be here long," she tells him and waves him back to the car.

Otherwise, there is only the sky, mostly the sky, a huge, blue-gray void always there behind the sometimes haze of humidity and mosquito spray. Nothing else remains that was ever here before. The Choctaws. The General. The horses and, then, the cattle. Big John. The children. The ducks are different than before and, too, every blade of grass and weed stalk. The oak tree has lived a long life but disease or age will claim it or, before then, lightning. Cape House. She almost laughs aloud, catching herself so that Sam will not come rushing to her. It will outlast her own life but the false suggestions of permanency inherent in every architectural contrivance do not mislead her. If any of history remains, she does not see it nor can she feel it as Big John had. It is the opposite for her, she realizes, not remembrance but expectancy, as if she were in a friend's parlor, kindly waiting for the other to speak, certain she would hear the words shortly. Here, though, no one has spoken for a very long time.

Margaret turns to retrace her path to the car. Sam watches, but lets her make her own way. So, that is it. There is nothing here for her, no reason to come. Only the one thing remains, the same rising expectation. She feels it clearly and, then, a relic—a fleeting intimation of utter confidence in her course and, as quickly, the feeling is gone. She stops, surprised, and looks back toward the pond. There is a memory here after all. She had felt that confidence here, in this place. She does not recall the circumstances, still, she is certain that it was the very last time she knew such sureness in her course, the last her path was clearly marked.

A movement of dark and light draws her attention to the water. "Something new, Sam," she calls out and Sam steps through the deep grass to where she stands on the bluff, pointing to the pond's north bank. A long-legged gray bird, black over white marking its watchful eyes, stands frozen, waiting for prey in the shallow waters at its feet.

"Look at that!" he says. "A big ol' blue heron. I guess he must've got lost."

"From Enid Lake?"

"Oh, no, ma'am. See, he probably heard about the catfish farms north and took a wrong turn. He best know it 'n move on. 'Less he eat shiners, he gonna starve here." Sam steps partway down the bank, searching in the sand. "Here," he says and picks up a rock the size of his fist.

"No!" Margaret whispers and falls to her knees. Sam reaches her in two steps. The bird flaps long wings rapidly and rises from the water, turning to the north at the same time. Margaret watches the disappearing gray, its thin, black legs trailing underneath. The thoughts crowd in and she is still dizzy. She opens her mouth, as if to speak, but she is silent and points to the rock in Sam's hand.

"Look there." Sam drops the rock, his voice solemn now, almost dark, and she turns to see his face and follow his gaze down the hill toward Cape House. The dark car emerges from the pecans and pulls sideways to the front of the house. She stares at it until Sam grasps her shoulders and turns her away. "Here. Let me help you, ma'am. Hold there on my arm." He nudges her firmly toward the car, where she slides onto the backseat, spent from the morning's effort. She closes her eyes, resting her head against the soft leather, and Sam rolls the window down perhaps two inches, then shuts the door and gets in front to start the car.

"It her again" is all he says.

28

Sam drives the Buick through the pasture gate, not stopping to close it. No cattle to watch for anymore, just a habit. At the kitchen porch door, he helps Margaret out of the car, then up the concrete steps into the house. Something has happened, she is so quiet, more so than usual. Little Mildred is already in the house, he can hear the rasp of her shuffling walk, the tap of the cane from the foyer. "Margaret? Is that you?" she calls, but he ignores her voice until he is certain Margaret is seated on the bed and safe.

"Miz Mildred? I comin'. Just a minute," he calls out in a pleasant voice.

"Sam. Where is Miss Margaret?"

"She restin' in her room. I don't think she up to a visit today, ma'am."

Little Mildred pushes past him into the back hall, peering in the kitchen, then along the hall to the kitchen porch. "Have you had any visits from anyone? That lawyer, Abbott?"

"No, ma'am. Can I help you with somethin', Miz Mildred?"

"Are the bedrooms open upstairs?"

"Yes, ma'am. Maybe you tell me what you lookin' for, I can get it."

Mildred hesitates, then sighs. "Yes. Why not? Do you recall

the painting that hung in the Front Hall many years ago? It was a soldier by his horse."

"Yes, ma'am. General Cape's picture it were."

Little Mildred seems surprised. "That's right. Where is it stored? I would like to take a look at it."

Sam goes to get the painting. He does not try to think through what is motivating Little Mildred's strange request, that is not his habit. He understands the request and he acts. He leaves Mildred in the hall and enters Margaret's bedroom, certain she will already be sleeping, but she is not. She sits where he left her and his heart grabs to see her in the same position, the same as she did before this waking. "Miz Marg'ret?" he whispers, but she does not move. He will come back to her later, get Miz Mildred what she wants and gone and then come back. He goes to the corner of the room, the little alcove out of which the side yard door opens, and he looks for the painting, but it is gone. Maybe he sat it someplace else. He looks around the walls. He is getting old and his memory fails him now and then, still he can see himself putting the painting, it was heavy, against this wall and when he looks at the wall again, he sees the gold mark from the gilt frame. "Miz Marg'ret, where the General's picture?" he asks her but she does not turn her head.

"Well?" Little Mildred asks him when he returns to the hall.

"I thought I knew where it were, but it's not there. I'll just have to look around some more."

"Have you looked upstairs? I don't think it was left in the bedroom."

Sam hesitates. "Well, I did see it up in Mr. Buie's room the other day, but Miss Marg'ret, she asked me to bring it down and I did, but it's not where I sat it at."

"Let me see her," Mildred demands and pushes past him into the open door of the bedroom. "Margaret, where is that painting? It belongs to the Cape family." She turns back to Sam. "What's wrong with her?"

"I don't know, ma'am. She just now got this way."

"Oh, good Lord. What next?" Little Mildred scans the perimeter of the room and the closet and bathroom. "Has anyone been here that might take it or she might give it to?"

"No, ma'am. Mr. Mall tryin' to get in awhile back but he ain't been back far as I know."

Sam looks in each of the upstairs bedrooms and each of the downstairs rooms while Little Mildred waits with Margaret in the bedroom. When he cannot find any sign of the painting, they walk together to the barn office. Little Mildred is heartened that, although the painting is not there, a desk and two filing cabinets filled with papers are. Perhaps, the will is in one of those instead.

"Keep looking for the painting, Sam. I'll have these papers fetched so I can sort through them."

He holds the front door for her and watches Albert drive her away—boldly going 'round the post at the locked gate in the same manner they had come in—then returns quickly to the bedroom. Margaret sits motionless on the edge of the bed and he leans close to her face, touching her shoulders and rocking her gently. "Miz Marg'ret, why you doin' this? Don't go away again. Please don't do it."

Cape Plantation, 1966 🙥 When Margaret returned from the pasture, John Buie was standing in the Front Hall near Junior Tierney next to the mantel. Little Mildred sat across with Frank III and Sara Cape. She stood back from the door, but Sara Love saw her and came to her arms outstretched. "My poor Margaret. I am so sorry, dear," she said, her arms encircling the smaller woman and the scent of Youth Dew strong in her hair when she pressed her cheek against Margaret's, then held her out by her shoulders to look at her with sad eyes. "Oh, my God! Margaret! Your dress, the blood!"

"Please excuse me," Margaret said, by rote. "I'm going to bed now."

"Of course you are! That's exactly what you should do. I don't know how you've managed to stay on your feet this long. I don't. Junior? I'm seein' Margaret to the bedroom. Fix me somethin' while I'm gone, would you, darlin'?"

She had waited until Sara Love softly closed the door, leaving for the Front Hall and, then, she made her way to the stairs and stepping on the edge of the risers for silence, climbed them and crossed to Buie's room. It was an hour or more before she heard his step on the stairway. "Margaret? Are you up here?" His voice was thick with drink and, for a moment, she doubted what she knew and thought, perhaps, he suffered with her and she was not as alone as it seemed. She stepped from the room into the upstairs hall and she saw the shadow of his head and shoulders as he neared the top of the stairs. She walked toward him, coming closer, until she was in the splash light of the foyer. "Margaret, is that you?" he said—he had said that so many times before—and she thought that she might speak to him, tell him, but how was that possible in this seamless path of pure action? She heard sound coming from her lips but it was low and guttural and there were no words. He stopped on the top step, holding the corner post to steady himself, then came all the way to the hall floor and stood facing her. She raised Buie's duck gun, a Winchester 12-gauge his father gave him on his twelfth birthday, and held the shotgun with both hands, her finger on the trigger and the gunstock braced on her thigh. John Buie's head jerked back when he saw what she had and his mouth opened as if to speak or to laugh but his eyes met hers and whatever he thought to say was lost. They stood there, eyes fixed each on the other's, and Margaret felt his touch on her soul and wondered at the pleasure such touching brought even when it was malevolent. He knew without her saying, without her moving, and he took the step back himself and again, and as his balance gave way, she saw his face contort without hearing the scream or anything at all until he was at the bottom and the crack of his neck and the softer

"oomph" of his collapsing chest rose up to her. Sam was suddenly there, bounding up the stairs and he took the gun from
her, carrying it back to Buie's room, and he removed the un-
used shell, putting the gun on its rack and the shell in the box,
then led her by the hand down the stairs and murmured soft
words. He nudged her away from John Buie's body sprawled
across the landing, but she turned and stepped across him, her
heel pressing his chest down so that a last sigh escaped.

THEY ARE SEATED in Charley's office. "Charley will be a little
late," Niles tells Mildred Melton and Frank Morgan Jr., who
occupy the blue club chairs. Niles has taken Charley's chair for
the meeting. "You understand I have no standing in this matter
at this point, nor do you," Niles says to them. "Judge Cordeman
has told me he doesn't plan to appoint me conservator of Mrs.
Cape on Friday. I'm not her lawyer. I have no role at all. I
only passed along Charley's information as a courtesy."

"He won't appoint you if the land belongs to Hardy?" Morgan is a slender, tall man with sheer, white skin and silky blond
hair. He is always moving and, now, he writes as he talks
although Niles can think of nothing said that needs notation.

"Right. The plantation, apparently, was the motivation for
the court's initial interest and, with that gone, the court has
decided a conservatorship is unnecessary." Niles's and Morgan's
faces are mirrors of their professional detachment, reasoned
analysis, demonstrating each to the other his grasp of the circumstances. Little Mildred shifts in her chair, grimacing from
the pain in her left hip, but says nothing.

"Frankly, absent new facts, some unknown aspect"—Niles
chooses his words carefully—"I don't know what else the court
can do." Little Mildred looks impatiently at Morgan, who continues to write, his long, thin arm hanging loosely over the chair
arm to balance.

"If there were something," Morgan says, "could we get some

extra time to develop that information, get the necessary papers together? Today is Wednesday and the hearing, Friday."

"I don't know, Frank. It would largely depend on the nature of the information. And, as I said, I really have no role here. I'm not the conservator. I don't represent Mrs. Cape. In fact, like I told you, now that Charley's client has a financial interest contingent on what happens to Cape Plantation, I may have a conflict of interest. At the very least, I would have to disclose all of this information fully to the court, should the chancellor change his mind and decide to appoint me conservator after all." Niles stops. They don't care. He is arguing with himself, trying to convince himself of what he already believes. He is not anyone in this matter and he need not do anything, no matter how much Mildred Melton or Frank Morgan Jr. or even Charley demands it. He had agreed to pass on the information, not seeing the harm in it—just see what comes up on the trotline, Charley said—supposing that it *was* somehow a proper courtesy, but then Morgan had called him Tuesday morning to set up this afternoon's meeting. Now Morgan tries to conduct himself as if they are indifferent, but the act spoke for itself and they have no reason even to think he may be interested. They do not know he has seen the files, seen the wills. And, so what if he has? He is not in a position to do anything.

Little Mildred's breathing is raspy and noticeable in the silence. She studies Niles, his face impassive, but he fiddles his fingers, snaps the edge of one thumbnail against another and she sees that he knows enough already. So. The only question is what he will do when told. She is not concerned for herself, being this old, and Frank Morgan Sr. is retired, playing golf and cards at the Greenville Country Club. What would be the point? No, it is the younger ones—Frank III, Sara Cape, and the grandchildren—they need protecting against the talk, the sudden assumptions of superiority by the others as if they were all descended from saints, as if they never cheated for less noble reasons. But he is Buddy Abbott's son and there is the other, too. He has feelings for Margaret—the woman has the devil in her!—and, like Big John and John Buie, it is a weakness.

"Tell him about the will, Frank." She ignores Morgan's shift forward in the chair. "We have a bit of a problem, Mr. Abbott. There is information as you say, but we don't have it."

Niles feels his heartbeat come stronger. He covers his mouth with the side of his hand in a contemplative gesture. He looks to Morgan and raises his eyebrows in the unspoken question and Morgan sighs.

"What Aunt Mildred—Mrs. Melton—refers to, well you have to understand that when Big John was alive, he must have written a hundred wills. He liked to write them himself, mostly, write them all out by hand."

"Holographic wills."

"Precisely. It got so it was hard to keep up with them or that's what Daddy always told me. This was before either of our times. He just always had some new idea, you see, he wanted to put in the will."

Little Mildred interrupts. "One thing never changed. He always wanted Cape to stay in the family, with Cape blood. There was never any question about that."

"When he married Margaret, he made another will. He had some idea that the two of them were going to have children. He wanted it all set up so the children would get their fair share and Margaret was so young, too, he wanted her cared for properly. Well, he wasn't deaf and dumb and he saw the possibilities for a fuss, so he went to Robert Sanders to draft something that would stand up. But they didn't have children and he died very suddenly."

Niles is impatient for the confession, but he is careful. "I'm not certain I see how this will help Mrs. Cape. Anyway, as I mentioned before..."

"You are not her lawyer," Little Mildred sarcastically finishes his sentence. "Cape land belongs to Capes, Mr. Abbott." She has moved forward in her chair and her fervor is such that it is intrusive ten feet away. He pushes his chair away from the desk, retreating to the window. "That's what Daddy wanted, what he always intended, don't you see? When he made that will he had no intention of giving away Cape Plantation outside the blood. He wanted to see that she had a roof over her head and she always has, despite everything. They didn't have children and that was mostly the point of even having the new will. The way it was written, Margaret was given some special life estate that tied up the land completely during her lifetime and some of the income, though mostly it was divided out among the children."

"So, you decided not to use it."

"Frank's father was our attorney and John Buie was back for the funeral. He was a bombardier in Italy. That was 1945 and they had already occupied the country, of course, although the Germans were still a problem, as I recall, and he flew bombing missions into Germany from Italy so many times right on into the next year, I think. Do you remember, Frank? No, you couldn't. Southern boys won that war, you know. So... well, the three of us discussed what Daddy would have wanted—John Buie was named executor—and we did exactly that."

They had substituted the wills, of course, not all of one for another, but the middle portion. Fortuitously, Big John had another Robert Sanders will and it had been so easy. Niles does not look at Morgan when his father's part is revealed, afraid he will see his own emotions played there. When John Buie was discharged in the spring, he sealed the deal with his marriage to Margaret. She would be cared for, but Cape stayed with the Capes. Except, now, it would be better, it turns out, if Margaret did own the property or have the life interest Big John had wanted to bequeath to her. If that were so, Chapin Finley's quitclaims to Hardy would amount to transfers of nothing at all. "I know John Buie kept the pages, although I told him to destroy them and he said he would. He always kept everything, but I've looked and I can't find them."

Niles blows out his cheeks and buries his face in his hands, weary of the pretense of detachment. The will had been tampered with—he was right—but there is nothing to replace it. "Where have you looked?"

"The warehouse, Cape House. Even the old barn office. He slipped things all sorts of places. I even checked under sofa cushions and behind the paintings. Of course, Chappy sold some things, so I suppose they could be lost forever."

"You're certain your father doesn't have the pages?" Niles asks Morgan.

"No. I asked him. You have to understand, he felt like he was doing the best thing for the family, Niles. Big John wanted Cape to stay with Capes, just take care of Margaret and what he wanted was done."

Niles recognizes the familiar argument. "Only now it seems that the only chance of keeping Cape with Capes is if you had done what he said to do in his will."

"There is no way anyone could know all of this would happen then," Morgan protests.

That's why it's best to follow the law; we don't know enough, he thinks but says, "Exactly."

"I've already researched the issue pretty well and there's nothing that limits bringing in a new will after another is probated. But, the fact remains I'm not her conservator, not her next of kin, nobody, and neither are y'all. Even if you had some basis to intervene, you don't even have the papers you need to prove what you're saying."

"Who needs to prove what? Is somebody going to court?" Charley Brandon sweeps into the office and stops to greet Mildred Melton. "Ma'am. Did my young associate offer you some coffee? No? Delores, bring some coffee for Mrs. Melton and is it Morgan? Mr. Morgan. Now, when's the trial?"

Niles looks at Morgan, who shrugs his shoulders. "Pages from a previous will were substituted when Big John Cape died. His actual will left a life estate in Cape to Margaret Cape. Mrs. Melton knows about the substitution, saw the original will, but the pages that prove it haven't been found."

Charley explodes in laughter. "Is that it? You two young guns ought to be ashamed of yourself probably scaring this lovely lady half to death. Although, when I think about it, I'll bet you didn't fall for it, did you, ma'am?"

"I beg your pardon." Little Mildred eyes Charley as she would a street drunk.

"They know, just the same as you and I know, that the last place you want to be fighting this battle is in court, making some poor elected chancellor, possibly Dewitt himself, decide this sensitive issue. Plus, you think those casino people want to be spendin' their time in a courtroom? Makes 'em nervous. Think about it. You got all you need now. Congratulations. For my own small contribution, I will personally call Vernon Pettis and get the meeting all set up. Niles, you available in the morning?"

"Charley, I don't know what kind of meeting you have in mind, but as I have explained to these folks, I'm not properly involved in any of this. I don't have a legal role that will allow me to participate."

"Niles, you have the most important role of all. What you are is the person that the chancellor was going to appoint Mrs. Cape's conservator before he decided she didn't need one. Now, if events develop—and they are likely to do so—that he changes his mind back again, you are the person most likely to still be appointed the conservator. So, I would say you are presently serving as a kind of conservator-in-waiting, a quasi-official status, and to avoid the appearance of an impropriety —I know you know your canons of professional ethics—it would be best for you to be present at any discussions that may bear on the interests of your potential ward. See? Plus, we are going to need your fertile brain to plow the legal ground, so to speak."

"Charley, could I speak to you in private for a minute?"

"Surely. Excuse us, ma'am, Mr. Morgan."

Niles walks with Charley past Delores's desk and down the hall until he is certain they will not be overheard. "Charley, I'll be the conservator-in-waiting or whatever that monstrosity is you came up with but I am not going to ask the court for any part of the money generated by Cape Plantation. There is no way to justify that. So, if that is your interest, forget it."

"Settle down, old man. My only interest is that Hardy will pay my client, Mrs. Blaylock, an inflated settlement if I can work out his casino-Cape problems, out of which inflated sum I get forty percent. You don't have to get a cent. In fact, I will stipulate for the record that you are completely untouched and pure of heart. I will stipulate you are the grandson of Jesus Christ himself, if that's what it takes. Satisfied?"

"Cordeman needs to appoint a guardian *ad litem* for her. I'll insist on that. I need to make certain Mrs. Melton and Morgan have no objection."

"Niles, you do whatever makes you happy. Run forty-one statutes up the flagpole and salute. I can assure you that the prospect of a few million dollars or more will be sufficient to make those two in there happy whatever you do. Meanwhile, buddy boy, I have some calls to make. You just keep tomorrow morning open."

Little Mildred and Morgan are waiting, silent, when Niles returns to the office. He looks at their hopeful faces looking at him and sees that Charley is right in assessing their interests. "Charley will try to set up a meeting with Mr. Mall and the casino people in the morning. In the meantime, I think it would be well for you to continue looking for the pages, Mrs. Melton. Maybe Sam can help you."

Mildred sucks in her cheeks, fluttering her eyelids in some

vestigial pattern of persuasion. "Oh, I don't think we should mention anything to Sam about the casino interest. I'm afraid he doesn't always think well. He may tell Margaret and it will only upset them both unnecessarily."

"I'm sorry, Mrs. Melton, but I've already told him. I drove out to Cape this morning and explained the situation to Mr. Adams in detail. He did seem upset, but I think he'll be fine." Niles holds up his palms in request for confirmation and Morgan nods his head, but Little Mildred is frozen in place.

"Well, then," she says at last and pulls a Salem from her purse, leaning toward Morgan for a light and Niles sees her hand is shaking.

29

The director of DACOM sits at her desk. There is a square, unpaned window to her left and she likes to look outside to the zoysia, still green the second of November. Her mother never let her go outside, except to walk to and from school three blocks away. The practice was begun so early and kept on in Tchula, then Greenwood, then Cleveland, she never thought to fight it until she was thirteen and other Negro girls went from school to the downtown stores to shop while she was ordered home. "I don't want you thinking like them, if they think at all," her mother told her.

"Who should I think like? I'm not like anyone I know," she demanded and her mother never gave her a sufficient answer, but held her ground with such ferocity that something in Emmaline knew it was futile to go on. MaMa was that way about a lot of things. There were only the two of them— her father never mentioned, never there—and once, when Emmaline got the fever, MaMa wailed in the doctor's office as if she had already died. "This is my baby! Don't take my baby. She's all I have." She went on until the doctor sat her down hard and told her Emmaline only had the flu and gave her a double dose of Valium. No questions were allowed. That was a rule Emmaline learned early. There were so many other rules to learn, the way through the maze of white domination, that her time seemed always filled. Her mother was forgiving of white bigotry. "Whites and us, I figure, have about the same portion of dumbasses and that means there's a right smart number. But, you're a good person, Emmaline, and there are good white people, too."

Gloria feels, strangely, the same as Emmaline's mother. Oh, she said nothing after the old white lady was in, Emmaline telling her to leave, watching her thin arm reach for the glass door, where she pushed, then pushed again. Still, Emmaline read the disapproval in her silence and there are other times, too, that she says, "Peoples jus' peoples," as if white and black skins no longer bring regard more than two colors of shirt but Emmaline thinks that a prayer Gloria recites to herself, nothing more. Does she think because the Handy Andy rings up her order without making her wait for the white man behind her that she is something more than what she is and that the rules are gone? They are not, but only resting out of sight in people's hearts, where no one can see what they are or how they are the same or different. It was easier, Emmaline thinks, when she knew exactly what to do, what was expected however unjust it might have been. Anyway, she opened the door for the lady, didn't she, crossing to her in three long strides. "Here, let me help you," she said, her voice soft and the woman sighed and smiled at her, in gratitude, she supposes, and Emmaline looked away from the aged eyes, ghostly pale, as odd-colored as her own, and held the door open until she was down the steps, not looking at Gloria, who she knew, nonetheless, was watching her and said, to no one in particular, "That would be just my luck. She have a stroke right on the premises my first week here."

A skinny Negro girl comes up the walk, her red skirt too tight and short and she wears a cropped black cotton sweater and earrings that dangle plastic fruit. Emmaline grimaces and closes her eyes when she sees the girl is chewing gum. "Gloria!

C'mon, girl. I am hungry!" the skinny girl yells from the front step and the two of them leave together for lunch and Emmaline declines to even consider what they will have. She takes the paper bag from the console behind her and spreads a small towel across her desk. An apple, low-fat yogurt, and a half sandwich, turkey and whole wheat with mustard. "White people's food." That's what Gloria would say, if she knew, but she doesn't.

This is not the job she thought to take when she worked for her degree in mathematics or her minor in English and music. She could have left the Delta. She has thought many times that she should have gone north or west like the many who left in the '40s and '50s when mechanical cotton pickers took their jobs and made the decision for them. She has been some places, to Las Vegas, where they sent her to train for this job, and New Orleans and Paris, once, with the university choir. It was strange, the feeling to be there rather than here, a certain lightness as if she had spent the day in a harness pulling a heavy load and suddenly the harness is removed. She wonders when the harness was put there and why she allowed it?

There are two things that keep her here nonetheless. Not MaMa, who left for Memphis ten years past, the same year Emmaline enrolled at Delta State. "I'm goin' to spend my life, a happy life. I'm not sittin' around down here bitchin' and moanin' about my hard lot and tryin' to make some field nigger feel like he's the king of Georgia," she told Emmaline and moved to midtown, landing a job as office supervisor for Dixie Health Support, Inc., and marrying Wilbur Watson, who owns the print shop in the same complex. In the evenings, they work together on recipe book compilations they contract from church groups and social clubs and Wilbur publishes from his shop. Both of them have grown children and, now, six-year-old twin boys, Emmaline's half-brothers. The boys work, too, and Emmaline is bitter when she reads the slurs against African Americans. She has rarely known a black person who worked less than two jobs or a white person who worked more than one. No, her mother left the Delta and she can leave, too, except she is twice held. For one, she still has people, kin, one anyway. But it is the other thing that pulls more.

Gloria comes back alone. She looks happy, content, and Emmaline resolves again to let her be, to give her no reason for disapproving looks when Emmaline is only trying to move forward, to make everything right. It was all that was given her by an invisible father, a no one her mother never mentioned except for his thought that it was best to face forward. "South—colored, uncolored alike makes no difference—we don't like change. That's why we get so attached to the land or to what's already dead and gone. It can't ever change. We forget that heaven has always been ahead of us, not behind." Her mother said nothing more, only that he said it and the saying became her father and the whole of him and that is the thing. She is south, of the South, too, and the Delta keeps her somehow, every badness and goodness of it pushing against her the same. A defining burden. Sisyphus and his rock and she is not yet ready to set it down. "I'm back. You got anything?" Gloria peeps through a crack in the door and Emmaline waves her inside.

"Here. Send these qualifications to our employment offices. They're still sending us too many waiters, not enough dealers, clerical staff. I put the cover letter in your directory." She hands the printed list to Gloria and refrains from a gratuitous lecture on black people aiming too low, underestimating themselves, the one Gloria has endured several times already. It will get better, she thinks, hopefully, and smiles at Gloria, who is suspicious and asks, "What is it?"

"Nothing," Emmaline sighs. "Thank you."

The dark car pulls up at the curb and Emmaline blinks her eyes, doubting what she sees. Why would he come here, she wonders? She goes to the front door, slowly, casually. "I'll be back in a minute, Gloria," and walks down the sidewalk, but he does not look at her, instead gripping the steering wheel with both hands and staring straight ahead as if he were still driving down the highway. She comes to the window and taps. His head jerks back and he looks at her, then opens the door. She leans over him and cups his shoulder in her hand. "What you doing here, Big Daddy? You OK?" she falls back into familiar dialect at the sight of him, and Sam Adams says nothing, but pulls her to him, wrapping his arms around her and holding her so tight she can scarcely breathe.

30

There is nothing more to say. It is not that she cannot speak, not that at all. That much is a relief to her; it had been unsettling when it happened in the pasture and the thoughts were rolling together—she can still hear their roar—and she feared she was slipping back into the dead years. But it is not that. It is only that the saying, the talking, is complete. She sits up in bed and turns her head from one side to the other, her neck crepitating noisily so that she laughs ruefully at her failing self. Just in time, she thinks.

What is left, comes tomorrow. "HOME—11/5" is what the list specifies and today is only the fourth and, so, there is today for nothing at all, pure moving, pure being without purpose. It is a light feeling, almost dizzying. Her dancing teacher told her that. "Hold your eye on the one point, Margaret, and turn and you won't fall," and that is the way it seems, as if she has let go of her turn point and is wild with motion.

"Miz Marg'ret! You up walkin'. That's good." Sam stands in the doorway and she stops to look at him. He is mostly bones, not aged from twenty-seven years before so much as eroded by the time lived, so much of it for her although she never asked him. And troubled. She has seen the look since her waking three months past and it had seemed a mere reflection of her own concern, but now the trouble shows on his face for what it is, his own. She walks to him, reaching for his hand and takes it in both of hers, lifting his bony fingers to her face, breathing the acid scent, pressing the dry, wrinkled skin to her own.

"If you're finished with the tray, ma'am, I'll take it, get it washed," he says as if he does not see and she nods, dropping his hand. He takes the supper tray from the bed and sets it to one side, straightening the covers and fluffing the pillows. He fills the water bottle on the nightstand and checks the glass to make certain it is clean. "I think everything OK. You stayin' in here, Miz Marg'ret? It's close to seven, your bedtime." Margaret walks to the bed and sits on the edge and he is satisfied with that. "I'm goin' out for a while and you can get your rest."

Rest. There has already been plenty of rest, it seems to her. Twenty-seven years of it and only now, clarity. Or, reassurance, at least. She has found her way after all, not by the markers of others or their instruction, but by her own halting progress, feeling her way through, letting her intuitions correct her course as she goes. There is no predetermined structure—she knew that much—but merely a purposeful giving of herself over to the movement of her own life. She moves, too, atop her life's shifting current, not toward a destination but toward completion. "It is enough to seek," her father had said and he never promised that her search would yield her a view of what she found. She sees, now, that there is no way for her to see the whole of it anyway, that her story persists beyond her, beyond the boundaries of her own life. It is for others to know in its entirety, not her. Still, in the pasture, she was pleased to view a part of it, enough to see that the order was there, that she had come this far. She had read and acted on the signs she recognized, there being only one that she never understood— the little Amazon girl. Now, she has remembered so much that she is confident of new thoughts and has renewed her determination. In the morning, she will retrieve the photograph from the library and bring it here in the light.

Sam leaves with the tray and she listens to his steps recede down the hall to the kitchen. It is only minutes later that he leaves, the front door scraping open and shut, the creak of the Buick's door and she is left alone again. She starts to rise, but her arm gives way before she can push upright. Sam is right. She needs to rest and, tonight, sleep comes quickly.

Cape Plantation, 1966 ✺ Sam sat her in the kitchen by the enamel-topped table and he was talking to her, his words tumbling out so fast she could not have understood them if she had been listening. But she was not listening. She was hearing and that is different, of course. She saw his hand, so large, placed over hers and the large rock over the small. She lifted the rocks, each in turn, and beneath was an opening into the earth not as wide as her side-turned hand, yet she slipped through into the earth and the pasture extended before her. It was pleasant to walk there to where the trees begin and she followed the narrow trail alongside the wall of a cliff. It was worn concave with many steps before and she reached her hand to the open side and woody bamboo that held her near the wall. A wailing called her and she moved toward it—it was louder each moment—until she reached steps spiraling up to the flat top of a tower. Her head was above the flat and she stepped onto the stone confidently, eager to see as far as she could, but there was only desert sand level with the tower itself. No harm to that, she supposed, stepping into the sand, soft sand with no sound and she followed it, directionless, for miles. The wailing was behind her now and that reassured, so that when she saw she had come to the ocean, she felt free to walk along the beach, purposeless.

"Miz Marg'ret. Get up now. Don't go!"

He was shaking her roughly and the white table scraped on the floor and the leg struck her knee, shocking her awake. She looked at Sam's dark face, his brown eyes filling with tears, and the room came into order. There were the windows, there. They looked out on the drive behind the house and the barn. Big John's office was there. And, there was Ella's sink. No, Ella was gone. "It goin' to be alright, ma'am. I won't let them hurt you, not nobody," and it was all very clear again and she was gone, back to the sand stretching along a woods and she turned left into it, following a dark path through. She was breathing deeply now and saw the large eyes, amber eyes, that walked with her. When she walked faster, at last running and out of breath, the eyes were beside her, gently rising and falling in cadence with her own stride. The trees ended and the flat top of the tower was before her, spiraling into the earth, she following the ridges around and slowly down. She was back, back at the large rock and the small rock, back to the very place she had entered, except now the world was black.

THE CAR IS almost driving itself, like an old stable horse that knows the road home. Sam Adams is solemn, both hands on the wheel. He has to make it to Cape House before the courage of the whiskey is gone, but careful, careful.

He lifts the fan lever to high and slides the vent to defrost. The front started through midafternoon and the temperature has dropped until he is certain frost will come. It will be the first time this fall. Late for this part of the Delta. The warm, dry air makes him sleepy and he cuts it off, cracking a window and turning up the radio. Big Joe Turner and Memphis Minnie McCoy sing blues for him and B.B. King and Bobby Bland and, with them, he feels safe inside the Buick, removed from anywhere at all, a traveler, an observer, no more than that.

Mr. Abbott told him straight, not talking slow like they did sometimes when they wanted to be certain to tell only the part that it was right for you to know, according to them, anyway. But, maybe he couldn't take it straight after all. Maybe all those years, being talked to slow had carved his senses, shaped them in a way, he couldn't take nothing else. Thirty million dollars, maybe more, the lawyer said, that's what the casinos would pay the owner and the fear gripped his belly so hard he couldn't speak, just nod. "If there's anything you can tell me, Sam, that might help us sort this out, I wish you would say it." He couldn't answer him then, just thinking about Emmaline and how it has never taken as much as a million dollars to justify killing even white folks.

He is going too fast, has to slow down, watch out for the drinking. He is still miles from the man's corner, but it is best to be careful and he is not accustomed to the road at this hour, the graveyard shift, and the moon full enough but in the wrong part of sky. He told Emmaline some things, but she too big now, too smart and he had finally told it all. Why hadn't she gone to Memphis with her mama? Or California. That would be a good place for her; he's heard no one is anyone at all there and she wouldn't scare no one the same way as here. But, no, she isn't going. Hardheaded like... well, just hardheaded.

Two miles ahead is the corner and he slows the car to fifty-two. He closes the window and turns the radio off. He has been going to the casinos nearly every night since he heard about Hardy Mall. After tomorrow he and Miz Marg'ret both be out a place to stay and he needs the money to support them, but his luck has been poor, the more he needed the money, the more it went away, then tonight he had a good sign when he came in and put a quarter in a near slot and hit the triple seven for $150. He went to the craps table and got a run and won $4,200. What would the old peoples say to that? he had asked himself, then, I am the old peoples now. What do I say?

He had decided cashing in his chips, decided while the lady sorted and stacked them by colors and fives. He would tell Miz Marg'ret, tell her straight out. She weren't there to tell for twenty-seven years and, if he is not certain why he waited this many weeks past her waking, he knows he needs to tell her now. There is trouble, danger for Emmaline, and who else has he trusted that served him right but her and not blindly because he has seen Miz Marg'ret when trouble visited and she were fierce to protect his Caraly, not even her own flesh and blood. She will do the same for Emmaline and not out of being forced, it suddenly occurs to him, and his mood lifts. No, she will be pleased. He knows her and he don't care what the old peoples say; they didn't know her. Why has he wasted time; he is eager to get home and let her know.

The interior light alters and he is suffused in soft blue light. At first, he thinks he is passing Blue's Grocery with the blue Christmas lights hung around the picture windows all year, but they don't flash and this light flashes. He looks at the speedometer—sixty-three—he has let the speed get away from him and he sees the four-way stop ahead and knows the man has fooled him, moving to the other side for this night. He pulls onto the gravel shoulder and waits.

31

Margaret has just wakened and her eyes are still closed. She sees the darkness, nonetheless, and fears she is already dead and lying in the coffin. She lies motionless, reluctant to know with certainty, until at last she wiggles the toes on one foot, hearing them scuff the sheet, and she knows she lives. She opens her eyes—the room is black—and looks to the side yard windows, where the three-quarter moon is setting, lighting the top of the white brick wall so that a narrow rectangle of gray light outlines the garden. She turns her body toward the windows, her shoulders first and then her legs, helping herself lift them with her right hand. The gray rim fades as she watches, not because the moon disappears, but because the sun is about to rise and even the dim light of dawn is brighter than the soft moonlight. At last, the top of the wall has reversed its role and becomes a black outline in the midst of everything else illuminated.

She feels a certain lightness herself. The dark has its own weight and, too, she is buoyed by the desire to know as much as she can before time is gone. She does not know when or in what way her life will end, but it seems clear enough that the end must be on this day. Still, there had been no need for a sign to tell that. What did her father call it? "The clear sky of a last day." Each is able to see his own, if he is willing to look.

Her father had died in the guest room and she returned to Massachusetts only days before his last. The room was poorly lit and she could not find his form when she first entered and went directly to open the green drapes. She thought the darkness her mother's peculiar notion of how he was best comforted, but it was he who lifted his hand to wave her away from the windows. They never spoke and he acknowledged her presence now and then with faint smiles and—she remembers this so clearly!—occasional prolonged gazing into her eyes as if he were placing his thoughts immediately with her own. It apparently required his great effort because such stares were always followed by fits of coughing and, then, deep sleep. She sat with her mother on the tufted loveseat recessed into the curved bay window overlooking an interior courtyard. They spoke in soft voices about her life with Big John in Mississippi and about her cousin, Rosemary, who once had been a fond friend. Sometimes they talked of Dr. Finley, lowering their voices further since he slept less than ten feet away, but the talk was the same each time—a recount of the pain that came this time, that put him here and what he had felt and ailed with since that time. There was no talk of his life until then or his imminent death but this moment which, Margaret suddenly understands, is of the least importance of all. Once, when her mother again told of finding him askew in the library and how he was weakened and seemed not to recognize her, Margaret caught her father watching them, his eyelids half open, and he closed them quickly when he realized she saw him. He wanted to listen, too. Listen to the specific circumstances of his dying. Understanding comes to her only this day, and she feels pleasure at the resolution of this mystery. One's death is the most intimate of the incidents of life and seeing another's dying is to share an intimacy so great that we are, at once, fascinated and, sometimes, shamed.

She listens for the music from the radio, the proof that Sam is in the kitchen preparing breakfast, but she does not hear it. She realizes, at this moment, that she has risen later than usual and, still, she has no hunger. She considers whether she should eat anything at all, whether time is well spent over meals taken for a body that no longer needs sustenance. She will have breakfast, she decides. Sam will be disturbed otherwise and she wants him to leave her to herself today without any concern. She has often foregone a midday meal and he will allow her that with no thought of it.

She crosses the hall to the kitchen porch and takes a seat at the long table. Sam will see her here to bring her tray. Big John had died only months after her father's death and it was altogether different since no one, including Big John, had thought his illness was his last. It had been the influenza and there was an epidemic in the county. The spring planting had just begun and he was in the midst of the field hands and in Rosamond at the stores and then, suddenly, he ached and was feverish and he died. He was an old man, but it was not time. They will not expect her death, but they will say it is time.

Sam is not here. She leans to look down the long hall through the lights on either side of the front door, but the car is gone. She steps up into the kitchen and sees the enamel-topped table and the counter bare of dishes. There is no sound, no one. She crosses the kitchen to the door to Sam's room and knocks. When there is no answer, she opens the door slowly and looks inside. The bed is made and the room is empty.

It is more than an hour before she can make the same distance to return to her bedroom and open the passage door to the library. She feels her way along the familiar shelves until she reaches the break and turns toward the cabinet's top, her arms extended, flailing. The metallic clatter of the small photograph's frame marks its fall. She takes it tightly in one hand and moves stiffly to the center of the room and the chair. Big John was puzzled when she pointed her camera at the little girl and she snapped the shutter, then answered his mute question, "I don't know," and she didn't. Today she remembers the moment clearly and every other moment of her life as well. Her back is pressed tightly against the chair and her head is full, but her skin is tingling on her arms and legs as they grow numb, their lost feeling fueling the fire of her memory.

Margaret reaches to touch the other frame, leaning against the chair's arm. It is a heavy weight and it had taken her four different trips to the library to bring the General's painting as far as here. She pulls the folded paper from her pocket and spreads it across her lap. Buie and Caraly. Their love was well hidden and the evidence hidden longer still. Not by Buie. He had told her directly then, that she must accept the consequences of who she is—he had accepted his own—but she could not act on the idea until now when she understands that she has never done as he suggested. Instead, she has retreated, hidden—pretending to be a person abiding by the rules of Rosamond and others at the same time she worked by other guides to be her own true self. She has come to this clear conviction: that the force of her life, moving inexorably and affecting more than she would know, cannot be forever contained from view, germinal and belowground, or else it must die. At least, she can remove the two lovers from hiding. She can do that much. Margaret pushes the paper between the canvas of the portrait and its backing, pushing firmly so that the framed picture of the little girl falls from her lap onto the frayed carpet. She spends minutes feeling for it with both hands, interrupting her search at short intervals to sit upright and get her breath. At last, she finds the sharp corner of the frame and feels the polish of the glass and the smooth back of the photograph on the floor next to it—the fall had been jarring and they are disassembled—and the thought comes, making her gasp. She leaves the frame and glass, taking only the girl's picture, and gently slides it between the folds of the other paper.

She stands, feeling for the hanging wire on the picture. Ah, there. She pushes the paper and photograph further between the portrait and its backing and grips the wire with both hands to pull the heavy frame upright. Slowly, she begins to move toward the passage door, dragging the weight of the portrait behind. She feels steady, powerful and is eager to bring everything back to the light of her room, where she can show Sam. As she walks and pulls, she is no longer alone. Now her past is with her and not in disordered patches of time and space, but arranged as a painting might be, aesthetically pleasing and meaningful. She can almost hold the view of it all in her mind's eye, letting it expand and contract with the increasing labor of her breathing. The events are the same as she has lived, has remembered before, but their previous pattern has dissolved and they are newly configured to show a new design. This new thought—wonder, really—is almost required to be true, else it would be discordant. Still, she will ask Sam. He will know with certainty and, if she asks him directly, he will tell her.

Niles comes to the jail as soon as Sam calls him shortly after eight A.M. He is at the office. "They wouldn't let me call any earlier. Said I might disturb your sleep." The deputy brings him up from the holding cell and throws a brown envelope on the desk. They had taken all his things, everything, the night before when the patrolman delivered him to their care, both of them whooping when they found the money. A black one and a white one, both the man, both the same look at the money. He told his children, "People ain't perfect in any skin," but he still hopes that, on his own, the Negro will be the one above anyone that could know the virtue of justice and that this one was just scared, being the white man's nigger.

"Where did you get this?" the white one asked him and he said playing at the casino and it was the two grins that made him add the lie. "I drove Mr. Niles Abbott the lawyer from over to Rosamond. I drove him there and he seen me do it, standing next to me." The smiles fixed on their faces then and they put the money in a separate envelope and threw it in the safe. "How much bond?" he asked, but they took him to the cell without answering and he knew better than to say more.

This morning he is brought to the desk and given the envelope without the money. "There were some cash," he says looking at the desk so as not to lose courage and hopeful since it is the black man that brings it. The deputy looks at Niles, who is reading the bulletin board, where Sam hopes he will occupy himself for the duration, then decides and pushes himself out of the chair and brings a smaller envelope and throws it toward Sam, across the desk. "Sign this property release and you can take it."

Sam counts it. There is $3,800, $400 short. He looks the deputy in the eye and the look is returned in silence. "It's all here," Sam says and signs the form that proves it.

Niles is beside him now. "What's the bond?" Niles asks and the deputy grins and shrugs. "We'll let it go this time."

"What do you mean? Sam, didn't you say this was a DUI? You had to book him when you brought him in. What about the ticket?"

The deputy leans forward, shrugs. "Lloyd was saying we might've lost that or something. You know, it gets busy so that happens." Niles's face mirrors the flat look of the deputy and they stare across at each other for a beat before the deputy shifts in his chair, looks down, and riffles papers. "If you want me to charge him with something, I will. Otherwise, we're through with him."

Niles reddens but says nothing, taking Sam's arm to direct him from the jail.

"Where is your car?" he asks, and Sam gives him directions to the turn-in where it was left. "They should've let you call last night. They never even booked you, did they? Then put you in a cell. They can't do that," he says hotly, at once feeling ridiculous because that is what they have already done. "Leave your car out, don't tow it. Somebody hit it and then what? Stupid is what that is."

"It's OK, Mr. Niles. I figure they run their own house. Just like the casino do. House rules, house got the advantage. You know?" Niles nods. He does know. They ride in silence for a few miles.

"I think we've got things worked out so Mrs. Cape won't have to move, Sam."

"Yes, sir." Sam waits for Niles to tell him more, if he wants, and when there is nothing said for another mile, "That's all I ever wanted was she be safe, no trouble."

"Good. That's good, Sam. Me, too. Now, you need to get her to the hearing by ten, a little before if you can. How does she seem?"

"Well, she been a lot better lately. Eatin' real well, for her anyway. I didn't leave until pretty late last night and she be gettin' up two hours before now, so I need to get on out there. Deputy wouldn't let me call nobody and wake 'em up, he said, or I would've got you sooner."

"Right. That's what you said. You'll be there by quarter after nine or so. Plenty of time. This it?" Niles pulls the Bronco onto the shoulder and behind the Buick, maneuvers a three-point turn, and backs alongside the car to let Sam out.

"I 'preciate all you done, Mr. Niles. I get Miz Cape to you in time. All dressed up and ready to go."

33

Before he leaves, Niles washes his hands at the tiny sink in his father's room. He had done the same when he arrived, scrupulously honoring Bayou Glen's request "to avoid contamination." He is on his way to appear in Dewitt Cordeman's courtroom, but he is suddenly relaxed. The tube has been put in place to feed Buddy and Niles can go. He had required himself to witness it, having sentenced himself to that payment for his decision, or the manner of it really. He had flipped a coin. "We have to know by the morning or you might as well forget it," the nurse told him last night and he was no closer to any reason one way or the other. At least he had not used just any coin, but the half eagle gold piece Buddy gave him for winning the state competition in Latin his freshman year in high school. Lady liberty was on the face and a heraldic eagle on the reverse. "Don't tell anybody about this. Just stick it away somewhere," Buddy told him and it was not until years later when he heard the news that ownership of gold coins was just made legal again that Niles knew what he meant. Miss Liberty, don't feed; the eagle, the tube. Eagle.

He has twenty minutes from the time he leaves Bayou Glen until he must appear in Dewitt Cordeman's courtroom. It is enough. He opens the ten-foot double doors to the courtroom and voices rebound from the high wood ceiling, beaded board painted white. The word has apparently spread and the presence of more than the usual clerk's staff witness the size of the case. The parties themselves comprise a substantial group anyway, Mildred Melton sitting on the front left pew beside Frank Morgan Jr., and Frank III and Sara Cape Melton Sims sit next to them. Vernon Pettis is already at counsel table and Hardy Mall stands beside him. Nathan Bass sits alone at the other counsel table, looking uncertain. There is a large box on the floor beside him. Sam is not here, but he had almost an hour's trip to Cape, then ten miles back again. He will probably cut it close to make it by ten. Along the near back row, three men sit in business suits, looking already bored by the proceedings before they have even begun. Niles recognizes the far man as the casino lawyer they negotiated with in Thursday's meeting and nods to him.

"Ready, set, go, old man." Charley comes up behind Niles and grabs his shoulders. "Remember, walk Dewitt through it. Don't go too fast or take too much at once. He gets confused, he could order anything. You and I might end up dealing blackjack with Mildred Melton as our pit boss," he says, then is past him, moving down the row to shake the casino hands, then the Meltons, and, finally, even Hardy's and Vernon's before seating himself at the far end of the front pew.

Bailiff calls the case and Cordeman ascends the bench. "In the matter of Margaret Cape, is counsel ready?"

"Yes, Your Honor," Pettis says.

"Niles, what are you doin' back there? Come on up here and help Nathan." Cordeman waves him to the front of the bar.

"Yes, Your Honor." While the others turn to watch him, Niles moves to the front of the courtroom, through the low swinging wood gates, and takes the chair next to Bass. Dewitt opens the court file and turns the pages, one by one, as though it is the first time he has seen them. The courtroom remains silent, patient for ten minutes while the review continues, Cordeman making frequent notes on a yellow legal pad he has placed to one side, and then he speaks.

"Now, the court has before it the Petition to Appoint Conservator of Margaret Finley Cape and for other relief, filed in this matter by Nathan Bass. You filed this, didn't you, Nathan?"

"Yes, sir," Nathan says from his seat and the chancellor looks meaningfully at Niles, who nudges Nathan to stand. "Oh, I'm sorry. Yes, sir. I did it."

"Alright, then. Let me ask this. Is Mr. Hardy Mall present?"

"Yes, sir. I am his counsel," Pettis answers for him.

"Yes. The court has your answer before it. Did you file this on behalf of Mr. Mall?"

"Yes, Your Honor."

"Very well. Mrs. Mildred Melton? Yes. And, your children, too. Very good." Cordeman writes the names on his pad. "And, Margaret Finley Cape?" No one answers. Cordeman looks at Niles. "Where's the lady?"

"Sam Adams, her employee, drove to Cape to bring her. He isn't back yet."

Cordeman nods, seemingly unconcerned. "Is anyone present in response to the published summons in this matter?" He turns the pages until he comes to the original copy of the notice, the proof of publication, filed with the court and reads, "Is any husband, wife, descendant, ascendant, next of kin, parent, or adult kin within the third degree computed in accordance with the civil law of the state of Mississippi of Margaret Finley Cape...is anyone like that present? Please state your name." The courtroom is silent and Cordeman makes more notes on the legal pad. "Alright. No one has answered the published summons. Now. Before we proceed with Mr. Bass's petition, it has come to the attention of the court that there have been discussions among the parties interested in certain of the issues presented by the petition and the answer filed by Mr. Mall; that a consensus has been reached among these parties that they may wish to present to the court for its consideration and approval." Niles looks over his shoulder at Charley, who returns the look, shrugging his shoulders. Niles stands.

"May it please the court, Your Honor is correct."

"For whom are you speaking, Mr. Abbott?"

"If it please the court, I do not presently represent anyone in this matter, but in view of the fact I would have standing should the court approve the proposed agreement, the parties have asked me to be a spokesman in setting forth the details of the agreement to Your Honor."

"Counselor, the court has, as stated, some understanding of what is being proposed but if counsel would, very briefly, summarize the salient portions, the court would be most appreciative."

"Yes, Your Honor. There has been some question, a cloud if you will, raised about the ownership of Cape Plantation. It was originally thought that the land passed to Margaret Cape on the death of her intestate son, Chapin Finley Cape. Mr. Mall then advised the court that Chapin Finley had quitclaimed all of his interest to him and he claimed ownership. However, Mrs. Mildred Melton has come forward, subsequently, with information that indicates that Chapin Finley did not have an ownership interest in Cape and, thus, claims that nothing passed to Mr. Mall by virtue of the quitclaim deeds."

"What information is this?"

"Your Honor, the family wishes to maintain as much privacy about the details as possible. However, I believe I may say that the information is in the form of an unprobated will and that testimony concerning its contents can be provided to the court as necessary."

"Very well, continue."

"Well, the bottom line is that Margaret Cape has a life estate in Cape with the discretion to liquidate the property should she decide to do so. Now, the family and Mr. Mall have been approached by Bali High Casino Corporation to lease Cape Plantation for its use for forty years, excluding the house itself and twenty acres surrounding it. The offer is substantial, but it is conditioned on the title to the property being clarified and the parties have gotten together and reached some agreement about how to do that."

"Yes. I see. What is the nature of the agreement?"

"If Your Honor grants the Petition to Appoint Conservator, naming me conservator, I have prepared a petition to file today with the court seeking authority to sell Mrs. Cape's life interest in Cape to Frank III and Sara Cape in return for monies sufficient to support Mrs. Cape and, also, to pay her employee a monthly stipend for their lifetimes. Prior to my filing this petition, Mr. Mall will quitclaim any interest he may have in Cape to Mrs. Cape in return for an agreement from the Meltons to give him one-fourth of any funds they receive from the Bali High lease. Additionally, I will ask the court to appoint a guardian *ad litem* for Mrs. Cape to consider her interest in the sale." Niles pauses and looks behind him, into the courtroom. Sam has not arrived. "However, Your Honor, I do not believe we can proceed further without Mrs. Cape."

"Mrs. Cape has been duly served with process and so, as far as the court is concerned, she is here. Petition to Appoint Conservator is granted and the court appoints Niles Abbott as the conservator of Margaret Finley Cape, ward. Additionally, as a precaution and in the interest of justice, the court appoints..." Cordeman pauses and looks at the collection of lawyers sitting in chairs in front of the bar, by the clerk's table. "Stewart Ellis is hereby appointed to serve as guardian *ad litem* of Margaret Cape for the sole purpose of assessing the potential transfer of real estate. Now, give me the next petition. No, wait. Hardy, do you have the quitclaims prepared?"

Vernon Pettis stands. "Yes, sir. May I approach the bench, Your Honor?"

"Yes. Give the deed here. OK. And this is the contract with the Meltons?"

"Yes, Your Honor."

"Very good. The court finds that Hardy Mall has delivered the quitclaim deed—here, Niles—to Margaret Cape and has entered into an agreement with Frank Melton III and Sara Cape Melton Sims whereby he 'is granted one-fourth of any and all sums they may receive from the Bali High Casino Corporation or any other such casino operation in return for the lease of portions of the property hereinafter described aka Cape Plantation.' Now, give me your petition, Niles."

"Your Honor, if I may, I believe my petition should wait until Mrs. Cape is actually present."

"What's the problem? She's been served."

Vernon Pettis is on his feet. "Your Honor, since Mr. Mall has delivered the quitclaim deed, it is incumbent on Mr. Abbott to file his petition. Otherwise, we are going to have a failure of consideration. Mr. Mall won't get what he bargained for."

Niles moves one step closer to the bench. "What Mr. Mall bargained for was the Meltons' promise to share proceeds from the Bali High. He has that. If we don't wait, I have misgivings about filing the petition without taking testimony from Mrs. Cape or, at least, letting her guardian *ad litem* have a talk with her about her wishes."

"What do you think, Stewart?"

"Whatever the court deems best, Your Honor, of course that is what I will follow."

Cordeman looks at Niles smugly. "Her guardian *ad litem* is happy, Mr. Abbott."

"If I may speak, Your Honor, my client is in favor of Mr. Abbott's more conservative approach. The project anticipated won't be completed for months. There is no reason we can't wait for the lady's appearance."

"And who might you be?"

"I am Joel Tacha, Your Honor, representing Bali High. We're the ones with the money."

34

They will not blame him, Sam is certain, and he is ashamed the concern has crossed his mind, but it was only habit and for a second, and he pushed it away knowing that, if anything, Miz Little Mildred will probably be so happy she go and send him another check. It is after eleven and somebody will come by, won't they, or when Miz Marg'ret don't show at the courthouse, it'll be they just keep on keepin' on, as if she never were at all. He pushes himself up from the enamel table and washes his hands in the kitchen sink, shaking them dry. Right about now is when he sweeps the kitchen and kitchen porch each day, but there is nothing to sweep because he did not make it home to prepare breakfast. He blames himself, letting her down, getting pulled over like he did, even if it was because he was hurrying to tell her what he kept secret it turned out too long. "You ain't the only somebody," the old peoples had reminded him often when he let his own concerns cost someone else and to get this old and forget a thing like that.

He takes the dust rag from the broom closet and carries it with him on another tour of the rooms. He has been to all of them twice over, the first time looking for her when he came in. It were just after nine, he knows that, and he did all the usual things when he couldn't turn her up right away. He slammed the front door again and sang his songs walking down the hall. He went to the bedroom itself and sang there and even said "Miz Marg'ret" pretty noisy, but she didn't come out. He knew where she was all the time, but that didn't mean he was right to tell her he knew or to go get her if that was where she wanted to be. "Don't go talkin' 'bout your family now," Big Mama told him often enough and he understood she weren't meaning his blood kin, since they were nobody and you had to be somebody to have people talkin' about you. His family were the Capes and he knew them up and down, living and working without notice for these sixty years, and he for sure knew he bricked up the library when Miz Marg'ret were in her misery after Mr. Big John, wouldn't even eat hardly.

He steps around the edge of the music room, careful to avoid Chapin Finley's excavations. The piano needs dusting, he always forgets it, not coming in here unless he has to. Miz Little Mildred will get her fur in a ball when she sees this, he knows that's right. But he's thinking now he don't particularly care what she thinks, he might not even tell her it were her own nephew done this, after she talked to Miz Marg'ret the way she did, putting those thoughts of dying in his lady's head that someone tender like she was you couldn't know how she might take it. Maybe she did know and maybe that's why she said it. He snaps the rag across the keys, causing a faint glissando. Still, he best tell her about Mr. Chappy and that they didn't know until the end how he wasn't right in the head or, at least, how much he wasn't right. Sam thinks how many times he left Miz Marg'ret alone, not knowing, and pushes further thinking down.

He hears the car coming and he puts on his white jacket before going to the bedroom to check a last time. She is lying on the bed where he left her, her apricot dress prettily draped. And he put her slippers on, too. He could not have left her the way he found her. After all these years, that would be a crime for sure. He didn't see her at first, even with the flashlight, when he came back with it. She were almost to the doorway and the rug was pushed out of line all the way from the other side of the break to there. Half under the General's picture, is the way she was, her dress pushed up over her thighs and nothing on her feet or underthings either. He combs a stray hair back from her face, then turns slowly in a circle surveying the remainder of the room. The General's portrait faces the wall next to the closet and he takes the papers from the night-stand and balances them atop the wide top of the gilt frame. That was the thing that gave him bumps like she talkin' to him from the dead. The whole back of that picture was covered with a kind of stiff paper and, underneath, bulging with a mess of stuff, and she had ripped it part open and stuck two of the papers in the crease. One were the marriage certificate for his Caraly and Mr. Buie from so many years back and he remembered they gave it to Mr. John Buie and that was the last anyone saw of it. But, the other, the photograph. He had never seen it before. A little, dark girl with light eyes and balanced on a log and the way she looked out at him. It were something.

PART FIVE

35

The dark is here before she knows it; it is the shortest day of the year and the sun sets in the afternoon it seems but she has the glow from the space heater at her feet, her own hearth, parumbling noisily on the slate floor. The bamboo shades are dropped on all the windows of the sunroom; still, she hears the peck-pecking of sleet, the closest the Delta will have to a white Christmas this year. There have only been a few in her life—one magical, deep snow when she was only six, the perfect age for magic, and another one when John Buie was still alive. Only tomorrow, the next day, then Friday, then Christmas and what a present she delivers to her children this time—Cape Plantation! The cold is past the blinds and she leans toward the heat, shivering. Perhaps it will be pneumonia that takes her. She takes the pack of Salems from the lamp table. Only one left and she is resolved this will be her last one. She lights the cigarette and inhales deeply. That warms her and she accepts the warmth as a reward for her service; she deserves this last pleasure before giving it up for good.

"You want another pack of them?" Albert's voice comes out of the dark, like the sound of her own conscience and she jerks back in the chair.

"Albert, I have told you not to come up on me that way,"

she says crossly and he says nothing, but turns on the lamp beside her, then the others, until the room is softly lit and the little heater returns to being a metal box.

"Do you, ma'am?" he asks again.

"No, I don't think so. Did you take the check to Sam?"

"Yes, ma'am."

"Well?"

"He gave it back to me, tore in half. Said he don't need it, you know, now."

Yes, Margaret is gone and no need for further concern by Sam or anyone at all. It could not have worked out better, except she hopes Margaret's will be the last death to occur on the premises of Cape House; it is not good for appearances to have too many demises under one roof.

"You need me tomorrow, Miss Mildred?"

"No, Albert, but tomorrow, we go to the Christmas bazaar at the Methodist meeting hall. One o'clock, I believe. And Thursday. I will need you to drive me Thursday. To the courthouse by two. When you go, get your Christmas. It's on the kitchen table."

"Thank you, ma'am. I 'preciate it, I really do. I be back for you Wednesday."

He leaves the sunroom to the hall and to the kitchen, where she hears him stop and pick up the card, tearing open the envelope on the spot, where she has left a card stuffed with a fresh one-hundred-dollar bill as his Christmas bonus. "Thank you, ma'am," he calls out and then he is gone.

Christmas already. It seems only a month ago that Albert took down last year's tree, wrapping each ornament in tissue paper while she supervised, then packing them in boxes with the correct labels and carrying them to the attic. What with everything, she has not decorated a tree this year and the children fussed, but she reminded them that a family member, of sorts anyway, had passed on and that calls for less decorating during the Christmas season immediately following, especially within three months. And, too, there is the casino money. Too much decoration and people will think the money enables them to afford more than they could before and that will never do. They will have their tinsel and lights at Frank III's house but on Sunday, of course. That is enough.

Cold air swipes her ankles and she realizes she has left her chair and is pacing the room. Is there something unsettled, something to worry? "This must please you," young Abbott said to her in the afternoon session when he returned to tell them about Margaret and that he found the will. They are always trying to bring those above down to their own level; it is the most difficult burden of being someone, rather than no one. "The Lord will care for us if we trust in Him," she told him, although it seems so clear as to go without saying. Unlike Margaret, she knew her duty to her family and, without regard to her own comforts, she has done it and Cape House will again be graced by a true Cape, while $30 million from the casino's temporary use of the rest of Cape Plantation will put Capes beyond reach of ordinary concern for generations.

Did she give Albert the correct time? She spies the folded document on the sofa table and sits while she unfolds it. "Summons" it says, the lawyer insisting on dragging everything out even longer, trying to get more money for himself, the more time that is wasted before Cape is delivered to Frank III and Sara Cape. Yes, two o'clock is when she is ordered to "appear and defend" as one of the beneficiaries of the will of Margaret Cape.

"Although it seems clear that Mrs. Melton's children are the beneficiaries of this will, the will does not name them by name but only gives a description. For that reason, we will have to have a determination of heirship, along with the necessary publications," Abbott had argued to the court and Dewitt might have dismissed him, but the casino lawyers, Yankees every one of them, agreed and the die was cast. The petition is attached to the summons and it shows the language of the will, all of the missing pages.

> I, JOHN BUIE CAPE II, being of sound and disposing mind, do devise, bequeath, and bestow unto MARGARET FINLEY CAPE, my wife, the use and benefit of Cape House, Cape Plantation, and all real property of which I may die possessed for her lifetime, including the power to dispose of said property at her discretion, and, upon the death of MARGARET FINLEY CAPE, said property or the fruits thereof I do devise, bequeath, and bestow, per stirpes, to the joint surviving heirs or descendants of MARGARET FINLEY CAPE and JOHN BUIE CAPE II, in any degree and, if there be none, then to the heirs or descendants of my children, JOHN BUIE CAPE III and MILDRED CAPE MELTON, of the closest degree per stirpes.

As a special bonus, there was a joint will executed by Margaret, disposing of all she might own to the same heirs. She should have trusted her father. Then again, how would it have been to have Margaret controlling Cape Plantation these many years. Too, there was the potential for problems with Sam, although they could not have guessed that at the time they altered the will. Good intuitions accounted for their foresight and God's grace, He knowing their motives were the best.

Sam came to the funeral but stayed his distance, almost as if he were snubbing her, but she knows better. He must have been embarrassed to come, bringing his young woman not even half his age, she dressed inappropriately in office clothes and wearing sunglasses as if she were some film star. No matter. Thursday it will be finally settled properly and, perhaps, that's why she caught herself pacing, the possibility Sam has something to be said. That is foolishness, now that she thinks about it openly. He hasn't said anything and, even were there something, he won't say anything now. Too much money scares them away. Two or three hundred dollars, they'll cut your throat, but millions of dollars scatters them like buckshot.

Margaret dead at last. Or again, really. She alive and seeing her child take his rightful place as master of Cape. Tears well in her eyes, not like her, and she smiles at herself. "You are a hopeless romantic, Mildred Cape," she says affectionately. The Lord is blessing the Capes and she is shy and humble before the bounty. It is enough to restore one's faith in Divine intervention, the Divine purpose, although hers has never wavered, only to see the proof of it is so very gratifying.

36

"Who's this?" Charley stops short of his usual drop onto Niles's sofa, occupied by an oil painting, two feet by four. "Can't even see it, you keep it so damn dark in here."

"That's the famous General Cape. I've been keeping it at the apartment. The hearing is this afternoon at two and Mrs. Melton will need to pick it up afterward."

Charley pushes the painting to one end and squeezes into the remaining space. "Have you decided what you're goin' to do?" Niles does not answer him but stares across his desk at the painting. "It's been almost a month since your daddy died and you haven't told me."

"Two weeks," Niles corrects him. "I haven't decided, Charley. I'll let you know by the first of the year, if that's OK."

"Well, I can really use you. We're sure to get our share of the casino business. You really impressed them, the way you were so meticulous with the old lady's stuff."

"I guess everybody's happy."

"Sure. I'm proud of you, buddy boy. It's hard to bring a file like that one to an end. Always some little thing popping up."

"Has Hardy paid the settlement to Mrs. Blaylock?"

"Nah. Vernon won't let him until after the hearing. He's cut from the same cloth as you, all concerned with following everything so thoroughly and driving those of us living in the real world half crazy. I like him. I was thinking I might bring him in with us."

Niles raises his eyebrows in surprise. "You would hire Pettis?"

Charley stands and tries to appear indignant. "What? You think I'm some redneck from the county can't be in the same room as a black person, excuse me, African American? I just have to operate with the way things are, Niles, and used to it wasn't possible or advisable. If I wanted to spend all my time working at making it work, maybe. And only maybe. Now, people are more accepting and it's possible to do the right thing. 'Course, there's an advantage, too, don't forget. You got over half the population coloreds and they get run over by cars and trucks as much as whites, maybe more, since they're driving all the farm equipment. Good for business and it isn't often we might get a chance at one of the good ones. Usually, some Yankee law firm steals them away. I never thought that was fair, us raising 'em up, schooling 'em, and taking care of the bad ones and then Wall Street comes in and skims off the cream, so to speak. Well, I need to get on over to Tony's. I know you'll make sure everything goes like it should today," he says, repositioning the General's portrait in the center of the sofa before he leaves Niles alone in the dark office.

Sam had given it to him almost the very first thing, after they both stood over Margaret's body, silently regarding her. Sam found her lying on the bed that way, he said, and it was no surprise to anyone. The timing was fortunate for the Meltons although Margaret's death had made it impossible for the chancellor to approve a sale of Cape to Frank III and Sara Cape. Now Cape will go to Margaret's heirs but, as it happens, it seems that is the Meltons anyway. Just as Mildred had predicted, the authentic will was in the bundle of papers stuffed in the back of the painting and gave Margaret a life estate. Chapin Finley had owned nothing to deed to Mall. On

Margaret's death, the will provided the property passed to the joint heirs of Big John and Margaret or, if none, to the heirs of Big John's children. A joint will by Margaret duplicated the bequest, should there be any question. Niles, of course, insisted on a full-blown determination of heirship to identify the proper heirs and, altogether, that has meant an additional six weeks' wait before Mildred's children can claim their millions. He is not certain whether he did it to follow the letter of the law as Charley thought or simply because he wanted to aggravate the Meltons, who seemed so pleased with themselves the way they were getting what they wanted, what they believed they deserved.

"Do we really need this, Counselor? You have the putative will that gives Cape Plantation to Mrs. Melton and her children."

"No, Your Honor, the will gives to the joint heirs of Big John and Margaret Cape and, if there are none, the heirs of Big John's children. Mrs. Melton's name is not mentioned. A determination of heirship for both Margaret Cape and Big John is required to be binding. There are millions of dollars at stake, Your Honor, and I would be remiss in my duty as conservator to do anything less." In truth, he does not know whether he is even the proper person to demand anything. Too many people are in the case, all moving around and changeable, and what the law requires of him less than certain. At least that uncertainty had been given an adjudication, the Meltons and Pettis, too, protesting vigorously against his position, but the casino lawyers again backed him and the mantle of $33 million gave their feelings priority.

Niles looks back to the computer screen. He needs to persuade Glen Thomas, the federal district judge, that his client, Equity Life Insurance Company, has denied coverage under the group policy for reasons fully justified under the authority of the governing Fifth Circuit opinion. It is a fairly straightforward argument and simply a matter of grinding it out, but he is struggling for an organizing principle, something that will bring it all together, a unity.

"Niles?" The voice on the intercom interrupts his thoughts.

"Delores, whoever it is, remember I'm in conference or at a deposition or anywhere but this office. I have got to finish this brief before two."

"I know, but Sam's here."

Niles can feel his temper rising. "Let me guess. Sam Hill?"

"Who's Sam Hill?"

"Just tell me who it is, Delores."

"Sam Adams. You know, Mrs. Cape's Sam."

Niles sits upright, excited for no reason that comes to him. "He's here?"

"Yes, he wants to talk to you."

"Tell him to come on up."

Cape Plantation, 1966 until 1993 ✍ To entertain himself, when other pastimes were out of reach. That was why he played with her, she supposed. And that was the surprising thing, that she supposed at all within her torpid life of so many years, but she did in those particular moments of Chapin Finley's fun. At the first, when she still moved unexpectedly, a moving target, he bothered her little. So much the worse, as the movement was only a leftover sign of living, not the living itself and without anything at all to feed that, even the motion disappeared. It was then he began, began to taunt and tease her, poking the ashes for some remaining ember, although he was cautious for a while, afraid, perhaps, that some errant spark would leap out and burn him.

She went the places the same as before, with the same air of purpose when she moved, but only that, an air, since there was no purpose, no thought of any kind. She sat in the bedroom chair where they had placed her, arms limp in her lap, her head lolling back against the padded surface and, then, she would be struck with an impulse to move. It was physical, not mental, something communicated to her muscles and skeleton directly and she followed along with her body wherever it might go. Several times she walked as far as the pasture, but mostly the excursions were shorter, to the office in the barn or into the pecan grove at the front of the house and Sam would fetch her, tut-tutting all the way back to where they had left her, but all that was gone before long and, for over twenty years, she never left Cape House, walking or being walked within its walls and not moving once placed.

"It's funny how things work out isn't it, Mother? You re-member how when Buie and me were first in school and we would be heading out the door and you would stop him, just him, and turn his collar so or adjust his hat or brush his hair from his face with your lovely, delicate fingers?" He waved his own long fingers in front of her face. "You always gave him that look. Taking care of him, Lord, you did that and what? He's lying worm-eaten in Rosamond cemetery with the others and here I am taking care of you and you, you'll be there with him ere long. That's how they say it in poems, isn't it? Ere long?" He leaned forward from his chair at the end of the kitchen porch table and pulled her arm, uprighting her. She had begun to lean. "Here. I don't like to drink alone," he giggled and poured a juice glass full of brandy, lifting it to her lips and wetting his fingers in the liquor then pushing them into her mouth and across her tongue. "Nevertheless, Margaret. Do you know I believe it made me stronger? I know I certainly became stronger when Buie died, as if I had at last feasted on his well-fed and favored blood." Her eyes flickered and he sat back, satisfied. "It's so very nice to have you all to myself now, dear," he said.

His confidence waxed and waned and it all was given to her, no matter which, for only the two of them were left to live at

Cape, together with Sam during the day. In the evenings, all evening, they were alone together and he carried her to different rooms, depending on his whim, setting her this way and that, in one place or another. He was a big man and that was the irony, that he possessed the lean menace of his father in the generous and loving form of his grandfather, Big John, except that his hair was white, silky-straight blond not dark and waving and he wore it long and thinning, combed over the top of his head.

"I saw Aunt Mildred today. She spoke of you. She usually doesn't, you know." But it was a holiday of some sort, New Year's Eve or St. Patrick's Day and Chapin Finley had instructed Sam to set the dining-room table for dinner. He sat back in his chair, balancing his plate on his chest while he ate and watched Sam feeding Margaret. "She said she imagined it would be a relief to you when you pass." He almost choked in a sudden explosion of laughter, which covered the sharp sound of Sam's bringing her spoon down hard against the table. Tears were in Chapin Finley's eyes and he could not stop the short spasms while he thought of it. "Little Mildred had those Chinesey eyes of hers all squinted up like she was so concerned. I mean. Trying to feed me that line of crap! Oh, God," and he had to set his plate back on the table because his chest was heaving and the peas were falling over the edge.

Once he wept in earnest, in a desperate moment of self-loathing, and he had almost suffocated the very small part of her left living. He was barely able to speak the words, "Why should my own mother hate me?" repeating them until they were a hushed chant, nothing more. He was bitter with it and could not let go. "What could I have done, I always wondered that. Even when I was four or five. I just got here, I thought, and, already, to be despised." It was an extra weight of almost-remorse that her fragile self was not set to bear. She had thought those same thoughts, for a time anyway and many years before. It was not he who had forced himself inside her, but John Buie, and he was only the result of the other's violation. Still, it was clear to her that he shared the part of his father that most threatened her, the predator's instinct for the secret nature of its prey. An uninvited intimacy to be sure and it seemed to her that John Buie had put himself inside her, in the guise of a child, to grow and feed on her and destroy her from within. She had no choice when it was done and didn't wild mothers cull the wrongly born babies from their care, leaving them on their own to survive if they could?

Still, his insistent prodding had the unintended effect of sustaining her life, making it move and take a breath from time to time, just enough not to leave completely and, at the end of the twenty-seven years, of waking her. The wakening began, really, almost eight years before when his conversations with her had at last changed over time until they were no longer about his own self or the persons close to him or her, but solely concerning money. Money and, inevitably, Cape Plantation. By that time, it was not that he was poking at her, so much as he had become accustomed to her company, to talking his thoughts aloud and times were difficult. It was during the time he was away for days at a time in New Orleans or Memphis, sometimes, and later when he left with Sam driving him several nights a week, it became the worst.

He saw the land as a place to give him more money and, yet, he appeared reluctant to sell it outright for some reason, looking to her, talking to her, a catatonic who was not the owner except that he knew, somehow, that she was. "You will end with me. There are no more. No more that count, anyway. Knowing that's worth some money in itself," he said, giggling. She heard the bang of the fall, but she could not move, if she had wanted. "He gone now, Miz Marg'ret. You'll see it for the best," Sam said to her, carrying her from the chapel and propping her up in her bed, the sunlight warm across the bed and she turned her eyes square to his face with the beginning of a smile.

"Miz Marg'ret! You here," Sam said, and she was.

THERE IS A light knock on the door. "Come on in, Sam." Niles rises to greet the old man, motioning him to the couch. He does not return to his chair with the desk between them, but sits on the front corner of the desk a few feet away. He waits patiently, then realizes Sam is waiting for permission to speak. "You needed to talk to me, Sam?"

Sam sits forward, his skinny knees spread. He holds his racing cap in both hands and he looks down at the floor. "Yes, sir. I do."

"Tell me what it is."

"Miz Marg'ret, she were good to me, to my family." He looks up at Niles for a second only before turning his gaze again downward. "I don't want to cause any trouble. I sure don't."

Niles ticks off a mental list of interests Sam might have in Mrs. Cape's estate, why he would come today. "You told me you didn't want to make a claim for the money you used for Mrs. Cape. Have you changed your mind?" Niles studies his face. "Is that why you need to talk to me?"

"No sir. That ain't it."

"You still can, you know. I know you supported yourself and Mrs. Cape for a good many months. I would be happy to amend my request to include reimbursement to you. Nathan Bass still had the silver that Mrs. Cape brought in to be resilvered. Tiffany Audubon, Gorham something or other. It's worth ten or fifteen thousand, so there's a little something that can be liquidated, pay you something."

"No, sir. I don't want none of Miz Cape's things." Sam removes a piece of folded paper from his jacket pocket and Niles leans over to take it, but it is not offered. Sam unfolds the paper and looks at it for minutes, his lips moving as he reads the print.

"I see you have the summons I sent you?"

"Yes, sir." Sam looks up, surprised. "This here."

Niles steals a look at his watch. It is nearly ten o'clock. "Sam, you're just goin' to have to tell me what's on your mind. The suspense is going to kill me otherwise and I can't be dead because I have to finish this brief before the hearing at two."

Sam looks up, startled, then shakes his head, smiling. "You somethin', Mr. Niles. Miz Cape, she liked you fine 'n she was real particular." Niles smiles, pleased.

"I'll try to help you, Sam, if you just tell me what concerns you."

"Well, what it is, I was wondering who these peoples were, the ones 'unknown heirs' it says up here at the top. They supposed to come today?"

It is not the question Niles expects and, yet, his stomach grabs, feels queasy, as if he already knows not only all that has been said before but what will be said after, too. "This is hypothetical, right?" Niles asks. Sam looks at him in puzzlement and Niles tries to bring them back to the law alone, give his answer there and no more than that. "It means if Margaret Cape has some descendant, child, grandchild, like that, who is also a descendant somehow of Big John Cape, that person should appear in the courtroom and make himself known. It's just a formality. We all know, of course, there isn't anyone, but this way there is an official finding by the court that will say the same thing. Do you understand now?"

"Uh-huh." Sam fidgets with his hat. "This person would have to come today or just don't never say nothin' more about it?"

"No, not exactly. There's actually a two-year grace period that somebody could show up and make a claim, but . . ." Niles's voice trails away. He has nothing more to say, only wanting to hear what he knows in some unfathomable way is going to be said.

"Ella. She wouldn't like it."

"Ella?"

"That were my wife. She died some years back."

"I'm sorry, Sam."

"Big Mama, neither. She always say, 'Don't put yourself in the light, it'll burn you,' and I kept it hidden all these years. But, then Miz Marg'ret waked up and I don't know. Then she died like she did—she good as they come—and she pulled out just those two papers special."

Niles knows immediately the papers meant, even six weeks after he came to Cape House and she was there already dead and Sam gave him the painting, then, solemnly handed him a folded paper and a snapshot. The paper was a marriage certificate for John Buie Cape IV and Caraly Adams, dated December 10, 1965, issued in Chicago, Illinois. My sister, Katy, lived there, Sam said. The photograph was no one he knew, nor Sam, he said, just a little girl with dark skin and pale eyes. On the back, in Margaret's distinctive writing, was a notation: "On the Amazon, July 1937." Niles returns to his desk chair. "The marriage certificate and the photograph?"

"Yes, sir. Those are the ones. And, I don't know, I got to thinking and maybe Big Mama say this and the old peoples say that, but what about what I say? You ever think like that, Mr. Niles? You think it's wrong to say that?" Niles shakes his head and Sam nods sharply. "That's what I was thinking, too. What I say is this, is you stay out of the light all that mean is you just sittin' around in the dark and what good is that?"

"Uh-huh." Niles makes no more effort to direct the conversation. He is flowing with the current and waiting to see what might come.

"I don't think you know her," Sam says. "My daughter, Caraly. She were just a baby when Miz Marg'ret had her own babies. They were together then, you see? Caraly and Mr. Buie.

That's the way it happens. More so nowadays. Well, I guess there were just something about them two. We tried to tell 'em to leave it. 'Course, I couldn't say nothing to him, but both of 'em were hardheaded, weren't nothing nobody could say or do." Sam appears immensely relieved, apparently feeling he has finally bared his soul. "She waiting downstairs. I told her, you just wait here. I be the one talk to you make sure what's what."

"Caraly?" Niles asks, disappointed. "She wouldn't qualify, Sam. She's not a blood descendant of both Margaret and Big John."

"No, sir. That not who I mean. No, Caraly be on up there now, older than you even. She married again, up in Memphis. This here's her daughter, Emmaline." Sam goes to the door of the office and opens it, leaning out and calling down the open stairwell. "Emmy, baby, you come on up."

Niles turns his chair to face the open door, a bright rectangle imposed on the dim light of his office. He watches the light expectantly, as if some certain and absolute vision of his own future might suddenly appear. She is tall, almost as tall as the opening, with coarse black hair slicked back from her gold-brown face over fine bones. Twenty-five, maybe more—no, twenty-seven years, of course—and she looks at him, unsmiling, from behind large aviator sunglasses. "Take your glasses off, baby. Let Mr. Niles take a look at you." She looks at Sam with affection, resignation and removes the glasses but the office is too dark and Niles stands from the chair, reaching out with one arm to switch on the ceiling lights. "Oh, Jesus," he breathes, barely aloud, when the recognition jolts him and he is looking, once again, into the blue-gray eyes of Margaret Cape.

EPILOGUE

In 1837 General James Seifert Foster, the former governor and the later senator of the state of Mississippi, led the founding of Rosamond. He said that it was an important thing for the people of Titus County to form a community in the same way that it was important for a man and his wife to bear fruit of their union. Rosamond was their child, borne of them and a reflection of what they are. The difference was that, unlike a human child, the town would never grow to the moment of independent life, but be reborn again and again to different parents. He insisted the schools should have three times the budget of the department of police. "We should favor at least that multiple for addressing the crimes of the mind, always greater than those of the body." He objected to naming anyone by their families, so at odds with the usual practice as to be startling. But it is the province of the Southern mind to have its genius by extremes. "There is the eternal ether, always moving, moving and it is an insult to pin it against the wall as if it could ever be fully understood." What then? His peers demanded an order from him, something to live inside, lean against, and he declined. He was a peculiar man.

Margaret Cape is dead and they know well enough what to do with her memory, to shape and mold it into a novelty and lesson teacher, making stronger the bindings that hold them together. But there is a difficulty with the girl here and now. Ranks have already broken what with Ches Cooper inviting her to his own home to a fund-raiser for the Republican candidate for Congress and, Billy McLaurin, not to be outmaneuvered in the banking circles had extended an invitation to dinner with him and his wife at the Rosamond Country Club. Fortunately, she declined both invitations—no one is certain what the club would do and that is another question. She is the wealthiest landowner in Titus County and shouldn't such a person, if anyone, belong to the country club? And, yet, really. It is so difficult to know what to do. George Carr suggested that the better whites form their own township, a kind of private town modeled on the high school academies of the '60s that would permit escape from these sorts of decisions, but there is something about the notion that has lost its appeal. So many questions, it is wearying. Who will she use for help? More is needed than her grandfather, old Sam Adams, who tends Cape House much as before, as though time goes on, and the Negroes are as disordered as the whites over the whole matter, not wanting to work for one of their own although she is not really their own, of course. And, that is another thing. Who will she marry and what if it is a white boy and what if the wall is broken and there is mixing? There has to be a way to tell who is somebody and who isn't and that will never do. Will it?

Emmaline Adams Cape feels the movement beneath her and steps delicately, toes from side to side to balance. Cape Fortune, that is what they call the casino and she is photographed to and from her car by persons who name her. What am I to do? she wonders and, so far, no one answers, Rosamond busy on its own, redirecting, balancing.

Niles Abbott stays, not deciding whether to leave. The *Cape* case, in any event, is not complete, since the Meltons, every one of them, filed suits to keep their mulatto kin from Cape House and when they were not successful, appealed them to the

Mississippi Supreme Court, which will rule in a few years, not before. Frank Melton III and his sister, Sara Cape Sims, have begun to talk of settlement and Little Mildred is churning the waters to sink that notion. "She's old, not thinking straight. We can't go back to how it was," Frank III told Niles at Tony's ten A.M. coffee club, where Niles gets by once a week. "How much is involved in getting a conservator, like you were for Margaret?" Niles demurs to comment. He is not certain he has any part there anymore, although he receives copies of every paper filed in the *Cape* cases as if he did. Not pretty, not pretty. General Foster most certainly would approve.

Rosamond swirls at the strangeness, the changes, the disorder. Hadn't they all done enough? Just three years ago Lila Turnipseed, first cousin to the Coopers, came back to Rosamond to have her wedding to a black man and the Turnipseeds and all of them gave her the proper bridesmaids' parties and the luncheon for out-of-town guests—not knowing who, for God's sake, might attend—and, then, gathered for the evening ceremony and reception at the Cooper's country club mansion, all done as formally and with as much fanfare as if he were white. They could commend themselves for their graciousness and Lila, for her part, had done the correct thing in taking the man back to California, where they could live among their own kind. But, this is something else altogether, right here rubbing their noses in it and it will bring Rosamond down to where good families won't be able to live here at all. If only Lee had known he had the federal troops surrounded that night in Gettysburg! Everything would be the lovely same as before and, sometimes, the longing for that unreality is so great as to be almost unbearable. There are even days, not all, when the Negroes and whites alike are joined in their wistful yearning for the past and, on those days, there is such a throbbing pulse across Rosamond and the hills on its east and the stark flat on the west that it can be felt swelling out, then in, by anyone who happens to be standing at the edge.